THE CHURCH
OF THE
COMIC SPIRIT

THE CHURCH
OF THE
COMIC SPIRIT

———

INCLUDING
THE BEAR LAKE SCROLLS

PAUL WIEBE

Komos Books

FORT COLLINS

Publisher's Cataloging-in-Publication
(Provided by Quality Books, Inc.)

Wiebe, Paul.
    The church of the comic spirit : including the Bear
Lake scrolls / Paul Wiebe. -- Rev. ed.
    p. cm.
    Includes bibliographical references.
    LCCN 2008905184
    ISBN-13: 978-0-9718599-4-4
    ISBN-10: 0-9718599-4-9

    1. Bible. O.T.--History of Biblical events--Fiction.
    2. Bible. O.T.--History of Biblical events--Humor.
    3. Prophets--Fiction. 4. Humorous stories, American.
    5. Picaresque literature. I. Title.

PS3623.I37C48 2008   813'.6
           QBI08-600174

Komos Books · Fort Collins

For Elly,
ministering angel

If you really want to make a million . . .
the quickest way is to start your own religion.
— *L. Ron Hubbard*

CONTENTS

AUTHOR'S PREFACE

THE BIBLE does not come with instructions for use. Why, then, should *The Church of the Comic Spirit*, which contains the Bible's earliest version, The Bear Lake Scrolls, be prefaced by directions on how to read it?

In pondering this question, I considered the average American reader. Now, I am as impressed as the next author with both his range and her skill. Both genders have a remarkable knowledge of the Western Canon, including the orthodox Bible, and it is all too easy to underestimate their ability to comprehend the hidden meanings of even the most demanding literary passages. In my view—and I am admittedly in the minority—the typical American could devour the complete comedies of Shakespeare in the course of an ordinary weekend and still have time on Sunday evening to enjoy an episode of *Masterpiece Theatre*. This is provided, of course, that he or she ignores the scholarly notes that sit uninvitingly at the feet of those grand, celebrated speeches, those To-be-or-not-to-be's, those Tomorrow-and-tomorrow-and-tomorrow's, to which our attention is spontaneously and quite properly drawn.

So if I choose to risk offending my readers, I do so with both the assurance that I hold them in the highest esteem and the promise that I will offer, not a complete set of instructions, but a pair of simple suggestions, for using this book.

My first suggestion is for that rare reader who does not every day spend half an hour reading the Bible. It is this: before reading each Scroll in the second part of this book, you may wish to refresh your memory by rereading the Bible story to which that Scroll bears some resemblance. My friend the editor has been kind enough to cite the relevant passages. (Should you for any reason have misplaced your Bible, I remind you that copies are available in bookstores, libraries, and motel rooms.)

The second suggestion is that you attend to the footnotes. I extend this advice, not only because the editor has taken great care in composing those notes, but also because hidden within them there is a subtle plot regarding a murder mystery.

FATHER LECHER

PROPHET, FOUNDER, SAINT

THAT A DROPOUT FROM A RABBINICAL SCHOOL in upstate New York, an ordinary young man with the ordinary young ambition of moving to Hollywood and becoming a film star, should be chosen to discover and translate the now-famous Bear Lake Scrolls and then to establish what quickly has become the fastest-growing religion in America, seems incredible. I must confess that when Father Lecher first told me his story, I too was skeptical. In fact, I thought it was a joke. But after spending eleven years in his illustrious presence and giving his testimony careful and prayerful study, I am convinced that Alazon Lecher was exactly whom he claimed to be: a true prophet, and, I would add, a bone fide saint.

Naturally, I do not expect anyone to embrace my claim without weighing the evidence. In our last private conversation, Father Lecher confided that he was depending on me, his most trustworthy and capable disciple, to confirm his legitimacy and to dispel the malicious rumors that were already beginning to arise about the origin of the Scrolls. He made it clear that he expected that when I came to publish this, the final and authoritative edition of the Scrolls, I would demonstrate both the truth of his story and the authenticity of the Scrolls themselves.

One rumor has it that the Bear Lake Scrolls were pirated by Father Lecher from the computer files of prominent comedians from the last half century (Mel Brooks, Woody Allen, the Monte Python lads, or Paula Poundstone). The "evidence" behind this spurious rumor is that the Scrolls slightly resemble some of the writings of these sources.

Spurious is indeed the word. All that need be said in rebuttal of this idle gossip is that neither Mr. Brooks nor Mr. Allen nor Ms. Poundstone nor, for that matter, any member of the old Python troupe, has filed a lawsuit alleging copyright infringement.

A second rumor is that the Scrolls are a spoof, and that Father Lecher himself was their author. The theory is that he conceived the plan while attending a convention of Biblical scholars in Anaheim, California; that a steady diet of listening to pedantic professors drearily debating the fine points of the Dead Sea Scrolls nearly drove him mad; that in order to maintain his sanity he fled the convention hotel and headed for a nearby theme park; that the sight of live cartoon characters tripping festively about the park created in his fertile but misguided mind the idea for composing twelve playful pieces and then passing them off to the world as "The Bear Lake Scrolls."

This rumor is false to its core. I have Father Lecher's word for it. In fact, when I first mentioned this fanciful theory to him, I was astonished to learn that he (innocent soul) had not even heard of the Dead Sea Scrolls! I had to explain to him that they were documents of great historical value, discovered in 1947 by a simple shepherd in caves above the Dead Sea on the Israel-Jordan border and sold to scholars for a large sum of money, documents over which succeeding generations of scholars have shed a large quantity of figurative blood.

According to a third and even more defamatory rumor, Alazon Lecher, far from being the saint for which his many followers and admirers take him, was an impostor with a history of fraud and had never even been near a rabbinical school. The "evidence" brought forward to support this flimsy conjecture is that he was the author of a self-help book that had a moment of notoriety some thirty years past, a manual in the Hidden Tax Breaks series entitled *How to Start Your Own Church.*

This rumor is based on a misunderstanding. Though there was such a book, its author was not our Alazon Lecher, but one Al

("Unlucky") Luciano,[1] a small-time con man who was swiftly apprehended by the authorities and charged with conspiracy to commit fraud, who subsequently pleaded innocent, was let out on bail, and promptly disappeared.

The fourth and most ludicrous rumor of all is that the Scrolls were written by Father Lecher himself; that he either borrowed some of Mr. Brooks's or Mr. Allen's or Ms. Poundstone's or the Python group's ideas or attended the Anaheim convention (or some combination of these items); that he was the impostor who wrote the manual for overtaxed citizens and later surfaced in order to perpetrate an elaborate hoax; and that he was a fraud who was not even a Jew but was in fact a Protestant!

This notion is merely a hodgepodge of the first three already-refuted rumors, with the added suspicion that Father Lecher was not Jewish. The further "evidence" is the frail assumption that, because of the Scrolls' linguistic dependence on that old Protestant favorite, the King James Bible, only a Protestant could have written them. In answer to this suspicion, I need only mention that "that old Protestant favorite" is widely recognized, even by Catholics and Jews, to say nothing of humanists, as the classical translation.

Why do these false rumors persist? In a word: persecution. This is not a novelty in the sad history of religion. New religions have always been subject to oppression by those they have sought to replace. The ancient Hebrews were persecuted by the Egyptians; the early Christians were persecuted, first by the Jews and later by the Romans; the original Protestants were persecuted by their Catholic foes, and returned the favor; the earliest Mormons were persecuted by both Protestants and Catholics, as were the Jews before them—the list has no end. Why would things be different in the case of Father Lecher's new church? One might even go so far as to say that those of us who have been converted to this new religion have every right to take these malicious attacks as badges of honor.

---

[1] Father Lecher never failed to remind me that Mr. Luciano was related neither to the American gangster "Lucky" Luciano nor to the Greek satirist Lucian, author of *Dialogues of the Gods*.

So much for the refutation of the rumors. What about positive proof? Is it possible to establish the truth of Father Lecher's story about the origin of the Bear Lake Scrolls?

2

THE OFFICIAL VERSION OF THE STORY is, of course, the one that astounded the American public when, on that memorable evening exactly one year ago as I write, Father Lecher related it on national television. A careful examination of that evening's transcript of the "Lenny Prince Live" show on which the good man appeared will be enough to establish the accuracy of his account.

PRINCE: Have *we* gotta show for you tonight. We'll lead off with an exclusive interview with The Most Reverend Alonzo Lecher. Rev. Lecher is the guy who came up with—get this—who came up with what by all accounts is gonna be the hottest property to come along in many a moon, the Bear Lake Scrolls! Later on, if we have time, we'll also touch base with the President of these United States, who'll stop by and give us the scoop on his plans to save America. But first, gotta go to this.

IT IS SIGNIFICANT that Mr. Prince considered Father Lecher's story significant enough to preempt the widely-advertised, highly-anticipated interview with the President. Though this fact proves nothing, it is, considering Mr. Prince's reputation for journalistic integrity and accuracy, powerful testimony in favor of the story's plausibility.[2]

PRINCE: We're back, and we're speaking with Father Al Lecher here. Mind if I call you Al?
LECHER: That's what my mother used to call me, Lenny.

---

[2]Note that Father Lecher's name is not Alonzo, as Mr. Prince calls him, but Alazon, from the Greek *alazon*, which refers to a type of comic hero. See Northrop Frye, *Anatomy of Criticism* (Princeton, 1957), pp. 172-73.

PRINCE: So how'd it happen, Al? How'd you happen to run across the Bear Lake Scrolls?

LECHER: You want the whole shtick?

PRINCE: That's what we're here for.

LECHER: It goes all the way back thirty-one years, March 31 to be exact.

PRINCE: That's, let's see, thirty-one years ago yesterday.

LECHER: I gotta hand it to you, Lenny, you got a head for figures. Anyway, at that time I was driving around this great land of ours, taking a vacation from Hebrew Theological Seminary, up in Buffalo on the shores of Lake Erie, and I happened to stop for the night at this little town called Bliss Beach on the shore of Bear Lake, when—

PRINCE: Some of our viewers might not know the whereabouts of Bear Lake.

LECHER: It's on the border between Utah and Idaho.

PRINCE: So what's a Jewish kid from Buffalo doing in Mormon country?

LECHER: I was in a state of great spiritual anguish, due to my "inadequate progress in the Hebrew language," to quote the good rabbi, and the thought crossed my mind that it'd be a great time to head out to the West Coast, where I had this uncle in Beverly Hills. Anyway, Uncle Jerry was gonna set me up with a screen test, and if that didn't pan out I thought I'd sell a screenplay or two, and if worse came to worst I figured God would show up and put me back on track, get me out of this major funk I was in, due, as I mentioned, to the lack of a decent background in Holyspeak, plus not having my special brand of humor appreciated by the rabbis.

PRINCE: Which is what happened. God came through for you.

LECHER: Did he! The story is, I enrolled for the night at this dump in Bliss Beach— . . . no, check that, first I had a bite to eat, etcetera, plus a coupla beers, and then I went over to this sleeping establishment, I cannot for the life of me remember its name, except that the word *Motel* figured prominently, and checked in.

PRINCE: You could buy beer in Utah?

LECHER: This was on the Idaho side.

19

PRINCE: And that's where the divine revelation took place? On the Idaho side?

LECHER: Right.

PRINCE: In case anybody's wondering, these details are important. Lotsa tourists dish out big bucks to be at the site where the Almighty has been known to drop down.

LECHER: Anyway, at the stroke of midnight this angel showed up in my room.

PRINCE: Out of the clear blue? No thunder, no lightning, no nuttin'?

LECHER: This is how it happened. I was in the process of calling upon the name of the Lord when suddenly there was this great and boundless light appearing at the foot of my bed and then all of a sudden, poof, this angel emerged out of thin air and just stood there, hovering about six inches off the ground and kinda smiling.

PRINCE: Tell me, Al. What'd he look like, this angel?

LECHER: He looked like a she, Lenny, a blonde, blue-eyed, willowy she, and I'd give her about a nine and a half.

PRINCE: Why not a ten? You'd think God wouldn't settle for anything less.

LECHER: Well, that maybe reflects my own personal taste, the nine and change, having mostly to do with the fact that I don't find thick glasses and an academic robe and a mortarboard headpiece that much of a turn-on. I guess you could say I'm from the old school.

PRINCE: You got lotsa company there, buddy. What about wings?

LECHER: Wings?

PRINCE: Angels are known for having wings, are they not? Isn't that what the pictures advertise? Did your angel have wings?

LECHER: Uh. . . .

PRINCE: Well, did she?

LECHER: Come to think about it, her shoulder blades stuck out a coupla inches more than the average.

PRINCE: You sure it was the shoulder blades?

LECHER: I could be mistaken. It was dark.

PRINCE: Maybe she wasn't really an angel, you ever stop to think? Maybe she was there to make a buck?

LECHER: No, she was an angel, all right.

PRINCE: How do ya know? She show you her feathers?

LECHER: She gave me her name and address.

PRINCE: Yeah?

LECHER: She introduced herself as Michelle and said she was sent by God, with a message.

PRINCE: A message, huh? I guess that proves your point.

LECHER: That, plus the name Michelle, which is the feminine derivative for Michael, which happens to be the name of one of the top ten archangels.

PRINCE: I'll say this, Al, you got a strong case. So how about the message?

LECHER: She had it all written out. There were these four major points. One, she says, go to this cave on a hill above Bear Lake—and she sits down next to me on the bed and points it out on a map—where you'll find a leather-bound dictionary of the Ur-Hebrew language, plus—

PRINCE: Pardon my French, but what the hell's Ur-Hebrew?

LECHER: It's the original form of Hebrew.[3]

PRINCE: How come I've never heard of it?

LECHER: Because I'm the only living person who knows it. That's the whole point, the instructions said I'm the one chosen to learn Ur-Hebrew, it'll come in handy later on, which is getting ahead of the story. Anyway, I'm to go to this cave and dig around for this dictionary, plus a granite slate which has chiseled on it a bunch of hieroglyphics, which is the key to the dictionary, being the Ur-Hebrew alphabet. Am I making myself clear?

PRINCE: Perfectly. Point two?

LECHER: Point two, I'm supposed to spend ten years learning the language, and keep in mind that languages aren't my ace up the sleeve, I'm more of a people person, which explains why I was headed out to the West Coast by way of Reno in my vintage '56 Chevy.

PRINCE: Hey, that was some automobile.

---

[3]The prefix *Ur* (German; from the Old High German) means primitive, or original. Thus, the term *Ur-Hebrew* refers to the original Hebrew language, as Father Lecher correctly informs Mr. Prince.

LECHER: They don't make 'em like that any more. Kids used to tie raccoon tails to the antennas, remember?

PRINCE: Yeah, and hang furry dice from the rear-view mirror, which they still do. Point three?

LECHER: Point three, I'm supposed to keep it all a secret, for the time being. "Tell no one," says Michelle, "not even your wife."

PRINCE: You had a wife.

LECHER: *Had* is the operative term. And point four, come back in exactly ten years to this same establishment, if they haven't closed it down.

PRINCE: Okay, so she gives you this message. Then what?

LECHER: So next morning bright and early I take the map and jump into my two-tone Chevy and head up the mountain high above beautiful Bear Lake and get out and stomp around in the sagebrush and find the cave and go inside and shine my flashlight around and locate the leather-bound Ur-Hebrew dictionary plus the granite slate that looks like a crippled chicken has tiptoed around on it while the cement was drying, both items exactly as advertised, except she forgot to mention there's a large animal guarding them, but luckily I happen to be carrying a box of popcorn, which I feed this unfriendly mammal, and when he's busy picking the hulls out of his teeth with his claws I grab the items, the dictionary and slate, and hightail it out of there, being allergic to bears.

PRINCE: What happened to Michelle?

LECHER: After delivering the message she ascended into heaven, whence she had come.

PRINCE: After? *Right* after?

LECHER: Well . . . next morning. After goodbyes were said.

PRINCE: Tell me, Al, what's it like to be said goodbye to by an angel?

LECHER: Lenny, it's outta this world.

PRINCE: Which reminds me, gotta go to this. Don't go 'way, we'll be right back.

DIVINE MANIFESTATIONS are not as common in the modern world as they once were. Classical cases include the revelations to Moses, to the prophet Isaiah, to suffering Job, to the three main disciples of Jesus, to St. Paul, to St. Augustine, to five of the Buddha's disciples, to Muhammad, and, in more recent centuries, to Joseph Smith, founder of the Church of Jesus Christ of Latter-Day Saints. Most of these displays of divine power are accompanied by miracles: burning bushes, the appearances of seraphim,[4] voices from whirlwinds, voices from undisclosed sources, shining faces, bright lights, claps of thunder, flashes of lightning, earthquakes, shouts reverberating from heaven to heaven, divine beings grasping the recipient of the revelation—the prophet—by the throat, angels floating alongside bedsides, et. The time of the revelation is also important. In almost every instance the revelation occurs while the prophet has been in a state of anguish or some other form of spiritual distress. And the substance of the manifestation is most often a marvelous, sometimes secret, message that is of extraordinary significance for a decadent but waiting world.

The prophet is commonly not a hero but is an ordinary, flawed human being. Moses had a speech impediment ("I am slow of speech," he admits, "and of a slow tongue") and was wanted for the murder of a rival gang member. Isaiah was foul-mouthed ("I am a man of unclean lips"). Job, by his own account, provided a poor role model for his children ("It may be that my sons have sinned"). St. Peter, the chief disciple of Jesus, lacked loyalty to his master. St. Paul persecuted the Christians before joining them. St. Augustine was a thief ("I stole pears," he confesses, "and threw them to the very swine") and had a son out of wedlock.

How, then, can one possibly doubt the truth of Father Lecher's story of *his* divine revelation? The miraculous events, the appearance of the angel, his state of great spiritual anguish, the message Michelle brings from above, his lowly status as a flunkout and class clown, his enjoyment of life's simple pleasures, his use of down-to-earth language—what do these items demonstrate if not the gospel truth of his account?

The next part of his story provides further confirmation.

---

[4]The seraphim is a species of angel possessing six wings. As Father Lecher once remarked, this is four above the minimum requirement.

PRINCE: Our guest is Reverend Al Lecher, and we're discussing what a lot of experts are calling the find of the last millennium, the Bear Lake Scrolls. So what happened next, Al? You do what the lady told you to? Follow the rest of her instructions?

LECHER: To the T. I spent the next ten years learning Ur-Hebrew.

PRINCE: This was in Beverly Hills?

LECHER: It was in Pocatello, Idaho.

PRINCE: Uncle Jerry didn't come through for you? No screen test?

LECHER: Oh yes, I had the screen test. In fact, they pointed out I had talent—was loaded with it, actually—but they said somebody else had already played the part I was cut out for.

PRINCE: Which was?

LECHER: Moses. In *The Ten Commandments*.

PRINCE: So Charlton, bless his ashes, beat you to it. Then?

LECHER: Then they suggested I get a job in the religion sector of the economy, which I ended up doing, having an uncle in Boise. This was Uncle Schlomo, who knew somebody who knew somebody in Pocatello, which is how I happened to spend the next ten years there as a rabbi, in deep scholarship, conjugating the Ur-Hebrew parts of speech, not much else to do, the ponies not being a big part of the Pocatello scene.

PRINCE: You ever get in touch with Michelle again?

LECHER: Exactly ten years later, on March 31, I go back to the same little village, Bliss Beach, and check into this sleeping establishment—

PRINCE: The one whose name slips your mind, except for the word *Motel*.

LECHER: No, that one is boarded up "By Orders of the Local Constabulary," quote unquote, so I settle for a Motel 6.

PRINCE: A real motel.

LECHER: Right. So I settle for a real motel, check in, then stroll down to the local café for a bite to eat and something that has the right combination of chemicals to wash it down with, all this time being in a state of deep spiritual despair, thinking about Michelle and wondering whether I am still on her schedule or whether I've wasted the last decade of a perfectly good life learning a dead language that's not gonna do me, or anybody else for that matter, a damn bit of good.

PRINCE: Lotsa people could identify.

LECHER: Then I sit down in a booth with a plastic seat split down the seams and look over the menu, which is sitting up straight and tall between the salt and pepper bookends, and suddenly there is a sound as of a rushing wind and my personal angel of the Lord appears at my elbow with a pencil behind her ear and chewing Wrigley's finest and she wipes off the leftover hamburger and Heinz products from the last customer and asks for my order.

PRINCE: This was Michelle.

LECHER: Right, and this time I'd give her about an eight.

PRINCE: Whatta ya got against waitresses, Al?

LECHER: I demand a certain level of class in my angels.

PRINCE: You're like God in that respect.[5] Go on.

LECHER: So I place an order for a Waldorf salad and a Manhattan, just to see her reaction, and then I ask her when she gets off work and what her plans are for the evening. Her reaction is, she scribbles down my order without batting an eyelid, then she says she gets off at ten but she'll appear in my room at the Motel 6 at the stroke of midnight, first she's got other business to attend to.

PRINCE: She show up on time?

LECHER: She's half an hour late, but I don't mind, I'm busy perusing some material placed there by the Gideons.

PRINCE: She knock, or she come in with all guns blazing?

LECHER: Same as before, same great and boundless light, same hovercraft act, same glasses, robe, and mortarboard, which I'm beginning to find less attractive.

PRINCE: Some women have a tendency to grow on ya. With some, it's the other way around.

LECHER: You have hit the proverbial nail on the head. This time she's all prepared to give me a test. An exam. On my knowledge of the Ur-Hebrew.

---

[5]Mr. Prince is acknowledging Father Lecher's divinely derived authority. Note that the host does not say that his guest *is* God, only that he is *like* God.

25

PRINCE: Which you ace.

LECHER: A-plus, he said proudly.

PRINCE: Which means you're ready for Message Number Two.

LECHER: Right. Then what she does is, she pulls this sheet of paper out from under her robe and reads me the latest instructions from On High.

PRINCE: Four major points?

LECHER: To the decimal. Point one, go back to the cave and find this briefcase, which will contain the Bear Lake Scrolls, in Ur-Hebrew. Point two—

PRINCE: No mention of the bear? No explanation? No apology?

LECHER: She didn't seem to consider it important, and I didn't bother to ask. Point two, spend the next ten years translating the Scrolls.

PRINCE: Into English.

LECHER: Into the going language.

PRINCE: This is all beginning to make sense. First the language lessons, then the translation—

LECHER: Shows good planning.

PRINCE: Restores your faith in God.

LECHER: God as all-knowing, God as the ever-present provider, God as the great taskmaster. Point three, I'm supposed to keep the whole project a secret again, for the time being. "Tell no one," whispers Michelle, "not even your lady friends."

PRINCE: That would be the tough part. Point four?

LECHER: Point four, when I'm done with the heavy work, come back and we'll see what's next.

PRINCE: Ten years? Same motel?

LECHER: Ten years, but a more upscale place.

PRINCE: You carry out the instructions?

LECHER: To the jot and tittle. Next morning bright and early I jump into my collector's edition fishtail Caddy and take off—

PRINCE: Cadillac? You've come up in the world.

LECHER: That's what ten years of hard work'll do for a guy. The good old American work ethic. So I drive up the mountain high above beautiful Bear Lake and get out and stomp around in the sagebrush and find the cave, it's still there, and I go inside and shine the flashlight around and locate the briefcase, exactly as advertised, and—

PRINCE: There's a bear guarding it, right?

LECHER: Good memory, Lenny.

PRINCE: Same bear?

LECHER: I didn't stop to ask.

PRINCE: You still allergic to large furry carnivores?

LECHER: Hey, once allergic to the big bruins, always allergic.

PRINCE: You remember to bring the popcorn?

LECHER: Forget the popcorn, but I remember the Remington Model 700, which I use to good advantage, and pretty soon I come strolling out of that cave with this large briefcase containing what turns out to be a dozen rolled-up sheepskins decorated with bits and pieces of the Ur-Hebrew alphabet.

PRINCE: What happened to Michelle? She ascend into heaven about the time you took off for the cave?

LECHER: Yes, but this time not as quickly.

PRINCE: Getting sentimentally attached, was she?

LECHER: That too, but mainly because she was lugging the dictionary, plus the granite slate covered with the chicken tracks.

PRINCE: Tomorrow night it's the Prez, the next night a hit man who's written a book on what's got to be the world's most misunderstood profession, Monday night we have the new Secretary of Space with her common-sense plan—get this—her plan to put a colony of chimpanzees on the planet Pluto by the year 2025. Don't go 'way.

THIS SECOND SECTION of the Lecher story provides more evidence that he did indeed experience a divine manifestation. Again the angel appears and delivers a momentous message, again the prophet attests to being in a state of anguish (now described as a "deep spiritual despair"), and again there are miracles, this time including "a sound as of a rushing wind." Beyond these proofs, there is Father Lecher's further testimony that "they [i.e., the movie moguls] said somebody [i.e., Mr. Hesston] had already done the part I was cut out for [i.e., the part of Moses]"—a statement that clearly puts Father Alazon Lecher in the company of the classical recipients of a divine revelation.

Then there is the matter of the Scrolls themselves.

27

The religions of the world all possess holy writ: the Vedas and the Upanishads (Hinduism), the Tipitaka (Theravada Buddhism), the Tao Te Ching (Taoism), the Analects (Confucianism), the Zend Avesta (Zoroastrianism), the Book of the Dead (ancient Egyptian religion), the Torah and the Talmud (Judaism), the Bible and the Church Fathers (Christianity), the Koran (Islam), and the Book of Mormon (the Latter-Day Saints), etc. These writings share many, sometimes all, of the following traits:

—they have a divine source;

—they are discovered or otherwise delivered by a prophet;

—they are perfect;

—they are authoritative;

—they contain a revelation that is of utmost importance;

—they were originally written on materials such as papyrus, stone, bamboo shoots, parchment, copper plates, etc.[6]

Judging by these traits, the Bear Lake Scrolls are clearly holy writings. They have a divine source, having been discovered by our devout[7] prophet through a message delivered by the angel (Father Lecher follows Michelle's instructions "to the jot and tittle"—clearly Biblical language). They were translated by a perfectly capable translator (his competence in Ur-Hebrew is graded as "A-plus") and are thus authoritative. They contain a revelation that is of utmost importance (Mr. Prince frankly acknowledges that "a lot of experts are calling [the Scrolls] the find of the last millennium"). And they were written on ancient sheepskin scrolls. Significant, too, is the fact that there are exactly twelve Scrolls—twelve being a sacred number (there were twelve tribes of Israel, Jesus had twelve disciples, there are twelve signs of the Zodiac, etc.; perhaps it is also significant that there

---

[6]For a brief treatment of holy writ, see G. van der Leeuw, "The Written Word," *Religion in Essence and Manifestation*, trans. J. E. Turner (New York, 1963), pp. 436-46.

[7]It is significant that, while waiting for the angel Michelle to appear in his motel room, Father Lecher does not waste his time looking at his watch, viewing television, or reading detective novels. He spends it devoutly and reverently, "perusing some material placed there by the Gideons."

are also twelve grades in the American school system). How, then, can one possibly doubt Father Lecher's authenticity, or the fact that the Scrolls are sacred writings?

But there is more to the demonstration, as we find in the next portion of the transcript.

PRINCE: We've got Al Lecher here, *Father* Al Lecher, I've been calling him Reverend but he prefers Father, and he's telling us about the Bear Lake Scrolls. You get 'em translated, Al?
LECHER: Ten years it took, Lenny.
PRINCE: Still working part time as a rabbi?
LECHER: No, about the time I started translating the sheepskins, I decided to go with the Catholics.
PRINCE: They cut you a better deal? You had this relative, Uncle Pete, who knew somebody who knew somebody in the hierarchy?
LECHER: No.
PRINCE: No?
LECHER: I won't go into details, I'll just say I was spending a great deal of time translating and neglecting my wife and I had a conversion experience and got an uncontested divorce and was fortunate enough to land this job as a Catholic priest in Salt Lake City.
PRINCE: Conversion, divorce, new job—these events happen in any particular order?
LECHER: The main point is, there were no kids involved, fortunately, and I got them all translated, the Scrolls, it took me the whole ten years but I finished the job, and on the evening of March 31 in the Year of Our Lord whatever it was I drove back to Bliss Beach in a Mercedes coupe with less than five thousand miles on it and checked into the finest motel in town toting a briefcase full of newly-translated sacred literature and some very musty, pored-over sheepskins that have seen better days.
PRINCE: Michelle still slinging hash?
LECHER: Michelle is nowhere to be found. I make the rounds of all the eateries and none of the guys have even heard of her.
PRINCE: Makes you wonder.
LECHER: It does, doesn't it, but I take it in stride, not really too worried, having great faith in the Man Upstairs to ship the hired

help down to do His bidding with a smile and further instructions regarding what's next on the agenda. I go back up to my room and hit the hot tub and crack open a carafe of aging grape fluid[8] and settle back with the Book of Mormon.

PRINCE: And about midnight Michelle shows up.

LECHER: At the stroke of midnight the strobe lights go on and poof, out of the midst of nowhere comes an angel, decked out in a Ph.D. robe and mortarboard but this time hovering a whole foot off the ground and without the glasses and now sporting a very nice ponytail. "Michelle," I whisper. "No," she whispers back, "It's not Michelle. It's Cheri."

PRINCE: Cheri?

LECHER: The diminutive of Cherubim.

PRINCE: Cherubim? Educate me here, wouldja?

LECHER: That's a certain species of angel, Cherubim. Aristotle puts them in the same category as the nymphet. But on with the story, so Cheri whispers back, "It's Cheri," and I say, "What happened to Michelle?" just out of idle curiosity, because I'm quickly losing interest in her present whereabouts anyway. "Michelle," she tells me, "is retired and living in Prescott, Arizona, and I'm her daughter."

PRINCE: She's a ten, is what you're saying.

LECHER: She's at least twelve, is what I'm saying, and she's there as a replacement for an aging parent.

PRINCE: I see. A Lolita.[9]

LECHER: A what?

PRINCE: That's a certain species of nymphet. She a fan of hot tubs?

LECHER: Actually, she spends most of the rest of the night

---

[8]Note that Father Lecher does not specify the brand. This "omission" is testimony to his great sensitivity. If he were to reveal, say, that it was Christian Brothers, his Jewish brothers and sisters might take offense; if Manichewitz, his Christian friends. And the fact that he uses the phrase *aging grape fluid* shows that he is mindful that faithful members of the Church of Jesus Christ of Latter-Day Saints, otherwise known as Mormons, abstain from all intoxicants.

[9]Mr. Prince is referring to Vladimir Nabokov's novel, *Lolita*.

sitting on the bed, cross-legged and in the lotus position,[10] grading my translations from the Ur-Hebrew.

PRINCE: How'd ya do?

LECHER: A-plus again, in spite of a few typos.

PRINCE: Then you're ready for Message Number Three.

LECHER: Right.

PRINCE: Again, four major points, which she reads from the instruction sheet she's been hiding in her training bra.

LECHER: How'd you know?

PRINCE: Lucky guess. Point number one?

LECHER: Point one, assemble a committee of four disciples, using affirmative action and ecumenical principles.

PRINCE: Makes sense. Keeps you on the side of the law. But why four? I thought disciples came in groups of twelve.

LECHER: Several reasons. One, corporate efficiency.

PRINCE: Downscaling is the name of the game.

LECHER: Stockholders expect it.

PRINCE: What's the other reason?

LECHER: She mentions that last time they went with twelve, it turned out to be a disaster.

PRINCE: Sharp cookie. Point two.

LECHER: Point two, convene this committee on a regular basis. Take ten years to study the translations prayerfully and figure out the theological meaning behind the Scrolls.

PRINCE: Point three, tell no one.

LECHER: Point three, write a letter of resignation and send it to the pope—

PRINCE: Solves the problem of divided loyalty.

LECHER:—plus, move to Reno with my disciples.

PRINCE: Why the move?

LECHER: Less competition, for one thing.

PRINCE: I guess Salt Lake City ain't the right town for starting a new religious enterprise.

LECHER: You got it. Also, Reno is a step up the career ladder.

---

[10]A meditative posture made famous by the Buddha. It need hardly be mentioned that this is yet more confirmation of the authenticity of Father Lecher's divine revelation.

PRINCE: Lotsa people would agree. Point four?

LECHER: Come back in ten years for further instructions.

PRINCE: What about the cave? You drive back up there in your slightly-used Mercedes coupe?

LECHER: I did. Wanted to see if there was anything I missed the first coupla times. You get a divine revelation, you can't be too thorough about it, they don't show up that often. Plus, I've always been curious about bear skeletons.

PRINCE: Mind telling us why?

LECHER: I had this hobby as a kid. Dead animals.

PRINCE: Probably kept you outta trouble.

LECHER: It did.

PRINCE: What about Cheri? She ascend into heaven next morning, like her momma?

LECHER: With about a dozen used sheepskins, which explains why I don't have them with me.

PRINCE: Too bad.

LECHER: Very unfortunate, yes.

PRINCE: They'd provide proof to any possible doubters.

LECHER: That, plus bring top dollar.

PRINCE: We have to take a break. Remember: tomorrow night the Prez, then the hit man, next week the Secretary of Space and her controversial plan for a gang of very lucky chimps.

THIS THIRD PART OF THE STORY supplies yet more confirmation of the legitimacy of both Father Lecher and the Scrolls. The appearance of Michelle's young daughter, the angel Cheri; her sitting in the sacred lotus position; his sitting in the hot tub (reminiscent, perhaps, of the holy sacrament of baptism?); his affirmation of his "great faith in the Man Upstairs"; his testimony that the newly-translated Scrolls are "sacred literature"; the reverence he shows for the Book of Mormon; the top grade he receives for a job well done; the thoroughness he exhibits by going back to double-check the cave—again, what can these facts indicate but that Father Lecher was the legitimate recipient of a bona fide revelation, and that the Bear Lake Scrolls are the new, genuine, and largely error-free scriptures for modern America?

But here we also find a new element in the story: disciples. In Hinduism, gurus of old had disciples to whom they taught the rudiments of yoga. In Buddhism, the Buddha had five disciples. In Christianity, Jesus had twelve. Of course all the religions of the world have had holy men. But as this short list shows, only the very holiest of those holy men, the crème de la crème, have had disciples. Thus it should come as no surprise that Father Lecher would also attract disciples—whom he, like Jesus before him, would send out into the world. The only surprise lies in the small number (four), which, of course, the angel Cheri explains in a perfectly logical way.

But to proceed to the fourth and final part of the story.

PRINCE: This is "Lenny Prince Live," and we're speaking with Al Lecher, the guy who's written—make that *translated*—the Bear Lake Scrolls, which is gonna sell a zillion copies when it gets beyond the draft stage.[11] Al, we got to the part where Cheri gives you the directions for the next ten years. Follow them to the T again, didja?

LECHER: Pretty much, Lenny. I spend the next ten years exchanging frank but friendly memos with the Vatican, organizing the committee of top-notch disciples, moving to Reno, and figuring out the meaning of the Scrolls.

PRINCE: The disciples. How'd you pick them up?

LECHER: I ran help-wanted ads in *The Wall Street Journal*, *The Chronicle of Higher Education*, *Poets & Writers*, and *Penthouse*.

PRINCE: And you started your church out there in Reno?

LECHER: Those weren't my instructions, remember?

PRINCE: So what'd you do, spend your time playing golf?

LECHER: Mostly I just made sure everybody showed up at the monthly meetings and prayerfully did the assignments. And of course on our free evenings we occasionally hit the tables.

PRINCE: Any truth to the rumor that you guys were known as the

---

[11]Mr. Prince is mistaken on this point. At that time the Scrolls themselves were well beyond the draft stage. All that remained was for me to complete the editing and compose the present introduction and the concluding catechism.

High Rollers?

LECHER: Actually, it was the High *Holy* Rollers, and there was also a lady.

PRINCE: So who exactly were these disciples?

LECHER: Just three guys and a gal.

PRINCE: Any well-known personalities?

LECHER: Uh . . .

PRINCE: Don't remember who they were?

LECHER: I'm not great with names.[12]

PRINCE: But you'd recognize their faces.

LECHER: Come to think of it, the woman's name was Emma something. Emma Emma Emma. . . .[13]

PRINCE: Gotta move on, not much time left. So on March 31 of that sacred year it's back to Bliss Beach in a fully-restored Rolls for a return engagement with Cheri.

LECHER: Right date, right automobile, wrong angel.

PRINCE: Who's the new flapper?

LECHER: Gabriella, which is the feminine for Gabriel.

PRINCE: Gabriel. . . . Why does that name sound familiar?

LECHER: He was the archangel who played the trombone.

PRINCE: Every family's gotta have a musician. What happened to Cheri?

---

[12] Father Lecher is being typically modest. He was in fact on a first-name basis with all his disciples.

[13] Father Lecher refers here to Ms. Emma LaFemme, C.H.M. (Certificate in Hotel Management). The other disciples were:

—Cardinal August Micromentis, Th.B., Th.D., C.P.A.

—Professor Mortimer Z. Z. Allbright, B.A., M.Ed., B.S., D.V.M., D.D.S., M.D., M.Mus., M.A., M.S.T., Th.M., Th.D., Ph.D., D.D., D.Litt.; and

—B. S. Buller, B.A., M.F.A.

Note the ecumenical nature of this small circle. Father Lecher had been a member in good standing of a Jewish synagogue. Professor Allbright had been a distinguished Protestant theologian. Cardinal Micromentis had been an important member of the Roman Catholic hierarchy (upon his conversion, Father Lecher allowed him to retain his title). Ms. LaFemme had been a respected leader in the Association of American Covens. Mr. Buller had embraced the tenets of agnosticism.

LECHER: She wasn't sufficiently musical, so they put Gabriella on the job.

PRINCE: Gabriella equally talented, generate a lot of voltage, bring an important message, capable of floating in the air, ascend into heaven without too much difficulty, that type of a thing?

LECHER: She was about everything you could hope for in all those categories.

PRINCE: We're running late, let's get to her message.

LECHER: Four points again. Point one, I'm to start a new religion, to be called the Church of the Comic Spirit, and I'm to serve as the Prophet, Founder, and Pontiff, with all the rights and perks pertaining thereto. Point two, I'm to spend the next year at Bear Lake building a theme park, where church members in good standing will be able to stay at the motel where the angel Michelle quizzed the Prophet on his knowledge of Ur-Hebrew, sit in the very same hot tub where the Founder received Message Number Three through the angel Cheri, and, for a nominal fee, visit the remains of The Motel Whose Name Father Lecher Forgot, view the relics of the unfriendly bear, and touch the glass case displaying an exact replica of the briefcase in which the Bear Lake Scrolls were first entrusted to the Pontiff's capable care. Point three, when the theme park is completed I'm to leak the story to the press, hire a major advertising agency, find a publisher, make the talk show circuit, and run a membership drive. And point four, I'm to come back in ten years for a reevaluation, do a cost/benefit analysis, check the cash flow situation, etc., then see where we go from there.

PRINCE: You heard the man, folks. When we come back, we'll take your calls.

RELIGIONS CAN BE SAID TO FALL WITHIN TWO CATEGORIES: (1) ethnic religions, in which the faithful augment their numbers largely in the biological manner and (2) missionary religions, in which the community also grows through proselytizing. As the demographic data show, missionary religions, such as Christianity, Islam, and the Latter-Day Saints, tend to grow more quickly than ethnic religions. Thus it should come as no surprise that the Church of the Comic Spirit, now the fastest-growing religion in

America, falls within the latter category. Its stunning successes can be attributed to its application of contemporary techniques in promotion, fundraising, the internet, etc., to the traditional formula of "spreading the gospel." (I must proudly add that the Church has had to rely, to date, on neither the sword, the rack, nor the bomb.)

Pilgrimage, the journey of the faithful to a holy shrine, is another widespread religious phenomenon.[14] It is common in Catholic Christianity, Islam, and Hinduism, and Bear Lake World promises to make the sacred act of pilgrimage a dominant feature of the Church of the Comic Spirit, thus ensuring the Church's long-term prosperity.[15] One has every right to expect that point four of the angel Gabriella's message, the ten-year check-up, will be a mere formality.

But to the conclusion of "Lenny Prince Live."

PRINCE: Berkeley, California, you're on.
BERKELEY: How do I join?
LECHER: Just call 1-800-COMICSPIRIT and give us your credit card number. We'll enroll you as a member of the Church of the Comic Spirit and send you a first-edition gilt-edged copy of the first edition of the *The Bear Lake Scrolls* at the discounted price of $99.95, plus shipping and handling. Please allow six months for delivery. As a bonus, you'll receive autographed and perfumed color photographs of the angels Michelle, Cheri, and Gabriella, with statistical data. You may examine your membership kit for twenty-four hours. If for any legitimate reason you are not completely satisfied within that time period, simply return the material and you'll be under no further obligation. Otherwise, each month you will receive the *Comic Spirit Monitor*. In it we

---

[14] See Victor Turner, "Pilgrimages as Social Processes," in *Dramas, Fields, and Metaphors* (Ithaca, 1974), pp. 166-230.

[15] Scoffers would do well to consider that Bear Lake World will provide great economic benefits, and not just for the Church of the Comic Spirit. As the late anthropologist Turner wisely pointed out, "the pilgrimage ethic helped to create the communications network that later made capitalism a viable national and international system. *Ibid.*, p. 226.

review our Main Selection and half a dozen other fine books. Current selections include the series on the Seven Main Virtues:[16] (1) *Proud to be an American;* (2) *Your Neighbor's Wife;* (3) *The Lecher Story;* (4) *Learning to Accept Your Rage;* (5) *Gorging Your Way to a Full Figure—A Guide for the Anorexic;* (6) *Green is My Favorite Color;* and (7) *Archaic Techniques of Stress Reduction.* If you want the Main Selection, do nothing and we will send it to you automatically. If you want one of the other selections, or nothing at all, send us the reply form within three days. In the next year you agree to buy twenty more books at the regular low Church prices, plus shipping and handling. Breaking up is easier than a Nevada divorce: just send us a signed and notarized statement indicating ninety-five points of theological disagreement with our religious institution, in triplicate. Hurry. This offer is for a limited time only. That number again is 1-800-COMICSPIRIT.

PRINCE: It's listed on the bottom of your screen. Cairo, Egypt, you're next.

CAIRO: What are your Five Pillars?[17]

LECHER: Unlike a major competitor, we do not have five pillars. In the interest of simplicity, we've reduced the number to three. One, the belief that God is God, and Father Lecher is his final prophet; two, the giving of tithes to the Church of the Comic Spirit; and three, a semi-annual pilgrimage to Bliss Beach.

PRINCE: Visitors welcome?

LECHER: Anybody who flashes plastic.

PRINCE: Rome, Italy, hello.

ROME, ITALY: What are members required to give up for Lent?

LECHER: We recommend giving up confession.

PRINCE: You'll get a lot of takers there. Kirkland, Kansas, you're

---

[16]Observant Catholics will recognize these virtues as inversions of the Seven Deadly Sins: (1) pride, (2) covetousness, (3) lust, (4) anger, (5) gluttony, (6) envy, and (7) sloth. Father Lecher's ten years as a priest undoubtedly influenced his reflections on these subjects.

[17]The caller is referring to the Five Pillars of Islam: (1) the creed, "There is no God but Allah, and Muhammed is His prophet," (2) prayer five times a day, (3) the giving of alms, (4) fasting during the month of Ramadan, and (5) at least one pilgrimage to Mecca per lifetime.

on. . . . Kirkland, Kansas?

KIRKLAND: Lenny, I must say I really enjoy your show. I watch it every chance I get. I am especially enjoying tonight's program, because I myself can identify with somebody who flunked out of a language course in college, plus I've always been interested in angels and the question whether they've got feathers and are sexless or the other way around, and I—

PRINCE: What's your question?

KIRKLAND, KANSAS: Actually, I have four questions for Reverend Lecher. One, what must I do to be saved? Two, what's it like to be saved? Three, what happens when you die? Four, I'm a little confused, is God a He or a She? Thank you.

PRINCE: Good questions.

LECHER: Join the church and buy the book. The answers are all in there.

PRINCE: Couldn't you give her at least a hint? For instance, what's it like to be saved, in three words or less?

LECHER: No more therapy.

PRINCE: What if you happen to be a therapist?

LECHER: Good question.

PRINCE: Cambridge, Mass., for Al Lecher.

CAMBRIDGE: *Where* does Aristotle put cherubim in the same category as the nymphet?

LECHER: In his chapter on nymphets.[18]

PRINCE: St. Thomas, Missouri, hello.

ST. THOMAS, MISSOURI: What I wanna know is, if Michelle and Cheri took off with the dictionary and granite slate and the Scrolls, where's the evidence for your claims?

LECHER: God doesn't require evidence. He requires faith. Also, how many religions still have their original scriptures? I defy you to show me a single religion that still has its original scriptures. There are no federal or state laws, that I know of, stating that a religion has to keep its original scriptures around for evidence. All the major religions are built on faith, not on evidence, and we are proud to stand within the traditions of the great religions of the world.

---

[18]Father Lecher is referring to Aristotle's lost treatise on comedy.

PRINCE: Time for one last caller. Beverly Hills, California.

BEVERLY HILLS: Say, aren't you the guy who got busted for statutory—

PRINCE: Sorry, musta got cut off. We're outta time, so we'll reschedule the President for sometime later. This has been "Lenny Prince Live," we've been talking to Father Al Lecher, gotta go now, remember, tomorrow night the hit man, next week the Secretary of Space with good news for the animal kingdom. Bye bye.

THERE IS LITTLE TO ADD to Father Lecher's comments, especially the one in response to the doubting Thomas. Like most of his public appearances, this performance was a tour de force. The last caller's insinuation of evil doings, however, calls for the rebuttal he was unable to give due to the constraint of time.

Many of the great prophets exhibit behavior that to our Puritanic sensibilities might seem extreme, even bizarre. The Biblical patriarch Abram offered his wife Sara's favors to the Egyptians. Lot's daughters slept with their inebriated father (Abram's nephew) in a cave. David, the first king of Israel, kept a substantial harem. Buddha's father furnished the young prince with 40,000 dancing girls. Brigham Young married twenty-seven women and proclaimed polygamy an official tenet of the Church of Jesus Christ of Latter-Day Saints. This is not of course to suggest that there is anything morally questionable about Father Lecher's behavior toward the angels; it is only to put the matter in perspective. As for the insinuation that he preferred the company of somewhat younger women, I can only cite the words of another great founder, Jesus: "Suffer the little children to come unto me, and forbid them not."[19]

3

THE PROOF, THEN, IS OVERWHELMING. Father Alazon Lecher was innocent of the vicious charges of those who have sought to

---

[19]Matthew 19:14. See also Mark 10:14, Luke 18:16.

defame him, to discredit the Bear Lake Scrolls, and to destroy the Church of the Comic Spirit.

To recapitulate the evidence I have cited would be tedious. It is enough to summarize the theme to which this mountain of evidence points: Father Lecher's narrative is no less plausible than the stories about the Buddha, Moses, Jesus, Muhammad, Joseph Smith, etc. The principal difference between the Lecher account and those others is that the divine manifestation he experienced supersedes theirs, that the Bear Lake Scrolls displace all prior scriptures, and that the Church of the Comic Spirit is destined to replace every other religion.

This not a cautious claim, but it is thoroughly reasonable. A close scrutiny of Father Lecher's account uncovers a well-conceived divine plan. He is visited by angels four times, at exactly ten year intervals; each time the angel delivers a message; each message contains exactly four instructions. Or, to put the matter in the most orderly terms:

- ORIGIN
  1. Find the dictionary
  2. Learn Ur-Hebrew
  3. Keep your activities a secret
  4. Return in ten years
- TENTH YEAR
  1. Find the Scrolls
  2. Translate them
  3. Keep them a secret
  4. Return in ten years
- TWENTIETH YEAR
  1. Gather four (4!) disciples
  2. Interpret the Scrolls
  3. Write a letter of resignation to the pope
  4. Return in ten years
- THIRTIETH YEAR
  1. Found the Church
  2. Build a theme park
  3. Proclaim the new gospel
  4. Return in ten years for a reevaluation.

Stated in this way, there is a highly logical structure, which is consistent with the time-honored belief that God operates according to a mysterious but well-organized plan. I need only add that there is also the matter of Father Lecher's material progress in life, from Buffalo to Pocatello to Salt Lake City to Reno,[20] from a long-forgotten motel to a Motel 6 to "a more upscale place" to the unnamed "finest motel in town," and, most importantly, from an old '56 Chevrolet to a "collector's edition fishtail Caddy" to a slightly-used Mercedes coupe to a restored Rolls-Royce—progress that is clearly a sign of divine favor.[21] Assuming that the diagram is accurate, and that the divine plan is rational, there can be no other conclusion than that the Church of the Comic Spirit is divinely ordained.

But one more proof should convince those with a scientific mind. Shortly after Father Lecher left us, I approached an organization that specializes in procuring CEOs for corporations, universities, and other bureaucratic enterprises—a so-called "head-hunters" organization. I described to them a "hypothetical" religion (I had in mind the Church of the Comic Spirit) and asked them to construct a profile of someone who could serve as prophet, founder, and pontiff. Their extensive research yielded the following criteria for that position:
—charisma;
—a common touch;
—an impressive track record;
—experience;
—honesty; and
—a sense of humor.
Then I presented them with the resumés of the founders of the

---

[20]One thinks of Horace Greeley's sage advice: "Go West, young man."

[21]Note that Father Lecher was a respected leader in several religions (Judaism, Catholicism, and Protestantism) before founding the Church of the Comic Spirit. This personal itinerary should not be construed as a "ranking" of these illustrious forerunners of his own religion; as is clear from his choice of disciples, the good father was possessed of a thoroughly ecumenical spirit.

great religions—preserving, of course, their anonymity—and invited them to rank these founders according to the six criteria. It should come as no surprise that Father Alazon Lecher was the candidate of choice, and by a wide margin. (Fully sensitive to the other religions, I must decline to present the actual data. I will note, however, that many of the candidates fell short on the third criterion, an impressive track record, and all but Father Lecher lacked the sixth, a sense of humor.)

If further proof were needed, it might come in the form of a brief recapitulation of the rest of the Lecher story. As is well known, the Friday after Father Alazon appeared on "Lenny Prince Live," he was martyred. This fact, as well as the fact that the assassination occurred at Bear Lake World, and in full view of thousands of newly-baptized church members and a large crowd of well-wishers, is beyond dispute. What are still not known are, of course, the details of his martyrdom. Who was the perpetrator of this despicable crime? One of his legions of persecutors? The hit man who cancelled his appearance on "Lenny Prince Live?" A former spouse or spouse-equivalent? An irate ex-disciple? The only evidence the FBI has been able to turn up to date has been an unregistered Remington 700.

What is not so well known is that beginning the following Sunday morning and lasting for a period of forty days, Father Lecher was sighted in and around Bear Lake by various of the faithful: first by three of the original disciples, then by five hundred members of the booster club who were enjoying an evening at The Motel Whose Name Father Lecher Forgot. I myself had the privilege of being the last to speak with him. His final message, whispered to me immediately before he ascended into heaven to be with his beloved angels, were the enigmatic words of the English novelist, George Orwell: "Saints should always be judged guilty until they are proved innocent."[22]

Reno, Nevada
B. S. Buller, Editor

---

[22]"Reflections on Gandhi," in *The Orwell Reader* (New York, 1956), p. 328.

THE BEAR LAKE
SCROLLS

INTRODUCTION

WHAT FATHER ALAZON LECHER DISCOVERED on April 1 some forty years ago in that hallowed cave overlooking Bear Lake was a set of twelve ancient sheepskin scrolls, neatly arranged within the folds of what he later described to his four disciples as "a very old briefcase." When we pressed him for an estimate of the age of that briefcase, he judged it to be four thousand years old, "give or take fifty years." He conceded that this was an estimate,[23] that the angel Michelle had provided him no information about the history of the documents. He added that the probable reason for her silence on this question was that, in order to preserve the aura of mystery with which divine manifestations are always attended, angels do not reveal their revelation's minor details to prophets.

The briefcase, he emphasized, had never been opened. He verified this opinion by citing the expert testimony of a certified Beverly Hills[24] locksmith (he could not remember her name).

---

[23]Father Lecher was being typically modest. His estimate on this matter was not that of an ordinary layperson. He possessed remarkable archaeological expertise, especially for one who had no formal training in the field. As he once told me, he had visited the Oriental Institute of the University of Chicago as a child, and on a trip to London at the age of twenty-four (a college graduation present from his father), he spent nearly half his waking hours in the British Museum, fascinated by the antiquities of the Ancient Near East.

[24]Ever mindful of his filial obligations, Father Lecher visited his uncle in Beverly Hills with regularity.

After she had disengaged the rusty clasp, Father Lecher said, he paid her, quietly left the back room of her establishment (secrecy, he emphasized, was of the utmost importance), went back to his uncle's mansion, stole unobserved into the wine cellar (secrecy again being the motive), opened the briefcase, and found a trove of twelve ancient sheepskin Scrolls, all of them perfectly preserved. Each scroll was secured with a royal blue waxen seal, on which was stamped a tiny Ur-Hebrew number, indicating, he surmised, the order in which the Scrolls were to be translated and positioned within the finished text.

What follows in the main body of this volume are Father Lecher's translations of the twelve sacred Scrolls, including the titles, which were present in the original. As the disciple chosen by the master to edit this volume, I have taken the liberty of writing an introduction to each Scroll and to add a few notes to the body of the text.

SO MUCH FOR THE HISTORY of the Bear Lake Scrolls. What about their subject matter?

After Father Lecher had translated the Scrolls, it did not take him long to discover that they contained eleven stories as well as a collection of maxims. Nor did it take him much time to discover that most of the stories are remarkably similar to some of the well-known stories found in the Hebrew Bible (or, as Christians call it, the Old Testament)—the stories of Eve and Adam, for example; of the Great Flood; of Abraham and Sarah; of the destruction of Sodom and Gomorrah; of Job and his sufferings; of Jonah and the whale—and that the collection of maxims is remarkably similar to some of the wisdom literature also found in the Bible.

The discovery of these resemblances led to a crucial question: Which were written first, the biblical stories and wisdom, or the stories and wisdom of the Scrolls? The committee of master and disciples spent seven of our ten years together debating this question. It is not necessary to record the particulars of those late-evening disputes. It is enough to say that our committee was divided on this question, but that our disagreements were expressed within a cordial atmosphere. Professor Allbright was originally of the opinion that the Scrolls were later restatements of the so-called "orthodox" stories and maxims. Father Lecher and I believed otherwise, insisting that the Scrolls were the originals, and that their likenesses were merely imitations, and inferior ones at that. Cardinal Micromentis was convinced that both sides in this argument were correct. (Ms. LaFemme did not participate in the majority of these evening discussions, being engaged in her lucrative business.)

Father Lecher and I were finally able to convince our colleagues of the superior logic of our position. Our primary argument was simple: because the Scrolls were composed in Ur-Hebrew, and because the word *Ur* means original (in the sense of chronological precedence), the Scrolls therefore must consist of the original, authentic form of the stories and the collection of aphorisms. Our secondary argument was more subtle: if the Scrolls did not consist of the original form, they could not have been divinely inspired; they were indeed divinely inspired; therefore, they must consist of the original form of the stories and wisdom.

We were forced to the conclusion that Judaism and Christianity, both of which accept the Hebrew Bible (or Old Testament) as scripture, are based on a tragic though understandable mistake. Committed as we were to the search for truth, we did not shrink from this conclusion, which, to many of our Jewish and Christian friends, will naturally cause discomfort.

Thus we disciples were later quite prepared to follow Father Lecher when, on that April day some ten years ago, he received the divine instructions to form the one true religion, the Church of the Comic Spirit.

1 | First Person Omniscient

THE STORY CONTAINED IN THE FIRST SCROLL bears a strong likeness to the later, orthodox story of the creation of the world and of our primordial parents (Genesis 1:1–3:24). But there are substantial differences between the two.

1. The original is narrated by God himself, a fact to which the title ("First Person Omniscient") calls attention. The orthodox version, however, is told from the third person point of view. This raises a question. How could anyone except God give an accurate account of his creation of the first human beings? Was anyone else there?

2. In the original, God provides a wealth of detail concerning the motives for his acts, as only he would be able to do. The later version is extremely spare in this matter; rarely if ever does it suggest the reasons for God's actions. Why, for example, did he prohibit Adam from eating the fruit of the tree of the knowledge of good and evil? Was it a mere whim? An immature need to "show who's boss"? An awareness of the presence of dangerous pesticides? One is only left to speculate.

3. God, in this original account, is a person with whom one can readily sympathize. He is vulnerable, self-deprecating, honest with himself, chauvinistic but capable of learning from his mistakes, and disarmingly ironic. In the later story, these traits vanish entirely. He is portrayed as distant, disengaged, and disapproving.

These differences show the vast superiority of the original to its pale imitation.

§

IN THE BEGINNING, there wasn't much of anything. Just the basics. There was earth, of course. Heaven, too—we needed a place to come home to, after our numerous trips down to earth. And when I say earth, I'm including the lakes, the rivers, the oceans, etc. Everything that comes under the category of water. But water was not why we made those excursions. None of us would have even *thought* of coming down for water. We associated water with ships and sailors. Nobody wanted to be a sailor. The sailor was considered the lowest form of life. No, the reason we came down was for the dry land. And when I say dry land, I'm including the vineyards.

Speaking of the basics, there were also the sun, the moon, the planets, the stars—things for the astrologers to study, I believe that was the plan, and for the poets to write about. Also, there were the birds and the fish, for the bird watchers and fishermen. (That's what they were called back then, *fishermen*. Nobody knew any better.) And I can't forget the animals. At that time they were all wild—not necessarily ferocious, just wild. Domestication was my later innovation, as were the Seven Wonders of the Ancient World, of which, they tell me, I have every right to be proud. They include—I'm reading from my notes here—(1) the Mausoleum of Halicarnassus; (2) the Artemision at Ephesus; (3) the Colossus of Rhodes; (4) the statue of Zeus (Zeus was my biggest rival, but we were instructed to be tolerant of other religions; besides, he was not a key player in the total scheme of things); (5) the lighthouse at Alexandria; (6) the Sphinx and the Pyramids, which counted as one (I especially enjoyed designing the Pyramids, because of the excellent retirement benefits); and (7) the Hanging Gardens of Babylon—not including the walls, which came later.

And oh yes. I also created an Eighth Wonder. That would be Eve. I once considered her my masterpiece.

§

LET ME TELL YOU ABOUT EVE. Built like a Venus statue: five foot

nine, with 128 pounds moulded within a 36–24–36 hourglass[25]—
exactly the stats that win beauty contests. Which of course she
never entered, for philosophical reasons. "What's the point of
entering the Miss Solar System Pageant," she'd say, "when I'd be
the only contestant? Where's the challenge?"[26] You had to be

---

[25]The original reads: "Built like a Venus statue: 3.83 cubits tall, with
38.9 minas poured into a 2–1.33–2 hourglass."

There was general agreement among members of our committee that
the modern equivalent of a cubit is 18 inches. There was disagreement,
however, about the modern equivalents of the ancient Ur-Hebrew
system of weights. According to Professor Allbright's calculations:
1 lb. (avoirdupois) = 16 oz. = 7000 grains (*Merriam Webster's Collegiate
Dictionary*, 10th ed., s.v. "weights and measures");
1 shekel = 420 grains (*Encyclopædia Britannica*, 1963 ed., s.v. "shekel"); 1
lb. (avoirdupois) = 16.6667 shekels;
1 mina = 60 shekels (*Oxford English Dictionary*, 1971 ed., s.v. "mina");
1 lb. (avoirdupois) = .2778 minas;
1 mina = 3.599712 lb. (avoirdupois).

Father Lecher pointed out that if this conclusion were accurate, Eve
would have weighed 140 lb. In his experience, he added, a 5'9" woman
who measures 36–24–36 will weigh 128 lb. Therefore, in the Ur-Hebrew
system, 1 mina must have been equivalent to 3.29 lb. (avoirdupois).

In support of Father Lecher's argument, Cardinal Micromentis added
the observation that:

a. the ancient Egyptians invented glass;

b. the ancient Egyptians must have invented the hourglass;

c. the ancient Egyptians were neighborly rivals to the ancient Ur-
Hebrews;

d. hence, the ancient Ur-Hebrews undoubtedly got their standards of
feminine beauty from the Egyptians.

Ms. LaFemme did not participate in this discussion, being on call.

The editor has chosen to depend on Father Lecher's experience in
this matter.

[26]The reader may wonder why Eve speaks of the Miss Solar System
Pageant and not the Miss Universe Pageant. Is not the universe more
encompassing than our tiny solar system?

The committee produced three possible explanations.

(1) In the opinion of Professor Allbright, God did not create the
entire universe; he created only our solar system, and both he and Eve
recognized the likelihood of life beyond it.

impressed with her ability to think those things through. Also, with her moral values, her refusal to parade her stunning attributes before a pack of my chauvinistic colleagues who had only one thing on their minds.

And talk about charm! I'll never forget how she'd raise her eyebrow ever so slightly and flash a hint of that very knowing, adult smile, which you could read all sorts of things into. The original Mona Lisa.

Except that she was blonde. In the evening, among palm trees on the moonlit beach, her hair shone ever so gloriously. We took many an evening stroll, Eve and I—she in her stunning evening gown, me in my diamond-studded white shirt and elegant tuxedo. Gazing into each other's starlit eyes, singing Italian aria duets, quoting portions of *Sonnets from the Portuguese*. Sharing inmost thoughts. Comparing metaphysical speculations. Making plans for the future. Until that fateful day . . . but I'm getting ahead of myself.

It's not often you get a chance to create the woman of your dreams, and I don't mind saying that I made the most of that opportunity. I gave her a double helping of id and held off on the superego. (Or is it the ego? I always get those two mixed up.) When there are going to be just the two of you, that can be done, experimenting with the id/superego/ego ratio. It's quite ethical, speaking of moral values, because you don't have to worry about the consequences. In that particular case, I don't have to tell you what the consequences were. Fabulous! That's all I can say. Here I am, omniscient, which includes an ample vocabulary, all sorts of words at my disposal (ornithology, ambidextrous, proclivity, etc.) plus the instinct about how to use them to the best effect, and I end up simply saying Fabulous! That'll give you some idea.

---

(2) According to Father Lecher, the Ur-Hebrew language does not have separate words for *solar system* and *universe*.

(3) In the opinion of Ms. LaFemme, who had just come back from an appointment, God had created Eve with a low self-esteem.

Cardinal Micromentis did not participate in this discussion, being asleep in the corner.

But we didn't always have sex. We also played lots of chess. I enjoy the game of chess, so I gave her a full complement of brains, as I may have mentioned. This is because I don't always like to win. In my opinion, long winning streaks get to be boring. I know most people dream of batting a thousand, hitting home runs with the bases loaded every time they come to bat, things like that. But I'm not like most people. I don't mind actually *losing* once in a while. It makes winning more meaningful. I know it sounds crazy, but that's the way I am, of the opinion that winning, winning, winning, nothing but winning, can get to be a big bore, because of the repetition involved. That's why I gave Eve a goodly measure of brains. Competition is the spice of life, I've always said. At least it's a strong second.

Of course I didn't *have* to create Eve. There were other options. For example, I could have created a computer chess game with a high level of difficulty. It would have been similar, in terms of the intellectual challenge. It would also have avoided a problem down the road. But it wouldn't have been the same, in terms of the romance and intimacy and high-powered ecstasy and everything. Not that I couldn't have done without the sexual element. I could have remained celibate. It was within my power. I could have made a substitution. I'm not sure what it would have been, but I could have done it. But I had free will, which happens to be one of my attributes. Omniscience, omnipotence, free will—I'd have to say these are my most outstanding qualities. I especially enjoy the free will. When you've got free will going for you, you sort of naturally lean toward expressing yourself romantically, which always seems to lead to sex. It's practically inevitable. That's why I decided I needed a woman. Not just any woman, of course. Somebody like Eve, the woman of my dreams.

We never had children, Eve and I. We took precautions. We weren't Catholic,[27] so we could do that. I wouldn't want to say any more on the topic. People might think I'm making recommendations, or they might suspect I'm getting a kickback from the

---

[27]This is not a negative judgment on Catholicism but a statement of fact. One must keep in mind that God was not a Christian but a Jew—more specifically, an Ur-Jew.

manufacturer, or taking sides on some important religious or moral issue. Also, I don't happen to think it's the kind of a thing that should be mentioned in mixed company. Traditional values, that's another thing I have.

Naturally, we thought about having kids, but we were practical people, Eve and I. We knew that when you have kids, you have to cut back on other things, like BMWs and Italian leather furniture and St. Moritz vacations and eating in the better restaurants. We were also planning ahead, thinking about the cost of tuition, which wasn't quite as bad as it is today but could still put a crimp in your budget. So we had to stop and ask ourselves if it would be worth it, having kids and everything. We decided no, we'd have pets instead.

This explains the wide open spaces you may have noticed. We needed a place for all those pets. If you've ever had a goodly number of pets, you'll know exactly what I'm talking about. They need lots of room outdoors, to roam free. Well, I took account of that need and created plenty of woods and pastures and gardens. They were getting underfoot in Eve's kitchen, the pets were, so I took a few extra days to design much of what you now enjoy as the great outdoors.

At the time, it didn't seem like such a bad idea.

§

Eve eventually got tired of eating Swiss chocolate and practicing her French while I was spending my day down at the office. So one evening during a stroll along the beach she looked up to me with fervor in her big blue innocent eyes and said, "Oh, my perfect, all-knowing one, can you guess what I'd really like for my birthday?"

"No, my lovely sweetheart," I said, pretending I hadn't forgotten that important occasion. I usually didn't. Forget, that is. The previous year, for instance, I'd remembered. I'd gotten her a novel by some French author. A gentleman by the name of Flaubert (the first name escapes me). "What would you really like for your birthday?" said I, finishing my sentence.

"A man," she whispered.

"What?" I said. I wasn't sure I'd heard her correctly.

"Wouldn't it be nice to have a man around the house?" she asked in her normal voice.

"What?" I repeated. This time I heard her, all right. I was just checking her sentence for grammatical errors.

"WOULDN'T IT BE NICE—"

"I heard you," I said. "You want a . . . a. . . ."

"A man around the house!" she said. Her excitement level was rising.

"A man?" I asked. "Around the house?" I asked.

"Right," she said, or maybe it would be better to say *she cooed.*

"A man," I said. This was a new concept for me. I knew the word *house,* but not *man.*

"Kind of like a . . . pet," she explained.

"Oh," I said. I knew about pets. I remembered having created them.

"A *talking* pet," she went on to explain.

"A talking pet," I said. "Like a parrot?"

She hesitated a moment. "Kind of," she said.

"You already have a parrot," I pointed out to her. I was referring to Eveline.

"But Eveline isn't quite. . . ." She was looking for words, Eve was. She sometimes did that, search for words, often with her hands, manually. It wasn't that she wasn't intelligent, she just wasn't, how shall I say, omniscient. I didn't make her to be omniscient. That would have created problems, with the chess games and everything.

"Eveline isn't quite what?"

"Eveline can't. . . ." She was going through another word search.

"Speak French?" I guessed.

"She can't. . . ."

"Sing Verdi arias?" I guessed.

She finally found her word. "Give massages," she said.

"Massages?"

"Massages," she repeated. "These bon bons are filling me out a little more than I'd like. You've probably noticed."

Yes, I had noticed, but I hadn't said anything, being sensitive by nature.

"So I was thinking," she went on, "I could use a masseur to work on the hips and thighs."

"Does it have to be a masseur?" I asked. "How about a nice masseuse? Wouldn't that do the trick?" I wasn't suspicious or potentially jealous or anything; these aren't desirable traits to have, and of course I didn't have them, being who I am. I was just making sure she was aware of all the options.

"No," she said, turning to me and flashing her lovely smile in the moonlight, "I'm not sure I could trust her with you."

This rather surprised me. But she had a point, I have to admit. If I were to design a masseuse, I'd probably make her perfect, because of my exacting standards. Which would mean I'd run the risk of getting involved with her, because of my attraction to perfection. And with two perfect women on my hands, I'd have a hard time choosing between them, and I'd probably end up choosing them both. If I know myself, that's exactly what I'd do. I'm referring to the fact that I'm very fair-minded, which is ordinarily a good trait to have, but in that particular situation it would probably lead to the problem of divided loyalty.

She presented me with a dilemma, Eve did. If I created a masseuse for her, we'd end up with, at best, a time-sharing plan, which would undoubtedly cause some friction, getting the schedules right and everything. If I created a masseur . . . well, I just had a sense it might not work out. Call it a premonition. On the other hand, if I didn't create either a masseuse or a masseur, her hips and thighs would *really* go to pot, which would cut down significantly on my appreciation and overtax my sensitivity.

So I created a masseur for her. I ignored the premonition and created the masseur. This was Adam. She liked the name *Adam*. Six foot four, 245 pounds, dark hair, straight nose, and he could bench press 495 pounds. Those were her specifications. Also, he had Mediterranean teeth and a voice like Pavarotti, R.I.P. Perfect again, except for one thing: not as smart as Eve. That's the way she wanted it.[28]

---

[28]The committee engaged in a lengthy dialogue on these last two

At first this seemed to be a decent enough arrangement. Adam did his job and was courteous and respectful and slept on the sofa downstairs. He even helped with the little chores around the house, like taking out the garbage, making the beds, even cooking dinner, crêpes and *boeuf bourguignon* and other delectable dishes. Eve was grateful to me for her birthday gift, as well as being extraordinarily affectionate. And of course she regained her youthful figure. Sex got to be even more fantastic. In fact, she kept thinking of different and exciting variations, which made me start coming home in the middle of the day occasionally, just to see what she'd dreamed up that morning while Adam was dutifully performing his main function.

That's how I found out.

§

ONE DAY I CAME HOME AT NOON, without calling first. I wanted to surprise her. All morning long I'd been thinking about her, my precious Eve, going through that distasteful regimen of reduction, having Adam rub off that excess flesh around the hips and thighs, just so she could enhance my pleasure. I have to admit I hadn't been attending to my business. At the time, I was working on the blueprints for the Hanging Gardens of Babylon, trying to decide whether to put a wall around them. But I just couldn't keep my mind on my work.

There was nobody home when I walked through the front door. That's funny, I said to myself. She's usually here this time of day.

Oh, I thought, she's probably out feeding the animals. That's what it is. The woman just *loves* animals. Adam is probably over on the couch taking a nap after his morning workout. I won't go

---

sentences. Ms. LaFemme remarked that they confirmed her faith in the authenticity of the Scrolls. Cardinal Micromentis took the position that Father Lecher had mistranslated this passage. Father Lecher took the position that he had not.

Professor Allbright did not participate in this discussion, having left the room to install some software on his new computer.

over and disturb him. I don't like to be awakened from my naps and neither, I'm sure, does he.

I know what I'll do, I continued. I'll take a bottle of champagne from the refrigerator, also a little basket of fresh strawberries, and go surprise her. It won't be moonlight, she'll be blonde, but this won't prevent us from walking among the hyacinths and discussing the deep meanings behind certain of our favorite poems. Then we'll find a private clearing out there in the garden, sit down in the grass, crack open the champagne, insert strawberries in each other's mouths, compliment each other on some of our most remarkable traits—her beauty and my powers of observation, for example—and finish it off with a refreshing bit of sex. Perfect. That's what I'll do. Then, if there's still time, I'll go back to the office and finish designing the Hanging Gardens, maybe even get a start on the Sphinx.

So out I went to the garden, loaded down with champagne and strawberries, whistling a happy tune—I believe it was a Bach fugue, but it could have been "On Top of Old Smokey"—and admiring my handiwork. I was quite pleased with myself, I have to confess. On top of the world, so to speak.

As I was strolling along, however, I suddenly heard a noise some twenty feet ahead of me and to my left, right off the garden path. A sigh. A damsel in distress! I quickly surmised. But then I remembered: no, the only damsel on the entire earth is the one I created. That would be . . . Eve.

Eve? I thought. No. She was a damsel, all right, but I could not imagine her being in distress. (1) Distress is a situation one finds oneself in when one has not thought of the dangers that lie ahead. (2) I had created Eve to think ahead (chess is a game that, played properly, requires the players to think ahead). (3) Therefore, Eve, though she was certainly a damsel, was not now, nor had she ever been, nor would she ever be, in distress—it would be an impossibility, metaphysically speaking. Besides, the sigh was too rapturous to qualify as a sign of distress.

On the other hand, it sounded like Eve.

By the time I had carefully thought this problem through, I was standing right next to the noise. It was coming from some thick bushes alongside the path. Next thing you know, I was sticking my cane into the very midst of those bushes. This wasn't part of any complicated reasoning process, it was just . . . instinctual, I guess you could say. In fact, I didn't know quite what to expect. I guess I was expecting to hit some animal or other. Eve was always the kind of a person who got a big kick out of playing with pets (see above). That's probably what's transpiring, I finally concluded. Eve is in the bushes, playing patta-cake with some simian creature.

It wasn't a pet, though, my target in the bushes wasn't. It was somewhat firmer than a soft, furry creature. It was a buttock. A hairy, muscular buttock. Hmmm, I thought. Male. That would be . . . Adam. He's the only male I've created. Therefore, Adam.

A male head stuck itself out of the bushes. Correct, I congratulated myself, thinking of my powers of deduction; it's Adam, all right. I'd know that dark hair and those gleaming Mediterranean teeth anywhere.

"What the hell's going on here?" inquired Adam.

What a coincidence! thought I. This was a question I myself was just then on the verge of asking, though I wasn't planning to put it quite that way.

"Oh," he said before I could think of an appropriate way to phrase it. "It's you."

"Right," I said. "I was just walking along this garden path, looking for my wife, Eve—your client—and I heard a noise in these bushes. So I stopped to investigate, just out of curiosity." I should point out that I like to keep up on all the new developments. I have an insatiable intellectual curiosity. It's probably a function of my omniscience.

"Haven't you ever heard of privacy?" he asked. He was being gruff.

"Privacy?" I asked.

"Privacy," he repeated. "Seclusion."

"Ah yes," I said. "'The state of being apart from company or observation'."

"Scram, Grandpa," he said.

"Who's that?" another voice from the bush suddenly inquired.

Unless I'm mistaken, I said to myself, that's Eve. Either Eve, or her pet parrot, Eveline.

"Shhh," I heard Adam whisper. "It's *him*."

Well, I stuck my cane into the bushes once more. The curiosity factor again. This time, however, I hit something soft. Soft, and feminine. And familiar. But definitely not a parrot.

"Ow!" said the voice. "What the hell do you think you're doing?"

"Eve!" I said. Now I knew for sure it was Eve. Eveline couldn't construct complicated sentences. She could swear, but she was incapable of constructing complex sentences, especially if they were in the interrogative mode. I had created parrots to repeat short, snappy aphorisms, not to ask long complicated questions. Long questions require curiosity, and I had reserved curiosity for myself and a few select human beings.

"What a coincidence," I continued, after I was satisfied that my conversation partner was none other than my perfect wife Eve. "I was just looking for you. You wouldn't care for some strawberries, would you?"

"Sorry," said the voice. "I just ate."

"Champagne?" I inquired. I was being thoughtful. Another one of my traits.

"Who needs champagne?" replied the voice.

This was not like Eve. One of her favorite pastimes, ranking right behind beating me in a hotly-contested game of chess and walking along the beach in the moonlight and attending to the animals and purchasing the latest fashions in negligee, was eating strawberries and drinking champagne. But here she was, Eve, my adoring wife, speaking to me out of a bush, telling me no thanks, she wasn't hungry, she wasn't even thirsty.

Maybe she'd change her mind, I thought to myself, if she stood up and faced me. Maybe that's the problem, she's lying down (or is it laying down?) and can't feel the full effects of my personal charisma.

"Say, Eve," I said to her. "Why don't you stand up so we can talk about this, face to face. If you're having a problem, I'd like to know—"

Well, she stood up, all right. She stood up for a face to face conversation with me, her ever-loving husband. But it wasn't her face I noticed. What I noticed was that she was naked from the waist up. And for all I knew, from the waist down.

Then Adam also stood up. I noticed the same thing about him.

"Excuse me," I said, and I turned completely around. To tell the truth, as I always do, I found this very embarrassing. This explains why I turned around 187 degrees. I'd seen them both in the buff before, Adam when I created him and Eve while we were working through the instructions in *The Joy of Sex,* but this was different, somehow. It must have been the combination.

Anyway, the fact remains that I was embarrassed. So I said, with my back to them, "Why don't you both get dressed, then we can go back to the house and discuss the matter." To tell the truth again, I had no idea what the matter was that we'd be discussing, but this seemed to be an appropriate sentence to speak in that situation.

They took me up on this casual suggestion. I was kind of surprised, but that's exactly what they did. They put on their rumpled clothes—he was wearing a pair of jeans and a muscle shirt, she was sporting cool muslin shorts and an undersized tank top from some Spring catalog; they were both barefoot—I was starting to say they put on their clothes, giggled a bit, and started to walk back to the house, holding hands.

I followed them. This seemed to be the appropriate thing to do. I had never been in a situation quite like this, but my instincts took over and told me, *follow that pair. It would be in your best interests to follow that pair and keep them in your sight.* Which is what I did.

As I was walking along behind them, humming the Funeral March from Chopin's Sonata in B flat minor, the word *flaunt* came to mind. That word had never entered my mind up to that point—in fact I had never even heard it before. But there it was, right on the tip of my tongue. They're *flaunting* it, I said to myself; that's how I'd describe them, *flaunters.*

This is one of the perks of being omniscient. You're always expanding your vocabulary to help you describe new situations. The point is that you don't start out with a full vocabulary; you gradually acquire it. A new situation will arise, and immediately the right word—*le mot juste,* I believe the French call it—will pop into your head. And once you acquire this word—French,

English, Greek, Ur-Hebrew—you never forget it.

It's the same thing, incidentally, with knowledge and wisdom. They, too, are traits a higher being acquires gradually. Once acquired, they, too, tend to stick with you.

If you ever have a chance to be omniscient, you'll see what I mean.

§

"WE CAN STILL BE FRIENDS," Eve was informing me. The three of us were seated around the kitchen table, finishing off the strawberries and champagne, and she was trying to make me feel better about the situation. She had switched from the flaunting mode to the concern mode.

Friend was another new word. I knew *spouse*, but up to that time I had not run across the word *friend*. I immediately knew what she meant by this word, however, as in the sentence, "We can still be friends." She meant goodbye.

What did I do wrong? was the thought that was crossing my all-knowing mind. Did I fail to be solicitous of her every need? Did I spend too much time at the office? Did I beat her too often at chess? Did I forget our anniversary again? Did I neglect to fold my pajamas?

No, I replied to myself, I just got old. That explains her original request for this Adam person. Now I knew what she had meant by the command, Make him youthful. At the time, I just assumed she meant she wanted somebody with plenty of energy for the long, arduous massages. That wasn't it at all. There was another dimension to it.

"Would it help," I asked, "if I shaved my beard and started to use Grecian Formula?"

"You can if you want to," she cooed, snuggling up closer to Adam, "but it won't make any difference."

"Just a suggestion," I replied ruefully. Another new word. *Ruefully*. I'm not saying I liked this new word, I'm just saying that all at once it occurred to me. I was suddenly learning a lot of new stuff, stuff they don't teach you in school.

"Excuse me," I said.

They didn't seem to notice.

I cleared my throat. "Excuse me," I repeated.

Again, no response. So I got up anyway and walked over to my study to pick up a yellow legal pad and a #2 pencil. At that time in my life I had a study, which I liked to call my home office. I used it for take-home work, writing romantic poetry, reading the *Review of Metaphysics* and *Mad Magazine,* keeping track of the family budget, figuring out our income tax. Things like that.

It was tax deductible, the home office was. That is, under the former tax laws. But with the new tax laws, new rules applied. The new rules said that in order to claim a deduction, (1) the home office must be used exclusively on a regular basis for business purposes; (2) it must be the taxpayer's principal place of business; and (3) it must be for the convenience of the employer. These rules appeared to disqualify my office as a tax deduction, but as I was scrounging around for the legal pad and the pencil, I began to see some possibilities. For example, I thought about cutting down drastically on the poetry and canceling my subscription to *Mad Magazine.* Since Eve was moving out to live in the tree house with Adam (Aha, I thought; maybe they'd qualify as dependents? It would certainly be worth a try.), I figured poetry would become a thing of the past, anyway, and all of a sudden life wasn't as humorous as I had first judged it to be. These moves wouldn't be too difficult, and they'd help to qualify my study as a legitimate home office. Another thing, I thought about giving up my job as an architect and becoming a full-time consultant. That way I could work out of my home and satisfy the new rules. I'd also save money on the rent.

Brilliant! I said to myself as these thoughts coursed through my ingenious, all-knowing brain. Absolutely brilliant! I'll make a note of it.

Which is what I did: I wrote a note to myself, reminding me to call my lawyer in the morning to work out the details.

Now, I asked myself, where was I?

Oh yes, I told myself, the *divorce*—another new word. I came in here to pick up a legal pad and #2 pencil so we can work out *an equitable division of the assets.*

§

DID I MENTION my Ninth Wonder? No?

Well, let me tell you about Ernestine. Built like a Buddha statue: 145 pounds distributed over a five foot four frame, with a jolly smile and white hair—exactly the qualities that win Grandmother of the Year awards. Which of course she never entered, not being a grandmother. We found out that it's very difficult to be a grandmother when you don't have kids. Or a grandfather, for that matter. Not that attempts weren't made. But when you get to be a certain age . . . well, you're satisfied to leave those things to the younger generation.

And talk about sensible! She had no use for lawyers and divorces and fancy phrases like *alienation of affections* and *in the best interests of both parties*. But I'm not the kind of a person who dwells on the negative. I'm the kind who knows how to put the past behind him and get on with his life. The kind who learns from his mistakes. Which is why I created Ernestine.[29]

Every night, after I've beaten her in a game of checkers, I wind the clock and we go to bed. She cuddles up to me and gives me a nice affectionate kiss. Then, after turning off the light, she turns over on her back and goes right to sleep, snoring and leaving me to lie—or is it lay?—there, wondering why it took me so long to put a wall around those Hanging Gardens of Babylon.[30]

---

[29] As Ms. LaFemme remarked, "Even the gray goose gets her gander."

[30] Note that in this original account, God first creates Eve, then Adam, whereas in the orthodox version, the order of their creation is inexplicably reversed. Father Lecher pointed out that this reversal is illogical, considering the fact that, as both stories agree, God is a male—and, it would seem, an aging one at that. Would not God, he argued, wish his first human companion to be a young female?

Ms. LaFemme disagreed. Might not both accounts be mistaken? she asked. Might not God be a female, for example—perhaps even a lesbian?

After giving this possibility a week's reflection, Professor Allbright proceeded to write the first of his many monographs, "On the Question Regarding Gender and Sexual Orientation in Scroll #1, 'First Person

Omniscient': the Definitive Answer to a Frivolous Objection," (Reno [Unpublished], n.d.). The argument is summarized on pp. 583ff.:

"1. If God had been an aging homosexual male, an aging heterosexual female, an aging homosexual female; or, again, a young heterosexual male, a young homosexual male, a young heterosexual female, a young homosexual female—if he (or she) had been any of these other logical possibilities, then the world would of course be quite different than it is. (Had God been a young homosexual female, for example, it would be quite reasonable to suppose that she would have created homosexual females—some young, some perhaps more mature—to be her companions. Equally reasonably, we would suppose that in that hypothetical event there would be no males, either through generation or through special acts of creation.)

"2. But the world is as it is. It contains both males and females, and aging heterosexual males naturally prefer young heterosexual females (I am indebted to Father Alazon Lecher for this insight, and to my octogenarian friend and colleague Cardinal Micromentis for the suggestion that the reason for this preference is the geriatric principle that, in his charmingly ingenuous words, 'old men need nice nurses'), etc.

"3. Therefore, God was, and most likely still is, an aging heterosexual male."

Ms. LaFemme remained unconvinced by this argument. She allowed it to stand, however, remarking, perhaps facetiously, that she could only shudder at the thought that God might have been nonexistent, autistic, or dead.

2 | The Secret of Long Life

THE SHORTEST STORY IN THE ORTHODOX BIBLE is found in Genesis 5:21–24:

"And Enoch lived sixty and five years, and begat Methuselah. And Enoch walked with God after he begat Methuselah three hundred years, and begat sons and daughters. And all the days of Enoch were three hundred sixty and five years. And Enoch walked with God: and he was not, for God took him."

This is a weak story, in three respects.

1. The character of Enoch is flat. We know next to nothing about him. What were his most heart-felt values? What was his philosophy of life? What was his tragic flaw? In short, who was this man Enoch, and why should we care about how he spent his walking hours?

2. There is hardly any plot. After setting the stage with a two names and dates, the author simply tells us that "Enoch walked with God: and he was not, for God took him." We are not told when Enoch walked with God, or why. We are not told where they walked, or how —whether they walked side by side, or in single file. We are not told whose idea it was. Nor are we told where God took Enoch.

3. The point of the story is obscure. The author evidently wishes to establish a connection between Enoch's strolls with God and his disappearance. But it is difficult to decipher that connection with any certainty. Is this a moral tale? A shaggy dog story?

The original story avoids these weaknesses.[31]

---

[31] As for the reason behind these flaws, one can only speculate.

Professor Allbright convinced himself that the author was merely

§

A Routine Ten-Year Physical

HE WANDERED INTO THE OFFICE and checked in at the front desk. He had an appointment, he reminded them; he was there for his ten-year physical.

A young nurse smiled at him sympathetically, gave him a form to fill out, and pointed him in the direction of the lounge. He shuffled over in that direction, bumping into a potted plant on the way. He steadied himself in front of an armchair before sitting down. He squinted at the grid of boxes requesting his vital facts. He sighed. This was the part he hated most, answering all those personal questions. But he had to do it. It was all part of the system.

Name: Enoch
Age: 365
Address: 7 Eden East Drive
Occupation: early retiree
Marital status: married, with children
Spouse: Beth ("Ma"), age classified
Eldest son: Methuselah, age 300
Eldest grandson: Lamech, age 113
Father: Jared, age 527
Paternal grandfather: Mahalaleel, age 592

---

summarizing the original. See his monograph, "On the Ancient Techniques of Recapitulation in the Interests of Brevity: A Case Study taken from a Certain Text of the Ancient Ur-Hebrews" (Reno [Unpublished], n.d.), especially the last section, "Summary, Recapitulation, and Cursory Synopsis," pp. 438-579.

Ms. LaFemme suspected that the piece was copied by a young man, possibly a college freshman, from the *Cliff's Notes* outline of the original story.

Cardinal Micromentis suggested that Genesis 5:21–24 was the epitaph on Enoch's tombstone.

Father Lecher theorized that the author was in a hurry.

Paternal great-grandfather: Cainan, a.k.a. Kenan, age 662
Paternal great-great-grandfather: Enos, age 752
Paternal great-great-great-grandfather: Seth, age 857
Paternal great-great-great-great-grandfather: Adam (deceased),
cause of death: homesickness
Family tradition: righteous living
Personal motto: "An apple a day"

After finishing this form, he cautiously pulled himself to a standing position and returned to the front desk. Another young nurse escorted him into the doctor's cubicle, joking with him about the onset of male baldness—very insensitive of her, he thought. She instructed him to sit down on the paper-covered table. He did so, taking pains to relax in order to keep his blood pressure from soaring into the danger zone. Breathe deeply, he told himself.

This technique soon put him to sleep.

As he slept, he dreamed about his prize possession, the nine-generation family photograph, taken by his great-great-great-great-grandmother Eve on the occasion of her husband's nine-hundredth birthday: there was Adam, gravely sitting in an armchair on a dunghill in the midst of a sheep pen, surrounded by seven generations of eldest sons (some scowling, some saying "cheese"), holding young Lamech (then age twenty-six) on his lap.

Suddenly he awoke. The nurse was caressing his wrist with the tips of her fingers at the point where a pulse was expected to exist. Finding distinct signs of life, she noted this fact on her chart. Then she left, but not before instructing him to remove most of his clothing.

He complied. Then he stretched out on the table and closed his eyes, waiting for the next stage of this dreaded ordeal.

He awoke to the sound of approaching footsteps. The door opened.

"Sit up," ordered the doctor.

Enoch sat up awkwardly, knocking over a costly Arabian lamp.

"Open wide," ordered the doctor.

He blinked and opened wide.

"Stick out your tongue and say ahhh," ordered the doctor.

He did as he was told.

"Stand up," ordered the doctor.

He eased himself into the standing position. "Sorry about the lamp," he said apologetically.

"We'll bill you," said the doctor inexpressively.

"Thank you," he replied meekly.

Dr. Gerry took the stethoscope that had been hanging around his neck like a vigilante's rope and pinned it to his chest, listening for signs of cardiac enthusiasm.

"Hmmm," observed the doctor.

"How's it sound, Doc?" he asked nervously.

The doctor ignored this question. "Drop your loincloth," he ordered.

[. . . . .][32]

"A little tender," remarked the doctor. "How old are you?"

He cleared his throat. "Just turned 365 last Tuesday."

"It figures," observed the doctor. "Get dressed."

He complied. "How'm I doing?" he inquired anxiously.

Dr. Gerry frowned. "Bad ticker," he said.

He experienced a brief panic attack. "So, what do you recommend?"

"Eat right. Sleep well. Cut down on the wind sprints."

"Maybe get myself a treadmill?" he suggested.

The doctor shook his head to and fro.

"Stationary bicycle?"

The doctor frowned and shook his head again. "At your age?"

"Well, I can't just sit and vegetate."

"You might try walking with God," suggested Dr. Gerry, and he abruptly left the room.

Ringing Up God

BACK HOME, Enoch pondered the question of walking with God versus not walking with God. Walking: was this to be taken in the literal or the metaphorical sense? They had been discussing the

---

[32]The text at this point is corrupt.

question of exercise, so it must be in the literal sense. . . . On the other hand, maybe Dr. Gerry was being ironic. Maybe Doc was trying to tell him something. Maybe "walking with God" was a metaphor. Maybe it meant. . . .

There was only one way to find out. He looked up God's number in the Yellow Stones and rang him up.

"God here," said a confident baritone voice. "I can't come to the phone right now, but at the tone please leave your message and I'll try to get back to you in the morning."

He faltered. "This is Enoch," he finally said. "I've got a health problem . . . it's a bad ticker, and doctor says wind sprints are out of the question . . . so he recommended walking with you . . . and I was just wondering—"

"Enoch, you say? I didn't catch the last name."

"God?" he said, taken aback. "Is that really you? I thought I was talking to an answering machine."

The voice chuckled. "Lots of people make that mistake."

This made him feel better. But he was still confused. "I don't get it," he said. "You leave a message on your machine, then you break in and say you didn't catch the last name. What's going on?"

"It wasn't really a message on my machine, it was really me, if you can believe it, and the point is, I like to screen my calls by telling people I can't come to the phone right now, but it's really me in the first place."

Enoch paused. "Could you run that by me again?"

"The basic point," explained God, "is that I get lots of unwanted calls."

"Oh yes," he nodded into the phone. "Telemarketers."

"Those, too," sighed God. "But the biggest pains are the people who want me to work them a miracle. 'Could you drop off a couple hundred sheep at my ranch? You did it for Sidon, and I do twice as many burnt offerings as he does.' 'My wife can't seem to get pregnant, help her out, would you?' 'It's my husband, Lord, he's fooling around with the maidservant, would you mind rolling him off a cliff? Tomorrow evening about nine would be fine—oh, and make it look like an accident.' That kind of stuff."

"I guess it goes with the territory," said Enoch sympathetically.

"I suppose so," sighed God. "But listen. I don't have all day. Let's get to the point. What's your last name?"

"Enoch," he said.

"Enoch Enoch, huh?"

"No, just plain Enoch."

"You mean you don't have a last name?"

He was confused by this question. "Am I supposed to?"

"You certainly are. Otherwise, how do you expect me to look you up?"

"All I know is, I was never assigned a last name."

"I could have sworn. . . . I'll have to talk to my secretary about that.[33] Anyway, Mr. Enoch, you were mentioning something about. . . ?"

"Right. I was saying I've got a health problem, it's a bad ticker, so my doctor recommended walking with you, and I was just wondering"—he did not want to appear too brazen—"I was just wondering if you might like to take time off from your busy schedule for a walk or two around the park."

"By park you presumably mean Eden."

"I'd prefer that to the Everglades," he said, trying for a laugh.

God ignored this bit of humor. "We've got us a slight problem here. As you may or may not know, I've put Eden off limits."

He found this perplexing. "Why?" he asked.

"People have been breaking in and eating the apples."

He couldn't understand this. "What's the point of having apple trees if people aren't allowed to eat the apples?"

"You've got a point there," said God, laughing the embarrassed laugh of a professor who has just been caught in a simple logical error by a C student. "Anyway, let's make it the Christian Country Club. Let's make it Sundays through Fridays. And instead of walking, let's make it jogging."

"Jogging?" he asked. "What's jogging?"

"It's halfway between running and walking."

---

[33]Ms. LaFemme remarked that God's secretary apparently made many such mistakes, because the majority of the Ur-Hebrews do not appear to have a family name. She conjectured that God's office staff was exclusively male.

He was confused. "What's the point?" he asked.

"There *is* no point," explained God. "I just thought you'd like to do something a little bit different."

Enoch thought about this proposition for a moment. "I kind of like my present routine," he said. "When you get to be my age, you're pretty much a creature of habit."

Can you *believe* this guy? thought God. Calls me up just as I'm getting ready for bed, wants my help on a longevity problem, which I give him, and then he has the nerve to turn around and say No thank you, I'm getting too old to try anything new.

"Think of it this way," said God in his most persuasive tone. "It'd be a chance for you to be the answer to a trivia quiz. Question: 'Who was the first human jogger? Answer: Enoch'."

A way to go down in history! thought Enoch. This was his big chance! It had always been difficult, being the great-great-great-great-grandson of the notorious pair who had been expelled from Eden for what everybody for generations had agreed was a minor infraction. He could be equally—maybe even more—notorious!

"Great!" agreed Enoch. He already felt a century younger.

Then he had a second thought. "What about the dogs? Won't they nip at my heels as I go jogging across the fairways?"

"Don't worry, I'll protect you," said God reassuringly. "I have a way with dogs."

Jogging Buddies

So Enoch jogged with God.

Next Sunday morning they jogged a few laps around the Christian Country Club. Just the two of them, he and God. It was nothing competitive. And to Enoch's surprise and relief, there was no deep theological conversation. Just a nice quiet friendly little jog. When they were through, they went back to the clubhouse and relaxed under a hot shower.

"Say, this is neat," said Enoch, awestruck by the marble walls. "How long you been coming here?"

"Oh, something like a thousand years,"[34] said God, adding, in a confidential tone, "but between the two of us, I'm not a member."

"I see. Low on cash," he nodded knowingly.

"No," said God, "I don't qualify."

"Why, what are the requirements?"

"You have to be Gentile."

"So how come they let you in to shower?"

God chuckled. "They think I'm one of them."

Enoch enjoyed this little joke. He was beginning to appreciate his new friend, who wasn't at all what he had been led to expect. Friendlier. Less threatening. More down-to-earth.

He shut off his shower. "Hand me a towel, wouldja?" he said. He was getting braver by the sentence.

"Here you go. . . . Say, how about a coupla whiskey sours?"

"Well. . . ."

"Hey kid!" called God to the locker room attendant. "A coupla rounds of whiskey sours for me and my jogging buddy!"

The young man left with the order.

"I'm not sure. . . ," said Enoch hesitantly.

"What's the matter?" said God incredulously. "You got a problem with a coupla whiskey sours?!"

"I'm thinking of the health angle," he explained—he didn't want God to think of him as maybe a little too moralistic. "You know, possible side effects."

"Where'd you get *that* idea?"

"I read an article in a medical journal," he lied.

"What the hell do doctors know?" scoffed God.

"If you say so," he said, with reservations in his voice. Was it his imagination, or was his new friend maybe a little . . . strange?

"Of course I say so! If you wanna know the truth, the whiskey sour is a health drink."

The young man came back with the health drinks. It was too late for Enoch to argue. And besides, who in their right mind could argue with God? Despite his friendliness, it was something you would think twice about doing. Even if you were beginning to

---

[34]As Professor Allbright pointed out, here God is merely estimating. The exact number is 980 years.

have your doubts.

"Ah, here we go," said God. "Thanks, kid. Just put it on my bill." Then, to his guest, "Cheers."

"Cheers," Enoch agreed, cautiously raising his glass.

"To the first jogger in human history."

"To the guy who keeps the springer spaniels off my heels."

Tragedy Strikes

FOR THE NEXT FOUR DAYS, God and his proud new friend followed the same routine: quietly jogging a few laps around the Christian Country Club, afterwards enjoying hot showers and quaffing off a pair of whiskey sours each.

But on Friday morning, as God was chasing away a pack of wild dachshunds, Enoch dropped in his tracks. At first God thought his new jogging buddy had simply tripped over a broken tee, but when he knelt down to check the pulse,[35] he could see that, to put it delicately, Enoch was not.

What to do? pondered God, who suddenly found himself in a panic. Do, do, do. Oh yes. The manuals all recommend, "Notify next-of-kin."

God left the former Enoch and walked over to the clubhouse in deep but anxious thought: *which* next-of-kin? Great-great-great-grandfather Seth? Great-great-grandfather Enos? Great-grand-father Cainan (a.k.a. Kenan)? Grandfather Mahalaleel? Father Jared? Son Methuselah? Grandson Lamech?

While reflecting on this problem, he showered, ordered a couple of whiskey sours, dried himself off, dressed, sat down at the bar, and requested a telephone.

After fortifying himself with the whiskey sours, he called young Methuselah.

"Hi," said a deep bass voice. "Methuselah here. I can't come to the phone right now, but if you leave your message on the

---

[35] Cardinal Micromentis noted that despite his distrust of doctors, God is here following the accepted medical procedure.

machine I'll try to get back to you in a year or so."

"Methuselah, did you say? Sorry, I didn't catch the last name."

"It's just plain Methuselah, and what's the matter, don'tcha understand plain English? I *told* you I can't come to the phone right now, and to leave your message on the machine."

"I've got some disturbing news," confessed God, "and I thought you might want to be consoled in person."

There was a lengthy pause.

"Who *is* this, anyway?" asked Methuselah.

"This is God."

"Yeah? God who?"

And God thought: Can you *believe* this younger generation?

"Let's just say I'm an old friend of the family," said God. "I used to run around with your father."

"How *is* Dad, anyway?" asked Methuselah, changing the subject. "I haven't seen him in a coon's age."

"Well, actually, last time I saw him, uh—"

"He's all right, isn't he?"

God paused, trying to think of a sensitive way to put it. He had never been in exactly this position before, but he knew enough to put the matter in a sensitive way. Don't panic, he advised himself, and keep it sensitive.

He cleared his throat.

This helped. It gave him time to come up with a sensitive way to put it—sensitive, but accurate. "Last time I saw him," he finally said, "the buzzards had not yet entered the picture."

It was Methuselah's turn to pause. But his was not the pause of one who is seeking a sentence hedged about with sensitivity. His was the pause of one who is wary. "Why do I have the sense," he said, "that you're trying to tell me something?"

"We were out jogging, Enoch and I—"

"Hold it right there. You were doing *what?*"

"We were jogging," said God.

"Jogging?!" exclaimed Methuselah. "What the hell is *jogging?*"

"It's halfway between running and walking," explained God.

"So what's the point?" asked Methuselah.

"It's supposed to be good for a bad ticker. Which your father had."

There was a long pause in the conversation. "Did you say *had?*"

God acknowledged that he had used the past tense.

"You mean Dad's dead?"

God thought about this word for a moment. It was an expression he did not like to use. Especially when the cause of . . . "death" . . . was jogging . . . and, perhaps, an overdose of whiskey sours. But then he had a sudden inspiration; a new expression crossed his mind. "I prefer the phrase *passed away*," he said. "More elegant. More poetic. Has more of a serene sound to it, don't you think?"

But Methuselah was not the sort of a man easily impressed with elegance and poetry. "You took a guy with a bad ticker out *running*, and he keeled over? From a coronary?"

"That is true, yes," admitted God. "Except we weren't running, exactly, we were more like . . . jogging—which is closer to walking—actually, more like strolling—and what has to be kept in mind was that I was protecting him from the dogs. I have a way with dogs."

"But not, apparently, with buzzards," replied Methuselah sarcastically.

"Nnnno," said God, not quite knowing how to respond but wanting to nudge the conversation onto a more comfortable course. "Buzzards are not in my job description. You're probably wondering why. It's all very complicated, but basically it has to do with my orchard and the apple tree and people always breaking in and stealing the apples, which got me thinking, there ought to be some kind of punishment for this infraction, and I thought to myself, buzzards. Let them strut their stuff. Buzzards will be buzzards, so why don't I—"

"Let's get this straight," interrupted Methuselah. "You're saying (1) Dad's dead (2) from jogging, (3) because you were punishing him for stealing apples from your off-limits orchard."

"Did I say that?" said God, trying to sound offended. "Did I mention anything about your father stealing apples? As far as I know he's never stolen an apple in his entire life. He was never an apple man. He was a whiskey sour man. After every jogging session we'd have ourselves a couple of whiskey sours. Does that sound like a man who'd break into an orchard and steal apples?

77

What would a man with a taste for whiskey sours want with a few worm-eaten—"

"What's Ma got to say about all this?" interrupted Methuselah. "Ma?"

"Dad's wife. Look in the phone book, under 'Enoch and Beth.'"

"Under 'Enoch and Beth'," murmured God.

"And while you're looking under the E's, I'll be looking under the A's."

"The A's?" asked God.

"As in 'Attorneys'."

A Happy Ending, with a Moral or Two

FORTUNATELY FOR GOD, this threat turned out to be idle. As Methuselah was soon to discover, the courts were not set up to handle lawsuits against higher beings.

But the son learned from his father's mistakes. Methuselah never took up jogging, he limited himself to one whiskey sour per diem, he avoided doctors like the plague, and he kept his distance from God. Then he proceeded to live to the ripe old age of 969, a record that still stands.

As for Enoch, never again was he forced to undergo the rigors and humiliations of a ten-year checkup. More importantly, he went down in history as the very first human jogger.

3 | The First Entrepreneur

ACCORDING TO THE ORTHODOX STORY of the Flood (Genesis 6:5–9:29), God, furious at man's evil, instructs righteous Noah to build an ark, which will protect him, his family, and a matched pair of every living species, from the coming deluge. Noah obeys. He builds the ark according to God's exacting specifications. He places his wife, his three sons and their wives, and two of every animal species (or seven pairs; the story is inconsistent) on the vessel. Then he battens down the hatches and waits for the rains to descend. Which they do for forty days and forty nights. When the waters finally abate and the arkless portion of the world's population—humans and beasts, birds and insects—has been drowned, Noah and his passengers emerge from the ship, dry and thankful. God then instructs Noah and his family to "be fruitful, and multiply, and replenish the earth." To commemorate this victory over human evil, and as a sign of his promise never to repeat this catastrophe, God creates the rainbow. Noah celebrates by getting drunk.

The contrast between this story and the original, "The First Entrepreneur," could hardly be more pronounced. The orthodox story inhabits a world of myth and legend; the original, of realism and social satire.

There is no need to say which of the two is more effective.

§

WHAT CAN SHE POSSIBLY SEE IN HIM? they wondered.

She, they said, was young, attractive, intelligent, ambitious, and vivacious. And, some would add, sociable to a fault.

He, they said, was old enough to be her great-grandfather. He never combed his beard, he walked with a limp he had picked up from being rear-ended by a goat, and he had lost his right eye while trying to trim the rear hoof of an impatient camel. He was four years older than anyone else in his middle school graduating class. He always seemed to be broke. Worst of all, they said, he was a grouch, misanthropic down to the last human being.

This was not, of course, how he would describe himself. He was fond of referring to himself as "a self-made man." And there was evidence to support this opinion. He had started his career by establishing a goat-milking service, which lasted until the butting incident, after which he decided that what the village needed was a pedicurist specializing in camels and catering to the wealthy camel drivers who lived on the highest sand dunes. This second profession lasted until he lost the perfectly good eye, at which point he suddenly saw the opportunity to set up a gerbil shop, which he owned and operated until he ran across an ad in the *Sinai Observer* for a correspondence course in futurology, offered by a hermit with Ph.D.s in both theology and astrology. He took the course, passed with distinction, and became an itinerant prophet, roaming from tent to tent wearing nothing but a sandwich board proclaiming the end of civilization, unless civilization returned to traditional family values.

What, then, did she see in him?

There were various theories on this subject: that he served as a subconscious replacement for the great-grandfather she had never known; that she had suffered from an earlier unrequited love and had concluded that the joys of the amorous life were significantly exaggerated; that she needed somebody to dominate; that she felt sorry for him; that there was more to the old guy than met the eye.

There was even talk, though few took it seriously, that she had come to share his appreciation for family values.

But these were only theories. No one could be certain, because no one quite knew how to ask a young, attractive, intelligent, enterprising, ambitious, vivacious, and sociable woman such an intimate question.

§

IT WAS IN THE LATTER STAGES of his stint as a prophet that she entered his life.

One morning, as she was walking to her job as a waitress at the local camel stop, she happened to notice him in his back yard, dressed in his sandwich board and hammering nails into boards. Curious, she stopped to kibbitz.

He ignored her and continued his pounding.

"What are you doing?" Elsie finally asked.

"Building a boat," said Noah gruffly.

"Yeah?" She smiled at him. "Taking up boat building, huh?"

"And just what's wrong with being a boat builder?" he asked.

"Oh, nothing," she said. "It's just that this is the middle of the desert."

He put aside his hammer. "There's a lot of job satisfaction in building boats," he explained. "A recent survey showed that ninety percent of the boat builders rated their job satisfaction—"

"Wouldn't that be more like 100 percent? Aren't you the only boat builder around?"

He stopped to recalculate. "Right," he agreed. "One hundred percent rated their job satisfaction as either 'good' or 'excellent.' But only about 66.8 percent of the camel drivers rated their—"

"So they get a little sand in their eyes." It was her turn to be defensive. Some of her best clients were camel drivers.

He resumed his hammering. She sat down and resumed her kibbitzing.

"Do you actually expect to sell this boat?" she finally asked.

"That's beside the point."

"Yeah?"

"Yeah."

There was a long silence.

"Well, then, what *is* the point?"

"The point is, I'm following orders."

She looked at him in disbelief.

"Yup," he said. "God instructed me to build a boat."

"Why would he want you to build a boat? Just out of curiosity."

Elsie's curiosity had nothing to do with a disbelief in the *existence* of God. It had to do with a different view of the *nature* of God. She believed in the necessity of God's existence, just as Noah did. Where they parted company was on the question of whether God believed in the necessity of boats in the desert.

Noah again put aside his hammer. "Why would he want me to build a boat?" he repeated with what he hoped was a knowing smile. "To protect me and my pets from the flood he's sending."

"Flood! Why would he send a flood?"

"Because of man's wickedness."

"Man's wickedness?"

"Well . . . woman's, too."

"And for *that* he's sending a flood?"

"I believe that's the plan."

"I'm sorry, I don't see the connection."

"The connection is the decline of family values."

"Let's get this straight," said Elsie. "God's going to wipe out ninety-nine percent of the population over a political issue, and you're going to *help* him?"

"It's not just a political issue, and he's asked for my cooperation, which I promised to give him."

Elsie stood up. "What it sounds like to me," she muttered to herself as she left for work, "is a case of ethnic cleansing."

It was hard for her to believe that God, as a person, would concern himself with what a man and a woman did within the privacy of a tent or behind some remote sand dune or in some out-of-the-way sheep pen. No doubt he had access to the information regarding who was keeping intimate company with whom—after all, those things have a way of becoming common knowledge. But having access to information and keeping up on the latest in sleeping arrangements were not the same as concerning oneself. And even supposing that he *did* concern himself with such trifles, it was hard to believe he'd take such drastic measures, when all he'd really have to do to straighten things out would be to send letters marked "Confidential" to the persons suspected, advising them of their rights and maybe suggesting ways to improve their behavior patterns.

And even if he *would* decide to get nasty about things, it was hard to believe he'd use somebody like Noah to help force his own personal preferences on those who were, after all, his children. Noah? Noah the Negev Nebbish?[36] Of course they were both males, God and Noah—that had to be taken into account. So even if they *were* somehow in partnership, which was extremely doubtful, but *if* they were, it was hard to believe that they'd be up to the task of sending a bona fide honest-to-God flood that would be capable of wiping out the entire camel driver population, just because of a few innocent—what was the Spanish word?—*peccadillos?*. . . And even if they *were* able, somehow, to send a little rain . . . well, there were ways to take advantage of *that* situation.

§

THAT EVENING AFTER WORK, Elsie returned to Noah's back yard. He was still dressed in his sandwich board and was working on his long-standing enterprise.

"Hand me a plank of that gopher wood, wouldja?" he asked as he finished hammering a nail into the stern.

She obliged him.

"Why couldn't you just use shittim wood?" she asked. "Isn't it a lot cheaper?"

"Those were God's specifications. Gopher wood, 450 feet long, seventy-five feet wide, and forty-five feet high. Plus the fact that it'll make a good impression."

"On whom?" she asked. "There'll be just be you and the pets. That is, unless. . . ."

"Hand me a wooden nail, wouldja?"

She handed him a wooden nail.

"I don't mean to be nosy," she said, "but how can you afford

---

[36]The Negev (or Negeb) is the hilly desert region of present day southern Israel. A "nebbish" (from the Yiddish, *nebakh*) is a timid or ineffectual person—or, in the vernacular, a "loser." See Professor Allbright, "On the Presence of a Quaint Alliterative Phrase in Scroll #3, 'The First Entrepreneur,'" (Reno [Unpublished], n.d.), esp. pp. 389-411 and 637-718.

this?"

Noah stopped and looked at her. "You think I'm doing it for nothing? God said something about 'a nice consideration'."

"A pot of gold at the end of the rainbow?" she suggested sarcastically.

"Exactly what I was thinking," said Noah. "Another nail?"

She handed him another nail. Great minds, etc., she was thinking.

"Say," she suggested, "won't it get pretty lonely on the boat? I mean, all by yourself?"

"I'll have the pets," he reminded her.

"Won't you need somebody to help feed them?"

"Exactly what I was thinking," said Noah. He paused and looked at her closely. He noticed that she was certainly young and attractive. "Say," he continued, "what are your thoughts on family values?"

§

AND SO NOAH AND ELSIE SIGNED a prenuptial agreement. He agreed to give up the sandwich board; she promised to give up her own lucrative job at the camel stop and become an apprentice boat builder and part-time homemaker. This part-time job consisted of raising three sons (two of which, she explained to him on their wedding night, she had recently adopted because of her position on family values) and a number of pets, including Spot, a dog, Puff, a cat, and three hundred or so anonymous gerbils that had not been snatched up by the public in Noah's last going-out-of-business sale.

Several years of marital harmony passed. Then, on the morning after Noah finally put the finishing touches on his and God's boat, it began to thunder and lightning and sprinkle.

Noah looked across the cot at his wife. "God's plan in action," he whispered with a knowing wink of his functioning eye.

She smiled back at her husband. "Elsie's plan in action," she thought to herself.

It was still sprinkling when Elsie approached her first client.

"Yoo-hoo!" she called as she rattled the camelskin flap. "Is the man of the tent in?"

"Yeah?" asked Hiram, sticking his head out of the tent. "Oh, it's you, Elsie. Long time no see. Come on in."

"Thanks, Hiram," she said as she ducked and entered the well-appointed tent in which Hiram and Ruth and their three children spent many a happy hour. Hiram, however, was the only one at home. He was a camel driver, but it was his day off. The children were in school, and Ruth, a sex therapist, was involved with her extensive clientele.

"What could I get for you, Elsie? A bottle of Liebfraumilch?"

"Not today, Hiram. How about a glass of goat milk?"

Hiram retreated into the kitchen to prepare this treat for his unexpected but welcome guest. "Coming right up," he called. "Want something in it? Chocolate? Strawberry? Vanilla? Maybe an aphrodisiac?"

"How about a cup of brandy?" she called back as she looked over the attractive brochure she had brought with her.

"Here we go," said Hiram, entering the room with two glasses of doctored goat milk. He handed one to Elsie and sat down on the rug next to her. "So, what's on your inventive mind?"

"I just wanted to be the first to warn you, Hiram, that if you want to be saved, you'd better trade in your camel for a cruise around the world in Noah's boat."

"Saved, huh?" said Hiram, sipping his goat milk. "You mean, in the religious sense?"

"More in the life insurance sense."

"Sorry, we're covered."

"Not from the coming flood, you're not." She handed him the brochure.

He looked it over. "Flood," he said. "What's a flood?"

"Look it up in your dictionary."

"I don't have one," he admitted.[37] "Just give me the definition."

"Flood, noun, from the Old English, 'to flow': 'An overwhelm-

---

[37]Professor Allbright pointed out that Noah was quite probably telling the truth. Dictionaries at that time, he recalled, were made of large tablets of stone, and many found it too hard to turn the pages.

ing quantity of fluid, especially water, caused by excessive precipitation'."

Hiram got up and went over to the tent flap and cast a gaze at the sky. "We could use a little rain," he observed.

"This isn't going to be a *little* rain, it's going to be a *lot*. According to my source, it's going to cover the earth."

"Yeah? What's the point?"

"God's handing out punishment for illegal camel-loading."

Hiram was skeptical. "I don't see how a few overloaded camels have anything to do with an overwhelming quantity of water. Everybody knows that excessive precipitation is caused by the groanings of the spirits of the dead."

"That's just one theory," Elsie replied diplomatically. "Some of the subtler observers of causal relationships have noticed that there's an intimate relation between legal infractions and weather patterns."

"More goat milk?" offered Hiram. She was getting out of his depth.

Elsie accepted his offer. And over their second glasses of goat milk they went on to discuss the crisis in the Middle East and its impact on the camel business. But no exchanges were performed, either with Hiram or with any other men of the tents that Elsie visited that day—that is, no camels or cruise tickets changed hands.

But the next day was another story. It continued to rain, and Elsie was again making her rounds. By late afternoon the water was three to four inches deep in the low-lying areas, a general panic had set in, and she suddenly had a ready market for her product.

"Yoo-hoo!" she called as she knocked on her first customer's canvas flap. "Is the man of the tent in?"

The tent flap opened, and Jason stuck his head out into the gentle drizzle. "Yeah?" he said. "Oh, it's you, Elsie. Can you believe this weather?"

"I certainly can. Remember yesterday? I was warning you about it."

"Oh yes," admitted Jason. "I'm beginning to see your point about the relation between camel cargo and the weather. Come on in."

"Starting to get religion, are you?" said Elsie as she entered her client's tent and looked around. Jason was home alone—too wet a day for camel driving. He and his wife were childless, and Xanthippe, a marriage counselor, was undoubtedly busy mending marital fences.

"Speaking of the advantages of boats versus camels, I was just wondering. Do you happen to have any cruise tickets left? The wife and I—"

"I might just have one or two," replied Elsie as she rummaged through her purse.

"Let's see," said Jason nervously, "what were you asking, one camel per ticket?"

"Prices have gone up since yesterday. A ticket now will run you two camels, plus tax."

"Two camels? Why suddenly *two* camels?"

"It's the law of supply and demand," explained Elsie, "and there suddenly seems to be a great demand for cruise tickets. But on the positive side, we're now giving the buyers two for the price of one. He and she are allowed to take along his and her favorite pets."

"Pets?"

"For instance, Hiram and Ruth are taking along a couple of goats, LeRoy and Eunice are taking along a matching pair of donkeys, Max and Hortense are taking along two turtle doves of opposite genders, Mitch and Norma Jean are taking along a bowl of goldfish."

"What about you and your toy husband?"

"Noah and I are taking along a herd of used camels. The cruise theme is going to be togetherness, family values. So how about it?"

"Well. . . ."

"What's the matter, you got a problem with animals on the boat?"

"Nnnno. . . ."

"You allergic or something?"

"Not really, but . . ."

"You're not wild about shoveling camel dung?"

"That too, but. . . ."

"So what's your problem?" she chided him. "Don't believe in family values?"

"Oh I do, up to a point, it's just that. . . ."

"Well?"

"I've only got two camels," explained Jason apologetically.

"So, that's exactly enough to buy one ticket."

"But what about Xanthippe?"

"I thought you two were having problems. Isn't that what you used to tell me?"

"Right, but . . . I just wouldn't feel right about leaving her. She can't swim."

Elsie began pacing up and down. "Tell you what I'm gonna do," she finally said. "You've always been a preferred customer, so I'm gonna let you take Xanthippe along instead of a pet."

"Xanthippe . . . *instead of* a pet?"

"Right. I'm making an important distinction."

Jason considered this proposition carefully. "Why not both?" he finally asked.

"If I did that for you, I'd have to do it for everybody."

"Please? For old times' sake?"

"Nope. Can't do it. It's either Xanthippe or, what? Your Arabian stallion?"

"Okay," sighed Jason, "you win."

"So, what'll it be?" asked Elsie impatiently. "I have to know now, we sail in ten minutes."

"First, do you happen to have a cage aboard?"

"Why, has Xanthippe been biting again?"

"It's for my spider monkey."

§

"Who are these people?" inquired Noah as Elsie ushered Hiram, Ruth, LeRoy, Eunice, Max, Hortense, Mitch, Norma Jean, Jason, and a spider monkey into his back yard. The group was followed by a menagerie of goats, donkeys, turtle doves, goldfish, children, and a herd of eighteen camels.

"These are recent converts," Elsie explained. "They've seen the light."

"Yes, the light," agreed the camel drivers and their wives as they glanced nervously up at the large grey clouds.

Noah stood at the door of his boat, playing an unaccustomed role as host. "Welcome aboard," he greeted each and every one of them as he heartily shook their extended, trembling paws.

"Forgive me," said Ruth with an anxious smile. "I was under the impression that you were building this thing for the job satisfaction."

"I thought it was just a hobby," said Eunice.

"I thought it was going to be a restaurant," said Hortense.

"I thought it was going to be a casino," said Norma Jean. "Not that I approved," she quickly added.

"No," said Noah, addressing the entire congregation of guests. "God instructed me to build it. He said he had a plan. 'Build yourself a boat,' he said, 'I'm sending a flood'."

"You call *this* a flood?" muttered Jason under his breath. "It hardly covers the back yard."

Though Noah had many failings, he was not hard-of-hearing. "Just wait," he replied with a sly smile.

They waited.

And as they waited, they whiled away the time. By day they fed goldfish and cleaned out gerbil cages and shoveled camel dung. By night they played Monopoly and discussed the importance of following the letter of the law and bemoaning the deterioration of family values, after which they retired to one or another bunk bed. These tasks occupied them for forty days and forty nights while it continued to drizzle intermittently.

On the forty-first day the sun came out.

Noah and his passengers went up to the forecastle to check the damage. Water was three or four feet deep in the low-lying areas, the villagers who had not been fortunate enough to own camels were scurrying about planting rice and vineyards, and the boat was still docked in Noah's back yard.

Various theories were advanced to account for this change in God's plan.

"It's a matter of public health," guessed Noah. "God didn't

want to mess up his creation with all those bloated bodies."

"Somebody—and I'm not mentioning any names—got cold feet," ventured LeRoy.

"It sure as hell wasn't *wet* feet," grumbled Jason.

"Maybe the spirits of the dead have quit groaning?" suggested Hiram.

"His ways are past finding out," explained Elsie confidently.

"So are hers," Ruth murmured to her husband.

§

AFTER THIS ADVENTURE, life did not return to normal. The desert was never the same. Elsie went on to become a major player in the camel business. The day after the flood abated, she became the sole owner and proprietor of her own camel fleet, which within two years was grossing four million shekels a year and was listed on the Tel Aviv Stock Exchange. She proceeded to set up a branch office in Cairo, manned by Hiram, assisted by her son Ham, one in Athens, manned by Jason, assisted by her son Japheth, and one in Jerusalem, manned by Noah, assisted by his son Shem.

As for the people of the village, they no longer wondered what she saw in him. She had seen something, they said, that they had missed. She had seen that some day his ship would come in.[38]

---

[38]Cardinal Micromentis theorized that "The First Entrepreneur" as it stands is incomplete. He insisted that there are missing pages. If they could be somehow recovered, he said, they would be a great aid to interpreters of this difficult scroll. Professor Allbright promised to research the matter fully, perhaps coming up with a reconstruction that would be useful to future scholars. Ms. LaFemme advised the professor not to bother, indicating that the meaning of the story was crystal clear. The only problem she had with it, she said, was that she had not written it herself. Father Lecher expressed support for Ms. LaFemme's position.

4 | Miss Holy Land

TWO OF THE MAIN CHARACTERS in the orthodox Bible are Abram and Sara (later renamed Abraham and Sarah), the subjects of numerous stories in Genesis 12 through 25.

It is clear that five of those stories were purloined from the original scroll discovered by Father Lecher:

(1) the story of their trip to Egypt, in which Abram advises Sara to pose as his sister in order to save his life (Genesis 12);

(2) the scandalous story of the triangle involving Abram, Sara, and Sara's maid, Hagar (Genesis 16);

(3) the story of God granting the Holy Land to Abram and his descendants, circumcising him, and changing his name to Abraham and Sara's to Sarah (Genesis 17);

(4) the story of God sending angels to inform the elderly couple of an impending happy occasion (Genesis 18); and

(5) the story of God ordering Abraham to sacrifice his beloved son, Isaac (Genesis 22).

But in revising these stories, the orthodox version does violence to the original and simple meaning, which shines forth clearly in Scroll #4, "Miss Holy Land."[39]

The most distinctive feature of this text is that it appears to be a

---

[39] Strictly speaking, Scroll #4 is not a single scroll but five. As Father Lecher explained to me in private, this fourth Scroll was actually composed of five sheepskins, which were sewn together with a material that he could only describe as "kind of like cat gut." In order to avoid unnecessary bickering, I did not inform my fellow disciples of this conversation.

screenplay. This feature became the subject of several intriguing theories. Cardinal Micromentis argued that this proved something he had long suspected, that the ancient Ur-Hebrews were far more technologically advanced than anyone has given them credit for being. He reasoned that, because "Miss Holy Land" was a screenplay, there must have been a thriving film industry even then.

Ms. LaFemme was convinced that Miss Holy Land was written by a woman. Women, she contended, have a natural cinematic imagination that their male counterparts lack; besides, the anonymous author shows a profound understanding of many of the subtleties of the feminine psyche, and of the baser qualities of the masculine mind. Professor Allbright was absent that morning with a migraine and could not be reached for comment.

Father Lecher took no position on this issue. He merely smiled and suggested we go on to more serious work.

§

ONE: THE HONEYMOON

THE SUN BEATS DOWN ON A VAST DESERT. A range of mountains is visible on the horizon. In the distance a car moves slowly over the sand dunes, left to right, followed closely by a camel.

NARRATOR'S VOICE: (Solemnly) And there was a famine in the Holy Land. And Abram took his wife Sara and went down into Egypt to sojourn there.

Driving the car, a battered Yugo, is Abram, a twenty-nine-year-old schlemiel dressed in traditional desert garb. On the seat next to him rests a leather saddlebag. Seated atop the camel, sidesaddle, is Sara, a voluptuous young woman of nineteen, also dressed in the traditional desert robe. The camel is burdened with her extensive trousseau— saddlebags, suitcases, hat boxes, etc.

The tiny caravan approaches a billboard, "Welcome to Egypt," beyond which lies another, "Visit Tut's Tomb," bearing the MasterCard and American Express logos.

NARRATOR'S VOICE: And it came to pass, when Abram was come near to enter into Egypt, that he said unto Sara his wife,

"Behold now, I know that thou art a fair woman to look upon."

The caravan stops. Abram shuts off the engine, stumbles out of the Yugo, and approaches Sara, who remains seated on her camel. She peers into a vanity mirror, carefully applying makeup. Abram looks around suspiciously, then motions for Sara to lean down. She does so. He whispers something to her.

SARA: Well, I *did* spend last year as Miss Holy Land.

NARRATOR'S VOICE: And Abram spake again unto Sara, saying, "When the king of Egypt shall see thee, he shall say, This is his wife, and he will kill me."

Abram whispers again.

Sara hurls the mirror to the ground, smashing the mirror to pieces.

SARA: Oh, Abe! Why are you so damned pessimistic? This is our honeymoon, fer crissake!

ABRAM: (*Defensively*) That's exactly why I started with the line, "fair woman to look upon."

SARA: Just a line, huh? You mean five years from now I won't be hearing it?

ABRAM: *Seven* years from now. Studies have shown it takes seven years for the newness to wear off. Seven being a sacred number.

SARA: (*Sighing*) Nobody can argue with that.

NARRATOR'S VOICE: And Abram continued his much speaking, saying, "Tell them, I pray thee, thou art my sister, that I shall live because of thee."

Abram picks up the broken mirror and hands it back to Sara, then whispers again.

SARA: What!? Are you ashamed of me or something?

ABRAM: You know how proud I am of you, sweetheart. Wow! Miss Holy Land! But that's just the point. Kings have a certain . . . reputation, plus they've got all this power, which makes them dangerous to fool with.

SARA: So?

ABRAM: Well, you're a woman and I'm a man, which means. . . .

SARA: Yes?

ABRAM: You know what they say. Power is the intimate African dizzy act.

SARA: So?

ABRAM: So, Egypt is in Africa, and Egypt has a king, and . . .

(*Losing his train of thought*) anyway, if we just happen to run across him, tell him you're my sister. Okay?

SARA: (*Shrugging*) It ain't gonna happen, Abe, but if you insist, okay.

Abram, grinning, goes back to the Yugo, starts the engine, and takes off across the border into Egypt, followed by his skeptical "sister."

The small caravan approaches a Rest Area.

ABRAM: (*Calling to Sara*) You need to stop?

SARA: (*Calling back*) This is as good a time as any.

The Yugo and the camel turn off the highway. They pass the signs, "Oxen Only," "Camels Only," "Cars Only," and turn into the parking lot marked "Camels and Cars."

NARRATOR'S VOICE: And it came to pass, that when they were come into Egypt, the Egyptians beheld Sara, that she was very fair.

Abram jumps out of the Yugo and makes a beeline for the men's room. Sara dismounts from the camel and walks leisurely towars the women's room, swinging her hips provocatively. She passes half a dozen men who are standing around. They welcome her with wolf whistles and suggestive remarks. She smiles coyly and disappears into the women's room. They follow her, continuing to ogle.

The door slams in the men's faces.

Outside a modest motel tent. The sign reads: "Cairo Rent-a-Tent." The Yugo and the camel are both tethered to a hitching post. It is now evening.

Inside the motel room. The wall is decorated with pictures of the Sphinx and the pyramids. The small leather saddlebag rests on the sandy floor. Abram, dressed in a bathrobe, lounges in an easy chair. His sandaled feet rest on a Gideon Bible, which is placed on the lone table. He is drinking beer and watching TV. Sara stands before a full-length mirror, hands on her hips, posing for herself. She sports a swim suit, across the front of which is a banner bearing the title, "MISS HOLY LAND," and underneath, in smaller print, "1995 B.C."

Sara struts over alongside the TV and strikes a seductive pose. Abram, intent on a baseball game, ignores her.

ANNOUNCER: He takes a strike.

ABRAM: (*To the batter*) Swing, you idiot!

Sara lounges over to Abram and stands behind him. She leans over and gently rubs her breasts on the back of his head. He bends forward, still preoccupied with the game, and takes a swig.

ANNOUNCER: Another strike, right down the middle. 0 and two, bases still loaded.

ABRAM: (*To the batter*) God! What are you *waiting* for?

Sara takes the beer out of Abram's hand and places it on the table. Then she sits down on his lap, puts her arms around him, and caresses him erotically. He leans sideways to get a better look at the game.

ANNOUNCER: Strike three, bat on his shoulder. So at the end of nine it's all tied up, one-one.

ABRAM: (*To Sara*) You see that? Three fat pitches, and the guy just stands there like a spectator!

Abram reaches over for his beer; Sara tumbles off his lap. He finishes off the beer. She picks herself off the floor, stands up, and displays a tantalizing Wonderbra stretch.

SARA: (*One last hint*) I think I'm going to bed.

ABRAM: (*Intent on the game*) Before you do, sweetheart, be a sport and get me another beer.

Sara sighs and goes over to a cooler. She retrieves a beer, tosses it at her "brother," and disappears into the back of the tent in a huff.

ABRAM: (*Calling*) I'll probably be in when the game's over. (*To himself*) That's funny. I thought she *liked* baseball.

He shrugs, then opens the can of beer, which fizzes over and spills on his primary erogenous zone.

Sara alone in bed. She gets up, yawns, and stretches, displaying a scant negligee to good effect. She strolls over to the tent flap and opens it, checking the morning sun. Then she goes over to the phone, sits down, and flips through the directory. She finds a number and dials. While waiting for an answer, she files her nails.

SARA: Pharaoh's Employment Agency? . . . What do you have in the way of jobs for immigrants? . . . A brother and a sister. . . . He? Yes, he's willing to start at the bottom. . . . Something with lots of physical exercise. . . . Oh, construction would be just the thing. . . . Her? Excellent credentials. In fact, last year she was

Miss Holy Land. . . . Willing to work in a what? . . . A harem? (*To herself*) Must be an Egyptian word. (*To the phone*) And just what would that involve? . . . Yes, she dances. . . . A fabulous voice. . . . Experience doing what? . . . Not yet, but she's very anxious to learn. . . . You'll send somebody right over? Good. . . . That's at Cairo Rent-a-Tent. Ask for Sara. . . . Thank *you*.

She picks up a scroll dictionary and looks up a word.

SARA: (*To herself*) Harem, harem. H-A-R-E-M . . . Ah, here it is.

She reads the definition with increasing fascination. Then she puts down the dictionary and smiles.

An ancient palace.

The Grand March from Verdi's Aïda. *Pharaoh's honor guard steps smartly out of the main entrance, forms a pair of parallel lines, and comes to attention. Pharaoh, dressed as a sheikh and wearing a crown, emerges from the palace. He struts magnificently to the end of the line, where one of the guards presents him with a camel, furnished with all the royal trappings. He hops onto the camel, wheels it around, and is soon galloping through the streets of Cairo.*

Pharaoh arrives at Cairo Rent-a-Tent. He dismounts, then wanders over to Sara's camel and Abram's Yugo. He stops to check the license plates. The tag on the camel's rump reads "Miss Holy Land"; that on the back of the Yugo, "Just Married." He smiles lustfully and heads for the tent flap.

Abram sits in an easy chair, eating popcorn and watching a baseball game on TV.

There is a knock at the tent flap. Abram ignores it.

ANNOUNCER: A ball, low and away.

ABRAM: (*Shaking fist at the umpire*) Ball, hell! That was a strike, you idiot!

Another knock.

ANNOUNCER: He swings . . . down the left field line . . . fair ball.

ABRAM: (*Shouting*) How in God's name can you call that fair? It was foul by a cubit!

A third knock.

Abram sighs, hits the mute button, puts his bag of popcorn on the

table, stands up, and stretches.
ABRAM: (*Calling*) Hold your camels, I'm coming.
Abram goes to the flap and opens it. Pharaoh enters.
ABRAM: Come on in, come on in. (*Extends a buttered hand*) The name's Abram, but my friends call me Abe.
PHARAOH: (*Shaking Abram's hand*) Glad to meet you, Abe. I'm Pharaoh.
ABRAM: Farrow, huh? That spelled F-A-R-R-O-W?
Pharaoh examines his newly-buttered hand.
PHARAOH: Close enough. . . . Say, I was just in the neighborhood and happened to notice a camel with a Holy Land tag. Thought I'd drop in and welcome you to Egypt.
ABRAM: Thanks. (*Indicating*) Sit down, wouldja?
PHARAOH: Don't mind if I do.
The two sit.
ABRAM: (*Offering*) Popcorn?
PHARAOH: (*Accepting*) Thanks . . . who's playing?
ABRAM: The Alexandria Librarians and the Ur of the Chaldeans Herdsmen.
A pause.
PHARAOH: Who you for?
ABRAM: Ur of the Chaldeans. My old haunts.
PHARAOH: Yeah?
ABRAM: Of course, that was way back when. But I still support the Herdsmen. . . . What about you?
PHARAOH: I'm a Sphinx fan.
A long, long pause. Pharaoh looks around.
PHARAOH: Say, nice little tent you got here.
ABRAM: Thanks. It's the honeymoon suite. Thought we'd come down to Egypt, get away from the famine back there in the Holy Land.
PHARAOH: (*Pretending ignorance*) We? Honeymoon suite?
ABRAM: (*Proudly*) Me and Sara. Sara's my wife. We're newlyweds.
Pharaoh extends his hand.
PHARAOH: Well congratulations!
Abram shakes Pharaoh's hand.
ABRAM: Thanks. (*Looks at Pharaoh's crown*) Say, I like your hat.
PHARAOH: Here in Egypt we call it a crown.

97

ABRAM: You mind telling me what it set you back, in terms of shekels?

PHARAOH: Here in Egypt the word is pounds.

ABRAM: Where are they on sale?

PHARAOH: Oh, you can't buy them. I have them specially made.

ABRAM: Gee, I'm im*pressed*. . . . Well, you gonna wear it in here? I could put it in the closet for you.

PHARAOH: (*Looking around*) That's funny, I don't see a closet.

ABRAM: Uhhh . . . Strictly speaking, you're probably right. Back in the Holy Land we have this custom, we call saddlebags closets.

PHARAOH: Well, this is Egypt, and we call saddlebags saddlebags.

ABRAM: Hmmm. What's that saying? When in Rome, do as the Romanovs?[40]

PHARAOH: Around here we like to say, when in Cairo, do as the Pharaoh suggests.

ABRAM: Oh? I guess you have to be Egyptian to understand that saying.

PHARAOH: It might help.

Sara listens at the door. Then, humming, she goes to her dressing table, dabs herself with perfume, and applies makeup. Finally, she dresses in a scarlet evening gown and puts on her Miss Holy Land banner.

Back to Abram and his Mystery Guest.

ABRAM: Just out of curiosity, what do *you* call closets?

PHARAOH: The lower class calls them closets. The middle class calls them wardrobes. The folks I hang around with call them pyramids.

ABRAM: Pyramids, huh? Don't think I know that concept.

PHARAOH: Just in from the Holy Land, did you say?

ABRAM: Right. Me and my wife, that's Sara, pulled into town just yesterday. (*Confidentially*) Frankly, we're looking for jobs.

---

[40]As Professor Allbright has indicated in his 318-page monograph, "Notes on a Reference in Scroll #4," (Reno [Unpublished], n.d.), the phrase derives from the English divine, Jeremy Taylor (1613-67), whose exact wording was: *Si fueris Romae, Romano vivito more*,

PHARAOH: What do you know! I happen to be looking for help.

ABRAM: (*Sitting up straight*) This must be my lucky day!

A pause.

PHARAOH: (*Smiling wickedly*) Say, Abe, how would you like to build me a pyramid?

Abram jumps up and turns off the TV.

ABRAM: (*Enthusiastically*) When do I start?

Pharaoh stands up.

PHARAOH: There's no time like the present.

ABRAM: That's always been my philosophy—that, plus my belief in the good ol' Holy Land work ethic. Where do I report?

PHARAOH: Just go down Tut Street till you hit Nefertiti. Tell 'em Pharaoh sent you.

Abram pullsout a notepad and pencil from under his robe.

ABRAM: (*Writing*) Tut . . . Nefertiti . . . Farrow. F-A-R-R-O-W.

Sara chooses this moment to make her grand entrance.

ABRAM: Oh hi, honey. Sara, I'd like you to meet Mr. Farrow. Mr. Farrow, I'd like you to meet Sara, the former Miss Holy Land. . . . Did I do that right?

Sara and Pharaoh ignore Abram. They lock eyes. Their mouths drop open simultaneously.

Flashback. The stage of a beauty pageant. Sara stands before an enraptured audience. She wears her scarlet dress; this time her banner proclaims her to be Miss Sinai. She is performing in the talent portion of the Miss Holy Land competition, favoring the audience with an amateur rendition of the aria "È strano" *from Verdi's* La Traviata. *Bad English subtitles.*

SARA: *È strano! è strano!*

[How strange! how strange!]

In core scolpiti ho quegli accenti!

[In my heart are sculpted those accents!]

Saria per me sventura un serio amore?

[Would to me true love bring bad luck?]

Che risolvi, o turbata anima mia?

[What think you, oh troubled spirit mine?]

Back in the tent, Sara continues to sing the aria. Pharaoh listens, enchanted; Abram looks on with pride.

SARA: *Oh, gioia*

[Oh, joy]

Ch'io non conobbi

[I've never felt this way before.]

Esser amata amando!

[To love and be loved!]

E sdegnarla poss'io

[Can I deny this]

Per l'aride follie del viver mio?

[For l'aride follie del my life?]

    Pharaoh raises Sara's hand to his lips and kisses it, gallantly but passionately.

ABRAM: (*Proudly*) She sang that at the pageant. That's when I fell in love with her.

    Pharaoh ignores Abram. He bursts into song, favoring Sara with an equally amateur rendition of the first stanza of "Un dì felice, eterea," *from* La Traviata. *This time it is Sara who is enchanted; Abram looks on in puzzlement.*

PHARAOH: *Un dì, felice, eterea*

[One day, happy]

Mi balenaste innante

[You flashed ethereally into my life;]

E da quel dì tremante

[And from that day forth]

Vissi d'ignoto amor.

[I've lived by that unspoken love.]

Di quell'amor chè palpito

[That day love became the pulse]

Dell'universo intero,

[Of the universe entire,]

Misterioso, altero,

[Mysterious, unattainable,]

Croce e delizia al cor.

[The cross and deliciousness of my heart.]

ABRAM: (*To Pharaoh; naively*) Is this how you always greet your newcomers?

PHARAOH: Only when they're auditioning for my harem.

ABRAM: Harem? . . . Oh, I see. An Egyptian word.

An awkward pause. Pharaoh and Sara gaze at each other.

ABRAM: (*To Sara*) Oh, sweetheart, Mr. Farrow just gave me a job!

SARA: How nice of him.

ABRAM: I'm gonna build him a large closet, a . . . (*Turning to Pharaoh*) what did you call it?

PHARAOH: A pyramid.

ABRAM: I'm gonna build him a pyramid. The job's only temporary, of course. But the main thing is, it's a job.

SARA: That's the best news I've heard in a long time. Better get to it.

ABRAM: I'm on my way!

Abram runs to the tent flap and exits.

PHARAOH: (*Taking Sara's hand*) What a lovely hand, oh fair one to look upon—

Abram sticks his head through the tent flap.

ABRAM: Sweetheart, is it all right if I take the camel?

SARA: (*Staring at Pharaoh*) Fine.

ABRAM: You won't be needing it?

SARA: (*Transfixed*) Not in the foreseeable future.

ABRAM: You sure?

SARA: (*Still transfixed*) Absolutely positive.

ABRAM: The humps are full?

SARA: (*Glancing over at Abram*) You might want to head down to the Nile and fill them.

ABRAM: Great! I'm off!

Abram exits.

PHARAOH: Say, pretty one, where have you been keeping yourself all these—

Abram sticks his head through the tent flap.

ABRAM: Corner of Tut and Nefertiti, did you say?

PHARAOH and SARA: Corner of Tut and Nefertiti.

Abram exits.

PHARAOH: Say, beautiful, haven't we met someplace be—

Abram sticks his head through the tent flap.

ABRAM: How many T's in Nefertiti?

PHARAOH and SARA: Two.

ABRAM: Just wanted to make sure. First day on the job, you

know . . . don't want to make a fox paw. (*To Pharaoh*) That's Latin for screwing up.

SARA: Better be off if you want to beat the rush hour traffic.

ABRAM: Right.

Abram exits.

PHARAOH: Say, pretty maiden . . . you don't mind if I call you pretty maiden, do you? . . . what do you do in your spare—

Abram sticks his head through the tent flap.

ABRAM: Just happened to think. Honey, you might ask Mr. Farrow if he has a job for *you*.

PHARAOH: That's the best idea I've heard in a long time.

SARA: Better get going before he changes his mind.

Abram gives the A-OK sign.

ABRAM: Gotcha!

Abram exits; this time Sara and Pharaoh go to the tent flap to make sure he has left.

Outside. Abram tries to hop onto the camel but falls. He tries again; same result. He looks around and notices a providential step ladder. He retrieves it, places it alongside the camel, and climbs aboard. He tries to get the beast to move, but no dice: the camel is still tethered to the hitching post. He climbs down the ladder and tries to untie the rope. No success. He spots the Yugo. He pauses to think. Then he runs over to the Yugo, jumps in, starts the engine, and roars off, "singing" (la, la, la) snatches of "Largo al factotum," *from Rossini's* Barber of Seville, *at the top of his voice.*

Pharaoh and Sara watch these antics from the tent flap. Then they return to the room.

Inside.

PHARAOH: How long have you been married to that idiot?

SARA: Back where I come from we call them schlemiels, and who said anything about being married? He's my brother.

The two embrace.

PHARAOH: Funny. I could have sworn he said you were his wife.

SARA: Well, there's this custom back in the Holy Land. Guys call their sisters their wives.

A lingering kiss.

PHARAOH: (*Coming up for air*) Doesn't that get confusing?

SARA: I handle confusion well.

She fiddles with his robe.

PHARAOH: I kinda like that custom. . . . (*Looking around*) Say, you wouldn't happen to have a boudoir around here, would you?

SARA: Boudoir? What's a boudoir?

Pharaoh fiddles with her zipper.

PHARAOH: It's a place where you express your deepest feelings to your mistress and then get on with it.

SARA: Oh, *those* things. Back in the Holy Land we call them sheep pens.

She removes the rope from around his waist.

PHARAOH: Here in Egypt we have this custom, we call them boudoirs. Wouldn't happen to have one, would you?

SARA: We didn't bring any sheep along.

PHARAOH: What about a plain old bedroom?

SARA: (*Giggling*) I thought you'd never ask.

She takes him by the hand. They disappear into the back of the tent.

A pyramid construction site. While the supervisors slap them with flyswatters, Abram and his fellow workers swing sledgehammers and sing parts of the Anvil Chorus *from Verdi's* Il Trovatore. *Again, English subtitles.*

WORKERS: *Vedi! Le fosche notturne spoglie*

[See! The immense heaven strips]

De' cieli sveste l'immensa volta;

[Herself of the dark night;]

Sembra una vedova che alfin si toglie

[Like a widow who finally removes]

I bruni panni ond'era involta.

[The black mourning veil.]

All'opra—dagli, martella!

[To work—strike, hammer!]

Chi del gitano i giorni abbella?

[Who brings light into our lives?]

La Zingarella!

[Women!]

The motel bedroom. Sara and Pharaoh sit up in bed, après sex. They take turns puffing on a water pipe. His crown is askew.

SARA: That was *nice.*

PHARAOH: (*Pleased with himself*) Was I really that good?

SARA: Oh, you *were.*

PHARAOH: (*Fishing*) On a scale of one to ten, you'd give me . . . what?

SARA: Eight . . . no, nine . . . Somewhere in there.

PHARAOH: Oh. . . .

SARA: (*Consoling him*) It's not an exact science, you know.

PHARAOH: (*Plaintively*) I was trying for a ten.

SARA: (*Sighing*) Okay. Nine and a half.

PHARAOH: Any pointers? I'm into self-improvement.

Sara props herself up on an elbow.

SARA: I wasn't gonna mention it, but—

PHARAOH: Come out of the tuck position sooner?

SARA: No. . . .

PHARAOH: Keep my head straight as I prepare for entry?

SARA: No. . . .

PHARAOH: Close my eyes at the moment of impact?

SARA: We don't have all day, so I'll tell you. Next time you might take off your crown.

PHARAOH: . . . But I've always considered my crown a turn-on.

SARA: Oh, it is . . . up to a point. But if you're gonna use a crown during these difficult maneuvers, you gotta keep it on your head.

Sara affectionately reaches over and adjusts Pharaoh's crown.

An earthquake suddenly rocks the tent. Terrified, Pharaoh and Sara grab each other.

NARRATOR'S VOICE: And God plagued Pharaoh and his house with great plagues because of Abram's wife Sara.

A cellular rings.

In a frenzy, Pharaoh and Sara chase around the room, looking for the source. Pharaoh finally locates a cellular in the pocket of his robe. He answers it, while Sara stands at his elbow in a state of great agitation.

PHARAOH: Pharaoh here . . . What do you mean, *which* Pharaoh? Didn't they teach you that in school? . . . Now, let's just think this through. Which age are we in? . . . That's right, the Middle Bronze age. Okay, which dynasties appear in the Middle Bronze Age? . . . Very good. Dynasties Roman numerals XII, XIII, XIV, XV, XVI, XVII, and XVIII. Now, what is *this* year? . . . Excellent. 1994 B.C. So, which dynasty is alive and well in this, the Year of Our Lord 1994 B.C.? . . . Brilliant! Dynasty XII. Be patient, we're almost there. Who is the first Pharaoh in Dynasty XII? . . . No no no, not Amenemhet IV, he's due in about a century. But you got the first name right. . . . No no, not III. . . . Not II, either. . . . Splendid! Amenemhet Numero Uno. See how easy it is when you stop to think things through?

Another earthquake rocks the tent. Pharaoh remains on the phone, with Sara clinging to his elbow.

PHARAOH: (*On the phone*) Did you feel what I felt?

SARA: Oh, I did!

PHARAOH: (*To Sara*) Not you, I'm talking to the palace. (*On the phone*) What was that on the Richter scale? . . . You can't read the Richter scale, it's covered with *frogs?*

The pyramid construction site. Abram and the other workers scurry about chasing hyperactive frogs. The supervisors are on their knees, praying.

The motel bedroom. Another earthquake rocks the tent. Pharaoh remains on the phone, with Sara still clinging to him.

PHARAOH: Now you can't read it because it's covered with *locusts?*

(*To Sara*) What the hell is a locust?

The pyramid construction site. Abram and workers scurry about with butterfly nets, chasing locusts. The supervisors are still on their knees, praying.

The motel bedroom. A fourth earthquake rocks the tent. Pharaoh remains on the phone. Sara now has her arms wrapped around his knees, begging for his attention.

PHARAOH: (Ignoring her) Now you can't read it because it's too dark?

The pyramid construction site. The supervisors are walking around, shining flashlights on Abram and workers, who are getting ready for bed. Some are brushing their teeth, some are putting on their pajamas, and some are climbing into their sleeping bags. Abram is kneeling beside his sleeping bag, saying his bedtime prayers.

ABRAM: . . . And God bless Mommy and Daddy and Adam and Eve . . . and oh yes, God bless Sara and Mr. Farrow.

The motel bedroom. Pharaoh is finally off the phone. Sara is still at his knees. He looks down at her.

PHARAOH: You wanted to say something?

   Sara nods guiltily.

Flashback. The pageant stage. Sara stands alongside the emcee. She is wearing her evening dress with the Miss Sinai banner; he is dressed in traditional desert garb, interviewing her for the final event of the competition. A short distance away Miss West Bank and Miss Dead Sea, the other two finalists, are stashed away in a pair of soundproof telephone booths, their ears to the glass, trying to hear the question.

EMCEE: (*To the audience*) And now, before the judges make their final decision on who will spend 1995 B.C. reigning as Miss Holy Land, we will ask the three finalists one and the same question. The judges will grade them on their poise, their originality, and their religious correctness. (*Melodramatically*) Are you ready, Miss Sinai?

   Sara nods nervously.

EMCEE: Here it is. The question is in two parts. First.

   Drum roll.

EMCEE: Which, in your own personal opinion, is the most important of the Ten Commandments . . . for Miss Holy Land?

   The audience applauds.

EMCEE: Quiet please. The second part of the question.

   Drum roll.

EMCEE: What, in your own personal opinion, should be the punishment for breaking that commandment?

   A hush falls over the audience. Sara shifts her weight from one foot to the other, then back again.

EMCEE: Would you like me to repeat the question?

Sara shakes her head no.
SARA: I think . . . the most important commandment for Miss Holy Land is . . . I can't remember the number.
EMCEE: That's all right, the ranking isn't important.
SARA: I think . . . the most important commandment . . . is. . . . Damn! I forget how it goes.
EMCEE: That's all right. The judges are only interested in the general concept.
SARA: This is so embarrassing. . . . In my opinion, the most important commandment . . . for Miss Holy Land . . . is . . . the one about . . . adultery!
The audience applauds wildly. A proud father and mother look at each other and nod their approval. The emcee raises his hand to quiet the audience.
EMCEE: (*To Sara*) Now . . . for the second part of the question.
SARA: I forget. . . .
The emcee puts his arm around her waist in an unfatherly way.
EMCEE: (*Gently*) What should be the punishment for committing adultery?
SARA: I think . . . in my personal opinion . . . the punishment for adultery should be . . . plagues!
Again the audience applauds. Again a proud father and mother look at each other and nod their approval.

The motel room. Sara and Pharaoh sit across a table from each other.
PHARAOH: So *that* explains it: the frogs, the locusts, the darkness . . . and who knows what else your god has up his sleeve? (*Angrily*) Why didn't you *warn* me?
Sara puts her face in her hands and sobs.
SARA: I didn't think . . . you'd mind . . . a few little . . . plagues.
Pharaoh, touched, reaches across the table and takes her hands in his.
PHARAOH: There, there. I understand. Now, the third question is . . .
Drum roll.
PHARAOH: What are we gonna do about it?
Sara quickly brightens up.
SARA: I have an idea.

The sun is setting over a cool, serene desert. A range of mountains is visible on the horizon. In the distance a stretch limo is moving slowly over the sand dunes, right to left, followed closely by a camel.

NARRATOR'S VOICE: And Pharaoh commanded his men concerning Abram; and they sent him away, and his wife Sara.

As in the initial scene, Abram is driving the vehicle, Sara is riding the camel. Trailing behind the limo and camel are sheep, oxen, he-asses, she-asses, and other camels.

Abram stops, climbs out of the limo, and goes back to Sara.

ABRAM: I forgot to ask, sweetheart. How was *your* day?

TWO: THE TRIANGLE

MORNING. *A thriving village spread over a barren desert. At the outskirts is a weather-beaten billboard: "Welcome to Abeville, Heart of the Holy Land—Celebrating* 26 36 46 *56 Years of Progress." Main Street is reminiscent of the Old West: storefronts, wooden sidewalks, hitching posts—everything but horses and buckboards, which have been replaced by camels and a few cars (a Model A Ford, a Kaiser, a vintage VW bug).*

The signs on the buildings announce:

"Abe's Grocery"
"Holy Land Post Office"
"Abe's Trading Post—We Specialize in Used Camels"
"Holy Land Federal Courthouse"
"Sears, Abe's, and Company"
"Abe's Video"
"HLND-TV"
"Abe's Souvenir Shop—We Cater to the Religious Tourist"
"Abe's Saloon"
"Holy Land Sheriff"

Behind Main Street are many residential tents. A sizeable percentage of the male citizens are loitering on Main Street, smoking, spitting tobacco, and chatting. They are dressed in traditional attire, except for the Western holsters and revolvers that are slung around their hips. They wear cowboy boots, which are decorated with spurs.

At the end of Main Street is a large red-and-white striped circus tent. Behind the tent is a sheep pen, which is in use. Ranging beyond the pen is a pasture on which are grazing an assortment of oxen, goats, asses, and camels. Alongside the tent is a satellite dish. Parked in front is a well-worn stretch limo and a mailbox marked "Abram, Mayor . . . Sara, Miss Holy Land, 1995 B.C."

Inside the tent. A calendar reads "May 1938 B.C." Three plaques decorate the tent walls: "God Bless Our Home"; Joyce Kilmer's poem, "Trees"; and the Ten Commandments ("Thou shalt not commit adultery" is underlined in red).

NARRATOR'S VOICE: Now Sara, Abram's wife, bare him no children.

Sara, now in her seventies, is rocking in a rocking chair, a parody of Whistler's mother. She is knitting pink booties and singing "Rock-a-Bye, Baby" in a melancholic tone.

NARRATOR'S VOICE: And Sara had a handmaid, an Egyptian, whose name was Hagar.

Hagar, young and beautiful, wearing a simple robe with a Queen Nefertiti headdress, enters from the rear of the tent. She scurries around, brandishing a feather duster.

SARA: (*Haughtily*) When you're through dusting, Hagar, I'd like you to scrub the floor.

Hagar desists from dusting and looks at the floor with a puzzled expression.

HAGAR: (*Deferentially; very British*) But Mum, it's nothing but sand.

Sara glances at the floor.

SARA: Oh. . . . So it is. . . . Well then, scrub *some*thing.

Hagar looks around, puzzled.

HAGAR: Begging your pardon, Mum, but do you have any suggestions?

SARA: . . . Have you done the dishes?

HAGAR: Dishes?

SARA: Yes, dishes. Are you deaf?

HAGAR: (*Diplomatically*) Perhaps Mum is referring to the earthen pots?

SARA: Oh . . . so I am. Have you done the earthen pots?

HAGAR: No, Mum, I haven't, Mum.

SARA: Well, hop to it.

HAGAR: Yes, Mum. Scrub them, did you say?

SARA: Yes! Scrub the damned earthen pots!

Hagar rolls her eyes and heads for the back of the tent.

HAGAR: (*To herself, no British accent*) It's *so* hard to find good management.

The front of Abe's Saloon. Abram, now in his eighties, comes hobbling out of the swinging doors of his saloon in a parody of John Wayne. He is dressed like the other men standing around, except that his holster contains a banana instead of a gun. He nods to the other men, takes a pack of Horse cigarettes out of his pocket, lights up, unhitches a camel, and mounts. He turns around and heads up the street toward home.

Abram approaches the tent. He gingerly dismounts from his camel and tethers it to a hitching post. He pauses, his thumbs hitched under his belt. He pulls the banana from his holster, awkwardly twirls it on his finger as if it were a revolver, then replaces it. He continues to approach, this time as if preparing for a shootout: hands at his side, ready to draw.

Inside the tent. Sara is still rocking, still knitting, still melancholy, still humming "Rock-a-Bye, Baby."

NARRATOR'S VOICE: And Sara said unto Abram, Behold now, the Lord hath restrained me from bearing. I pray thee, go in unto my maid; it may be that I may obtain children of her.

There is a knock at the tent flap.

ABRAM: (*Calling*) Sara, honey, I'm home!

Abram enters. He notices that Sara is crying.

ABRAM: (*Under his breath*) Oh hell. What did I do *this* time?

SARA: Boo hoo.

Abram hobbles over to Sara and gives her a peck on the forehead.

ABRAM: So, how's my beautiful young bride?

SARA: (*Bitterly*) I'm seventy-five, Abram. You call *that* young?

ABRAM: Well, I'm eighty-five, and I feel great! Remember, this is the age of patriarchs. Life expectancy must be about, what, two hundred years?

SARA: (*Starting to be consoled*) It's one hundred and ninety-six . . . (*Sniffling*) which makes me middle-aged.

Abram sits down in a rocking chair.

ABRAM: Well, you're still my beautiful bride.

SARA: Oh boo hoo.

ABRAM: *Now* what'd I say wrong?

SARA: Don't you get it? I'm still your *bride*.

ABRAM: You're my *beautiful* bride.

SARA: But I'm still just a *bride*. I'm not a *mother*.

ABRAM: I keep telling you, if you wanna celebrate Mothers' Day, you gotta get pregnant.

SARA: And I keep telling *you*, you gotta *get* me pregnant.

ABRAM: (*Throwing up his hands*) It's always the man's fault.

SARA: Well, if you'd do something more than feed me watermelon seeds.

ABRAM: (*Naively*) Like what, for example? Besides putting mustard on my hot dog?

SARA: That was a metaphor. You weren't supposed to take it literally.

ABRAM: I was never great at poetry.

SARA: Oh, Abe! Do I have to draw you a picture?

ABRAM: I'm not much for art, either.

SARA: Oh God!

ABRAM: (*Perplexed*) . . . You suggesting I turn it over to *him?*

SARA: (*Ironically*) Maybe that wouldn't be a bad idea.

Abram gets up from his chair and goes over to comfort his wife.

ABRAM: Look at it this way, sweetheart. There are advantages to being middle-aged and childless.

SARA: Like what, for example?

ABRAM: Think of all the shekels we've saved on things like diapers . . . toys . . . robes and sandals . . . camels . . . college tuition . . . bail money.

SARA: And what are we gonna do with all those shekels?

ABRAM: (*Thinking*) . . . You've been wanting a new camel.

SARA: (*Interested*) With power steering?

ABRAM: Power steering, cruise control—you name it.

SARA: (*Hopefully*) And could we finally take that vacation to Paris?

ABRAM: Paris, Cairo—anywhere your heart desires. . . . Speaking of Cairo, how's your new handmaid working out?

SARA: You mean Hagar?

ABRAM: (*Too innocently*) Hagar? Is that her name?

SARA: (*Sarcastically*) The former Miss Egypt.

ABRAM: (*Missing the sarcasm*) Is that right? Miss Egypt, huh? I hadn't realized.

SARA: You sure couldn't tell by looking.

ABRAM: Well, she doesn't hold a candle to the former Miss Holy Land.

SARA: You think so too?

ABRAM: Of course. . . . So, how's she working out?

SARA: I haven't really been keeping tabs on the little bitch.

ABRAM: Too busy trying to get pregnant?

SARA: (*Ironically*) That's probably it.

ABRAM: Maybe I should run downtown, ask her how she's working out. . . . You wouldn't mind, would you, darling?

SARA: Not at all, dear. (*To herself*) Can't imagine it wouldn't be safe.

Abram emerges energetically from the tent, unhitches his camel, and mounts. Then he rides off toward Main Street. This time his holster contains a real revolver.

NARRATOR'S VOICE: And Abram hearkened to the voice of Sara.

Abram stops before Abe's Trading Post and dismounts, continuing his John Wayne impression. He tethers his camel, acknowledges a few loiterers with a hand gesture, makes a big spit, and swaggers across the street toward the saloon.

Inside the saloon. Half a dozen men stand at the bar, attired in traditional garb, drinking from earthen pots. Hagar, now a barmaid, is serving them.

MAN 1: (*To Hagar*) Say, sweetie, when do ya get off work?

She winks at him.

OTHER MEN: Ooooh!

MAN 2: Better not let Abe catch ya doin' that.

Outside the saloon. Abram continues to approach. Then he pauses, his thumbs hitched over his belt. He takes the revolver from his holster, twirls it on his finger, drops it, picks it up, then replaces it. He continues to approach, again as if preparing for a shootout: hands at his side, ready to draw.

The loiterers watch in dread anticipation.

Inside the saloon. Half a dozen men are sitting at a table, smoking cigarillos and playing poker.

MAN 3: (*Glaring at Man 4*) I'll see ya.

Man 4 lays down his five cards, on which are printed the names of the first five books of the Bible: Genesis, Exodus, Leviticus, Numbers, Deuteronomy.

MAN 5: Holy Moses! A straight!

The holders of the losing hands all shake their heads in wonderment. The holder of the straight smiles slightly and gathers in his chips.

Outside. Abram approaches the saloon, bounds onto the wooden sidewalk.

Inside. The saloon doors swing open, and in strides Abram. He spots Man 1 and draws his revolver. The men in the bar are terrified. Hagar rushes over to him and grabs his shooting arm.

HAGAR: (*Melodramatically*) Don't! Please don't!

Abram shrugs her off and fires a quick succession of five shots over the head of Man 1. The men dive for cover. Abram then saunters over to an empty table, nodding for Hagar to follow him. She does. They sit down. He motions for the bartender to come over to their table. He does so, frightened.

ABRAM: (*Very macho*) Two goat milks.

The bartender scurries over behind the bar to prepare the drinks.

MAN 1: (*A terrified whisper*) Goat milk? Why goat milk?

MAN 2: (*To Man 1*) You idiot! It's an aphrodisiac.

The bartender scurries back to the table with two goat milks. Abram and Hagar drink while the crowd watches. The two gaze intently at each other. They stand. They walk upstairs, his arm around her.

NARRATOR'S VOICE: And Abram went in unto Hagar.

They disappear into a bedroom. The men look around at each other and begin to speak in hushed tones.

A shot rings out from the upstairs bedroom.

NARRATOR'S VOICE: And she conceived.

The men look at each other for a moment. Then they break into boisterous laughter.

A biology classroom. An elderly nun stands before a class of semi-attentive pre-adolescent school children, who are dressed in the traditional desert garb. She points with her ruler at charts of the male and female reproductive systems.

NUN: . . . And in the female, the ovum, which is the Latin word for egg, passes from the ovary, which is this round thing here, into the fallopian tube . . . this thing here, which is almost as ugly as this naughty thing on the male chart. . . .

A boy raises his hand.

NUN: Yes, Adam?

BOY: What's the naughty thing called, in Latin?

NUN: (*Quickly*) God only knows, next question?

The living room of the tent. Sara is dressed as before, except that her hair is in curlers. She again knits pink booties, again stifles sobs. The calendar reads "June 1938 B.C."

NARRATOR'S VOICE: And when Hagar saw that she had conceived, she looked with contempt on her mistress.

There is a respectful knock on the tent flap.

SARA: (*Calling*) Come in.

Hagar enters.

SARA: (*Looking up*) Oh it's you, Hagar.

HAGAR: Yes Mum, it's me, Mum, your loyal handmaid Hagar, Mum.

SARA: (*Angrily*) Where have you been? You're five hours late.

HAGAR: I have been out sacrificing an animal, Mum, to the pagan goddess Isis, Mum.

SARA: Who the hell is Isis?

Hagar starts dusting the furniture.

HAGAR: She's not in hell, Mum, she's a nature goddess. Worship of Isis originated in ancient Egypt. It's destined, Mum, to extend throughout the Mediterranean world, or I miss my guess.

SARA: And what animal have you been sacrificing, my good handmaid Hagar? Not one of my husband Abram's sheep, I hope?

HAGAR: (*Innocently*) Oh no, Mum. It was a rabbit, Mum, an itty-bitty rabbit.[41]

SARA: (*Interested*) A rabbit, huh? Tell me, how do you do it? I've been trying to kill a rabbit for nearly sixty years.

HAGAR: It's easy, Mum.

SARA: Yes?

Hagar stops dusting to explain.

HAGAR: If I may be so bold, Mum, there are three simple steps.

SARA: (*With great curiosity*) And what is the first step?

HAGAR: If I was you, Mum, I'd first hold off on the bon-bons.

SARA: And what do you expect Miss Holy Land to eat while she's reading her Harlequin Romances and knitting booties?

HAGAR: I'd recommend alfalfa sprouts, Mum, between a pair of salt-free crackers.

SARA: Sounds terrible. And what is the second step?

HAGAR: The curlers, Mum. They've got to go.

SARA: But my raven tresses are the glory of my womanhood, the essence of my sexuality! Plus the fact that they make me feel good about myself.

Hagar takes a vanity mirror and holds it before Sara's eyes. She fluffs Sara's hair.

HAGAR: I'm sure they do, Mum, but your beautiful hair has a natural wave to it, Mum, rendering curlers quite superfluous.

SARA: Well . . . I'll think about it. And the third step?

HAGAR: Begging your pardon, Mum, but they've got some real nice teddies down at Frederick's of Hollywood.

SARA: And how would *that* look on the former Miss Holy Land?

HAGAR: Right now, Mum, not so good, but after six months on alfalfa sprouts and salt-free crackers . . .

SARA: (*Sighing*) I suppose you're right.

HAGAR: (*Pushing her luck*) Don't want to appear too boastful, Mum, but it's what worked for me.

SARA: (*Suspiciously*) It did, huh?

---

[41] Cardinal Micromentis mentioned that Hagar is probably referring to a jackrabbit, not a cottontail.

HAGAR: Oh yes, Mum, it did, Mum. And when a woman gets to be your age—
Sara clears her throat.
HAGAR: When she gets—
SARA: (*Icily*) That will be all, my loyal handmaid Hagar.
HAGAR: Mum?
SARA: The former Miss Holy Land thanks you for your advice and gives you the rest of the day off.
HAGAR: Oh thank you, Mum.
Hagar starts to leave. Sara raises her index finger.
SARA: One more thing.
Hagar stops in her tracks and turns around.
HAGAR: Mum?
SARA: Run down to Abe's saloon and tell him I'd like a word with him.
Hagar curtsies and exits.

Inside the saloon. Hagar and Abram are huddled at a corner table, whispering inaudibly. She is intense, he is nervous. No goat milk.

Main Street. Abram heads home on his camel, this time in slow motion. He looks very much his eighty-five years. His holster now contains a dozen red roses.

The tent living room. Sara is in her rocking chair. On her lap she has a Harlequin romance, which she isn't reading. She is clenching and unclenching her fists.
NARRATOR'S VOICE: And Sara said unto Abram, My maid, Hagar, has looked on me with contempt.
There is a tentative knock at the tent flap.
ABRAM: (*Calling*) Sara, honey, I'm home!
Abram enters with the roses. He notices that Sara is irate, but does not appear to be surprised.
ABRAM: (*Apologetically*) Hi, honey, I brought you some flowers.
SARA: (*Controlled fury*) Abram. . . .
ABRAM: They're roses.
SARA: . . . You know what that damned little bitch said to me?
ABRAM: Uh . . . let's see . . . Hmmm, Hmmm, Hmmm . . . that you

116

don't look a day over seventy?

SARA: She said I was fat.

ABRAM: Maybe she was referring to the fatted calf?

SARA: She said I was ugly.

ABRAM: You? Miss Holy Land? Ugly?

SARA: She said I was dowdy.

ABRAM: Dowdy? Is that an Egyptian word?

SARA: And then . . . she had the gall to tell me I wasn't pregnant!

Abram's mouth slowly opens. He slaps his forehead.

ABRAM: (*Extending rose-filled hand*) Well congratulations, sweetheart! How did this come about? Divine intervention?

Sara slaps the roses from his hand. He is startled.

SARA: What are you gonna do about it?

ABRAM: (*Puzzled*) . . . Hand out cigars? . . . Give you a baby shower? . . . Make a burnt offering?

SARA: You fool! I mean, what are you gonna do about that little bitch?

ABRAM: Oh . . . her.

Abram paces about the room, thinking. Hmmm, Hmmm, Hmmm.

NARRATOR'S VOICE: Abram said unto Sara, his wife, Behold, thy maid is in thy hand; do unto her as it pleaseth thee.

Abram ceases his pacing.

ABRAM: It's really not my problem, is it?

SARA: (*Rising fury*) You mean to tell me you're gonna sit around and do *nothing* after that little tart insulted your poor wife?

ABRAM: There are of course . . . legal issues.

SARA: Such as?

ABRAM: . . . Give me time. . . .

Abram resumes pacing.

Sara stands up.

SARA: (*Full fury*) Well, if you're not gonna do anything, I guess it's up to me.

Abram ceases pacing.

ABRAM: (*Meekly*) Very well, dear. You know best.

Sara heads for the tent flap. She pauses, then turns and heads for the back of the tent. A moment later she returns, wearing her Miss Holy Land banner. She heads directly for the tent flap.

Outside. Sara storms from the tent, jumps into the limo, and takes off in a cloud of dust, her banner flying in the wind. She comes to a screeching halt in front of the saloon, jumps out of the limo, and makes a beeline for the swinging door.

Inside the saloon. Men are busy ogling Hagar, who is now wearing a Miss Egypt banner.

  Sara bursts through the swinging doors.

NARRATOR'S VOICE: Then Sara dealt harshly with Hagar, and Hagar fled from her.

  Sara confronts her adversary.

SARA: Bitch!

  Hagar stands her ground.

HAGAR: Fat! Ugly! Dowdy! Unpregnant!

SARA: When you call me that, *smile!*

  Hagar obligingly smiles. Then, in a parody of the stock Western barroom brawl, the two women engage in an extended fistfight. The men take sides, and soon tables are turned over, chairs are broken over men's backs, and bodies are strewn on the ground. Finally, Sara stands over her defeated foe, panting and pointing to the swinging doors.

SARA: I give you till sundown to get out of town.

  Hagar picks herself off the floor. She stumbles toward the doors. She exits.

  The men look at Sara in astonishment. She walks over to the bar. The bartender's anxious face slowly rises from behind his workplace.

SARA: (*Nonchalantly*) Goat milk all around.

The wilderness. Day. Hagar is sitting on a rock beside a fountain, holding her tummy.

NARRATOR'S VOICE: And an angel of the Lord found her by a fountain of water in the wilderness.

  An angel descends from heaven with a briefcase. She trips lightly among the rocks and then stands before Hagar.

ANGEL: (*Dramatically*) Hagar, former handmaid of one Sara, and close personal friend of one Abram, and before that, Miss Egypt and the third runner-up in the Miss Universe Pageant.

HAGAR: And who, pray tell, might thou be?

ANGEL: I am an angel of the Lord, sent to comfort and instruct thee in this, thine hour of trial.

HAGAR: (*Suspiciously*) What's it gonna cost me?

ANGEL: Fifty shekels an hour for the backrub and prenatal care, and that includes five minutes of legal advice.

HAGAR: *An* angel of the Lord, did you say? Not *the* angel of the Lord?

ANGEL: Right. But one of the top ten angels, if I may blow mine own horn.

HAGAR: . . . Tell you what. I'll give you twenty-five shekels, payable when the advice bears fruit.

ANGEL: (*Thinking this over*) Angels aren't supposed to haggle . . . but . . . okay . . . just don't let this be known, or I could end up in deep doo-doo with the Boss.

HAGAR: Don't know if I'm acquainted with your boss. I'm more or less committed to Isis, being Egyptian and all.

ANGEL: We have no problem with that. We're not prejudiced against other religions, just as long as the cash register keeps playing its merry tune.

HAGAR: Good.

She starts to lie down.

HAGAR: Let's get to the backrub.

ANGEL: Not so fast.

The angel produces a #2 pencil and a legal pad from her briefcase.

ANGEL: First we've got to fill out a form. Your name and Social Security number?

Hagar sits up.

HAGAR: I'm Hagar, as well thou knowest, and to tell the truth I'm an illegal alien.

ANGEL: (*To herself; writing*) Hagar . . . illegal alien. (*To Hagar*) Got that. Now, Question Number Two, whence camest thou?

HAGAR: If you're really an angel, you know damn well whence I camest.

ANGEL: Right. But this is for the record.

HAGAR: Well, I was working for Sara, see, and we had this argument about her not paying my Social Security, and . . . (*Tearfully*) and all of a sudden she hit me and kicked me out of the tent.

ANGEL: (*To herself; writing*) Sara . . . non-payment . . . Social

Security. (*To Hagar*) Got that. Now—

HAGAR: (*Anxiously*) Did you get the part about the assault and battery, also about her firing me without giving cause?

ANGEL: Those aren't my areas of expertise. Gabe does the cases of domestic violence, and Mike's in charge of employment litigation.

HAGAR: (*Disappointed*) Oh . . .

ANGEL: Don't worry, sister. I think we've got enough on the old bitch with just the illegal alien and non-payment angles.

HAGAR: Well, if you say so . . .

ANGEL: You don't believe me? Here, let me give you a number to call.

She produces a slate and chisel from her briefcase.

HAGAR: Why don't you just use pen and paper?

ANGEL: (*Chiseling*) The Boss likes us to use chisel and stone.

HAGAR: Why?

ANGEL: (*Chiseling*) More permanent . . . at least that's the theory.

HAGAR: What about when you were filling out the form? Why didn't you use chisel and stone then?

ANGEL: (*Chiseling*) Beats me.

HAGAR: It's a matter of consistency.

The angel keeps chiseling. Hagar keeps watching.

HAGAR: How long's this gonna take?

ANGEL: It's only three digits.

HAGAR: Forget it.

The angel tosses the chisel and slate into the fountain, then takes up the pencil and legal pad.

ANGEL: (*Sighing*) Just when I'm halfway through. Okay, Question Number Three. What about Abe?

HAGAR: (*Defensively*) What *about* Abe?

ANGEL: You're pregnant, aren't you?

HAGAR: That's what the rabbit has led me to believe.

ANGEL: He's the father, I take it?

HAGAR: (*Indignant*) Who do you think I am? I like rabbits, but—

ANGEL: What I meant was, Abram's the father?

HAGAR: Oh. . . . Well, if he isn't, what we have here is a case of good old divine intervention.

ANGEL: And if he is, what we have here is a case of good old sexual harassment.[42]

A pause.

HAGAR: (*Suddenly enthusiastic*) I think you're gonna be worth every penny!

Inside the Holy Land Courthouse. Abram is seated at the defense table. Hagar is seated at the plaintiff table, holding a crying Baby Ishmael. Abram's lawyer, representing Abram, and the angel, representing Hagar, are standing at their lecterns. God, dressed in the traditional black robe, is seated in the judge's seat, behind a sign saying "GOD."

NARRATOR'S VOICE: And Hagar bare Abram a son. And she called her son's name, which Abram gave her, Ishmael, because he was a child of controversy.

God bangs his gavel. Baby Ishmael stops crying.

GOD: Have the two parties reached an agreement?

LAWYER and ANGEL: We have, Your Honor . . .

Hagar smiles broadly and glances in the direction of Abram.
Abram stares at the floor.

The tent living room. Sara sits in her rocking chair, watching TV and sobbing.

On the TV screen:

JIM: Greta, what about these procedures? Do you think God should have let Abram and Hagar work it out for themselves?

GRETA: Jim, I think God clearly abdicated his responsibilities. I don't know Holy Land law to the extent Roger does, but it seems to me he set a dangerous precedent by throwing the decision back in their faces.

JIM: Roger, what about what Greta just said? And what about the agreement itself? Who in your opinion was the big winner here?

ROGER: Jim, I'm gonna have to disagree with Greta. Under Holy Land law, as I understand it, God can pretty well do anything he

---

[42]Father Lecher was quick to inform us that this unnamed angel was not one of those who appeared to him at any of the Bear Lake motels. Ms. LaFemme was equally quick to reply that lawyer angels make better role models.

darn well pleases. As for who was the really big winner, I think Abram clearly gave up way, way too many camels.

JIM: What about it, Greta? Where do you stand on the camel issue?

GRETA: Jim, I don't see that Abram was in a strong bargaining position. The baby looks just like him.

JIM: Thank you, Greta and Roger. Now, back to our studio in Jerusalem for a late-breaking story about a real estate deal.

THREE: THE DEAL

ABRAM'S BEDROOM. Midnight. Abram, dressed in pajamas, sleeps on a cot. He is snoring gently and enjoying a happy dream.

NARRATOR'S VOICE: And when Abram was ninety years old and nine, the Lord appeared unto him.

God approaches the tent, carrying a battered briefcase and supporting himself with a cane. He sports an unkempt white beard, is now dressed in a white sheet, and wears a pair of Nike runners.

He pauses at the tent flap.

GOD: (*Softly*) Abram!

ABRAM: (*From inside*) Whazzat? Whoozzer?

God sticks his head inside the tent flap.

GOD: (*More loudly*) Abram. It's me.

ABRAM: (*Groggily*) Me? . . . Me who?

GOD: ME, THE ALMIGHTY GOD.

ABRAM: (*Wide awake*) Oh! It's You!

Inside the tent. Abram rolls off the cot and onto the floor, then quickly crawls to the tent flap and opens it.

ABRAM: Come on in, sir, come right on in!

God enters and look around.

GOD: Say, nice little tent you've got here.

Abram stands up and rearranges his pajamas.

ABRAM: Thank You, Sir, and is there anything I can do for You, Sir?

GOD: Relax, Abe, you don't have to use the upper case.

ABRAM: I'll try to keep that in mind. . . . Anything I can do for you, sir? Get you a drink, maybe? I've got some Mogen David hidden down here someplace.

Abram gets down on his hands and knees and searches frantically in the sand for a bottle, which he cannot find.

GOD: Forget it, Abe. When I drink, I can't sleep.

God stretches and yawns.

NARRATOR'S VOICE: And the Lord said unto Abram, walk thou before me and be thou perfect.

GOD: Know what I'd really like you to do for me, Abe?

ABRAM: Anything you say, sir.

GOD: (*Confidentially*) Think you could, say, walk thou before me, and be thou perfect?

Abram gingerly gets up from the floor.

ABRAM: You want me to do *both*? Keep in mind, I'm not as young as I used to be.

GOD: So which would you prefer? Number One, walking thou before me, or Number Two, being thou perfect?

A long pause.

ABRAM: Uh . . . let's go with Number One, okay?

GOD: Fine. Ready?

ABRAM: Ready.

Abram begins to walk around in circles with God at his heels. Then, looking over his shoulder and terrified, he stumbles over the furniture and falls on his face.

GOD: (*Chuckling*) Am I making you nervous?

Abram picks himself off the floor and starts walking again.

ABRAM: (*Near anxiety attack*) Oh no no. I'm just naturally a klutz.

GOD: Maybe we should try Number Two, being thou perfect.

Abram abruptly stops walking.

ABRAM: Well. . . .

GOD: (*Astonished*) Don't tell me you got a problem with being perfect?!

ABRAM: What are we talking here, perfect, in what sense perfect, is that in the moral sense, the physical sense, the spiritual sense, the Boy-Scout-helping-old-ladies-across-the-street sense. . . .

GOD: (*Scratching his whiskers*) Hmmm. I hadn't really stopped to think about it . . . but yes, I'd say in the moral sense, certainly . . . because considering your age, which is, what? Maybe ninety-nine, or so? . . . Didn't I read that someplace? . . . Probably in the Bible. Let's see, where was I? . . . Oh yes, I was starting to say, it shouldn't be too difficult, this being-perfect shtick. It gets easier with age, because of the temptation factor dropping off the charts. At least that's been my experience.

ABRAM: Tell you what. If it means that much to you, I'll give it a shot.

GOD: Fine.

ABRAM: Just as long as I don't have to give up TV.

GOD: Hey, I watch that crap myself.

ABRAM: Really?

GOD: Everything but the mud wrestling.

ABRAM: You gotta draw the line somewhere.

God sits down, puts his briefcase on the table, opens it.

NARRATOR'S VOICE: And the Lord said, I will make a covenant with thee. I will give unto thee, and to thy descendants after thee, the land wherein thou art a stranger, for an everlasting possession.

God puts his feet up on the table.

GOD: Now, let's get to the point.

Abram cautiously sits down across from God.

ABRAM: . . . The . . . point?

GOD: You don't think I came by just to talk about stuff like morals and perfection and TV junk, do you? What I really came by for was to make us a covenant . . . just between me and thee and thy descendants.

God rifles through his briefcase.

ABRAM: A cov— . . . a what?

GOD: A covenant. . . . A deal. A fantastic bargain.

ABRAM: (*Warily*) I don't know if I like the sound of this.

GOD: Wait'll you hear the details.

God produces a shiny real estate brochure. Abram remains skeptical.

ABRAM: Okay, what's in it for me and my descendants?

God hands Abram the brochure.

GOD: The land wherein thou art a stranger.

Abram looks over the brochure.

ABRAM: You referring to the Holy Land?

GOD: Exactly. For an everlasting possession. So whaddya think?

ABRAM: (*Scratching his chin*) Hmmm. . . . Everlasting, huh? What else?

GOD: (*Faking astonishment*) Whaddya mean, what else? Most guys I know would *jump* at the chance for a long-term lease on this place, and you're running around saying What else? You got any idea what this tract of real estate runs?

ABRAM: Ah, go on. You know it's nothing but a pile of rocks.

GOD: . . . Tell you what, let's take a look at it.

God and Abram stand on a hill outside the village, surveying the distant property.

GOD: There are a few boulders, true, but you also gotta take into account the strategically-located oases.

ABRAM: (*Scornfully*) Oases! (*Pointing*) Is that what you call those watering holes?

GOD: (*Con game*) Listen, Abe, you can't look at them as watering holes. You gotta look at them in terms of (*Gesturing grandiosely*) swimming pools . . . palm trees . . . hotels . . . American tourists!

ABRAM: (*Scratching his chin*) Interesting proposition. Verrry interesting. . . . Tell you what. I'll talk it over with the wife, then get back with you.

GOD: Fine, fine. You might point out the central location. It's close to all the nice shopping centers—Cairo, Beirut, Baghdad. She'll know a good thing. So meetcha later.

ABRAM: Your dream or mine?

GOD: Let's make it yours. I don't dream . . . actually, don't even sleep.

ABRAM: Insomnia, huh?

GOD: Yeah. My omniscience keeps me awake.

ABRAM: Huh? Omniscience?

GOD: That's what the theologians call it. I like to refer to it as my all-knowingness. As I was saying, that's what keeps me awake.

ABRAM: I thought it was the wine.

   A long pause.

GOD: (*Skeptically*) Did I say that?

ABRAM: That's what I *thought* you said—of course, I could be mistaken.

GOD: No no—it was probably my mistake.

ABRAM: Irregardless. Meetcha later. My dream.

GOD: Right. I hope you don't mind.

They shake hands. God hobbles off into the distance, and Abram shuffles back in the direction of his tent.

Abram's bedroom. He is still snoring peacefully, and dreaming. Sara shuffles in from her bedroom, dressed in a frowzy nightgown, with her hair in curlers, and carrying a pot of coffee and two mugs.

SARA: Abram!

ABRAM: Whazzat? Whoozzer?

SARA: It's just me.

ABRAM: (*Half awake*) Me? The Almighty God?

SARA: Me, Sara. Thy beautiful wife.

Abram sits up and rubs his eyes.

ABRAM: (*Disappointed*) Oh . . . Sara. Guess who just showed up in my dream?

SARA: Hagar, that little bitch! I thought we'd settled out of court!

ABRAM: No, it was God.

A long pause.

SARA: God? . . . What'd *he* want?

ABRAM: He wanted to give the Holy Land to me and my descendants. I said I'd talk it over with you and get back to him.

Sara pours a mug of coffee for Abram and one for herself.

SARA: Your *descendants*? Who's he referring to, Hagar's little brat Ishmael?

ABRAM: I hadn't really thought about it, but that'd be one interpretation.

SARA: (*Hands on hips*) And what's in it for me? Did you think to ask him that?

ABRAM: (*Apologetically*) I was about to bring up the subject, but he had to go to the bathroom.

Sara paces back and forth, thinking of a plan of action. Then she sits down at the table across from her husband.

SARA: Here's what I want you to do, Abe. Hold out for a baby. You know how much I've always wanted a baby.

ABRAM: (*Laughing*) At the age of eighty-nine? What do you expect, a miracle?

SARA: Exactly. Remember who we're dealing with.

ABRAM: . . . I guess that makes sense . . . . So what should I put in for, a boy or a girl?

SARA: A girl, obviously . . . but come to think of it, maybe I should handle this. Next time you see him, tell him to show up in *my* dream.

ABRAM: Are you kidding? He doesn't reveal himself to women.

SARA: (*Ironically*) I wonder why.

ABRAM: (*Missing the irony*) Probably has something to do with sexual harassment.

SARA: I think you're projecting, Abram.

ABRAM: Projecting? Me?

SARA: (*Icily*) The Hagar incident?

ABRAM: Oh.

SARA: (*Sighing*) Well . . . next time he shows up in your dream, try to remember two things. One, tell him I want a baby, and two, ask him what's the catch? . . . Got that?

ABRAM: Got it.

SARA: Repeat after me. One. Sara wants a baby. Two. What's the catch?

ABRAM: Sara wants one baby to play catch with.

SARA: I'd better write this down.

Sara writes, while Abram counts to two on his fingers.

Abe's bedroom. As before, he sleeps alone on a cot, snoring gently, enjoying a happy dream.

NARRATOR'S VOICE: And the Lord appeared again unto Abram, and said, Neither shalt thy name any more be called Abram, but thy name shall be Abraham. And ye shall be circumcised in the flesh of your foreskin, and it shall be a sign of the covenant betwixt me and thee. As for Sara thy wife, thou shalt not call her name Sara, but Sarah (spelled with an H at the end) shalt her name be.

God, dressed as before and carrying the same briefcase, sticks his head through the tent flap.

GOD: (*Softly*) Abram!

ABRAM: Whazzat? Whoozzer?

GOD: (*More loudly*) Abram. It's me.

ABRAM: (*Groggily*) Me? Hagar?

127

GOD: ME, THE ALMIGHTY GOD.

Abram sits up and rubs his eyes.

ABRAM: (*Disappointed*) Oh. . . . Guess who just showed up in my dream?

GOD: Hagar.

ABRAM: God, you *are* omniscient.

GOD: Omnipotent, too. I believe that means all-powerful. . . . Well? Aren't you going to invite me in? It's *cold* out here.

Abram falls off the cot, picks himself off the floor, and goes over to the tent flap.

ABRAM: Come right in, sir, come right on in.

God comes in and sits down at the table.

ABRAM: Getcha a glass of Mogen David, sir? . . . Oh I forgot, you don't drink.

GOD: Now that you mention it, I think I will have an earthen pot of the stuff . . . just to celebrate the deal.

Abram retrieves a bottle and mugs. The bottle reads "Christian Brothers." He pours two drinks and hands one to God.

ABRAM: Here you go, sir.

He joins God at the table.

GOD: (*Sniffing*) Hey, this smells like Christian Brothers!

ABRAM: (*To himself*) Ohmigod, wrong bottle. (*To God*) You must have a cold, sir. (*Sniffing*) It smells okay to me.

GOD: Hmmm. I could have sworn. . . .

ABRAM: (*Laughing nervously*) I mean, what would *I* be doing with a bottle of Christian Brothers?

GOD: (*Chuckling*) Yeah, I guess the old nose just ain't what it used to be. . . . Well, here's to our covenant. (*Offering a toast*) Cheers.

ABRAM: (*Clinking God's mug*) Cheers.

God takes a sip.

GOD: Funny, but it *tastes* like Christian Brothers.

ABRAM: I wouldn't know. Never tried the stuff.

GOD: Of course I'm just going by hearsay.

ABRAM: Of course.

GOD: . . . Lemme take a look at that bottle, wouldja?

Abram hides the bottle behind his back.

ABRAM: I seem to have misplaced it.

GOD: You got that problem too, huh? Misplacing things? Also, short attention span? . . . Well, did you talk over my proposition with the little woman?

ABRAM: I certainly did, and she had a coupla suggestions.

GOD: (*Testily*) Oh? Like what, for instance?

Abram fumbles under his robe for the instruction sheet.

ABRAM: Where'd I put it? . . . Damn. (*Locates it*) Oh, here it is. (*Reading*) Number One: a . . . B-A-B-Y? I believe that spells *baby*.

GOD: Baby?!

ABRAM: Sara's always wanted a baby. We're a childless couple, ya know, and she'd really like to have a baby.

GOD: (*To himself*) A baby.

ABRAM: It's . . . only a suggestion.

GOD: I don't know. . . .

ABRAM: (*Laughing nervously*) You know how they are, women.

GOD: Children. So many things can go wrong.

ABRAM: (*Hopefully*) I think we'd make good parents.

GOD: Hmmm. . . .

ABRAM: Sara, at least.

God thinks this over.

GOD: Okay, okay. Boy or girl?

ABRAM: It doesn't matter, you take what God gives you. . . .

GOD: (*A sage nod*) Good thought.

ABRAM: . . . but if it's all the same to you, she'd prefer a boy.

GOD: (*Frowning*) Hmmm. We'll see what we can do. Now, the second suggestion.

ABRAM: Right . . . The second suggestion . . . Ah . . . Here we go: What's . . . the . . . C-A-T-C-H? I believe that spells *catch*.

GOD: The catch! Who do you think you're dealing with?

ABRAM: (*Meekly*) I was just reading what's written.

GOD: The catch! I have half a mind—

ABRAM: Just a minor suggestion.

GOD: The catch indeed!

ABRAM: Sorry I even brought it up.

GOD: Well I should think you would be!

ABRAM: (*Cautiously*) So I guess what you're saying is, there's no catch, huh?

GOD: Right.

ABRAM: You just give the Holy Land to me and my descendants

everlastingly, and you give Sara the baby, no strings attached?

GOD: Exactly.

ABRAM: Great.

GOD: Plus the fact that neither shall thy name any more be called Abram, but thy name shall be Abraham.

A long pause.

ABRAM: (*Warily*) What's the point?

GOD: (*Reassuringly*) I'm just adding two letters to your name, that's all. H and A. I believe that spells *ha*. That's for laughing when Sara said she wanted a baby.

ABRAM: It doesn't strike you as funny that a eighty-nine-year-old woman wants to have a baby?

GOD: Strike me as *funny?* It strikes me as a chance to work a *miracle.* . . . But if you're gonna get bent outta shape over it, tell you what. We'll add an H to Sara's name, too. That way you won't stick out like a sore thumb.

ABRAM: (*Suspiciously*) Well . . . okay. When's this new name take effect? I gotta change the registration on a few stocks.

GOD: After the operation.

A long pause.

ABRAM: The . . . what?

GOD: The operation.

ABRAM: The . . . operation?

GOD: The name-change operation.

A longer pause.

ABRAM: (*Warily*) Am I missing something here? Name-change . . . operation?

GOD: Right. The circumcision.

ABRAM: (*Laughing nervously*) That's a new one to me. How do you spell it?

GOD: C-I-R . . . Uh. Hmmm. Tell you what, I don't have time to go into it. All you have to know is the address.

God takes a pencil and legal pad out of his briefcase. He jots down a number and hands it to Abram.

GOD: Here. I've set up an appointment for tomorrow morning.

ABRAM: (*Looking at the number*) Thank you very much, sir. For this, also for the real estate, plus the baby . . . you might keep in mind, she wants a boy.

God gets up to leave.

GOD: You're welcome, and I'll try to remember. . . . Well, keep in touch.

They shake hands. God exits.

ABRAM: (*Calling after God*) I'll work on that perfection thing, sir. (*To himself*) Morning, did he say?

A doctor's office. Morning. The nurse enters, dressed appropriately, followed by Abram, popping breath mints.

NURSE: (*Sweetly*) Here we go, Mr. Abram. Let's see, we're here for a . . . (*Reading a chart*) name-change operation, right?

ABRAM: Right. A quote-unquote name-change operation. . . . Say, I like your dress. White looks very good on you.

NURSE: Thank you.

ABRAM: Very nice shoes, too. You don't see white shoes that often. Or stockings, for that matter. Clever color combination.

NURSE: Now, if you could just step up on this scale (*Indicating*) so we can get your weight.

Abram steps on the scale. Nurse reads it.

NURSE: (*Frowning*) Have you ever considered a weight-loss program, Mr. Abram?

ABRAM: You sound just like my wife, Sara. Actually, it's scheduled to be *Sarah,* spelled with an H. She's gonna have a name-change operation, too.

NURSE: (*Aside*) I wouldn't bet on it. (*To Abram*) Now, if you could roll up your sleeve.

Abram rolls up his sleeve.

ABRAM: You don't waste any time, do you? I *like* that in a woman.

Nurse takes Abram's blood pressure.

NURSE: (*Frowning*) Have you ever considered an exercise program, Mr. Abram?

ABRAM: What a coincidence! That's what Hagar used to say.

NURSE: Hagar?

ABRAM: (*Proudly*) My *last* mistress. We settled out of court.

NURSE: . . . Now, if you could let your hand go limp, Mr. Abram.

ABRAM: (*Becoming soft butter*) My hand, did you say?

Abram lets his hand go limp; Nurse takes his pulse.

NURSE: (*Frowning*) Hmmm. Have you ever considered taking a long vacation, Mr. Abram?

ABRAM: (*Grinning*) What did you have in mind?

NURSE: Maybe . . . some monastery?

Abram does some fanny patting.

ABRAM: Mona who? Could you spell it out for me?

NURSE: If you get your hand off my dress.

Abram ceases and desists.

ABRAM: Just admiring the whiteness.

Nurse gives him a look and walks toward the door.

NURSE: Doctor will be with you in a minute.

ABRAM: Doctor?

NURSE: Dr. Chop.

Nurse leaves. The clock shows ten o'clock.

Doctor's office. The clock shows eleven o'clock. Dr. Chop arrives. She is young and beautiful and is wearing a white surgeon's coat and face mask. As she comes in, Abram is shining the tiny flashlight at a mirror and does not notice her.

ABRAM: I didn't realize it'd be such a complicated—(*Seeing Dr. Chop*) . . . Oh. I thought you were Dr. Chop.

DR. CHOP: I am.

A long pause.

ABRAM: Say, I like your coat. White looks very good on you.

Dr. Chop ignores him and inspects the chart.

DR. CHOP: Let's see, we're here for a . . . Hmmm . . . name-change operation, is that right?

ABRAM: (*Full of enthusiasm*) Right. A quote unquote name-change operation.

DR. CHOP: Now, Mr. Abram, if you could just drop your loin cloth.

ABRAM: (*To the camera*) I think I'm gonna like this!

The desert. High noon. Abraham rides toward home very slowly. Once home, he dismounts, in great pain, and hobbles towards the tent flap.

The tent living room. Sara sits in her rocking chair, humming and knitting pink booties. She hears someone approaching.

SARA: (*Calling*) That you, Abram?
Abraham enters, lacking in enthusiasm.
ABRAHAM: No . . . It's me, Abra*ham*.
SARA: So how did the negotiations go? I've been dying to know.
ABRAHAM: Perfect, except . . .
SARA: Except?
ABRAHAM: . . . except that you're gonna have to add an H to your name.
SARA: I don't see a problem there . . . Do *you* see a problem?
Abraham sits down and sighs.
ABRAHAM: It ain't as simple as it sounds.

FOUR: ENTERTAINING ANGELS

OUTSIDE THE TENT. Abraham, still ninety-nine, sits in the shade. A dromedary is tethered nearby.
NARRATOR'S VOICE: Now Abraham and Sarah were old and well stricken in age; and it ceased to be with Sarah after the manner of women. And Abraham sat in the tent door in the heat of the day.
Abraham closes his eyes and begins to snooze. And dream.

A desert well. Abraham and his thirteen-year-old son sit in a pair of lounge chairs beside a well, fishing. The son feels a tug on his pole. He yanks and is soon fighting the fish he has just hooked. He slowly reels it in, while Abraham prepares a net to retrieve it. They finally land an octopus.
A baseball diamond in a desert pasture. Abraham sits behind the home dugout with a camcorder, pointing it at the action on the field. Abraham's son, dressed in a Camel League uniform with the team name "He-Asses," is at the plate, pointing with his bat, à la Babe Ruth, at a distant target. The pitcher, wearing a uniform bearing the nickname "Librarians," pitches; the son hits the ball 400 feet, scattering a herd of sheep. Abraham bounds onto the field and records his son rounding the bases.

The saloon. Evening. Abraham's young son and a thirteen-year-old girl sit at a table, drinking goat milk. The two gaze intently at each other. They stand. They walk upstairs, his arm around her. They disappear into an upstairs bedroom. A moment later, a cap gun rings out.

The tent living room. Sarah, now eighty-nine, sits in her rocking chair. She is knitting pink booties and daydreaming.

A bazaar. Sarah and her thirteen-year-old daughter stand at a booth. In pantomime, Sarah haggles with a merchant over the price of a training bra.

The pageant stage. Sara's daughter stands before an enraptured audience. She wears a scarlet dress; her banner proclaims her to be Miss Sinai. She is performing in the talent portion of the Miss Holy Land competition, favoring the crowd with a superb rendition of the aria "È strano" from Verdi's La Traviata. *English subtitles.*

DAUGHTER: *È strano! è strano!*
[How strange! how strange!]
In core scolpiti ho quegli accenti!
[In my heart are sculpted those words!]
Saria per me sventura un serio amore?
[Would to me true love bring bad luck?]
Che risolvi, o turbata anima mia?
[What think you, oh troubled spirit mine?]
   The audience applauds wildly. Sarah and Abraham look at each other and nod their proud approval.

A tent bedroom. Afternoon. Sarah's daughter and a thirteen-year-old Pharaoh are in bed, après sex. They are sucking on suckers, which they hold like cigarettes. His crown is askew.

DAUGHTER: That was *nice.*

PHARAOH: (*Pleased with himself*) Was I really that good?

DAUGHTER: Oh, you *were.*

PHARAOH: (*Fishing*) On a scale of one to ten, you'd give me . . . what?

   She props herself up on one elbow.

DAUGHTER: Definitely a ten!

   Pharaoh smiles immodestly. They smoke their suckers.

134

PHARAOH: Anybody wanna go for eleven?

DAUGHTER: Mathematically impossible, but . . .

A dreamy smile crosses her face. She sits up quickly (covering herself, of course), yanks off his crown, tosses it on the floor, and throws herself on his tender young body.

Back to the real world. Main Street. A pair of young American tourists, George and Sandy, ride down the street toward the tent. He is driving a jeep, she is following on a dromedary, sidesaddle. The camel is laden with her extensive trousseau. Both wear Hawkeye caps and sunglasses, and both have cameras dangling from straps around their necks.

NARRATOR'S VOICE: And Abraham lifted up his eyes and looked, and lo, three men stood by him.

GOD'S VOICE: No no no. There weren't three, there were two. And one of them was a woman. And they didn't stand by him. They approached him.

NARRATOR'S VOICE: But it is written—

GOD'S VOICE: Written, schmitten. I've got eyes in my head. *I* say there are two, and *I* say one of them is a woman.

NARRATOR'S VOICE: *(Sighing)* Okay, you're the boss. . . . And Abraham lifted up his eyes and looked, and lo, a man and a woman approached him.

GOD'S VOICE: That's better.

Abraham stands up, shades his eyes, and takes a look.

ABRAHAM: *(Calling)* Sweetheart . . . come here.

Sarah appears at the tent flap.

ABRAHAM: It looks like we've got visitors.

SARAH: Are you kidding? I haven't had a "visitor" in fifty years.

ABRAHAM: Well, you've got two now. . . . Wonder who they are?

Sarah looks.

SARAH: *(Sarcastically)* They're probably messengers from God, bringing the baby.

ABRAHAM: *(Missing the sarcasm)* Angels! That would explain the wings!

Sarah shades her eyes for a better look.

SARAH: They look to me like ordinary shoulder blades.

ABRAHAM: How clever! He's disguising his angels with ordinary shoulder blades!

SARAH: They seem to be a young married couple. . . . Gentiles.

George and Sandy come nearer.

ABRAHAM: Seem! Exactly! Oh, his ways are past finding out! (*Whispering*) Quick, into the tent! Rustle up some hors d'oeuvres for our guests.

SARAH: But Abe—

ABRAHAM: (*Whispering*) Trust me, I know how to deal with these people. You gotta put your best foot forward.

Sarah sighs, then goes into the tent to rustle up some hors d'oeuvres.

George and Sandy come to a stop in front of the tent.

ABRAHAM: Howdy, strangers! The name's Abraham, formerly Abram . . . (*Winking*) as if you didn't know the whole story!

George and Sandy dismount and greet Abraham.

GEORGE: (*Bright-eyed*) Hi. I'm George, and this is my new bride Sandy.

SANDY: (*Naively*) We're American tourists, and we're lost.

ABRAHAM: (*To himself*) How sly of God! Sending quote-unquote American tourists!

GEORGE: Honey, I know exactly where we are.

SANDY: And I know exactly where we're *supposed* to be. In Bethlehem of Judea.

ABRAHAM: (*To himself*) How cunning of him! Disguising them as Christians!

GEORGE: You wouldn't happen to have a telephone around here, wouldja?

ABRAHAM: (*To himself*) They want to report to The Boss! I've already made an impression! (*To George and Sandy*) No I wouldn't, but could I interest you in a glass of water? Or a large plate of hors d'oeuvres? . . . Maybe a fatted calf?

GEORGE: You know what'd really hit the spot? A bottle of Blue Nun.

SANDY: And a coupla ham sandwiches.

ABRAHAM: (*To himself*) Uh oh . . . they're testing me! (*To George and Sandy*) Sorry, it's against our religion.

GEORGE: Oh, we didn't mean . . .

SANDY: We're really sensitive, basically.

ABRAHAM: (*To himself*) Sensitive? Of course! They're angels! (*To George and Sandy*) We're sensitive, too. (*Chuckling*) Not as much as you folks, but then, who is?

Sarah comes out of the tent with a plate of hors d'oeuvres.

ABRAHAM: Oh. Sarah. I'd like you to meet George and Sandy.

SANDY: (*Enthusiastically*) We're tourists, and this is our first trip abroad.

SARAH: (*Looking them over*) I'm sure it is.

ABRAHAM: George and Sandy, this is Sarah, my wife. She's the former Miss Holy Land!

Sarah curtsies.

GEORGE: Well, I can see why!

SANDY: (*Proudly*) I was the runner-up for Miss Dubuque.

SARAH: Abe thought you might like some hors d'oeuvres.

Sarah offers the plate around. Sandy and George take several each. Abraham takes the remainder.

GEORGE: Our favorites! Pork balls wrapped in bacon!

SANDY: You must of figured out we was from Iowa.

Abraham quickly puts his generous portion back on the plate. He wipes his hands on his robe.

ABRAHAM: (*Sniffing; to Sarah*) Do you smell something burning?

SARAH: We haven't done a burnt offering for ages.

ABRAHAM: (*To George and Sandy*) Excuse us. We've got to go check . . . something.

Abraham steers Sarah into the tent.

Inside the tent. Abraham and Sara engage in a major domestic dispute.

ABRAHAM: What's the matter with you, serving them pork balls? And then saying we're behind on our burnt offerings! Didn't I say they're angels?

SARAH: He may be cute, but he's no angel.

ABRAHAM: The hell he's not! He was sent by God!

SARAH: That still doesn't make him an angel.

ABRAHAM: You should have heard them! They were dropping clues left and right!

SARAH: For example?

ABRAHAM: (*Counting on fingers*) One, she said they're American tourists and two, they're looking for Bethlehem and three, he said he wanted to use our phone and four, he asked for a bottle of Blue Nun and five, she wanted a ham sandwich and six, she said they're basically sensitive!

SARAH: So?

ABRAHAM: That's six clues! What more do you want?

SARAH: Come on, Abe! They're just a coupla wet-behind-the-ears Iowa farm kids on a honeymoon.

ABRAHAM: (*Confused*) . . . I thought you agreed they were messengers from God, bringing the baby.

SARAH: . . . A baby? (*Suddenly enthusiastic*) Now that you mention it, there *was* a gleam in his eye.

Outside the tent. George and Sandy inspect their host's camel.

GEORGE: Can you *believe* that idiot?

SANDY: (*Giggling*) I think he's kinda cute.

GEORGE: If you wanna know the truth, he reminds me of your great-grandpa.

SANDY: (*Defensively*) What's wrong with Great-grandpa? He's wise and considerate, plus, he's been all the way to Des Moines without getting lost.

GEORGE: So you prefer older men, do you? The guy must be a hundred!

SANDY: Who're *you* to talk? I saw the way you looked at her.

GEORGE: What's wrong with older women? Besides, she *was* Miss Holy Land.

SANDY: *Was* is the operative word. She's ninety if she's a day.

GEORGE: I know a certain person who didn't even make it to Miss Iowa.

SANDY: And I know—

GEORGE: Shhh. . . .

Abraham emerges from the tent bringing a bottle of wine, two mugs, and a bottle of pickles. He smiles hospitably.

ABRAHAM: Would you like some Mogen David? Maybe a few kosher pickles?

GEORGE: I think—

ABRAHAM: "Therefore, I am." Plato, right?

SANDY: (*To George; whispering*) What'd I tell you? He's a philosopher, just like Great-grandpa.

GEORGE: (*To Sandy; whispering*) He's crazy, like your mother.

ABRAHAM: Speaking of philosophy, have you ever noticed how appearance is often mistaken for reality? For instance, sometimes pork balls can be confused with matzos balls, and bacon can be . . . etcetera.

GEORGE: (*To Abraham*) Speaking of pork balls, you think maybe Sarah's got any more of them whore dwarfs?

SANDY: (*To George; hinting*) Why don't you go and find out? Mr. Abraham was just about to show me his ranch . . . weren't you, Mr. Abraham?

George gladly takes Sandy's hint and goes inside the tent.

ABRAHAM: (*To Sandy*) Are you interested in sheep?

The sheep pens. Abraham gives Sandy a tour, pointing out the main attractions. They come across ewes being suckled by kids, then a ram tupping a ewe.

SANDY: I'm so excited! . . . You know what this reminds me of, Mr. Abraham?

ABRAHAM: (*Chortling*) I can only guess.

SANDY: Bach. Johann Sebastian Bach. "Sheep May Safely Graze."

ABRAHAM: Bock? . . . Isn't that a beer?

SANDY: You're so witty, Mr. Abraham.

Abraham pats her hand.

ABRAHAM: Just call me Abe.

SANDY: Oh, I couldn't do that, Mr. Abraham. . . . Say, betcha can't guess who you remind me of!

ABRAHAM: Paul Newman?

SANDY: Oh Mr. Abraham. You're being clever! Just like Great-grandpa . . . he's the one you remind me of.

ABRAHAM: Your great-grandfather?

SANDY: That's because you're both so wise.

ABRAHAM: Well, I *do* usually ace the *Jerusalem Times* crossword.

SANDY: Really? I'm *so* impressed! I'm *terrible* at crosswords. (*Sighing*) I guess I just don't have the mind for it.

ABRAHAM: Well, there are minds, and . . . there are bodies.

SANDY: That's *so* philosophical!

ABRAHAM: Your talent probably lies in your body.

SANDY: (*Blushing*) Oh, you're just saying that! I'm not even good at shucking corn!

ABRAHAM: Well, bodies can do more than shuck corn. (*Under his breath*) I wonder if angels come fully-equipped?

SANDY: What did you say?

ABRAHAM: I said, Bodies are good for more than shucking corn. I was just repeating myself, putting it in a different way. Us witty philosophers do that a lot. We're always trying to find the best combination of words. (*Under his breath*) I wonder if God would mind if I got to "know" her? In the Biblical sense?

SANDY: And what was that combination of words?

ABRAHAM: I was saying, Bodies should get to know each other. I was starting a new thought. That's another thing us wise philosophers do a lot of. (*Under his breath*) Why not get to "know" her? Isn't that why God sent her?

SANDY: That's exactly what Great-grandpa used to say. He'd say, "Y'know, bodies rilly oughtta get ta know each other better."

ABRAHAM: Your great-grandpa was a very wise man.

SANDY: (*Giggling*) Like somebody else I know.

ABRAHAM: You know what they say . . . great minds run in similar canals.

SANDY: Isn't it channels? Or trenches? Could it be ditches? (*To herself*) Maybe it's gutters.

Inside the tent. Sarah and George sit around a table, eating hors d'oeuvres and flirting.

GEORGE: I don't know why, but I have this thing about older women.

SARAH: Funny, but I've always preferred younger men.

GEORGE: Say, how'd you ever end up with a clown like Abe?

SARAH: Here in the Holy Land we call them schlemiels, and how'd *you* ever end up with an innocent like Sandy?

GEORGE: (*Proudly*) I got her pregnant.

An office. Sarah sits behind a desk, with paper and pen. She is interviewing George for a position. She is dressed in the modern style and is wearing a pair of stylish glasses; he is dressed as a young American businessman. Their manner is extremely formal.

SARAH: Does this happen often—the getting of older women pregnant?

GEORGE: I've had a modest share of success along those lines.

SARAH: What about older women? Have you had good luck with them also?

GEORGE: As a matter of fact, they're something of a specialty with me.

SARAH: Within what basic parameters do you normally operate, age-wise?

GEORGE: I seem to function most effectively in the fifty-to-eighty-year-old bracket.

SARAH: What is your personal best?

GEORGE: I have been clocked, unofficially, at eighty-seven years and three months.

SARAH: Was that the moment of conception or the moment of birth?

GEORGE: The former, though I must add that she brought the child to full term.

SARAH: Still, you have every right to be proud of yourself.

GEORGE: I had great cooperation from the lady involved. She was a wealthy spinster who needed a quick heir to whom she could leave her not-inconsiderable fortune.

SARAH: Are spinsters a significant percentage of your clientele?

GEORGE: Indeed they are. In fact, that's my sub-specialty. I have expensive tastes, and they pay well above the going rate.

SARAH: Speaking of which, what is your preferred mode of payment?

GEORGE: Ordinarily I favor a secret donation to my Swiss bank account, but I also take American Express.

SARAH: Do you take payment in kind? Sheep, for example?

GEORGE: New Zealand sheep, certainly. Also, African elephants, Peruvian llamas, German shepherds, trained St. Bernards, albino peacocks (in matched pairs), assorted carnivores of the Serengeti, and parrots with the vocabulary of, say, a modest spell-check program.

SARAH: What about camels?

GEORGE: I've been known to take camels, yes, though I am loath to accept the one-humped variety, also known as the dromedary.

SARAH: Suppose the lady were the former Miss Holy Land?

GEORGE: Under those circumstances, I'd certainly consider a one-humper.

SARAH: Fine. Am I to assume you guarantee your work?

GEORGE: Up to the limits prescribed by law.

SARAH: Do you operate according to contract?

GEORGE: I rely upon the handshake.

Sarah and George stand. She walks around the desk. They shake hands, formally. He begins to leave.

SARAH: Oh. One final question. When would be a good time to consummate the deal?

George pulls a notebook from his vest pocket, and consults it.

GEORGE: Let's see . . . Amazing! I seem to have an immediate opening.

He begins to chase her around the desk. They play the cat and mouse routine for some time. Finally he catches her. She giggles. They embrace. They kiss, passionately. They begin to disrobe each other, frantically. They roll on the floor.

God suddenly appears. He takes a long look at the pair, then walks over to the camera and covers it with his hand.

In the bedroom. Sara and George sit up in bed, après sex. They are puffing on corncob pipes. His Hawkeye cap is askew.

SARAH: That was *nice.*

GEORGE: (*Pleased with himself*) Was I really that good?

SARAH: Oh, you *were.*

GEORGE: (*Fishing*) On a scale of one to ten, you'd give me . . . what?

SARAH: Definitely an eleven!

A long pause.

GEORGE: You wouldn't consider throwing in a peacock?

Outside the tent. Sandy sits on her camel, George is in his jeep. Abraham's camel is tethered to the jeep. They are saying goodbye to Abraham and Sarah. A peacock struts along behind.

SANDY: (*Calling and waving*) Bye, Mr. Abraham.

ABRAHAM: (*Calling and waving*) Bye, Sandy. Write some time, wouldja?

SARAH: (*Calling and waving*) Bye, George.
GEORGE: (*Calling and waving*) Bye, Sarah. Keep in touch, okay?
George and Sandy slowly disappear over a sand dune, waving and blowing kisses.
ABRAHAM: (*Beaming*) What a nice young couple.
SARAH: Aren't they? . . . Say, Abe, I have to admit, you were right.
ABRAHAM: Oh?
SARAH: (*Sighing*) He *was* an angel.
ABRAHAM: Except that he didn't bring the baby . . . HEY . . . HE'S RUNNING OFF WITH MY CAMEL!

The tent living room. Sarah is rocking, watching TV, knitting pink booties, and smiling. She is pregnant. The set shows the interior of an American TV studio. George and Sandy are seated side by side. She is dabbing at her eyes with a handkerchief; he looks uncomfortable. A subtitle reads: "He Got Another Woman Pregnant On Their Honeymoon." An attractive young hostess appears on the screen, caressing a microphone.
HOSTESS: You've heard the story, audience. What do *you* think?
The audience thinks hard about it.
WOMAN 1: (*To George*) What if she'd of done that to *you?*
George and Sandy glance at each other.
GEORGE: For all I know, she did.
AUDIENCE: Oooooh!
Sandy sobs into her handkerchief.
SANDY: No I didn't. I just *thought* about it. There's a great big difference.
The audience applauds.
WOMAN 2: (*To George*) I think you're trash. Not for getting somebody else *pregnant*, but on your *honeymoon*?
SALLY: Let's not be too judgmental. Maybe he had a reason. (*To George*) Why *did* you do it, George?
George sits up straight and looks serious.
GEORGE: She was eighty-nine years old, and she was childless. Besides, God had promised her a baby.
The women in the audience look at each other and nod sympathetically.
GEORGE: So I figured it was my Christian duty.

143

The audience bursts into spontaneous and sustained applause.

FIVE: THE SACRIFICE

THE TENT LIVING ROOM. Morning. Sarah rocks a cradle, smiling and knitting blue booties. She leans over and fusses with Baby Isaac. The calendar reads "July 1923 B.C."

NARRATOR'S VOICE: And the Lord visited Sarah as he had said, and the Lord did unto Sarah as he had spoken.

GOD'S VOICE: What's that? "The Lord *did unto* Sarah"? . . . I'm not sure I like the way you put it.

NARRATOR'S VOICE: That's the way you put it in the Bible.

GOD'S VOICE: Really? Are you sure?

NARRATOR'S VOICE: Genesis 21, verse 1.

GOD'S VOICE: (*Musing*) "Did unto Sarah." Huh . . . Gotta be more careful what I say. People might get the wrong impression.

NARRATOR'S VOICE: Then it goes on, "For Sarah conceived, and bare Abraham a son in his old age."

GOD'S VOICE: (*Still musing*) They might think I didn't admire her for her *mind*.[43]

Abraham enters in a squeaky wheelchair.

SARAH: That you, Abe?

ABRAHAM: Yes, Sarah, my bride of, what? must be nearly sixty-nine years.

SARAH: (*Hinting*) It's seventy years today. Exactly.

ABRAHAM: Seventy years! Well, well . . . Exactly, did you say?

SARAH: Ex . . . act . . . ly.

ABRAHAM: I'll take your word for it. You're the one who keeps track of things like birthdays and . . . what's the word I'm looking for?

SARAH: (*Icily*) Try anniversaries.

ABRAHAM: Ah. Anniversaries. I'd forgotten. Must be getting old.

SARAH: You've been using that excuse for sixty-nine years.

ABRAHAM: And, if memory serves, each one of those years I was

---

[43] The text here is corrupt. Ms. LaFemme suggested the interpolation.

getting older.

Sarah sighs.

SARAH: Anyway, that's not what I wanted to discuss.

ABRAHAM: You wanted to discuss my squeaky wheelchair, right?

SARAH: How did you know?

ABRAHAM: That's what we talked about yesterday. And the day before. And the day before that. And the day—

SARAH: You remember, do you?

ABRAHAM: (*Indignantly*) Listen, I may be getting old, but I'm still sharp as a tack.

SARAH: (*Sarcastically*) I never doubted it.

ABRAHAM: (*Missing the sarcasm*) You want me to oil my wheels because they always wake up little Ishmael. How's that for memory?

SARAH: (*Supreme iciness*) Brilliant. Except that his name is Isaac. Ishmael is the son of Hagar, my former handmaid.

ABRAHAM: Hagar, Hagar . . . oh yes, the former Miss Egypt, right?

SARAH: I've never seen how they chose the little tramp, but . . . right.

Abraham points at his forehead and grins.

ABRAHAM: See? Memory like a top-end computer.

Main Street. Evening. Thirteen-year-old Isaac and his buddy, Augie, stroll nonchalantly down the board sidewalk, dressed in traditional garb.

NARRATOR'S VOICE: And it came to pass, that Isaac grew in wisdom and stature.

The pair spot an elderly woman peering into the window of Abe's Saloon. They glance at each other; Augie gives a signal. They swoop down on her, knock her down, grab her purse, and take off running.

Inside Abe's Grocery. Evening. Isaac and Augie saunter down the aisle. They come across the magazine rack, on which are displayed The Holy Land Enquirer; Holy Land News and World Report; Playperson; Pent Tent; Hot Camels; Judaism Today; The Christian Century. *They glance around furtively, then slip copies of* Playperson, Hot Camels, *and* The Christian Century *under their robes. Then they walk casually out the door.*

*Isaac's bedroom. Evening. Isaac, reclining on the bed, watches MTV,
which is on at full volume. He is dressed in leather pants and wears
gold earrings, a gold nose ring, gold nipple rings, and etc.*
   Abraham enters in his wheelchair.
ABRAHAM: Ike! Turn that damn noise down.
   Using his remote, Isaac turns the damn noise down several decibels.
ISAAC: So what's the rap, Papa Time?
ABRAHAM: What's this I hear about you and Augie racing a
coupla stolen camels?
ISAAC: It wasn't my idea, it was Augie's.[44]
   Isaac climbs out of bed.
ABRAHAM: (*Grumpily*) Always blaming your Christian friends.
   Isaac stretches and yawns.
ISAAC: Listen, Gramps, I gotta blow this pop stand. Augie's set us
up for a coupla rounds of Satan worship. Then we're scheduled
for an interfaith orgy.
   Isaac starts to leave.
ABRAHAM: (*Wagging a finger*) Listen, young man, when I was
your age. . . .
   Isaac exits.
ABRAHAM: (*Calling after Isaac*) . . . I didn't run around with
Christians . . . (*Muttering to himself*) and when I did, I took the
leadership role.

Abraham's bedroom. Night. Abraham picks up the phone and dials.
NARRATOR'S VOICE: It came to pass after these things, that God
did tempt Abraham. And God said, take now thy only son Isaac,
whom thou lovest, and get thee into the land of Moriah; and
offer him for a burnt offering.
   Intercut. A two-way conversation with Abraham in his bedroom,

---

[44]As Cardinal Micromentis pointed out, Augie is short for Augustine,
the name of one of the most important theologians in Christendom.
(The good cardinal could not explain the significance of this fact,
however; unfortunately, Professor Allbright could not assist him, being
at the time busy working on a monograph).

God at a computer.
GOD: Hi, God here.
ABRAHAM: This is Abraham, and I've got—
GOD: Abraham? How's that spelled?
ABRAHAM: A-B-R-A-H-A-M. (*To himself*) How soon they forget.
GOD: What's your account number, beginning with the letter J, as in Jerusalem?
ABRAHAM: J-1.
GOD: Wait . . . it's coming up on the screen . . . there . . . fine. Now, what's your maiden name?
ABRAHAM: Abram, that's A-B-R-A-M.
GOD: Age?
ABRAHAM: One hundred and thirteen.
GOD: Fine . . . it all seems to check out. Now, how many children do you have living at home, and what are their names and ages?
ABRAHAM: One boy, Isaac, age thirteen.
GOD: And that's what you called to talk about, right?
ABRAHAM: (*Amazed*) How did you know?
GOD: An educated guess . . . maybe it was my omniscience. And how much time have you been spending with Ike?
ABRAHAM: Just three minutes a day—but that's all quality time.
GOD: What do you do with him?
ABRAHAM: Discuss physics.
GOD: More specifically?
ABRAHAM: We talk decibel levels.
GOD: Hmmm . . . Ever considered taking him hunting?
ABRAHAM: Hunting?
GOD: Sure. He needs some male bonding, and I'd recommend hunting as a great way for father and son to connect.
ABRAHAM: Wait a minute. I gotta write this down.
Abraham takes a pencil and paper from under his robe.
ABRAHAM: (*To himself; writing*) Bond . . . ing. (*To God*) Gotcha.
GOD: Anyway, it's just an idea. You might take a stab at it.
ABRAHAM: (*To himself; writing*) A . . . stab. (*To God*) Got it. What else?
GOD: That's it, basically. All it requires is that you sacrifice a little of your time.
ABRAHAM: (*To himself; writing*) Sac-ri-fice . . . spelled with two

C's. (*To God*) Could you be more specific?

GOD: Listen, Abe, I've got another client on Hold. Tell you what, just figure it out for yourself.

The desert wilderness. Morning. Abraham and Isaac climb a mountain. Abraham is in his wheelchair, carrying a hunting knife and a rope. Isaac is carrying a handgun.

ISAAC: (*Breathless*) Why we gotta go hunting, Pops? I was just on my way to school.

ABRAHAM: God's orders.

They continue to climb. They finally stop to rest.

ISAAC: (*Breathless*) What are we hunting for?

ABRAHAM: A goat.

They toil until they reach the summit. Then Abraham climbs out of his wheelchair and begins to bind Isaac.

ISAAC: (*Petrified*) What kind of a goat?

Abraham sharpens his knife.

ABRAHAM: I believe the technical term is *scape*.

GOD'S VOICE: (*To Abraham*) That's enough. Hold it right there. The rest of this scene is too explicit for family viewing.

ABRAHAM: (*To God*) You mean I come all the way up here and I don't get to finish the job?

GOD'S VOICE: (*To Abraham*) Oh, you can finish the job. But you have to do it off-screen.

Isaac unties himself and sneaks away, unobserved by Abraham.

ABRAHAM: I know how *that* goes. I get off screen and then you give me all sorts of excuses to keep me from—

GOD'S VOICE: I promise.

ABRAHAM: How do I know I can trust you?

GOD'S VOICE: Listen, Abe, we go back a long way.

ABRAHAM: True, but—

GOD'S VOICE: Haven't I always been there for you?

ABRAHAM: Yes, but—

GOD'S VOICE: Didn't I set you up with Miss Holy Land?

ABRAHAM: Yes, but—

GOD'S VOICE: Didn't I throw in Miss Egypt as a bonus?

ABRAHAM: Yes, but—

GOD'S VOICE: Didn't I make you a very nice real estate deal?

ABRAHAM: Yes, but—

GOD'S VOICE: And didn't I send an angel to give you and Sarah a son?

ABRAHAM: Yes, but—

GOD'S VOICE: So what's this shtick about not trusting me?

ABRAHAM: I don't know . . . can't quite put my finger on it.

Abraham suddenly looks around and discovers Isaac missing.

ABRAHAM: My God! He's gone!

Abraham looks heavenward.

GOD'S VOICE: Don't look at *me*.

The sheriff's office. Noon. The sheriff sits back in a chair with his feet on a desk, snoozing. In a parody of the silent movies, a piano plays offscreen, tempo largo. Isaac rushes into the office; the piano switches to tempo allegro. He gesticulates wildly, indicating, in pantomime, what has just happened to him. The sheriff rushes out the door, followed by Isaac.

Main Street. The sheriff and Isaac come running out of the Sheriff's Office, tempo presto. The sheriff hops on his camel, wheels around, and gallops off down Main Street toward the wilderness. Isaac runs down the street to the door of HLND-TV and enters.

The wilderness. The sheriff charges up the mountain. Tempo presto.

The wilderness. Abraham sits in his wheelchair at the summit, smoking a cigar and enjoying the sun. Tempo largo. He sees the sheriff charging up Mt. Moriah on his camel. Abraham spins his wheelchair around and takes off down the mountain. Tempo presto.

Office of HLND-TV. Isaac rushes in and again tells his story in pantomime. Tempo presto.

The sheriff chases Abraham across the desert, swinging a lasso. Tempo presto.

Living room of the tent. Sarah sits in her chair, watching TV. She is wearing her Miss Holy Land banner.

BENJAMIN: This just in. We have word that a prominent political figure is being sought by the Holy Land sheriff. What have you got for us, Esther?

ESTHER: We have reason to believe that an unidentified celebrity has been accused of child abuse.

Desert wilderness. Abraham and the sheriff sit at a chessboard, musing. Tempo largo. Abraham makes a move, then turns his wheelchair around and takes off, tempto presto. The sheriff quickly mounts his camel and resumes his pursuit.

Tent living room. Sarah sits in her chair, watching TV.

BENJAMIN: Could you be more specific, Esther?

ESTHER: Benjamin, word has it that this morning, about ten a.m., the man attempted to sacrifice his son with a knife.

BENJAMIN: And as many of you are well aware, child sacrifice, as traditionally practiced, is regarded with raised eyebrows in some circles.

  Sarah raises her eyebrows.

An amusement park, the revolving merry-go-round. Abraham, riding a horse, looks behind himself in fear. The sheriff rides another horse, behind his prey, swinging his lasso. Tempo moderato.

The tent living room. Sarah sits in her chair, watching TV.

BENJAMIN: Esther, do we have any positive identification of the suspect?

ESTHER: A source close to the action tells us that the suspect is the mayor of Abeville.

BENJAMIN: If I'm not mistaken, that would be Abraham.

  Sarah sits on the edge of her chair, her mouth open.

A baseball diamond. Abraham circles the bases in his wheelchair, with the sheriff and his camel in hot pursuit. A large crowd urges Abraham on, and cheers as he crosses home plate. Tempo prestissimo.

The tent living room. Sarah sits on the edge of her chair, eating a banana and watching TV.

BENJAMIN: Esther, any thoughts on what this will do to Abraham's political career?

ESTHER: Benjamin, our on-the-spot poll shows that thirty-eight percent of the probable voters approve of his behavior, nine percent disapprove, and fifty-three percent are too busy enjoying the action to express an opinion.

Sarah throws the banana at the TV.

A graveyard. Abraham enters the Holy Land Cemetery on his wheelchair, pursued by the sheriff. They pass headstones bearing the names of Adam, Eve, Cain, and Abel. Prestissimo.

Abraham and wheelchair suddenly disappear into a large open grave. The sheriff pulls his camel to a halt at the edge. Abraham's head slowly appears from the grave, covered by a wreath of flowers. Largo. The camel, if it is well-trained, reaches down and munches on the flowers. The headstone at the end of the grave reads: "Abraham (née Abram): 2023 B.C.-1910 B.C."

The courthouse. Late afternoon. A judge sits behind her bench, armed with a gavel. Abraham enters in his wheelchair and takes a position directly before the judge. He is accompanied by his lawyer and the sheriff.

The judge adjusts her glasses, clears her throat.

JUDGE: Mr. Abraham, I believe?

ABRAHAM: That's right . . . if I remember correctly.

JUDGE: (*Shuffling papers*) Hmmm. Let's see . . . Oh yes. A case of, Hmmm . . . child sacrifice. (*Reading*) You are charged with, number one, binding said child to a large boulder, number two, brandished a knife in his or her presence, and number three, threatened said child with dismemberment and/or death. How do you plead?

LAWYER: I believe said child's name is Isaac, and it was blown out of proportion by the media.

JUDGE: This is not a media report. It's a report from the arresting officer. How does your client plead?

ABRAHAM: Keep in mind that I am old and well stricken in age.

LAWYER: My client is old and well stricken in age.

JUDGE: What's that got to do with anything?

ABRAHAM: The point is. . . . That's funny, I forgot what I was gonna say.

JUDGE: You were saying that you are old and well stricken in age.

Abraham sits back in his wheelchair, hands behind his head.

ABRAHAM: Very poetic, don'tcha think? "Old and well stricken in age," if I may savor the phrase. You don't hear that kind of language anymore. They tend to use trite clichés like "over the hill" and "the golden years" and "senior citizens" . . . not clichés but . . . what's the word I'm looking for? . . . Bromides? (*To himself*) No, that's the med you take when you can't sleep. . . . Maybe it's for hemorrhoids? . . . (*To judge*) Excuse me, Your Honor, my memory isn't what it was, which is what happens when you're over the—

JUDGE: Mr. Abraham.

ABRAHAM:—hill, don't interrupt me, please, you're supposed to humor senior citizens. . . . Now I forget what I was gonna say. . . . Help me out here, wouldja?

JUDGE: (*Losing patience*) Did you or did you not bind an innocent child to an immense boulder, brandish a knife, and threaten his life?

ABRAHAM: Ah yes, now I remember. We were out hunting. . . . We needed some male bonding, you see, and a well-known expert recommended hunting as an excellent way for father and son to connect.

JUDGE: (*Shouting*) What do you plead?

ABRAHAM: Oh, let's say . . . ninety-five percent not guilty.

The lawyer whispers to Abraham.

ABRAHAM: (*To the judge*) Let's make that 100 percent . . . of course, that's a ball-park figure.

The lawyer whispers to Abraham.

ABRAHAM: (*To the lawyer*) Really? (*To the judge*) Let's make that 100 percent on the button . . . somewhere in that general neighborhood.

The tent living room. Sarah sits on the edge of her chair, wearing her Miss Holy Land Banner. She is watching TV. Abraham is being interviewed, rapid-fire, by reporters.

REPORTER 1: Has Ike been a problem child?

REPORTER 2: Was he raised according to Dr. Spock?

152

REPORTER 3: Has he been diagnosed with ADHD?
Sarah throws one of her sandals at the TV.

Outside the courthouse. Abraham and his lawyer stand in front of the courthouse, facing a battery of camera crews and raucous reporters.
LAWYER: Ladies and gentlemen, one question at a time.
The reporters reduce the decibel level slightly.
REPORTER 4: Is it true that you tied the kid up and scared the hell out of him?
Abraham and his lawyer exchange whispers.
ABRAHAM: God told me to.

The living room. Sarah rises from the chair and turns off the TV. She disappears into her bedroom, but soon returns with a revolver. She heads for the tent flap with homicide in her eye.

Outside the courthouse. Same personnel.
REPORTER 5: You admit it, then?
Abraham smiles mysteriously.
REPORTER 1: Let's get this straight. You admit to the facts that you brandished a deadly weapon—
LAWYER: To wit, a knife.
REPORTER 1: . . . and threatened your son—
LAWYER: Said Isaac, also known as Ike.
REPORTER 1: . . . with great bodily harm.
ABRAHAM: Your argument isn't with me, it's with God.

Main Street. Sarah drives the limo toward the courthouse at full tilt.

Outside the courthouse, as before.
REPORTER 2: Mr. Abraham, why do you keep bringing God into the picture?
ABRAHAM: What's the matter, you an atheist or something?
REPORTER 2: (*Indignantly*) Not at all. I cast my lot with the ninety-six percent of Holy Landers who believe in the existence of a Higher Power but wouldn't want to be more specific about it.
REPORTER 3: What proof do you have that you were following God's orders?

The lawyer leans over and whispers to Abraham. Abraham reaches inside his robe and unsuccessfully frisks himself.

ABRAHAM: It's in here someplace . . .

Sarah appears on the scene in the limo.

She points a revolver at Abraham and shoots him.

Abraham falls.

Hue and cry.

Sarah's limo redistributes the sand. The sheriff hops on his camel, digs in his spurs, and is soon in torrid pursuit.

The camera crews gather around Abraham and put their equipment to good use. The reporters push ice cream cones in his face as if they were microphones. Abraham refuses a vanilla cone.

ABRAHAM: (*Dying*) Anybody got . . . tutti-frutti?

Reporter 2 provides a tutti-frutti. Abraham licks on it.

REPORTER 4: Could you explain for us, sir, why your wife just shot you?

The lawyer whispers in Abraham's ear.

ABRAHAM: I decline to answer . . . on the grounds . . . that it may tend . . . to incriminate me. . . . Say . . . did anybody happen to bring . . . the last . . . cigarette?

Reporter 3 lights a cigarette, inserts it between the victim's lips. The victim takes a long drag, looks noble.

REPORTER 5: Any last words?

The lawyer whispers in Abraham's ear.

ABRAHAM: (*Beatific smile*) I rest . . . my . . . case.

Dies.

REPORTER 1: (*Shaking his head sadly*) Such a waste.

REPORTER 2: (*Shaking his head sadly*) Had his best years ahead of him.

Mournful strains of Chopin's Funeral March.

The sheriff chases Sarah across the desert, swinging a lasso. Tempo presto.

Isaac's bedroom. Evening. Isaac reclines on the bed, watching loud TV and smoking hashish. He is dressed as before, gold rings covering three-quarters of his body.

JIM: Roger, your reactions to today's events.

ROGER: I'll say this, Jim, that was certainly an ingenious defense, using God as a scapegoat. The problem is, is that it places the blame directly on God. I just can't see how the court can have jurisdiction over a higher being.

JIM: Interesting point, Roger. Greta, what about Sarah's defense? What's the strategy gonna be in *her* case . . . that is, in the event she is apprehended?

GRETA: Jim, I disagree with Roger. You can *blame* God, but that doesn't mean you have to bring him to *trial*. So I don't see why she can't use the scapegoat defense. If he can use it, anybody can. It's as simple as that.

Isaac sits bolt upright. He shuts off the TV with his remote. He quickly reaches over, picks up the telephone, and dials.

ISAAC: Augie, my man! Do I gotta plan or do I gotta plan!

The sheriff chases Sarah into a Rest Area. Tempo presto. They pass the signs "Oxen Only," "Camels Only," "Stretch Limos Only," and turn into the parking lot marked "Camels and Stretch Limos."

The sheriff jumps off of his camel and makes a beeline for the men's room. Prestissimo.

Sarah climbs out of the limo and walks leisurely toward the women's room. Adagio.

Abe's Souvenir Shop. Morning. Isaac and Augie stand at the cash register. A gaggle of American tourists pours into the shop, grabs black T-shirts with white lettering from the racks, and rush to ring up their purchases.

Morning. The sheriff is propped up outside the women's room, asleep. Largo. Sarah emerges from the women's room. He wakes up and yawns. She walks leisurely toward the limo, swinging her hips provocatively. He follows her, making suggestive remarks. Andante.

Sarah climbs into the limo and takes off. The sheriff jumps on his camel and chases her. Presto.

American tourists pour out of the souvenir shop, trying on their black T-shirts and looking delighted.

The sheriff chases Sarah down Main Street in the direction of her tent, this time more slowly. Tempo moderato.

Sarah reaches her tent, stops, gets out of the limo, and walks over to the flap. She enters the tent, followed closely by the panting sheriff.

Main Street. Morning. American tourists promenade up and down the wooden sidewalks, toting holstered revolvers and sheathed knives and proudly wearing black T-shirts with white lettering: "The Lord Is My Scapegoat."[45]

SARAH'S VOICE: (*Indignantly*) . . . and on our honeymoon, all he could think of was watching baseball, can you believe it? He preferred the Ur of the Chaldeans Herdsmen to Miss Holy Land! And that was when I started to . . . well, a girl has to take care of herself, wouldn't you agree? . . .

Sarah's bedroom. Sarah and the sheriff sit up in bed, après sex. He is rolling a cigarette. His ten gallon hat is askew.

SARAH: . . . because the reason we're put here on God's gray earth is to be fruitful and multiply, and I take that to be an order, but was *he* interested in following it? . . . Well, he was, but not within the marriage covenant. . . . Speaking of which, God promised us a baby, plus the Holy Land, which *I* thought we already owned, clear and free, and I put in for a girl . . .

The sheriff looks bored. He puts the unlit cigarette in his mouth.

SARAH: . . . but what did I get? you guessed it, a boy, and I know

---

[45]The committee had a spirited discussion on the meaning of this line. Cardinal Micromentis suggested that it refers, somehow, to the profound spiritual quest of the American tourist. Professor Allbright disagreed; he concluded that, though he could not yet fathom its meaning, he would be able to demonstrate that there was a perfectly plausible interpretation, if he were given a three-year federal grant. Father Lecher predicted that later generations would come to consider the line as one of the great climaxes in the history of literature. Ms. LaFemme pointed out that it was not a climax, and that the script did not contain a single climax; she maintained, perhaps facetiously, that this was because the producers were hoping for a G rating and promised to write an extensive monograph on the subject.

just who's to blame . . . and I doubt very seriously that he was punishing me for . . . well, let's just say you can't always do things in the orthodox way, sometimes you've got to take what's available, even if he's young enough to be your son, or grandson, or whatever . . .

The sheriff wearily lights the cigarette with a match.

SARAH: . . . I'm not saying he wasn't cute, oh, he *was* . . . George, that was his name. . . . I'm also not saying boys aren't as important as girls, but they're just a lot more trouble, especially in the teen years . . . .

The sheriff is suddenly fascinated by his cigarette, holding it at arm's length, deep in thought.

SARAH: . . . which doesn't excuse what he did, with the rope and knife and everything, and you know what the worst part of the whole thing is, it's. . . .

The sheriff inserts the cigarette between Sara's lips, to shut her up. She takes a few puffs, then takes it out of her mouth and blows a smoke ring.

SARAH: Thanks. . . . By the way, I'd give you about a twelve . . . even better than George . . . Pharaoh, too, for that matter. . . .

The sheriff rolls over on his side, away from Sarah, and places a pillow over his ears.

Outside the tent. The sheriff's camel sleeps alongside the limo, which now has a flat tire.

SARAH'S VOICE: . . . As I was saying, the worst thing is, he marries me, Miss Holy Land! and then he can't even remember our anniversary, not once in the whole eighty-some years! . . . And that's why I did it. . . . You can't blame me, can you? . . . I bet God would've done exactly the same thing himself . . . if he'd have been a woman. . . .

THE END

157

5 | The Tragedy at Sodom/Gomorrah

THE ORTHODOX ACCOUNT of the destruction of Sodom and Gomorrah (Genesis 18:16–19:38) tends to evoke two quite different responses. In the one case, our most serious moralists are consoled by the thought that the world is in the hands of a just God, who rewards the righteous and punishes the perverse. In the other case, those who take pains to read it are mystified by its many inconsistencies.

Father Lecher and his disciples were surprised to learn that the original story, "The Tragedy at Sodom/Gomorrah," is much longer than the orthodox version. They were gratified to discover, however, that this unexpurgated story places the controversial issue of sin in a clearer, more comprehensive light.

§

From The Bethlehem Star-Herald[46]
April 27, 1993 B. C.
NEWS AND VIEWS
Official Account Lacks Credibility

WHAT DO WE REALLY KNOW about the recent tragedy at Sodom and Gomorrah?

Not much. We know that in its aftermath, God himself read a statement accepting full responsibility. We know that during the

---

[46]Cardinal Micromentis suggested that the name of this newspaper points to the existence of an Ur-Christianity.

following five days, his press secretary, Jonathan, presented a series of hastily-called news conferences, at which he attempted to answer many of the questions put to him by the media. And we know that on the seventh day, God read another statement that called for an end to "this obsessive interest in rehashing ancient history," which, he warned, "is tearing our beloved nation apart."

But from Jonathan's many confused, often contradictory explanations, the *Star-Herald* has been able to piece together the administration's version of that horrible catastrophe.[47]

Early this year, God asked for a legal opinion on whether Abram should be informed of the administration's plans for Sodom and Gomorrah. His Temple counsel responded in the positive, citing the facts (1) that Abram was "chosen" and (2) that the planned Sodom/Gomorrah "incident" would serve as an example for future generations of Abram's heirs.

As a result of these communications, God decided to "go down" (note the autocratic choice of words) to see whether the moral outcry against the two cities was justified. He then informed Abram that the "grievous sin" of Sodom and Gomorrah required their destruction. Abram, whose nephew Lot was an inhabitant of Sodom, tried to persuade God not to destroy that city, pointing out that not all Sodomites are wicked. He asked God how many righteous Sodomites he would need to produce in order to keep the plan from being implemented. The two haggled over the number, finally settling on ten.

Then, early on the evening of the calamity, two anonymous angels came to visit Lot. He offered them hospitality, but the men of Sodom surrounded his house, knocked at the door, and asked for access to the so-called "men" (angels?), that they might "know" them. To appease the mob's lust, Lot offered them his two virgin daughters instead. When the mob refused this generous proposition and began to attack him, the two guests struck them with blindness, leaving them in utter confusion.

---

[47]The following paragraphs tell a story that is almost identical to the later Biblical story, as recounted in Genesis 18:16–19:35.

The guests then alerted Lot to the coming destruction, advising him to leave town. When he informed his sons-in-law of this warning, however, they suspected a prank. The next morning, the angels (men?) urged Lot to leave, with his wife and two daughters. But he procrastinated. So the men seized him and his family and led them by the hand outside the city walls, where they advised them to flee to the hills for their lives, emphasizing that they dare not stop, or even look back. Lot, who had no wish to live in the hills, suggested the village of Zoar as an alternative. This suggestion was accepted. Then God, true to his promise, destroyed Sodom and Gomorrah, raining down "fire and brimstone" from heaven. Unfortunately, Lot's wife looked back and became a pillar of salt. Next morning, Abraham discovered the destruction, which he later described to the press "as the smoke from a furnace."

Meanwhile Lot, finding Zoar unfit for habitation, took his two daughters and fled to the hills, where the three took up residence in a cave. The daughters, assuming that all other men had been destroyed, became concerned about the problem of the perpetuation of the human race. They solved this problem, it seems, by getting their father drunk and then taking turns sleeping with him. They are now pregnant.

In our opinion, this official version of the Sodom/Gomorrah debacle smells of a cover-up. It raises far more questions than it answers—questions concerning the actual facts, concerning favoritism, and especially concerning the administration's harsh policy on the sensitive issue of sin.

Holy Landers expect and deserve answers to these questions. We call upon Senator Samuel of the majority Theocratic Party to join Senator Shur of the Freedom Party in conducting a complete, bipartisan investigation.

GOD'S REFUSAL TO APPEAR before the Senate Sodom/Gomorrah Committee by appealing to the doctrine of executive privilege does not surprise us. Nor are we surprised that Senator Shur has been unable to convince his counterpart on the Theocratic side of the aisle, Senator Samuel, to join him in challenging that dubious doctrine. After all, if God were to subject himself to questioning by representatives of the people, he would have to answer a series of potentially-embarrassing questions.

•Was there sufficient reason to rain down fire and brimstone on the sleepy agricultural communities of Sodom and Gomorrah? Could not this needless loss of precious lives have been avoided?
•Exactly what was the "grievous sin" of which the two cities were accused? Could it have been any worse than Job's offering his virgin daughters to a lusty mob? Were innocent women and children being punished for the sin of their sons, husbands, and fathers?[48] Is this standard administration policy?
•What was the source of the original rumor concerning the sin of the two villages? Did God, or any member of his administration, take adequate steps to determine the accuracy of that rumor?
•Even if Sodom were proved to have been a cesspool of sin, what about Gomorrah? Did it deserve to share the fate of its neighbor and rival? Or is this a classic example of overkill?
•What is brimstone, and why was it used? Wasn't fire enough?
•Why wasn't Lot punished for taking indecent liberties with his daughters, however willing they may have been?

We can only hope that God will come to his senses and recognize that, if these questions remain unanswered, they could

---

[48]Ms. LaFemme suggested that this sentence points to the existence of an Ur-feminism.

become the main issue in the upcoming congressional elections. And, as more-than-casual observers of the current political scene, we would suppose that God's own Theocratic Party could very well lose its majority status, leaving him something of a lame duck.

September 28, 1993 B. C.
NEWS AND VIEWS
What's Been Going On in the Temple?

UNDER A STIFF CROSS-EXAMINATION yesterday by Senator Shur, Temple Chief Counsel Fox in effect conceded that he had reminded God that Abram was indeed chosen. He also admitted to having recommended that the Sodom/Gomorrah incident might well serve as an example to later generations.

We quote the relevant parts of the testimony.

SENATOR SHUR: Is it true, Mr. Fox, that God considered Mr. Abram chosen?

MR. FOX: No.

SENATOR SHUR: Are you telling this committee that Abram was *not* chosen?

MR. FOX: Yes.

SENATOR SHUR: How, then, would you describe Mr. Abram's status, vis-à-vis God?

MR. FOX: I would use the term *selected*.

SENATOR SHUR: Could you explain to us, Mr. Fox, why God selected Mr. Abram?

MR. FOX: We used to play a little poker, up at the Temple.[49] We sometimes needed an extra hand at the table. So we'd invite Mr. Abram to help us out.

---

[49]Father Lecher suggested that the mention of poker in the Temple points to the existence of an Ur-casino.

SENATOR SHUR: And why Mr. Abram, specifically?

MR. FOX: We were impressed by his track record.

SENATOR SHUR: I wasn't aware that Mr. Abram was an athlete.

MR. FOX: I'm referring to the story of how he went down into Egypt in a beat-up Yugo and soon returned driving a stretch limo. That's what caught our attention.

SENATOR SHUR: And is this not an example of preferential treatment?

MR. FOX: No it is not.

SENATOR SHUR: No? Please tell this committee why a special invitation to the Temple to play "a little poker," in your words, is *not* an example of preferential treatment.

MR. FOX: Because God seldom lost.

SENATOR SHUR: I see. . . . Now, moving on to another subject, it is reported that you referred to the planned Sodom/Gomorrah tragedy as an "incident." Is that true?

MR. FOX: Yes.

SENATOR SHUR: And why did you refer to it as an "incident"?

MR. FOX: I figured it wouldn't take very long. It didn't.

SENATOR SHUR: But it *was* planned?

MR. FOX: That's correct.

SENATOR SHUR: And who planned it?

MR. FOX: God.

SENATOR SHUR: Are you telling us, Mr. Fox, that your client planned the destruction of Sodom and Gomorrah?

MR. FOX: Every good administrator has plans.

SENATOR SHUR: Does God have a plan for each and every one of us?

MR. FOX: That is my understanding.

SENATOR SHUR: Do these plans involve fire and brimstone?

MR. FOX: They did in this case.

SENATOR SHUR: And what about other cases?

MR. FOX: I'm not at liberty to discuss other cases, for reasons of national security.

SENATOR SHUR: I understand. . . . Is it also true, Mr. Fox, that you advised your client that the Sodom/Gomorrah incident would serve as an example for future generations of Abram's heirs?

MR. FOX: That is true.

SENATOR SHUR: And why did you make that recommendation?

MR. FOX: My thinking was that he might want to leave a few examples scattered here and there.

SENATOR SHUR: And why did you think that, Mr. Fox?

MR. FOX: I figured he's like everybody else. He'd like to be remembered when he's gone.

Mr. Fox is a lawyer, and an extremely clever one. Whether or not he was being completely candid about the gambling in the Temple (which, incidentally, would place the taxpayers' hard-earned money at risk), we agree with him on one point: God will almost certainly be remembered for the tragedy at Sodom and Gomorrah.

September 29, 1993 B. C.
NEWS AND VIEWS
Are Angels Getting out of Hand?

YESTERDAY'S SENATE HEARINGS on the Sodom/Gomorrah affair focused on the roles of Mr. Dogberry, of the HLBI (Holy Land Bureau of Investigation), and Mr. Verges, of the BAPB (Bureau of Alcohol, Perversity, and Bombs), the two hitherto-unnamed agents who warned Lot of the impending calamity.

Again, we quote the relevant parts of the testimony.

SENATOR SAMUEL: The question has arisen concerning the identity of the two—some have hinted, but without just and adequate cause, three—men, or perhaps angels (I believe that has yet to be determined), who took the extraordinary precaution, far above and beyond the call of duty, of warning Mr. Lot and his family, including his wife, his two virgin daughters, and his two sons-in-law, of the coming destruction—I think we would all admit that it was quote/unquote "planned," in some trivial, innocuous sense—of the two former cities—some have called them villages—of Sodom, located at the southern end of the

Dead Sea, so-called because of the sheep and camel excrement that certain extreme environmentalists have claimed—falsely, I might add—has been draining into it from the neighboring pasturelands, and Gomorrah, which was, until very recently, a neighbor of its co-conspirator and partner in sin, as I am certain we will eventually find. Now, without further ado, let me get straight to the point, Mr. Dogberry—how are you this morning? in good health, I trust?—and ask you this question—I see that you are also accompanied by your associate, if I am not mistaken, and good morning to you too, Mr. Verges—do I have the name right?—The question, sirs, is this: Are you now, or have you ever been, or have you ever considered being, or has anyone every approached you and twisted your arm and forced you to become, an angel?

MR. VERGES: No.

MR. DOGBERRY: Yes.

SENATOR SAMUEL: I sense a slight discrepancy of opinion. Let me, if I may, put the question in another, slightly different way. It has been bruited about by certain irresponsible members of the press—and, I hasten to add, not all members of the Fourth Estate are irresponsible, that is to say, reckless in their disregard of the truth. As I was beginning to mention, before I was rudely interrupted, it has been bruited about by the aforementioned journalists, if I may use that word without fear of being falsely accused of insensitivity, that—

SENATOR SHUR: Are you angels?

SENATOR SAMUEL: Thank you, Senator Shur. Let me clarify, gentlemen—and ladies; I thought I saw several ladies as I came in—no?—Not to put too fine a point upon it, but are you now, or have you ever been, or have you ever considered being, or has anyone or anybody, living or dead, higher being or lower being, ever—

MR. DOGBERRY: No.

MR. VERGES: Not to speak of.

SENATOR SHUR: What do you mean, "not to speak of"?

MR. DOGBERRY: He means, those are our instructions. Not to speak of this, that, and the other. Including the angel part.

MR. VERGES: He means, we could admit we had training.

MR. DOGBERRY: If pressed.

MR. VERGES: *Only* if pressed.

MR. DOGBERRY: If, and only if.

SENATOR SAMUEL: If. Ah. That reminds me. If you'll excuse me, my good friends and colleagues, and Mr. Dogberry and your associate, Mr. Verges—do I have the name right?—I am forced to leave now. I am, as you may be aware, chairperson of the Foreign Relations Committee, there's a pressing matter that needs attending to, vital—I might say *equally* vital—to the people of this nation, of the Ancient Near East, of Asia, both Major and Minor, and, indeed, of all mankind—and, lest I be accused of—what's the word? . . . Insensitivity? Thank you—and of all womankind.

SENATOR SHUR: Certainly, senator. Now, sirs, let's get this straight. You had *training*?

MR. VERGES: As angels.

MR. DOGBERRY: But we didn't use it.

MR. VERGES: Not at Sodom.

MR. DOGBERRY: Not at Gomorrah, either.

MR. VERGES: We weren't *at* Gomorrah. Remember?

MR. DOGBERRY: Now that you mention it, yes, I *do* remember not being there.

SENATOR SHUR: Could you tell this committee, sirs, of what your training as angels consisted?

MR. VERGES: Just the basics.

MR. DOGBERRY: Flying.

MR. VERGES: For example, landing.

MR. DOGBERRY: What he means is, coming down to earth.

MR. VERGES: That's always the hardest part.

MR. DOGBERRY: You can get hurt if you do it wrong.

MR. VERGES: *Badly* hurt. They recommend you use parachutes.

SENATOR SHUR: I understand. And what are the other basics?

MR. DOGBERRY: Good grooming, for one thing.

MR. VERGES: For example, keeping the feathers preened.

MR. DOGBERRY: Obeying, for another.

MR. VERGES: For example, doing the will of the Lord.

MR. DOGBERRY: So, just the basics.

SENATOR SHUR: Is that all?

MR. VERGES: I swear to God.

SENATOR SHUR: Nothing else?

MR. DOGBERRY: Absolutely nothing.

MR. VERGES: Right.

MR. DOGBERRY: Except for the techniques of interrogation.

SENATOR SHUR: Techniques of interrogation?

MR VERGES: Oh, that's just fancy language.

MR. DOGBERRY: Basically, it refers to the methods of torture.

SENATOR SHUR: Methods of torture?!

MR. VERGES: What he means is, tickling the armpits.

MR. DOGBERRY: And the bottom of the feet.

MR. VERGES: Just harmless stuff.

SENATOR SHUR: Is that all?

MR. DOGBERRY: That's about it.

MR. VERGES: Right.

MR. DOGBERRY: Except for the Chinese water torture.

MR. VERGES: Plus, driving toothpicks under fingernails.

MR. DOGBERRY: The rack, too.

MR. VERGES: Can't forget the rack.

MR. DOGBERRY: Did we mention dismemberment?

MR. VERGES: The trick is, take your time.

SENATOR SHUR: What about striking men blind?

MR. DOGBERRY: Oh, we seldom do that.

MR. VERGES: Only when the situation calls for it.

SENATOR SHUR: Which it did in this case?

MR. DOGBERRY: Well . . . yes.

MR. VERGES: He's referring to Sodom.

MR. DOGBERRY: Not Gomorrah.

MR. VERGES: You'll find no blind men in Gomorrah.

MR. DOGBERRY: If you don't believe him, check the skeletons and skulls.

SENATOR SHUR: Speaking of skeletons, what about weapons of mass destruction?

MR. VERGES: We don't know nothing about 'em.

MR. DOGBERRY: Especially the incendiary devices.

MR. VERGES: Fancy language again. It refers to the firebombs, mainly.

MR. DOGBERRY: Which we don't know nothing about, neither.

MR. VERGES: Including the method of delivery.

MR. DOGBERRY: Catapults are seldom used.

MR. VERGES: Only when our safety is at stake.

SENATOR SHUR: The people of the Holy Land should be pleased to hear that. Now, what about brimstone?

MR. VERGES: We're totally ignorant.

MR. DOGBERRY: That's because it's state-of-the-art.

MR. VERGES: Top secret.

MR. DOGBERRY: A special scientific formula.

MR. VERGES: Only God knows.

SENATOR SHUR: I'm sure he does. Well, thank you, gentlemen. You've been extremely helpful.

MR. DOGBERRY: Thank you for helping us be helpful.

MR. VERGES: Remember, only God knows.

MR. DOGBERRY: He means, about the brimstone.

MR. VERGES: Nothing else.

MR. DOGBERRY: The buck stops here.

MR. VERGES: He means, we were acting on our own.

MR. DOGBERRY: Those were our instructions, to act on our own.

This testimony, a mixture of evasiveness and inadvertent candor, piques our curiosity about brimstone. It also raises the question of whether the HLBI and the BAPB have become rogue agencies.

September 30, 1993 B. C.
NEWS AND VIEWS
A "Missing" Witness

YESTERDAY'S SCHEDULED SENATE HEARINGS on the Sodom/Gomorrah affair were postponed when Mr. Abram, considered by some knowledgeable observers to be the central witness to the tragedy, was reported missing. Abram, the recently anointed mayor of the neighboring town of Abeville, is said to be vacationing in Egypt with his wife Sara, celebrating their first wedding anniversary.

We are frankly skeptical about this alibi. Especially since court records show that the marriage took place in June (!) of 1994.

Mr. Abram's reluctance to testify is, we think, quite understandable. He would face a formidable battery of questions concerning his role in this entire affair.

• Why did God consult him, and him alone, before destroying the two cities? Was he indeed a regular in the card games, as Mr. Fox claims?

• Did he do enough to persuade God to stop the planned destruction? Why was he unable—perhaps unwilling?—to bargain God down to a lesser number of righteous Sodomites?

• How many such righteous was he finally able to locate in Sodom?

•Why did he not show a similar concern for the fate of Gomorrah? Is this another example of favoritism?

These are important questions. The Senate Committee should not rest until answers are forthcoming.

October 1, 1993 B. C.
NEWS AND VIEWS
How Many Righteous Does It Take
to Satisfy This Administration?

YESTERDAY, SENATOR SHUR INTRODUCED a surprise witness to the Sodom/Gomorrah Committee. This witness, who would testify only on the condition that she remain anonymous, painted a much brighter picture of the moral conditions in Sodom than has the Holy Land administration.

Here is the relevant portion of her testimony.

SENATOR SHUR: Good morning, Mrs. X.
MISS X: It's *Miss* X, if you'll recall, sir, and a very good morning to you. I hope you're feeling well. I know we are, sir, despite the tragedy, which we're learning to put behind us. Wasn't it just *awful*?
SENATOR SHUR: It certainly was. I think I can speak for this en-

tire committee in offering you our deepest, most heartfelt sympathy.

MISS X: Thank you, sir. You have no idea how much this means to us.

SENATOR SHUR: Now, could you please tell this committee the precise nature of your affiliation with Sodom?

MISS X: I was a law-abiding citizen of Sodom, sir, from my birth in 2180 B.C. to April 16 of the present year, just before the tragedy.

SENATOR SHUR: That would make you. . . .

MISS X: Just celebrated my 187th birthday last Tuesday, sir. If you can call it a celebration, with just Miss Y—isn't that what we decided to call my twin sister, Miss Y?—and myself. What I mean is, there was no party. It's not the way we were brought up. No sir, we were always brought up, number one, to respect our elders, number two, to be kind to our neighbors, take an interest in their affairs, and number three, to forego parties, including centennial celebrations. And if I may say so, sir, our parents would be proud, if they were still with us, God rest their souls.

SENATOR SHUR: I'm sure they would. Now, Ms. X, could you tell us, for the record, how you escaped the tragedy at Sodom?

MISS. X: We could see it coming, sir. Miss Y—that's my sister, also 187 years of age; we're twins—Miss Y and I were out for our morning constitutional—we never miss it, sir, it's the way we were brought up—when we noticed something very, very unusual going on. You see, sir, they were setting up the artillery on a hill west of town. This was last April—April 19, to be exact. "That's strange," I said to Miss Y. "It's more than strange," said Miss Y to me, "I do believe we're in for a conflagration." Those were her exact words, sir, she does a lot of reading, taking after our father. "Conflagration?" I said, being inquisitive, like our mother. "Fire and brimstone," she explained. "Brimstone?" I said—it was the first time I'd heard that word. "It's a newfangled weapon system," she said, "I don't have time to explain." So—

SENATOR SHUR: So to make a long story short. . . .

MISS X: So to make a long story short, sir, as you recommended when we were going through my testimony, what I should say and what I should leave out—anyway, to make a long story short, we went back home—we lived together, Miss Y and I, always have, always will, till we draw our last breaths together, God willing—

SENATOR SHUR: God willing.

MISS X: Anyway, to make a long story short, sir, we went back home—it's not exactly a palace, but it has served us well for lo these 187 years—we went back home and gathered up our most precious belongings—you'd be amazed, sir, at the number of precious belongings a person can accumulate in 187 years—and left the place we had learned to call home—for good, sir, as it turns out—and headed into the hills, where we waited for the fire and brimstone to cool off.

SENATOR SHUR: That must have been a very wrenching experience, Miss X, having your home needlessly destroyed. I think I speak for the entire Freedom Party when I offer you our deep and sincere condolences. But let us get to the point. When you left Sodom, what was the total population, approximately, and how many of that total population would you characterize as righteous?

MISS X: How many righteous? . . . Well, sir, I'd have to break it down into categories. First of all, sir, there are the *perfectly* righteous. I'd say there were two—of course that was before we left town, Miss Y and I—Miss Y being my sister, who was brought up the same way as I, which accounts for our righteousness. So, to answer your question, sir, there were exactly two perfectly righteous in Sodom before April 19—of course that's *after* our parents passed away, God rest their sin-free souls. Two righteous, sir, out of a total population of fifty. Which comes to four percent, not counting the second category, which is the *semi-*righteous. Those were the people who observed the Sabbath, for the most part, also the holy days, did the burnt offerings, gave to the United Way, were hospitable—didn't always kill the *fatted* calf, mind you, sir, sometimes served up the scrawny one, especially when it came to entertaining the semi-righteous. Yes, sir, you had to admit they did all those things, but when it came to other forms of behavior . . . well, that's a different story entirely. There was lots of carrying-on, sir, if you know what I mean, judging by who was sneaking out and going over to visit whose tent after sundown and staying God only knows how long, often till the wee hours, several times as late as 3 a.m.—not to mention all the activity at the sheep pens. For example—

SENATOR SHUR: I don't think we need to get into the details. Just tell us, please, Miss X, your estimate of the number of semi-righteous.

MISS X: There were forty-seven, sir, counting their children, who were heading down the same road as their parents—you could already tell by the way they were brought up. As my great-great-great-great-grandmother Eve used to say, sir, the apple never falls very far from the tree.

SENATOR SHUR: So that leaves only one perfectly *un*righteous.

MISS X: Heavens, no, sir! How do you get one unrighteous?

SENATOR SHUR: Well, if there were fifty people in Sodom, predestruction, and two of them were perfectly righteous, and forty-seven were semi-righteous, that would leave one unrighteous. Am I correct?

MISS X: If I may disagree, sir, that leaves one *ex*-righteous. She came from a good family, too, almost as righteous as any other. But she strayed, somehow—tried the path of the truly righteous, didn't like it—her excuse was, it didn't pay as well. She started out so righteous, too—even belonged to a support group for singles. Then she married that terrible man—I'm not allowed to mention his name, because of the potential lawsuits—and became like the rest of them—tent-swapping, sheep pen activity, you name it, sir, she did it all, everything Miss Y refers to as prurient behavior—not to speak of that . . . magazine she was putting out—pure trash, if you ask me, enough to make a perfectly righteous person blush, and I speak from experience.

SENATOR SHUR: So the bottom line, Miss X, is this, is it not: there were *exactly no perfectly unrighteous living in Sodom at the time of its destruction.*

MISS X: That's right, sir, that's exactly right, we wouldn't have stood for it. Now, Gomorrah was another story. . . .

We remain curious about brimstone, which "Miss Y" referred to as "a newfangled weapons system." As far as we know, there has been no appropriations bill for any such system. (Could the monies for these weapons of mass destruction be coming from the winnings at a certain poker table?)

But what is most important about this testimony is that "Miss X" established, beyond a reasonable doubt, that Sodom was, if not a model city, certainly a respectable and God-fearing one. As for Gomorrah, we remain unconvinced by what Senator Samuel, in his cross-examination, was able to elicit from the witness. Was Gomorrah's degree of righteousness so minimal as to justify its destruction? We think not. We remain unconvinced that this administration had a legal basis for destroying either village.

On the positive side, we now have a good idea about the source of the original rumor concerning that undefined "grievous sin."

October 2, 1993 B. C.
NEWS AND VIEWS
Is the Cost of Therapy Getting out of Hand?

YESTERDAY MR. LOT, the central figure in the tragedy at Sodom and Gomorrah, finally appeared before the Senate S/G Committee, providing a plausible, if controversial, theory of the disaster.

We quote the relevant portions of his testimony.

SENATOR SHUR: I understand, Mr. Lot, that you were once in the employment of your uncle, Mr. Abram. Is that correct?

MR. LOT: That's exactly right, senator. I worked for him a coupla months, herding sheep.

SENATOR SHUR: And then you quit and moved to Sodom?

MR. LOT: I did, senator, yes. I was getting tired of the shepherd life style. I'm not anti-sheep, you understand, I just don't happen to think they're the be-all and end-all. I suppose they're okay, as animals go—maybe the wool *does* get a little scratchy, for my sensitive skin, but I enjoy mutton as much as the next person. Other than that, they don't have a whole lot to offer. I mean, *you* try holding a decent conversation with a band of the bleating bastards. My point is, if you're a shepherd, you find yourself with lots of excessive time on your hands. Even if your parents had you figured as musically inclined as a kid and made you take flute lessons, which lasted about a year. But if you've ever tried playing nothing but scales all day, and to a bunch of sheep that don't know the difference between C major and D minor, or a flute and a piccolo. . . . You see my point? Anyway, I ran across this ad in *Pent Tent,* describing the glories of Sodom. It seemed like a nice place to enjoy life—you know, get away from the desert routine, settle down, have kids, get married, go into counseling. And I've never been sorry.

SENATOR SHUR: It has been reported that it was because of you, Mr. Lot, that Mr. Abram tried to persuade God not to destroy Sodom. Do you have any idea why your uncle would intervene on your behalf?

MR. LOT: He was probably protecting his investment.

SENATOR SHUR: Please explain, if you would.

MR. LOT: When I quit the job and moved to Sodom, senator, I took along a few of his sheep. Not many, just a very tiny little flock, which I kept in the back yard. This was for the wool, no mutton involved. I figured Uncle Abe owed me something for all the psychological damage. Don't get me wrong, I'm not denying there's an upside to herding sheep, especially if you value your independence, which I did. But there's also a downside. They call it shepherd stress syndrome. Very expensive to treat. So as I mentioned, I figured Uncle owed me a few, due to the cost of therapy. He didn't see it that way.

SENATOR SHUR: Interesting train of thought. . . . Now, moving on to another subject, if I may. Is it true that, on the evening of the tragedy, you offered hospitality to several men and/or angels?

MR. LOT: I thought they were girls, in disguise. I'd never met a *male* angel. Didn't even know they existed.

SENATOR SHUR: Are you telling this committee that you had previous experience with female angels?

MR. LOT: Not per se. I mean, I'd *fantasized* about them. That's a thing you tend to do when you're out in the desert by yourself, herding a couple thousand head of sheep, you fantasize a lot. They say it's one of the symptoms of the stress syndrome. Some shepherds talk to themselves. Some talk to the sheep. Some talk to God. Some fantasize. I happened to be one of those who spent a lot of time fantasizing. Mostly about angels. Which is probably why I developed the idea they were exclusively female. Man, was I wrong.

SENATOR SHUR: Now, about the male population of Sodom. Did you notice that they showed any unusual interest in your guests?

MR. LOT: Can you blame them? Most of them were suffering from the same syndrome.

SENATOR SHUR: And did you try to protect your guests from the unwanted sexual advances of your fellow citizens?

MR. LOT: Right. I didn't want my fellow citizens to make the same mistake. We'd been through a lot together, in terms of the syndrome. That's shepherd stress, the nation's Number One Killer.

SENATOR SHUR: What about the rumor concerning your two daughters? Is it true that you offered *them* to the male inhabitants of Sodom, instead of the angels?

MR. LOT: I did, senator, yes. You see, they don't get out as often as they should. That's always been one of their weaknesses— probably due to our failure as parents. My wife, God bless her salty soul, used to call it the wallflower syndrome. We started to have it treated, but that can get to be pretty expensive. Anyway, I figured I'd offer the girls around, kill two birds with one stone. Bird one, get them out of the house. Bird two, cut the therapy budget.

SENATOR SHUR: Do you have any theories as to why the men of Sodom refused your offer?

MR. LOT: Have you ever seen my daughters? . . . Yes? . . . No?

SENATOR SHUR: I believe I'll let that pass. Now, why did the mob of male Sodomites then proceed to attack you?

MR. LOT: They found out who they were dealing with and took it out on me. You can't really blame them, senator. I mean, you hear this rumor about angels, you flock over to your buddy's house to check them out, you find out they're nothing but a coupla guys with maybe a few months of so-called "angel training." Then your buddy turns around and offers you a coupla wallflowers. Like he's doing you a big flavor! That would bring out the anger in anyone.

SENATOR SHUR: And did your guest angels then turn right around and strike the mob members with blindness?

MR. LOT: Well, live and learn! Is *that* why they were staggering around, clawing at the walls? I thought they were just playing a game—you know, the one where you swing at the piñata, to get at the goodies? Either that, or suffering from another syndrome.

SENATOR SHUR: Do you have any idea, Mr. Lot, why your angel guests warned you and your family of the coming catastrophe?

MR. LOT: I really don't know. I guess I assumed it was on account of my wife. I knew it wasn't on account of my daughters, and it sure as hell wasn't on account of me. . . . Come to think of it, though, it could have been the sheep. I mean, my guests could have been helping Uncle Abe protect his investment. Keep him in chips, you know, for the poker games. Which would explain why they showed so much concern for the sheep. Making sure we took them along when we escaped.

SENATOR SHUR: And why wouldn't the angels warn anyone else in Sodom?

MR. LOT: You know, senator, I never really thought about it. But if they really *did* strike all the guys with blindness, like you said, they were probably wanting to destroy the evidence. Wouldn't that make sense?

SENATOR SHUR: I'm here to ask questions, Mr. Lot, not to speculate. Now, I'd like to ask you a . . . delicate question. I don't wish to embarrass you, but . . . did you, or did you not, sleep with your daughters?

MR. LOT: Not while I was sober.

SENATOR SHUR: And while you were drunk?

MR. LOT: I don't remember. That's another thing I suffer from, the impaired memory syndrome.

SENATOR SHUR: I'm sorry to hear that, Mr. Lot. Now, one last question. Why, in your opinion, did God destroy Sodom?

MR. LOT: If you ask me, senator, it was because of those two prudes. The one you had in here yesterday, plus her sister. You see, they never quite fit in with the rest of us. Sodom has always prided itself on being a live-and-let-live kind of a place, and they had a hard time accepting those rules. Victims of the snoopy syndrome. There are no known methods of treatment. God probably figured this out and opted for a drastic solution.

In our opinion, Mr. Lot was a disarmingly candid and perceptive witness. The one point of his testimony about which we have questions is his theory of the destruction of Sodom. Not only did he offer no compelling evidence for his accusation, and not only did he fail to take the fate of Gomorrah into account, but he was unable to explain why Miss X and Miss Y, along with himself and his daughters, were the only known survivors.

October 5, 1993 B. C.
NEWS AND VIEWS
To Testify, or Not to Testify?

YESTERDAY'S SODOM/GOMORRAH HEARINGS were devoted to legal wrangling over the question of whether Mr. Lot's two daughters could be compelled to testify. They are both minors, a circumstance that, at least as some senators interpret Holy Land law, exempts them from providing testimony against their father's will.

Whether or not this interpretation is "a travesty," as one senator characterized it, it appears to have won the day.

So we are left to wonder. How can Mr. Lot's daughters have been virgin wallflowers if, as the administration claims, their father had sons-in-law? Is it true, as appears likely, that they got their father drunk and slept with him—were they so unattractive to him that this was their only recourse? Hadn't God warned them of the dangers of consanguinity, or him of the penalties for sexual abuse? Are these "children" currently pregnant, and do they plan to offer the children up for adoption? These may be slight matters, compared to the larger issue of the wanton destruction of loyal Holy Land citizens, but one can be forgiven for speculating.

THE SENATE SODOM/GOMORRAH COMMITTEE spent yesterday's session questioning Professor Blazer, the international expert on fire and brimstone. Professor Blazer took his doctoral degree at the University of Bologna, where he wrote his ground-breaking dissertation, "The Mud Pots and Geysers of Yellowstone." He has done extensive research at Mounts Vesuvius, Aetna, Pelée, Saint Helens, and Pinatubo. He now chairs the Department of Physics, Sin, and Punishment at the University of Sinai.

Here, in brief, are the highlights of Professor Blazer's long-awaited testimony.

SENATOR SHUR: In your expert opinion, Professor Blazer, what is brimstone?

PROFESSOR BLAZER: Brimstone, Senator Shur, is a compound of two sub-elements: namely, brim and stone. The word *brim,* noun, from the Middle English *brimme,* is defined by Webster, in one of its various usages—albeit archaic—as "the upper surface of a body of water." Notice that the latter term is taken to refer to a common aqueous solution, namely, a drinkable fluid, an imbibable liquid—that is to say, the hydrous element. On the other hand, the word *stone,* also noun, from the Old English *stan,* mediated to us through the Middle English and akin to the Old High German *stein,* also (though Webster unaccountably neglects to mention this) to the Middle Yiddish *shteyn*—from which, incidentally, we acquire our term *stone*—is defined, also by the usually learned and sagacious Webster, in its primary usage— which, I might add, is still current—as "a concretion of earthy or mineral matter." In this second definition, I believe you will find that the term *earthy* is central. An adjective, it is derived from the noun *earth,* if I may express myself in the vernacular. Thus, to put this very complex matter in its simplest, most rudimentary form, brimstone is, at base and fundamentally, merely a peculiar, distinctive—one is tempted to employ the term *idiosyncratic* (though one must be circumspect here about the danger—the very real danger, I must add—of oversimplification). . . . Now, where was I? Oh yes. In summary, brimstone is a distinctive compound of the two basic elements of (1) water and (2) earth, as they have come to be known to the undiscriminating multitudes.

SENATOR SHUR: And fire is fire?

PROFESSOR BLAZER: That is quite so, senator, quite so. A fine logical point. "Fire is fire." I would not have expressed myself in such a succinct, concise, and pithy form, but yes. You have, if I may again revert to the vernacular, hit the nail on the head.

SENATOR SHUR: Air is air?

PROFESSOR BLAZER: Again, senator, I must compliment your way with words.

SENATOR SHUR: Air, earth, fire, and water. Those are the four elements?

PROFESSOR BLAZER: Precisely so. I see that you yourself have done advanced work in the basic discipline of physics, in which, I would submit—and, I think, with good reason—the Greeks have always excelled. The four you enumerated, to wit, earth, air, fire, and water, are indeed the basic elements, the so-called "building blocks" of the visible creation. The Greeks, alas, have beaten us to them. But of course the search for truth continues. Taking into account the invisible creation, as well as the visible, there may in fact be five, six, even seven elements![50] If I may speak without being accused of immodesty, I am convinced that we in the Holy Land (I may, I hope, be forgiven for thinking specifically of my own university) are in the very vanguard of research into what I am wont, perhaps I should say inclined, to call "the missing elements," which we can now only imagine and of which we currently have only the slightest premonition.

SENATOR SHUR: Thank you, professor. Now, to turn once again to the subject of this committee's investigation. In your expert opinion, did Mr. Lot's wife become a pillar of salt?

PROFESSOR BLAZER: Senator, I have no specific knowledge of

---

[50]See Professor Allbright's monograph, "Are There Three Invisible Elements? Rethinking the Science of Chemistry" (Reno [Unpublished], n.d.).

that case. I must point out that, as a scientist, I deal exclusively with the formulation and testing of scientific, that is to say general, as opposed to specific, hypotheses.

SENATOR SHUR: But professor, aren't you the Chairman of the University of Sinai's entire Department of Physics, Sin, and Punishment?

PROFESSOR BLAZER: We must at this juncture, I think, make a critical distinction. Let me put it as clearly and simply as I can. Now, senator. Here is Physics, correct? Here is Sin, correct? Here is Punishment, correct? So. Three distinct, autonomous disciplines. Now, if you will follow me further in my argument. Professor Blazer is a physicist, correct? From this rudimentary fact it follows that he is not necessarily an authority on either sin, on the one hand, or punishment, on the other. Both of which disciplines are, incidentally, concerned with questions pertaining to specific cases—such as, should Mrs. Lot be punished for contravening the angels' express directive not to look back at a burning city, or, perhaps, for some other grievous transgression?

SENATOR SHUR: Let me rephrase. Is it possible, scientifically speaking, for a person to become a pillar of salt? Yes or no?

PROFESSOR BLAZER: That, senator, is much better. Now you have put the question in the proper, that is to say hypothetical, mode. "Is it possible," etcetera. By this, I would presume you mean, Is it possible, in general—as it were, theoretically. My interpretation of your words is, I believe, borne out by your employment of the indefinite article *a*, rather than designating a specific person—Person X, for example; or, for that matter, Person Y; or even Person Z—in the phrase, "for a person," etc.

SENATOR SHUR: Well, is it?

PROFESSOR BLAZER: I cannot speak to that question. It is beyond the strictly defined boundaries of my expertise. . . .

We would concede that we now have a somewhat better idea of the nature of brimstone. But we suspect that the good professor knows more than he was willing to say.

October 7, 1993 B. C.
NEWS AND VIEWS
Mystery Witness Explains All

No ONE IN RECENT MEMORY had ever heard or seen anything like it. We are referring, of course, to yesterday's session of the Senate Sodom/Gomorrah Committee, which has now completed its work, leaving the Holy Land in a buzz and the present administration in a state of chaos.

In a stunning move that still has the opposition Theocratic Party scratching their grizzled heads, Senator Shur produced a surprise witness, who was able to provide definitive answers to all the many questions the Sodom/Gomorrah affair has raised.

We quote the testimony in its entirety.

SENATOR SHUR: Good morning, madam.

MS. JANE: Good morning, senator.

SENATOR SHUR: Could you please reveal your identity to this committee?

MS. JANE: Certainly. I am Ms. Jane.

SENATOR SHUR: Were you ever known by another name?

MS. JANE: I was.

SENATOR SHUR: And by what name were you formerly known?

MS. JANE: I was known as Mrs. Lot.

SENATOR SHUR: May we have gasps from the opposition Theocrats, please?

SENATOR SAMUEL: Certainly, Senator Shur, my good friend and sometime adversary. Would you prefer that they be gasps of disbelief?

SENATOR SHUR: I believe the situation calls for a mixture of disbelief, awe, and anger.

SENATOR SAMUEL: We'll take up your offer at our next caucus. However, I make no promises.

SENATOR SHUR: Now, Ms. Jane. I would like to ask a most personal question. Are you, or have you ever been, a pillar of salt?

SENATOR SAMUEL: I object to that question.

SENATOR SHUR: Then let me rephrase it. Are you *now,* or have you ever been, a pillar of salt? Is that better, senator?

SENATOR SAMUEL: That's much better, senator.

MS. JANE: I am not now a pillar of salt. I was, however, a pillar of salt in a previous existence.

SENATOR SHUR: Was that by choice, or was it by the hand of God, fate, or some metaphysical power of which we have only the slightest of inklings?

MS. JANE: It was by choice.

SENATOR SHUR: And just why did you choose to become a pillar of salt?

MS. JANE: I wanted to know what it was like to be licked by a cow.

SENATOR SHUR: And what *was* it like to be licked by a cow?

MS. JANE: I've had better.

SENATOR SAMUEL: Then you wouldn't recommend it?

MS. JANE: Not to the connoisseur. In your case, however. . . .

SENATOR SHUR: Let us move on. Why have you come before this committee?

MS. JANE: I have come to explain the mystery of Sodom and Gomorrah.

SENATOR SHUR: Is that once and for all?

MS. JANE: Pardon me, senator. Yes. I have come to explain the mystery of Sodom and Gomorrah once and for all.

SENATOR SHUR: I believe the situation now calls for a short series of brief, stunning speeches that will answer all outstanding questions, put to rest all ugly rumors, and reveal that you, once a lowly beggar, have either recently and unexpectedly come into the possession of an immense fortune or are the long-lost daughter of some royal personage, thus making you fit to marry a prince and live happily ever after.

MS. JANE: That is also my understanding. Proceed, senator.

SENATOR SHUR: Question number one. Why were Sodom and Gomorrah destroyed?

MS. JANE: In April of the year 2000 B.C., I founded an underground magazine, entitled *Blasphemy* and subtitled *A Journal of Political Satire*. It served a narrow but discriminating clientele. In fact, one of the charter subscribers was God himself. He often wrote letters to the editor, cheerfully congratulating us on our sketches of his eccentricities and peccadillos and saying such things as, "Very good, ladies. You've got me down to a T!" But as we gained in popularity, his advisors began to worry about our growing influence. One night early this year he was warned in a dream of our danger to his prestige. Against his better judgment, he was finally persuaded to put out a hit on Sodom, of which I was at that time a resident, and Gomorrah, which was the secret base of our operations.

SENATOR SHUR: Now, question the second. Why was Lot not punished?

MS. JANE: Lot was not punished because the sins of which he stands falsely accused were common practice in the Temple. I say falsely because, contrary to his heroic, selfless testimony, he did not offer our daughters to a lusty mob, nor did they accept his generous offer, nor are our daughters, who, incidentally, take after their mother, unattractive, nor did they get him drunk with wine—he has always preferred beer—nor did he ever show a prurient interest in them, even when they were tiny tots. In fact, he refused to change their diapers.

SENATOR SHUR: Question the third. How did you escape the destruction?

MS. JANE: On the night in question, I was in Athens, where I was filing for divorce on the grounds of irreconcilable differences— Lot enjoyed the smell of sheep, I did not—and where I was scheduled to elope with a rich, handsome young playwright who shared with me a sense of the world's absurdity. That man was none other than Aristophanes the Eldest, to whom, I might add, I am now happily wed.

SENATOR SHUR: Question the fourth. Why was brimstone used?

MS. JANE: As all oppressed women know, brimstone, noun, is a common household disinfectant. It was used to rid the vicinity of the odor of sheep.

It is clear from this stunning testimony that the blame for the tragedy at Sodom and Gomorrah should be placed at the feet, not of God himself, but of his priestly advisors. What is most appalling about the behavior of this so-called "brain" trust is their shameless disregard of the benefits of satire. And what we find especially alarming is that the average Holy Lander is more concerned about the escalating price of mutton than about the number one issue we as a nation face, the preservation of our cultural heritage of blasphemy.

Have we come to the point where everything is sacred?

6 | Moshe's Diary

*T*HE DOMINANT FIGURE *in the first five book of the orthodox Bible, the Pentateuch (also known as the Torah, or Law), is Moses. He is reported to have led the Hebrews (the early Israelites) out of Egyptian captivity and in the direction of Israel, the Promised Land. He is also said to have been the one chosen by God to receive the Ten Commandments.*

According to the account in the book of Exodus, an anonymous child is born to a pair of anonymous parents of the house of Levi (the priestly caste among the Hebrews). This child escapes death as an infant: an anonymous Pharaoh, alarmed by a population explosion among his Hebrew slaves, has ordered that all their newborn sons be cast into the Nile and drowned. But the mother hides the baby in a basket alongside the river and appoints his anonymous sister (later identified as Miriam) to guard him; when Pharaoh's anonymous daughter discovers the baby and takes pity on him, his sister cleverly offers the services of her mother as a salaried nurse. Pharaoh's daughter accepts this kind offer; she takes him as her son and names him Moses (a.k.a. Moshe).

One day Moses sees an Egyptian beating a Hebrew slave. Incensed by this atrocity, he murders the Egyptian and flees to the land of Midian, where he meets a man named Reuel, who presents him with a gift, his daughter Zipporah. She, in turn, bears Moses a son, Gershom. While herding sheep for his father-in-law, Moses approaches a burning bush, where he is addressed by a disembodied voice, who introduces himself as God and commands Moses to return to Egypt and lead his people out of slavery into "a land flowing with milk and honey." Moses is unwilling, citing his lack of self-esteem due to an alleged speech defect. God, not to be denied, replies that Moses should commission his oratorically-gifted brother Aaron to be his mouthpiece.

Deprived of his best excuse, Moses returns to Egypt, becomes leader of the Israelites, and, with Aaron as his spokesman and with God behind him, plays political hardball with a new and even crueler Pharaoh by threatening him with a variety of plagues (polluting the Nile with blood, sending scourges of frogs, gnats, and flies, infecting the cattle with boils, sending hail and thunderstorms and locusts, visiting the earth with darkness, killing the Egyptians' firstborn), which God does not hesitate to visit upon the sadistic ruler. Using this tactic, Moses is eventually able to effect the release of the Hebrews.

Free from their captivity, the Israelites wander for forty years in the wilderness. During this time God calls Moses to the top of Mount Sinai and presents him with the Ten Commandments. Later, after much complaining among the people because their squalid living conditions, which keeps them from achieving the Israelite dream of a Promised Land, Moses passes the torch of leadership to Joshua, son of Nun. Then he dies and is buried in an unmarked grave.

This story is inferior in many ways to the original from which it is undoubtedly derived. Unlike the long, complex, often-repetitive story given in the Bible, the original is brief and to the point. It is recounted in the first person, so that the personality and motives of Moshe are more transparent to the contemporary reader. The diary form gives us a less fantastic, more accurate and immediate picture of the actual events. And last but far from least, its portrait of God is much more accessible to the average American.

§

GOT IN A FIGHT TODAY. Guy came to pick up his kid at the day-care center. Off work early, I guess, so his wife sent him over to retrieve little Tut. Little Tut tinkling at the time, which meant daddy had to wait, make small talk with Miriam at the front desk. Guy made a remark. Must be about a 36B, right? he says to her as I happen to walk in the door. Knock it off, says I. Who the hell do you think you are? says he. Moshe, house of Levi, says I. Sorry, didn't catch the last name, says the arrogant s.o.b. Which is the point in time at which I let him have it. Uppercut. Landed flush.

Have to quit being so sensitive about being a priest's kid.

26 Elul, 2422
Piece in the paper mentioned the incident with Tut's daddy. Guy's been admitted to Mt. Sinai Hospital. Severe concussion. Critical condition. Altercation at Pharaoh's Daughter's Day Care Center. Assailant being sought by police. Five foot three, 200 pounds, dark features and a pencil-slim moustachio. Answers to the name of Moshe.

That kills me: "pencil-slim moustachio."

27 Elul, 2422
Started new job here in Midian. Herding sheep. Shaved the

---

[51]Professor Allbright was the first to notice that the dates in this scroll are given in the Ur-Hebrew. He pointed out that this was inconsistent with the usual practice in the Scrolls, that of citing dates using the B.C. scheme. Father Lecher, when pressed for an explanation, was unable to provide one and could only insist that he was here, as everywhere, being faithful to the text as he found it. Unsatisfied with this reply, the professor offered to compose, not a monograph, but an entire series of volumes on this apparent inconsistency. Father Lecher was finally able to dissuade him from pursuing this avenue, pointing out that there were other and more pressing issues in the text to which he could apply his vast skills and learning. The good father's invitation for the rest of us to be on the lookout for such issues was met with enthusiasm.

moustachio, put lifts in my sandals. I'm learning to write with a cramped hand. Going by the name of Mose.

28 Elul, 2422
Got a note from Miriam. Enclosed information on Tut's daddy. Good news is, he was a bouncer. (Imagine that! Moshe took out a bouncer!) Bad news is, the information was his obit.

29 Elul, 2422
Boss is named Reuel. Also answers to the name of Jethro. Doesn't ask questions. Seven daughters, all nice-looking. Especially Zipporah. Must be about a 40D. Quite mature for her age. Probably about fifteen.

8 Heshvan, 2423
Helped Zipporah with the chores today. Drawing water for the camels. Got off on the subject of water. She told me about Sinbad. I told her about Noah.[52] What's an ark? she says, all innocence.

21 Sivan, 2423
This Jethro character is some kind of a nut. Excessively religious. Believes in bush gods. Regularly burns bushes to keep them (the gods) warm. Says they appreciate it, always pay you back. I find this hilarious but keep my mouth shut. I also keep the sheep away from the bushes.

4 Kislev, 2424
Brought up the subject of Zippy with her old man. Jethro. That's some daughter you've got, says I. Which one? says he, I've got seven. Zipporah, says I, the one who's not married. What's this about an ark? says he, She's been going on and on about an ark; water; Noah. Private joke, says I. Hidden sexual overtones? says he. I change the subject to bushes.

---

[52]Ms. LaFemme moved that Professor Allbright write a monograph on the subject, "Navigational Techniques in the Ancient Middle East: Sinbad and Noah." The motion died for lack of a second.

17 Adar, 2424
Jethro's a man of few words. Speaks only of sheep, gods, bushes, daughters.

9 Tammuz, 2425
Zippy winked at me today. Or maybe she just got sand in her eye.

10 Tammuz, 2425
Brought up the subject of Zippy with Jethro again. Eased into it. Started with sheep, moved to bushes, then gods, then daughters, finally narrowed it down to Zippy. You fancy her? says he. Reminds me of my first wife, says I.[53]
  Big mistake.

11 Tammuz, 2425
Jethro brought up subject of Zippy. Tell you what, says he. You work for me till 2466, herding sheep, I'll let you have her. Throw in a couple hundred sheep, says I, and we've got us a deal. Let's sleep on it, says he.

12 Tammuz, 2425
Did a little math with Jethro. In 2466, says I, I'll be sixty-five. Out of the danger zone, says he. What about the sheep? says I. We settle on a hundred.

10 Adar, 2466
Married Zippy.
  Misnomer.

15 Kislev, 2467
Nine pound miracle. Pretty sure it's mine. Wanted to call him Geraldhotep, Zippy big on Shaun. Jethro settled for Gershom. Old family name.

---

[53]As Father Lecher pointed out, Moshe is naturally reluctant to discuss this topic in greater detail.

26 Nisan, 2471
News on the radio says Seti the First finally died. Old age. New guy is Rameses the Second. Said to be soft on capital punishment.

27 Nisan, 2471
Thinking of going back to Egypt. Beginning to miss the pyramids.

28 Nisan, 2471
Asked Jethro for a leave of absence. Why? says he. Footloose, says I. Wrong thing to say. No, says he, I'd like to be near my grandson.
    Guess he wants to teach the kid about sheep and religion.

29 Nisan, 2471
Had a bright idea. Told Jethro I talked to one of his bush gods. B. G. wants me to go back to Egypt, says I. What for? says he. He has big plans for me, says I, thinks I'm a leader of men. You gotta be kidding, says he. No, says I, that's definitely what your bush god has in mind. A leader of men, did he say? says Jethro. The exact words, says I. What about Zipporah and little Gershom? says he. They're also invited, says I. Go in peace, says he, shaking my hand, his head.

18 Iyar, 2471
Applied for a job. Personnel manager for the Israelites. They're looking for somebody with a bachelor's degree and at least four years' experience. Somebody who can "facilitate and monitor dispute resolution systems."

25 Iyar, 2471
Guy looked over my resumé. Where's Peninsula State? says he, frowning. Otherwise known as Penn State, says I, gambling. Oh yes, says he, nodding. Seemed quite impressed. Especially liked my leadership experience and skills. They used to follow me like sheep, I said.
    Didn't mention that they *were* sheep.

26 Iyar, 2471
Got the job.

2 Sivan, 2477
There's an opening in labor negotiations. Aaron says go for it.
Miriam says go for it. Gershom says go for it. Zippy says think it
over carefully. Consider your age.

3 Sivan, 2477
Played tennis with the boss. Lost in straight sets.

4 Sivan, 2477
Got the job.

1 Shebat, 2481
Played golf with Rameses Number Two. Needed a stress-free environment to work out the sticky details in a contract. Took
Aaron along as a caddie. He warned me beforehand that Rameses
is a tough nut to crack. A real walnut, he says. Wrong. Guy's a
peanut. Like taking candy from Gershom. Easier than Jethro.

Pulled the golf-club-into-snake trick. Threw the driver into the
marsh, waded in, came up with a water moccasin. Tried it again,
came up with a frog. Handed it to him. Gave him warts, scared
the hell out of him.

So. Allergic to frogs, is Rameses the Second. Could be a campaign issue in the upcoming election.

Thinking of running against him. Pros: he'd be an easy mark, I
could use the money, I'd make a relatively decent pharaoh. Cons:
don't have the energy to campaign twenty hours a day, not the
greatest public speaker in the world. Then there's that tiff with
little Tut's father.

Cons win. Prefer low profile, anyway. Safer.

15 Nisan, 2481
Underestimated Rameses. Got wind that he was planning to feed
us to the alligators, Aaron and me. So we gathered the troops together this a.m. and took off for the peninsula. Everybody loaded
the kids on the camels while Rameses was still asleep, and headed

for the border. The guards were inside the booth playing chess, so we just went right on through.

Rameses sent the Coast Guard after us. Didn't stop to think that Egypt doesn't have a coast guard. An army and a navy, but not a hint of a coast guard. With enemies like Rameses II, who needs friends? Or bush gods?

28 Nisan, 2481
Troops starting to complain. So I promised them "a land flowing with milk and honey." Not the most poetic phrase in the world, makes you think of breakfast cereal, but they believed every word. Now I'll have to come up with some real estate with goats and bees. Either that, or spend the rest of my life in this godforsaken desert thinking up explanations.

2 Elul, 2490
Found some manna in the middle of the desert. Everybody's going around saying, Manna, manna, the answer to our prayers. Not so. Manna's a laxative.[54]

6 Sivan, 2497
Had an interesting experience. Met God.

Couldn't sleep, because of last night's ghost stories, so got up early and climbed the mountain. Sinai, I believe it's called. When I got near the summit I heard this fipple flute being played—"I Gave My Love a Cherry," something like that. Looked up, saw a naked figure sitting on a rock. Long white hair blowing in the breeze. Kind of skinny. Gaunt shoulder blades, slender white buttocks. Old as the hills. His back was to me. Tried to work myself in a position to see his frontside, just out of curiosity— not really interested in making comparisons—but no dice. He

---

[54]In the view of Cardinal Micromentis, this incident was very likely the real cause of the political turmoil among the Israelites, as recorded in Exodus 32. Ms. LaFemme raised the question of whether the manna was a natural fiber laxative. Professor Allbright's suggestion that this was the subject on which he might well compose a monograph was met with silence admixed with stifled laughter.

kept turning around, didn't seem to want me to get a good look at him. Hey, I yell at him, people down there just might want to get a little sleep. Moshe, says he. Jethro? says I. No, says he, is not Jethro, Jethro plays a violin, stringed instrument, this is a fipple flute, wind instrument, very plaintive, good for the melancholy in us all. If not Jethro, who? says I. Give you three guesses, says he. Father Time? Close, but no. The Ghost of Christmas Past? Wrong religion. The god of Abraham, Isaac, and Jacob? Among others.

He's not a bit like I'd have expected. Less bossy. Less transcendental. More . . . down-to-earth. Ethical, of course. Also, has the larger view of things. Not much of a detail man, but that's because of his overall perspective. What strikes me most about him is his comic side, which never gets emphasized. A certain . . . wistful comic spirit. Or maybe a sad comic spirit. . . . No, that suggests the adjective *Chaplinesque,* which is misleading. Chaplin is Chaplin. God is God. That's about all you can say. Very hard to describe. You think you have the right word, you immediately sense its inadequacy. You end up saying you'd have had to actually *be* there to know what I'm talking about.

Quite approachable, however, except that I couldn't really get a decent look at him. An odd mix of approachability and mystery. It's like we're long-lost friends, except that when I try to go up and shake hands he just turns around, like he's on a Lazy Susan. Always showing me his backside. Which isn't terribly attractive. Very shriveled. Lots and lots of moles, hairs growing out of them, that kind of a thing. Extremely pale. Needs a good suntan.

Winsome personality. Don't think it's just because of the contrast between what I'd have expected and what I got. Even if I'd have expected a friendly though comic figure, I'd have been pleasantly surprised. For instance, he doesn't seem to be especially disturbed about the incident with little Tut's father. Got the impression he'd have done pretty much the same thing himself, given the parameters of that particular situation.

Don't feel bad about it, says he, after all, the guy *was* messing with your sister. Oh, I don't feel bad, says I, I just wonder if I shouldn't have sent some money to the family, or at least a sympathy card. You've got a point there, says he, except I happen to know that the guy left his widow well provided for, member-ship in the Cairo Country Club, 300 feet of riverfront property, 5,000 shares in the Sphinx, even a small pyramid. Also, at that time the wife was happy to get rid of the guy, she was having a serious thing with his best friend. Relieved to hear that, says I, the paper didn't mention those things. It never does, says he, if you want the real scoop, you've got to know somebody who knows somebody.

Also talked about other things. The divine attributes. The problem of evil. Don't remember too much about that part of the conversation. Metaphysics and theology aren't my strong point. I'm more of a sheep and conflict resolution man. Also, I was more or less in awe, in spite of his approachability and winsome personality and sense of humor.

Do however remember the discussion on ethics. Fact is, I took notes when we got to the subject. Hey, are you taking notes? says he in an offhand way. Didn't bring a pencil, says I. Got a chisel and a hammer? says he. Just happen to have one of each in my briefcase, says I, but I didn't bring a legal-sized notepad. Here, use this rock, says he, and he tosses a stone slate over his shoulder. So I write the main points down. Ten of them. There was only room for ten on that slate. Which is a good thing, because by the time we get to the part about coveting this, coveting that, I'm exhausted, my fingers are bloody, my hands are shaking, I'm a nervous wreck from all the mistakes. Don't take it so seriously, says he, they're only suggestions. Of course, says I, but they're *your* suggestions. If I'd have known you were going to take everything I say so seriously, says he, I'd have brought up the subject that lies closest to my heart. Turns out the subject closest to his heart was comedy. Don't remember his thoughts on the topic, but I do remember that he also gave ten rules for aspiring comedians. Don't recall what they are. I know they're important, but I'm tired from taking notes on public morality, so I decide to rely on my memory. Big mistake, at my age (98).

All in all, I'd have to rank this confab as among the most memorable of my life. Right up there with the ones I used to have with Jethro. Infinitely higher than the arguments with Rameses the Second and little Tut's father.

27 Ab, 2521
The word's out. They're looking for a tombstone. Shouldn't be hard to find one out here in the desert.

28 Ab, 2521
Can't find quite the right tombstone, I hear. They want to make a shrine to me.

Told them not to bother. Rather be left to the buzzards. Prefer them to the tourists.

29 Ab, 2521
Well, this is it. I've had 120 years of a good life, with the possible exception of the last forty years. Tribal politics and manna I can do without. But no major complaints. Got to (1) herd sheep, (2) sit at the feet of my pappy-in-law Jethro, (3) play golf with Rameses Número Segundo, (4) talk to God. Not many can make those claims.

Just hope they find themselves a nice place to settle down— pasture for the goats, clover for the bees. I expect they will. First thing, they've got to elect my replacement. Frontrunner seems to be Josh. Nun's kid. Impressive resumé. Has spent a lot of time scouting. But a little too warlike, for my taste. Gets it from his old man.

Before I go, should have a friendly sitdown with the kid. Advise him to rely more on his wits.[55]

---

[55]The committee unanimously agreed that by far the most significant entry in "Moshe's Diary" is Moshe's conversation with God. Cardinal Micromentis was pleased that God is not nearly as industrious as the orthodox has led us to believe. Professor Allbright immediately wrote a 575-page monograph, "Notes on the So-Called 'Forgotten' Commandments: A Speculative Inquiry." (Unfortunately, he pushed a wrong key on his computer and accidentally erased the manuscript.) Father Lecher was content to point out that God is not spirit, but body, and that his natural persona is not one of high seriousness, as the orthodox account suggests, but of low comedy. Ms. LaFemme agreed, adding that both God and the author of this scroll appear to be engaging in self-parody.

7 | The Wager

*T*HOUGH THE *B*IBLICAL STORY OF *J*OB *and his sufferings has been read and enjoyed by millions for thousands of years, it has left most readers bewildered. The obvious puzzle is, Why would an all-good, all-powerful God allow a decent man like Job to suffer? But there are others.*

1. Job is portrayed as "perfect and upright," although he himself admits, "It may be that my sons have sinned, and cursed God in their hearts." How can he be both a model of virtue and a poor parent? And if he is really perfect and upright, why does he feel the need to "repent in dust and ashes" after God speaks to him out of a whirlwind? Is this not a case of misplaced guilt?

2. How could an all-wise God allow himself to be lured by Satan into the wager over whether a needless dose of suffering will cause Job to "curse God to his face?"

3. Who actually wins the wager? After his bout of cruel and unusual suffering, Job "curses his day." Who can blame him? More to the point, is cursing one's day the same as cursing God to his face? If so, why would any all-wise, all-powerful, self-respecting higher being permit himself to lose to someone the likes of Satan?

4. What are the underlying motives of the three so-called "friends" who come to "comfort" Job? What are their therapeutic credentials?

5. Why, in the end, does God give Job "twice as much as he had before?" Perhaps he feels guilty about the whole affair?

As Father Lecher insisted, there is a perfectly plausible explanation for all these loose ends. Scroll #7 was the original story; a later writer got hold of it and, for whatever reason (incompetence? excessive piety?), transformed it into the perplexing muddle that is the orthodox Book of Job. The proof of this theory, the good father pointed out, is that "The Wager" is completely intelligible, that it leaves the reader unmystified, that it solves the puzzles that have baffled theologians for millennia.

§

THERE WAS A MAN IN THE LAND OF OZ whose name was Job. And he had a reputation as a perfect and upright man, who spent his Sabbaths fearing God and eschewing evil. He was a wealthy man, numbering among his possessions 7,000 sheep, 3,000 camels, 500 yoke of oxen, 500 she-asses, 100 goats, four maids, two cooks, a butler, a wife, three children, and an account with Bildad the Broker.[56]

And just down the road from Job's ranch lived Satan, who spent his weekdays going to and fro in the earth, and walking up and down in it, being an international lawyer as well as a member of the Sierra Club.[57] And Satan was also successful in his chosen line of work, numbering among his clients Rameses the Second, Alexander the Great, the crown princes of half a dozen oil-rich nations, and the Queen of Sheba, at whose seaside retreat he spent the better part of his Sabbaths gamboling about in the surf with the beautiful people and closing deals and devising how he might fleece the unwary.

§

ONE BLUSTERY SPRING DAY, after tramping five miles through Job's impressive spread, Satan appeared at the door of God, his

---

[56] Job 1:1–3 duplicates this opening paragraph, with several significant changes. (1) The list of Job's possessions does not include the one hundred goats, nor do they specify the maids, cooks, butler, wife, children, and the brokerage account, the author being content to mention Job's "very great household." (2) The setting of the story is mistakenly given as Uz, not Oz, the land of "whirlwinds" (i.e., tornados).

[57] Job 1:7 fails to mention the reasons for Job's hiking expeditions.

friendly adversary.

"Just make yourself at home," said God, inviting Satan into his sanctuary. "A pot of coffee would hit the spot, don'tcha think?"

Satan unbuttoned his windbreaker, took off his gloves, and sat down in front of the hot stove. "Make mine black," he said, rubbing his hands in anticipation.

"Black it is," said God, pouring his guest a drink.

"Now then," continued God as he joined Satan at the stove, which doubled as a bargaining table. "What's on your mind?"

"Good and evil."

"Speaking of good. Have you considered my servant Job, that there is none like him in the earth, a perfect and upright man?"

Satan frowned and lit his pipe and blew a smoke ring. "Frankly," he said, "I'm not impressed."

"Not impressed?" replied God. "How can you fail to be impressed by a guy who owns 7,000 sheep? The average in Oz[58] is a thousand sheep per family unit. My man beats the averages seven times over, and you fail to be impressed?"

"I'm referring to his so-called 'uprightness.' Who wouldn't be upright with all those sheep? Excessive sheep is leading cause of uprightness."

"I fail to see the connection between the uprightness of a man and the quantity of sheep he has grazing out there on the rolling hills of Oz."

"It's a well-known fact."

"I've never heard of it."

"Studies have shown—"

"Don't talk 'studies have shown' with *me*," interrupted God testily. "As far as I'm concerned, they're nothing but a lot of oxen droppings."[59]

"How in hell's name can you call yourself an educated man," protested Satan, "and not be aware that sheep are the root cause of uprightness?"

---

[58] Population seven (7) families, according to the calculations of Cardinal Micromentis.

[59] Father Lecher cited this paragraph as proof of God's wisdom. Cardinal Micromentis cited the last phrase as proof of his delicacy.

And so the argument raged. Do large quantities of sheep cause uprightness, or do they not? Two hours later, Satan came up with a stunning proposal. "Say," he suddenly suggested with a cunning smile, "what do you suppose would happen if Job went bankrupt and had to go through a harrowing divorce?"

"It's not the kind of thing I like to think about," admitted God. "My guess, however, is that he'd bounce right back. He'd rebuild his fortune and work out a deal regarding visitation rights and turn right around and find a woman who was even more beautiful and talented and supportive—"

"No no," interrupted Satan. "You know what'd happen? He'd lose interest in the uprightness lifestyle in about two seconds."

"You seem pretty sure of yourself," observed God.

"You're damned right I'm sure of myself," replied Satan. "When you travel to and fro in the earth as much as I do, you're bound to pick up some self-esteem."

"I guess that's true," mused God. "Maybe *I* should try to get around more."

"Might help you keep up on things," suggested Satan diplomatically.

"Improve the circulation," added God.

"Also, keep you regular."

"There's that, too, isn't there."

"Well, what do you say? Are you game for testing my hypothesis?"

"Which hypothesis was that?"

"God, you *are* getting old," said Satan under his breath. Then, more loudly: "I'M REFERRING TO THE HYPOTHESIS ABOUT THE CORRELATION BETWEEN THE NUMBER OF SHEEP AND THE DEGREE OF UPRIGHTNESS."

"Oh yes," nodded God. "*That* hypothesis. Okay. I'm game. But how do you suggest we proceed, and you don't have to shout."

"What I'd suggest," replied Satan, "—and I'm just playing devil's advocate—is that thou put forth thy hand and touch all that he hath. . . . There. Is that better?"

"Fine," said God, who in the meantime had turned up his hearing aid, "except could you be more specific, and use plain Ur-Hebrew?"

"Specifically," suggested Satan, "you might start by stampeding his sheep over a cliff, moving on to the other livestock, rattling his ranch with a few earthquakes, then afflicting him with boils from head to foot."

God was aghast at this proposal. "That's not the way I like to treat my trusted servants," he protested. "It's hard these days to find good help."

"Which is more important," asked Satan, "good help, or the testing of scientific hypotheses?"

God thought about this question for a moment. "Good help," he finally replied. "Of course," he added quickly, "that's from the perspective of an employer."

"And a *major* employer."

"Yes," agreed God modestly.

"I've got a million shekels here that say that if somebody"— and here Satan gave his host a significant look—"if somebody should just happen to destroy Job's possessions, he'd give up his uprightness and perfection and re-evaluate his lifestyle."

God shook his head. "I'm not a betting man," he protested.

"Tell you what I'm gonna do," replied Satan, pursing his lips and squinting his eyes. "I'm gonna give you odds. I put a million shekels on this stove, you put down half a million, winner take all. Deal?"

God pondered this proposition. "A million shekels, did you say? Versus 500,000?" He paused to reflect and strum his fingers. "Okay. You're on."

§

AND SO THE WAGER WAS MADE. In no time at all Oz was inundated with suffering. As per the agreement, God stampeded Job's livestock over a cliff, rattled his ranch with several earthquakes, and afflicted him grievously with boils from head to foot. He even went the extra mile, planting skeptical thoughts in the mind of Job's wife, Dorothy (the mother of Leo, age six; skinny little Oscar, nicknamed "Scarecrow," age nine; and Tim Woodman, age thirteen, a son by a previous marriage). For shortly after God took action, Job came back home from the "natural disaster" to confront a suspicious helpmeet.

Q: Where have you been all day?

A: I have been going to and fro in the earth, and walking up and down in it.

Q: Do I smell perfume?

A: What you're smelling is sheep dip. I tried to tackle several of the dumb beasts as they were stampeding over the cliff.

Q: Am I supposed to believe that? Why on earth would your sheep—

A: They're *our* sheep, darling. What's mine is thine.

Q: Could I have that in writing?

A: Certainly. Hmmm. . . . I seem to have misplaced my pen. It was probably knocked out of my pocket in the stampede.

Q: Why on earth would *our* sheep suddenly take off and dive over a cliff?

A: How should I know? I was just out in the meadows of Oz herding them, playing my guitar, minding my own business, being more or less upright and perfect and eschewing evil, as is my wont, when bam, out of the clear blue, they and other of my livestock panicked and took off and began leaping over the cliff. It was your classic stampede.

Q: Are you suggesting they thought they were lemmings?[60]

A: What I'm suggesting is, they were just following orders.

Q: Orders? From whom?

A: I suspect it was from God.

Q: Where did you get *that* idea?

A: It had all the earmarks of a supernatural operation. Quick. Unexpected. Vengeful. Besides, how else would you explain it? Or those earthquakes we had this afternoon?

---

[60]In the view of Cardinal Micromentis, this question strongly suggests the existence of lemmings in the Ancient Near East. Professor Allbright disagreed. See his 496-page monograph, "Lambs, Lemmings, and Lunacy: Mr. Micromentis' Misguided Madness," (Reno [Unpublished], n.d.). Ms. LaFemme insisted that this dispute was distracting our attention from the major point of this section of the text, which is that men are notoriously poor liars.

Q: [*Sarcastically*] Low-flying aircraft?

A: [*Seriously*] Keep in mind that aircraft have not yet been invented. Balloons have been invented, but I wouldn't put them in the same category as aircraft. They don't rumble or shake the earth. They float. Serenely and gracefully, they float. Over hill, over dale—

Q: What's that red stuff on your collar?

A: Red stuff? What red stuff?

Q: [*Indicating the position of the "red stuff"*] There.

A: Oh, *that*. Looks like blood, doesn't it? It's probably from the boils.

On hearing this explanation, Dorothy went on a stampede of her own, calling her mother, loading the kids on the camels, and taking off. But fortunately for Job, he had three close friends who were accomplished in the art of consolation. And so immediately after this Q and A session, he telephoned his three friends and invited them to come over to comfort him.

§

"I KNOW EXACTLY what you're going through," Bildad the Broker consoled Job as the cards were being dealt. "I've been there myself. I lost a bundle in the Crash of '00."

"How can you possibly know exactly what it's like?" protested Job. "That was a crashette, comparatively speaking."

"It's like comparing figs and grapes," observed Bildad as he checked his hand. "The point is, the Big Crash almost took me down the tube. If I wouldn't have had a thirty percent cash position, I wouldn't be here consoling you now. They'd have had to scrape me off the sidewalk."

"That's nothing," replied Job. "*I* was fully invested."

"I *told* you to get out of sheep," said Bildad.

"The hell you did," said Job, his voice rising. "Four days before the stampede, you told me to purchase an extra 5,000 head of the woolly creatures."

Bildad gazed expressionlessly at his friend across the top of his cards. "I encouraged you to purchase 5,000 head of emus," he replied without the least hint of emotion in his voice.

"Sheep," insisted Job.

"Emus."

"Sheep!"

"Emus!"

"*Sheep!!*"

"*Emus!!*" cried Bildad, removing a derringer from his belt and placing it on the table that separated them.

"*SHEEP!!!*" cried Job, removing a Turkish gilt-edged scimitar from its sheath and placing it atop the firearm.

At this point Zophar the Physician broke the mounting tension. "Let's talk about the boils, shall we?" he suggested in a calm tone of voice. "Where does it hurt?"

Job indicated the location of the pain.

"Hmmm. . . ," said Zophar, examining his patient closely. "I'm going to give you a prescription for doxycycline, a broad spectrum antibiotic. Take one pill three times a day, at mealtime. If the problem doesn't clear up in three weeks, just give me a call and we'll schedule you for a vas."

"Vas?" protested Job. "I don't see the connection. You might as well amputate both my legs and pull all my wisdom teeth."

"We don't like to do those things," explained Zophar, "if the patient has just suffered a serious financial setback."

"Speaking of setbacks," interrupted Rabbi Eliphaz Woodman. "I know just the thing to solve your marital problem."

"I think I'd like that," said Job.

"As you may or may not remember," continued Rabbi Woodman, "I used to be married to Dorothy."

"Oh yes," replied Job, "I seem to recall that fact, now that you mention it. You are Eliphaz Woodman. When I married her, Dorothy was a Woodman. And if I am not mistaken, her oldest son, Tim, age thirteen, also bears the proud Woodman name. This suggests that she, Dorothy, must have been previously married. Either that, or living in sin. However, judging by her many comments on the subject, she was not one to live in sin. Therefore, she must have been married. Since her last name was Woodman, she must have been married to a Woodman. And since you are the only Woodman in these parts, it would seem to follow that yes, Dorothy, my estranged wife, must have been married to you, and that you were formerly married to her."

"Remarkable powers of deduction," observed Bildad the broker.

"Elementary, my dear Bildad" said Job. "As you were saying, Rabbi Woodman?"

"I was saying that I used to be married to Dorothy. The thing you should know about her is that she was in the habit of leaving her spouse at the drop of a Dow. She'd load the kids onto the camels and take off for Mama. She had the act down pat. When the Dow took a technical bounce, however, she'd come back. Except on the third crash. Her rule of thumb was, on the third crash, don't bother to come back. On the third crash, just file."

"That sounds like something she'd do," agreed Job.

"This is only your first crash," Woodman pointed out.

"Stampede."

"Stampede, crash, it makes no difference. My point is that she'll come back when you're in a position to purchase, say, 14,000 head of fine New Zealand sheep."

"I understand the theory behind this," said Job. "The problem is, how do I avoid the second and third stampedes?"

"That's something you're going to have to work out with God," counseled Rabbi Woodman.

"My advice," broke in Zophar playfully, "would be to cut down on the perfection and uprightness. Lower your standards. Be like the rest of us."

"Are you saying perfection and uprightness are the cause of suffering?" asked Job sarcastically.

"It's a well-known medical fact," explained Zophar, winking at his colleagues Bildad and Eliphaz. "If you come across as too perfect and upright, you're asking Satan to approach God and suggest the introduction of suffering into the picture."

"Why is this so?" inquired Job.

"Nobody really knows," admitted Zophar. "Some of the best minds in captivity have been working on this problem for centuries. It's known as the problem of suffering."

"One theory," offered Bildad the Broker, "is the ups and downs of the market."

"Another theory," offered Rabbi Eliphaz Woodman, "is Satanic jealousy."

"A third theory," offered Zophar the Physician, "is a chemical imbalance in the brain."

"But nobody knows for sure," admitted Bildad.

"I suppose if I want to find out," sighed Job, "I'll just have to go straight to the top."

§

AND STRAIGHT TO THE TOP Job went. He requested an audience with God. But God quickly put things in perspective. He came rolling through the Land of Oz and spake to Job out of a tornado.

"Look, Job, look. Look and see. See me spin."

"Gee whiz!" cried Job.

"Can you top this?"

"Not with the present software."

"So?"

"So," acknowledged Job, "I get your point."

"So?" persisted God. At this point in the conversation he had Job's right arm in a half nelson.[61]

"Oww," replied Job. "I *said* I got your point."

"What I meant was, so, what are you going to do about it?"

By this time God had his foe wrapped in a full nelson.[62]

"I'm sure you have some suggestions," replied Job sarcastically.

"You're absolutely right," conceded God, secure in his identity as the Master of the Universe. "The first thing I'd do if I were you is, I'd abhor myself."

Job, who by this time had been allowed to ease himself from the vice-like hold of his more powerful adversary, took a pencil

---

[61]An effective wrestling hold in which the arm of the assailant is thrust under the corresponding arm of the victim while the hand is pressed firmly against the back of his or her neck. (The editor is indebted to Father Lecher for this explanation.)

[62]An even more effective wrestling hold in which the assailant thrusts both his or her arms under the arms of the victim while clasping the hands behind his or her head. (The editor is indebted to Father Lecher for providing a demonstration on Cardinal Micromentis.)

and notepad from his vest pocket. "Abhor . . . myself," he repeated as he wrote down the prescription. "Got that. Then what?"

"Then what I usually recommend is that the patient repent in dust and ashes."

"Repent . . . in dust . . . and ashes," Job muttered to himself.

"Fine. Anything else?"

"What's the recommended dosage?"

"Start with three bouts of self-abhorrence every day, one before each meal. The dust and ashes should be taken at bedtime, with an eight-ounce glass of goat milk."

"Goat milk?!" cried Job. "Where the hell am I supposed to get *goat* milk? You killed all my goats."

"Correction," replied God. "I killed all your *sheep* . . . Also, the oxen . . . Camels too, I have to admit . . . Plus most of the she asses. But I left the goats alone."

"I think you'll find you got the goats, too."

"Why would I do that?" asked God. "I'm very proud of the job I did on the creation of goats."

"I won't argue with you on that point," acknowledged Job. "But it doesn't change the fact that I'm now a zero-goat rancher." At this point he rose, dusted himself off from the recent fray, and prepared to leave.

"Goats too, huh?" mused God. "An endangered species . . . wonder what I could have been thinking of?"

But Job did not hear these last remarks. He was already walking down the yellow brick road that leads to the drug store and the cessation of suffering.

"Stop!" God cried after him.

Job turned around, puzzled.

"Can't you take a joke?" asked God.

This question piqued Job's curiosity, He returned to the scene of his recent humiliation. "Pardon me?" he said.

"The truth of the matter," explained God, "is that I am not really a terrifying, awesome personage, as the rabbis, priests, and ministers take pleasure in depicting me. My closest friends know me as a lover of practical jokes; as always on the lookout for life's little incongruities; as someone whose oft-stern countenance hides an ever-so-slight twinkle in his eye—in short, as a rather merry, even impish, sort of fellow."

"Then you, too, are misunderstood?"

"Alas," responded God sadly. "It's the cross I have to bear."

Job considered this surprising revelation for a long moment. "I'll take your word for it," he finally said. "But how does this affect *me*?"

"Good question," acknowledged God. "The point is, I didn't really come to exact repentance of you."

"What about the self-abhorrence, the dust and ashes, the goat milk . . . ?"

"Oh, you can follow that prescription if you want to," replied God. "But just between the two of us, self-abhorrence is not conducive to mental health, dust and ashes wreak havoc on the alimentary canal, and goat milk has become a gourmet drink and is thus rather expensive."

"But what about my iniquities?"

"You mean your mistresses?"

"Actually, there are only three of them."

"Who am I to judge?" asked God, shrugging his shoulders. "That's a matter between you and your wife."

"But if you are not come to judge me," asked a confused Job, "why *are* you come?"

"I am come," said God, "to pay off."

At this, God reached into his camel-hide purse and pulled out a certified check, in Job's name, for half a million shekels.

Thus it happened that Job was able to purchase 14,000 head of New Zealand sheep. Dorothy then decided she had been too hasty and came back to her prosperous husband and became pregnant and began to knit booties for tiny Toto.

§

SOME TIME LATER, God returned home from a busy day at the office to confront his own suspicious helpmeet.

Q: What's this canceled check for half a million shekels?

A: Canceled check?

Q: For half a million.

A: Half a million?

Q: The one made out to Job.

A: Oh *that.* Job was down on his luck—livestock stampede, ill health, a recent separation—and I just gave him a little something to tide him over.

Q: A *little* something?

A: Well, you know how it is, when they get used to a certain lifestyle—

Q: But how can we afford it?

A: If I'm not mistaken, I recently deposited a million shekels in our account.

Q: And where, may I ask, did *that* come from?

A: I got it . . . let's see . . . from a fellow by the name of . . . Satan.

Q: Satan? *The* Satan? Your adversary?

A: I think we're talking about the same guy.

Q: And since when was that con man Satan so generous with his money?

A: Aren't we being a little judgmental here?

Q: You've been gambling!

A: Me? Gamble? You know I only bet on sure things.

Q: Okay, I want the full story.

And so God told Ernestine how he had made a wager with Satan over whether if someone should just happen to destroy Job's possessions, he'd give up his uprightness and perfection; and how God had caused Job to suffer (intending all along, of course, to pay him back); and how Job didn't give up his uprightness, for the simple and logical reason that *you can't give up something you never had;* and how Satan, because of his busy weekday schedule, didn't know about the mistresses.

Ernestine was curious. "Isn't that what they call a *sting?*"

And God laughed.

8 | Love Boat

THE ORTHODOX STORY OF JONAH begins by informing the reader that "the word of the Lord came unto Jonah . . . saying, Arise, go to Nineveh, that great city, and cry against it; for their wickedness is come up before me" (Jonah 1:1–2). But Jonah had a mind of his own: He fled to Tarshish by ship. God, not one to be resisted, sent a great storm into the sea. The ship's mariners feared for their lives; they cast lots to find on whose account the storm had been sent. Not surprisingly, the lot fell upon Jonah, who was asleep in the hold. When he was awakened, he confessed. Then the sailors threw him overboard, and God appointed a great fish to swallow him. Jonah, being naturally depressed by this turn of events, prayed for deliverance. After three days and three nights, God instructed the fish to disgorge his unhappy cargo onto dry land. The fish obeyed. Then "the word of the Lord came unto Jonah the second time, saying, Arise, go unto Nineveh, that great city, and preach unto it the preaching that I bid thee (3:1–2)." And Jonah did as he was told, with excellent results.

This story neglects to report the most striking feature of the entire affair: the hue and cry it caused. It was the public's passionate but varied reaction that gives "Love Boat" its intensity, and that made Jonah a rallying hero for the anti-theocratic Freedom Party.

Note that the original story does not bother to reprint the initial editorial as background for these letters to the editor. The reason for this is undoubtedly that the Jonah tale was so well-known that its repetition was unnecessary.

To the Editor:

Hurrah for the *Mediterranean Daily!* At last you've taken a firm editorial stand ["Torture Takes a New Twist," 16 August] against the reigning theocracy and its flouting of the Geneva Conventions (See Convention 3, Armed Forces at Sea). Finally, finally, somebody has the fortitude to name a Name! Perhaps the people at this end of the Sea will wake up and speak out against the common practice of incarcerating political prisoners—now, we hear, in the bellies of whales!—for the (apparently theological!) "crime" of fleeing an oppressive authoritarian régime.

The activities of the sailors in this sad affair were equally barbarous. Imagine: rousting a poor man from his slumber, forcing him to pray, subjecting him to an inquisition, and then tossing him overboard! Pawns those animals may have been in this philistine activity, but according to the principles laid down at Nuremberg, they are not blameless on that account.

Here's hoping you have the courage to continue your dauntless editorial policy, and that others will fearlessly join in the protest. Keep the faith!

Name withheld by request

ED. NOTE: *God is not a signatory to the Geneva conventions.*

§

Editor:

And you call yourselves a civilized people! Free Jonah!

H. Melville NEW YORK CITY[63]

---

[63] See Professor Allbright's extensive 838-page monograph, "*Moby Dick* and 'Love Boat': The Question of Literary Influence Raised and Resolved," (Reno [Unpublished], n.d.).

§

Sirs:

Once again the *Mediterranean Daily* has engaged in the practice of misplacing blame. If, as the scientific (*wissenschaftlich*) evidence suggests, the very idea of God is nothing but the fulfillment of a wish (*Wunsch*), how can "He" (note the ironic emphasis!) be at fault in this admittedly unfortunate affair? Look to the mariners! Look to the whale!

S. Freud
VIENNA

§

Editor(s):

I have read with some interest the editorial in which you mention the curious phenomenon of a cetacean ingesting a human being. For the record, and apart from any and all political or theological considerations, permit me to make the following points:

1) Conditions inside a so-called "whale," while admittedly far from ideal, are in fact not incompatible with regular human functioning. Normal cetacean temperature approximates that of many land-based mammals and stomach acidity is moderate. True, flatulence is present in a higher degree than in ordinary mammals (witness the "spout"), but it is plausible to assume that, to a man or a woman in a state of extreme sensory deprivation, this condition is not totally unpleasant and may even be a welcome diversion.

2) When a cetacean ingests a large, or even medium-sized, mammal, it often regurgitates that mammal within a relatively short period of time, usually a matter of days.

Assuming, then, that the subject is at least in the median range both longitudinally and latitudinally[64] and is not made of wood,[65] his prognosis must be considered excellent.

Professor Harold Seabody
LAJOLLA, CALIFORNIA, USA

§

Herr Redakteur:

A Message I write concerning your editorial Word of 16 August, in which you seem a Statement to make, that a notorious Higher Being was responsible for the Typhoon that raped the eastern Mediterranean Region the Twilight of 14 August. Although it once was considered that certain Typhoons are to a Primary Cause attributable, current Meteorology declares that such Occurrences are "caused," as if that Expression can any longer be used even, by long-term global Wind Configurations. To determine the Nature of these Wind Configurations with any Correctness is, of course, the most disputed Dilemma that our fastidious Branch of Science faces. Yet the Fact remains, that a vigorous Majority of Meteorologists are convinced that this Dilemma is capable of Solution within the Restrictions of the sovereign Paradigm.

Werner Sturm
FRANKFURT

ED. NOTE: *We await anxiously that Solution.*

---

[64] According to Father Lecher, the author is referring to Jonah's size.
[65] According to Ms. LaFemme, the author is alluding to Pinocchio.

216

§

Dear Editor:

Your editorial leaves the unsuspecting reader with the impression that taking a Mediterranean cruise would be one of the most dangerous activities he or she could ever engage in. This is far from the truth.

We at Philo Cruises are extremely proud of our safety record. Our crew has never thrown a single one of our customers overboard, regardless of his or her theological convictions. In fact, we carefully screen the applicants for jobs on our boats, which insures that our staff is free of religious extremists. Emergency situations such as the storm are always handled with calmness and courtesy, though I hasten to add that in the seventeen years we have been in the business we have had few if any such situations occur, to my knowledge.

Why not give Philo Cruises a chance to prove itself? Call today for a free brochure. . . .

Philo Schiff
CEO, Philo Cruises

ED. NOTE: *Editorial policy prohibits the listing of telephone numbers.*

§

Editor, the *Mediterranean Daily:*

Your recent editorial and the spate of letters it has engendered have, I think, overlooked certain critical facts to which only Mr. Jonah and I are privy. But since you have seen fit to publicize this matter, I am, alas, left with no recourse but to reveal the true state of affairs regarding the originally private dealings.

On August 13 past I requested of Mr. Jonah that he journey to Nineveh, Assyria, for the purpose of crying against her. (I hasten to point out that I was perfectly within my legal rights to make such a request: Mr. Jonah has been an employee of mine for thirteen [13] years and three [3] months, serving first as an apprentice, then as a junior prophet.) I made known my wishes to Mr. Jonah by way of an intra-office memorandum, which, as I am certain my employees will attest, is my preferred way of communicating with them. Mr. Jonah responded with a memorandum of his own, in which he requested the details of the assignment; he wished particularly to know the purpose of the journey. Again, this is standard practice in our office (which is the oldest and, I would modestly hazard, the most venerable, in Jerusalem). My response, again through a memorandum, was that, if I may quote myself, "their [referring specifically to the Ninevites] wickedness is come up before me."

I expected no reply to this final memo, and I received none. Thus I was surprised to find, in routinely checking with our Nineveh embassy the next morning, that Mr. Jonah had not arrived. A further check by my executive secretary revealed that Mr. Jonah had indeed purchased a ticket, not by air, to Nineveh, but by oil tanker, to Tarshish, in Spain, where we do not even have an office!

My immediate suspicion was that Mr. Jonah was acting as a double agent, and that he was in the secret employ of our Tarshish competitors. Thus I instructed a trusted assistant, Miss Drew (we are an equal-opportunity employer), to investigate the matter, naturally advising her to keep her sleuthing within the strict parameters of the law. Miss Drew did so, and came up with certain evidence that confirmed my suspicion. (That evidence is now ensconced in a safe-deposit box, and will remain there until such time as the occasion might call for it to be set forth in a court of law.)

Faced with this incontrovertible evidence, I consulted with the District Attorney to determine what our legal recourse might be. He pointed out to me that the oil tanker *Vengeance* could by that time be well beyond the twelve-mile limit recognized by international law, and was thus beyond Holy Land jurisdiction. I next called Captain Pius Maximus of said ship to ascertain her location, as well as to certify that Mr. Jonah was indeed on board.

The notes of our conversation show that Captain Maximus informed me of the following:

(1) that the ship was indeed outside the twelve-mile limit,

(2) that it had run into a small squall—not, as your editorial inaccurately reported, a major hurricane,

(3) that his crew was currently at vespers, and that

(4) Mr. Jonah was safely asleep in Compartment V.

Captain Maximus then inquired as to my wishes regarding the disposal of Mr. Jonah. I instructed him that when the *Vengeance* reached Tarshish, he should deliver Mr. Jonah into the hands of the port authorities until such time as the extradition papers had been drawn up and properly delivered, and that he should take care not to cause the suspect any physical, emotional, or spiritual distress. *At no time during this conversation did I suggest, request, or order that Captain Maximus jettison, heave overboard, or otherwise dispose of, Mr. Jonah; nor did I prepare a great fish, a whale, or any species of the genus* cetus, *to swallow my formerly-trusted employee. Nor, for that matter, did I send out a tempest, hurricane, or any other great wind, into the sea (as the letter from Herr Sturm attests, storms are brought about, precipitated, or otherwise caused by long-term global wind patterns, not by what he terms a "Primary Cause," by which he apparently means me).*

I am confident that Captain Maximus will certify the accuracy of these claims.

Almighty God
1 East Temple
JERUSALEM

ED. NOTE: *We sincerely regret any errors we may have made in commenting on these events.*

§

E<small>DITOR</small>, THE *M<small>EDITERRANEAN</small> D<small>AILY</small>:*

The gentleman is absolutely right, he didn't tell me to throw anybody in the sea, and even if he had, I wouldn't have done it, being law-abiding. And even if I would have done it, the guy would have deserved it, from what I know about him by his reputation as a troublemaker. Besides, what would've been so bad about *that,* because like the American professor said, the whale's probably chucked him up by now, and he got a free ride anyway.

What really happened was, the guy just plain up and jumped overboard. We thought he was going swimming.

Pius Maximus, Captain
H.M.S. *Vengeance*

§

To the Editor:

I note that in a recent letter, a well-known Higher Power has impugned the name and reputation of our fair city.

Let me just point out that Nineveh has recently been ranked #13 out of 107 cities by Rand McNally in their *Places Rated Retirement Guide to the Ancient Middle East.* They especially noted our all-season climate (#17), affordable housing (#6), availability of part-time jobs (#18), moderate health-care costs (#25), and leisure living facilities (#2).[66] Had it not been for our crime rate—and we have a special task force working to cut down on the hashish trade—we almost certainly would have been one of the top five communities, in terms of senior-citizen livability.

If this is "wickedness," maybe we should all go to hell!

His Honor Assurbanipal, Mayor
NINEVEH, ASSYRIA

---

[66]Professor Allbright was quick to point out that Ninevah had an extensive cuneiform library.

§

EDITOR:
GOD'S RIGHT STOP IT'S BETWEEN HIM AND ME STOP IT'S
ALL BEEN STRAIGHTENED OUT STOP

JONAH
EN ROUTE TO NINEVEH

9 | The Big Man in the Middle

THE TALE OF BRAVE YOUNG DAVID *challenging the giant Goliath is one of the most celebrated stories in the entire orthodox Bible. It is popular with lovers of the underdog, with those who delight in gargantuan challenges, and with the generals of small armies. It is especially well-received by short persons.*

Recall the circumstances of the conflict, as described in I Samuel 17: Philistines and Israelites drawn up for combat; Goliath loudly challenging any man of Israel to personal combat; every man of Israel cowering before the massive bully. Then onto the field of battle wanders innocent David, whose father Jesse had interrupted his lowly work as a shepherd and instructed him to carry food to his older brothers at the front. Upon his arrival, David hears Goliath's boastful challenge, accepts it, and goes forth to meet the heavily-armed giant, dressed in the simple garb of a shepherd boy and carrying only a sling and five stones. The two antagonists exchange insults and threats. Then little David flings a single rock, which strikes the giant on the forehead, killing him instantly. The triumphant youth strides over to the fallen foe, straddles him, and cuts off Goliath's head with his own sword. The remaining Philistines escape, pursued by the newly-emboldened Israelite army. David, now a hero, carries the ogre's head to Jerusalem and presents it to King Saul as a trophy.

Despite its undeniable human appeal, one senses that this later but simplified version lacks something. Is it drama? Of course not. Is it conflict? Impossible. Is it morality? No; virtue wins out in the end. What is missing from the orthodox story is a sense of presence: a sense of excitement, of immediacy, of being there. It is just this sense that pervades the original story, "The Big Man in the Middle."[67]

§

ABNER: THIS IS IT. The seventh and deciding game of the Ancient Middle East Basketball Association Championship Series. Who's going to come away the winner? The eleven-time defending champion Gath Philistines, coached by Genghis Khan, Jr., or the upstart Jerusalem Godfearers, coached by King Saul? I'm Abner, son of Ner, here with my colleague Joel, son of Samuel, who's with me to provide commentary on tonight's crucial game.

JOEL: Listen to that crowd, Ab.

ABNER: There's no tomorrow, and they know it.

JOEL: Do they ever.

ABNER: Joel, what can we expect from the Philistines tonight?

JOEL: Ab, the Philistines like to go to their man in the middle. If you want to stop the defending champions, you've got to find some way to neutralize Goliath. He's the heart and soul of this team. Their bread and butter. The one who got them here. Their go-to guy. The Godfearers have had difficulty in stopping the big man, especially in the first three games, which went to the Philistines by the scores of 300-0, 301-0, and 302-0. Of course he's not the only weapon Coach Khan has in his well-stocked arsenal. Ashdad can also crash the offensive boards, as can Gaza. Ashkelon isn't afraid to mix it up in there, either. Ekron's is more of a finesse game. He's the guy they rely on to run the offense, also the one they go to when they need a bomb from downtown.

ABNER: The Godfearers. What do they have to do to be successful tonight?

JOEL: The big story here is David. Didn't play in the first three games, because as everyone is well aware by now he was not considered by the Godfearer brain trust to be quite ready for the big time. He was languishing in the farm system, herding sheep. But the moment Coach Saul inserted him into the lineup in the last quarter of Game Four, the Godfearers became another team.

---

[67]Closed caption.

The young man, just turned fourteen, was suddenly their inspirational leader, scoring 303 straight points to take the game into overtime, and then of course going on to lead his teammates to eventual victory.

ABNER: What about his supporting cast?

JOEL: To be quite honest, the other Godfearers have had difficulty matching up with the likes of Ashdad, Ashkelon, Gaza, and Ekron.

ABNER: Let me ask you this, Joel. What's been their major problem, and what steps has Coach Saul taken to counteract it?

JOEL: They've been a little weak in the three C's: concentration, chemistry, and courage. The Philistines have been running up and down the court unchallenged, scoring practically at will. But Coach Saul has had a long talk with his team, so it's highly unlikely we'll continue to see things like Chico standing around taking snapshots of Goliath's mammoth dunks, Zeppo turning cartwheels and leading cheers for the opposition, Harpo scurrying up and down the aisles selling popcorn, or Groucho strolling the sidelines and rolling his eyeballs to impress the ladies[68] in the crowd.

ABNER: In summary, Joel, what can we expect tonight, in this, the seventh and deciding game of the AMEBA Championship Series?

JOEL: What it all boils down to, Ab, is a battle between Goliath, everybody's Most Valuable Terrorist eleven years running, and the unheralded David, whom even the aficionados of the hardwood sport didn't know existed until Coach Saul inserted him into the lineup for Gummo but who in just the last week, because of his continuously astounding heroics, has become the toast of this town.

ABNER: Speaking of Gummo, what's the injury report, and can we expect to see anything of him tonight?

JOEL: It doesn't look good, Ab. Just this afternoon I discussed the matter with Dr. Luke, the Godfearers' team physician, who took pains to point out that spear wounds take a long time to

---

[68] There was some good-natured banter between Father Lecher and Ms. LaFemme concerning the accuracy of this translation.

heal, especially when the heart is penetrated. In fact, Gummo is not even dressed for the game. So I would not expect to see much of him tonight, unless as rumor has it his extraordinary talents are used in the singing of Our National Anthem.

ABNER: So the whole season comes down to this, ladies and gentlemen. The seventh and deciding game of the AMEBA Championship Series. We'll be back for the introduction of the starting lineups right after this.

§

ABNER: ABNER, SON OF NER, back with you. Now, let's go down to courtside for the introduction of tonight's starting lineups.

ANNOUNCER: Ladies. And. Gentlemen. Your attention. Please. The starting lineups. For tonight's game. For the visiting Philistines. At point guard. Standing just a little over seven foot six. From the University of Socah. Ek . . . ran. At the two guard. Standing eight foot three. From Azekah State. Ash . . . ke . . . lan. At small forward. Standing an even nine foot. From Ephesdammim Tech. Ash . . . dad. At power forward. Standing nine foot four. From Elah Community College. Ga . . . za. And. At center. Standing nine foot nine and a quarter. From the San Quentin Correctional Facility. The big man. In the middle. Go . . . li . . . ath.

ABNER: The hometown fans showing their disapproval.

JOEL: Over the years this has been one of the great rivalries.

ANNOUNCER: Aaaannnd now. For your very own. Jerusalem. Godfearers. At center. Standing five foot nine. The lead romantic role in *Monkey Business*. Zep . . . po Marrrxxx! . . . At small forward. Standing five foot seven and an eighth. The peanut vendor in *Duck Soup*. Chi . . . co Marrrxxx! . . . At tiny forward. Standing just five foot five. The winning jockey in *A Day at the Races*. Har . . . po Marrrxxx! . . . At off guard. Standing five foot something. You loved the way he captured hearts in *A Night at the Opera*. Grou . . . cho Marrrxxx! . . . And. At point guard. Standing just a shade under four foot six. Author of "The Twenty-Third Psalm" and *An Introduction to Animal Husbandry*. Da . . . vid, son of Jes . . . se!

ABNER: Just listen to that crowd. Have you ever heard anything like it, Joel?

JOEL: Never, Ab. Pandemonium has broken loose.

ABNER: Not an empty seat in the house.

JOEL: You couldn't beg, borrow, or steal a ticket.

ABNER: The crowd senses a victory.

JOEL: They've been waiting a long time for this occasion.

ABNER: They're pinning their hopes on little David.

JOEL: Little, yes, but only in terms of stature. In terms of heart, he's a giant.

ABNER: This young man gives you sooooo many things. Scoring. Quickness.

JOEL: Ball-handling ability.

ABNER: A truly multidimensional player.

JOEL: His only negatives are size and inexperience.

ABNER: Which he makes up for with a tremendous work ethic.

JOEL: He's the spiritual leader of this club.

ABNER: Charismatic is the word that comes to mind.

JOEL: Jerusalem has become in a sense his town.

ABNER: And now, this.

§

ABNER: REFEREES FOR TONIGHT'S GAME are Shadrach and Meshach. The official scorer is Abednego. We're ready to begin. Goliath and Chico to jump it up. Tip goes to the Philistines. Ekron controls. Waits for Goliath to post up Chico. Lobs a pass into the big guy, who puts it down. Tonight, as every night, Arnold's Goat Milk[69] will donate 100 shekels for each and every slam dunk, to the Pituitary Research Division of the Ancient

---

[69]Compare with Scroll #3, "The First Entrepreneur," where Elsie's friend Arnold offers her a glass of goat milk. As Professor Allbright astutely pointed out in his 437-page monograph, "Arnold I, Arnold II, and the Problem of the Lactic/Capra Connection: A Solution," (Reno [Unpublished], n.d.), Elsie's Arnold is very probably a distant ancestor of this philanthropic Arnold.

Israelite Medical Society.[70] Your analysis, Joel.

JOEL: Coach Khan has to be pleased with what he's seen so far.

ABNER: Now the Godfearers quickly up court. Here's David for three. Nothing but fishnet. Listen to that ovation as the home team takes an early 3-2 lead.

JOEL: The crowd is enjoying every minute.

ABNER: Ekron controlling. Waits for Goliath to post up Chico. Hits him with a lob pass. The big guy puts it down.

JOEL: Two slams so far.

ABNER: Already two hundred shekels for AIMS. Joel?

JOEL: I sense another big night for pituitary research.

ABNER: Godfearers quickly up court. David for a three. Yessss.

JOEL: Now they're saying his right foot was on the line.

ABNER: Here's another look on the replay.

JOEL: Could have gone either way.

ABNER: I don't know.

JOEL: The referee was right there.

ABNER: Now Ekron up court. Taking his sweet time. Goliath sets up, guarded by Chico. Lob. Another slam for the big guy.

JOEL: I sure hope Arnold's been selling lots of goat milk lately.

ABNER: Now Chico calls a 20-second timeout.

JOEL: Coach Saul wants to talk things over. He doesn't like the way things are going. He may sense that Chico is overmatched.

ABNER: Let's talk about that, Joel. Don't you think the God-fearers have got to find a way to stop the big guy?

JOEL: I discussed this with Coach Saul before the game. Here's what he had to say.

JOEL: Coach, what are your plans for stopping Goliath, everybody's Most Valuable Terrorist for the last eleven years?

COACH SAUL: You can't stop a guy like Goliath. There's no way. You've got to figure he'll get his points. All you can really do is, you can try to minimize the impact of his supporting cast.

JOEL: Any plans for putting David on the big man, the strategy that worked so well in Game Four?

COACH SAUL: Well, you can only go to the well so often. The

---

[70] In the view of Cardinal Micromentis, this reference is yet more evidence of the advanced technology enjoyed by the ancient Ur-Hebrews.

reason that strategy worked so well in Game Four was the element of surprise.

JOEL: Thanks, Coach.

ABNER: That was Coach Saul before the game, discussing the problem of stopping Goliath. Joel, your analysis.

JOEL: I really feel in spite of what Coach Saul says that somewhere along the line they've got to put David on the big guy. You've got to go with what works, that's a cardinal rule in this game of basketball, and putting David on Goliath worked so very very well in the crucial Game Four, the game that turned this entire series around.

ABNER: Let's see what happens. David at the top of the key. Shoots. A three.

JOEL: Listen to this crowd.

ABNER: Godfearers back on top, 8-6.

JOEL: This is going to be a see-saw battle all the way.

ABNER: Ekron controls. Goliath posts up David. Coach Saul has made a prophet of you, Joel. The smaller David is now guarding the big man. A lob over David's head. Jam.

JOEL: David was hanging all over him.

ABNER: Apparently the refs didn't see it that way.

JOEL: They're letting 'em play. The seventh and deciding game in this crucial series, and they're letting 'em play. That's as it should be in a game of this importance.

ABNER: All tied up at eight apiece. Now David with the ball. A whistle. They're calling an illegal defense. That's only the first illegal defense, so the Godfearers get the ball out of bounds. Joel, explain for us, if you will, the rule on illegal defense.

JOEL: The rule on illegal defense is very clear. If you brandish a spear, they're going to call you for it every time. In this case, as you can see on the replay, the big man was clearly brandishing his spear. There's Goliath. There's his spear. A clearcut case of brandishment.

ABNER: In other words, it's okay to carry a spear, you just can't brandish it.

JOEL: That's the major difference. They're trying to put a stop to the sort of thing that happened in the crucial fourth game, when things got out of hand and Gummo received that severe spear wound, unintentional of course, which put him out of commission for the remainder of this championship series.

ABNER: Back to the action. Now here's Harpo in a surprise move, heading over to the stands. He's starting to sell popcorn again.

JOEL: Apparently that sword-brandishing incident did not go unnoticed.

ABNER: David looks for Harpo, can't find him, drives the lane and draws the foul. That's number one on Goliath. Joel, why would David do that? Why would he venture into the enemy's bastion of strength when he's been three for three from downtown for a total of eight?

JOEL: Number one, he's sending a message. He's saying I will not be intimidated. Intimidation is the name of the game as far as the Philistines are concerned, and by driving the lane young David is saying he will not be intimidated.

ABNER: David hits the first of two from the charity stripe.

JOEL: He's also, number two, providing much-needed leadership. He's showing his teammates that the way to beat the Philistines is not to run off into the stands and sell popcorn, the way to beat them is to show them that you are incapable of being intimidated.

ABNER: David hits the second as well. Godfearers up 10-8 with a little over eleven minutes to go in the first period.

JOEL: Time is not yet a factor in this contest.

ABNER: A whistle. Oh oh. This time it's a technical. Appears to be on David.

JOEL: They're calling it unsportsmanlike conduct.

ABNER: David is very, very unhappy about that call, and he's showing it. He's got to be careful or he may be gone for good. The Godfearers can ill afford to lose a boy of his stature. Joel, your comment.

JOEL: Ab, what you had there was just a little trash talk. The refs want to put a stop to it right here and now. They don't want to let things get out of hand, as they did in Games Five and Six.

ABNER: Joel, what's going on between the two men? The veteran of eleven years and the young phenom upstart with a world of potential?

JOEL: Ab, I talked to David about that subject before the game. I asked him if it was just a part of the game, all the trash talk, or whether there was indeed something of a personal nature going on between him and his taller rival. Here's what he had to say.

JOEL: David, there's all the trash talk. Is there something personal going on between you and Goliath, something the fans might want to know about? Or is it all just part of the game?

DAVID: It's all part of the game. He says something, then I say something. It goes back and forth like that. It's nothing personal. It's part of the game.

JOEL: *The Jerusalem Witness* reports that you've been giving him the needle on the subject of circumcision.

DAVID: It's nothing personal. It's a matter of hygiene. I just happen to believe that all male children under a certain age, and I don't want to be too legalistic about the exact age, should be circumcised, as a matter of hygiene.

JOEL: So it's not a religious thing with you.

DAVID: Not at all. It's a matter of hygiene, pure and simple.

JOEL: Glad to clear that up.

DAVID: Glad for the chance to clear it up.

JOEL: Thanks, David.

ABNER: Fascinating interview, Joel. This young man is so well spoken. He's a credit to his team, to the entire community, to the AMEBA, and to his father Jesse, who incidentally is here in the stands to cheer his son on—there he is in the middle of your screen, the man with the wide smile. Incidentally, Goliath missed the technical foul shot while we were away hearing David's explanation of their, shall we say, friendly rivalry. Now Chico steals the ball on the inbound pass. Over to David. David slows it down, waits for his team to set up. Harpo now back on the court, returning from his stint as a vendor. Apparently, and I say apparently, he's been heartened by his teammate David's refusal to be intimidated by the rough stuff under the boards. Now here's David from twenty. Rejected by Goliath.

JOEL: They're calling it goal-tending. They're saying the ball was on its downward arc.

ABNER: Here's another look.

JOEL: I don't know about that call.

ABNER: We'll let the viewers at home decide.

JOEL: The officiating in this series has been excellent overall.

ABNER: Timeout, Philistines. They're down by four, 12-8, and Coach Khan wants to stop to talk things over with his team.

JOEL: He doesn't want to let things get out of hand, as they did in Games Five and Six.

ABNER: He remembers all too well. While there's a timeout on the court, we go to this.

§

ABNER: JOEL HAD A CHANCE to talk to Junior Khan before the game about his plans for stopping, or at least neutralizing, David. This is what he had to say.

JOEL: Coach Khan, what are your plans for stopping or at least neutralizing David, the young man who has materialized out of nowhere to become the inspirational leader of the Godfearers?

COACH KHAN: You can't really stop a guy with the talent of a David. There's no way. You've got to figure he'll get his points. All you can really do is, you can try to minimize the impact of his supporting cast.

JOEL: Any plans for putting Goliath on him, the strategy that worked so well in the fourth quarter of Games Five and Six?

COACH KHAN: Well, you can go to the well only so often. The reason that strategy worked so well back then was the element of intimidation. But the young man seems to be adjusting. He's quickly learning that if you're going to be successful in this AMEBA Championship Series, you've got to show a total dis-regard for your own personal safety and just go ahead and mix it up with the big boys in the war zone. He knows there's no tomor-row, that you have all summer to recover from your wounds.

JOEL: Thanks, Coach.

ABNER: That was Coach Khan of the Philistines, discussing the matter of his plans to defend the small but crafty, charismatic David. Joel, your analysis.

JOEL: I really think that somewhere along the line they've got to put Goliath on the little guy. You've got to go with what works, and putting Goliath on David worked so very well in the final moments of both Games Five and Six, when it was too late.

ABNER: What about foul trouble? You don't want to jeopardize your big man, your go-to guy, by putting him in foul trouble, do you?

JOEL: I don't really see that Coach Khan has much of a choice in the matter. Sooner or later he's got to bite the sword and put the giant on the boy.

ABNER: We'll see. Back to the action. Ekran brings the ball up-court. Waits for Goliath to set up. Goliath now being guarded by Harpo. Apparently Coach Saul had a strategy session of his own and has decided to try Harpo on Goliath. Your analysis of that move, Joel, covering the big man with a much smaller Harpo.

JOEL: Ab, apparently Coach Saul has decided that if Harpo can be successful selling popcorn to the fans, he can also be successful handling Goliath one on one. We'll see how astute that reasoning turns out to be.

ABNER: Goliath with another jam. A whistle on the play. Foul on Harpo, his first. Which gives Goliath a golden opportunity to complete a three-point play. As you can see on this rerun, Harpo is hounding the big guy.

JOEL: Seems to be inspecting the big guy's underwear.

ABNER: He does appear to be peeking, doesn't he.

JOEL: You're not allowed to do that.

ABNER: They'll call it every time.

JOEL: Ab, I just don't see the Harpo-Goliath matchup. If I were Coach Saul, I'd send Harpo back to the popcorn enterprise. You go with what's been successful in the past, and Harpo has had much more success in selling popcorn than in covering the big man. He does not match up well. Has to resort to questionable tactics, tactics that can get him into early foul trouble and provide an early exit from the game. The Godfearers cannot afford to lose a man like Harpo, with the special talents he brings to this game of basketball.

ABNER: Goliath at the charity stripe. Throws up an air ball. The fans are chanting air ball, air ball. Philistines remain down by two with just two minutes gone in the first period. Now the Philistines, surprisingly, take another timeout. Apparently Harpo's harassment has shaken up the big man, has gotten to him, and

Coach Khan wants to spend a precious timeout to give him a chance to cool off. Your analysis, Joel.

JOEL: Goliath is visibly upset by Harpo's tactics, Ab, which he may have misunderstood. Those who know Harpo, and know him well, know that it was nothing personal. Probably all Harpo was doing was attempting to check out the hygiene story, see whether the big man is or is not circumcised.

ABNER: Back after this message.

§

ABNER: SOME FAMILIAR FACES at courtside, as the camera pans around. Malachi, star of this network's long-running afternoon drama, *The Tall and the Lonely,* with several very attractive lady friends. Joshua, former Godfearer great, now in the AMEBA Hall of Fame, always a great favorite here at Temple Square Garden, accompanied by various members of his harem. That's Rabbi Hillel, waving to us, obviously enjoying the action with his wife Ruth and their twelve sons and four lovely daughters. And of course, sitting there in his box high above the court, the owner and general manager of the Jerusalem Godfearers, God himself, very knowledgeable about this game of basketball, never missing a chance to see his team when they are in town, with his wife Ernestine next to him.

JOEL: A delightful couple.

ABNER: While we were away our own everpresent Abigail, wife of Nabal the Calebite,[71] had a chance to talk with God and his better half, get their reactions to the game and how it's gone so far.

ABIGAIL: Are you enjoying the game, Ernestine, wife of God?

ERNESTINE: I haven't been paying much attention, truthfully. I've been reading a novel.

ABIGAIL: Let's see, that would be.

ERNESTINE: *The Source.*

ABIGAIL: Oh yes, the bestseller. Is it as good as they say it is?

---

[71] According to the orthodox Bible (I Samuel 25), as well as to Scroll #10, Abigail, wife of the churlish Nabal, later became one of David's wives.

ERNESTINE: I'm only in the first chapter, but it promises to be as engrossing as *Exodus*. Maybe even *The Chosen*.

ABIGAIL: What about you, Sir? Are you enjoying the game?

GOD: Immensely.

ABIGAIL: Any surprises?

GOD: Not really.

ABIGAIL: Aren't you maybe a little disappointed by Groucho's performance so far? The fact that we haven't really heard much from him up until now?

GOD: We're in some very difficult contract negotiations with Groucho. That's all I wish to say at this particular time.

ABIGAIL: What about Harpo? Aren't you surprised that Harpo has apparently ignored Coach Saul's, King Saul's, directives and has gone back to selling popcorn?

GOD: I think Harpo's doing just fine.

ABIGAIL: One final question. Any predictions as to the final score of this game?

GOD: I'm really not in the business of making predictions. I leave that to the prophets. I will venture the opinion, however, that Godfearer fans will be pleased by the ultimate outcome.

ABIGAIL: Thank you, Sir.

GOD: Thank you, Abigail. I enjoyed talking to you.

ABIGAIL: My pleasure.

ABNER: So there you have it, Joel. Abigail's interview, first with Ernestine, then with the owner and general manager of the Godfearers, God himself. Your comments?

JOEL: Interesting to note that Abigail ranked *The Chosen* above *Exodus*. I myself thought *Exodus* had a better ending.

ABNER: What about God's remarks? Did you find anything interesting in them?

JOEL: I was intrigued by the mention of Groucho's name. The reference to contract negotiations might just shed some light on why Groucho has not been a factor in this game. You'll notice that while Groucho has indeed been strolling the sidelines, he has not been rolling his eyeballs at the ladies to the extent that he did in the previous games.

ABNER: Perhaps it's an ophthalmological problem. That's speculation, of course. We'll try to have Abigail talk to him about this matter as the game progresses. Get the real story on the immobile eyeballs.

JOEL: Whatever the reason, the fact remains that Groucho has not been a factor in this ball game. Chico has been a factor, Harpo has been a factor, and of course David has been a factor. But Groucho has simply not been a factor.

ABNER: Neither has Zeppo.

JOEL: Nor, on the other side of the court, have Ashdad, Gaza, and Ashkelon. Now, getting back to the God interview. You'll notice that he seemed pleased with Harpo's performance so far.

ABNER: Your interpretation?

JOEL: I'd venture to say that Harpo's sideline activity will gross the Godfearer organization somewhere in the neighborhood of, oh, 5,000 giant-size buckets of popcorn by the end of the game.

ABNER: Have you seen the latest figures?

JOEL: No I have not. That's simply a guess. But getting back once more to the interview. Another intriguing comment God made was that Godfearer fans will be pleased by the ultimate outcome.

ABNER: Do you think, Joel, that maybe he knows something the rest of us don't?

JOEL: I thought I noticed a twinkle in his eye.

ABNER: On that note, an official timeout.

§

ABNER: BACK TO THE ACTION as the teams return to the floor. Godfearers' ball. David upcourt in the uptempo fashion he brings to this ball club. Flips the ball to Zeppo, who fumbles it out of bounds.

JOEL: Zeppo has suddenly become a factor in this ball game.

ABNER: Ekron across the center line. Takes his time. Waits for Goliath to post up Harpo. Lobs the ball in to Goliath. Thunderous slam. Score all knotted up at an even dozen. Joel, I notice that Goliath has changed uniforms. He now appears to be wearing a coat of mail, plus greaves and targets of brass, topped off with a large helmet, also of brass. What do league rules have to say about this matter of unusual uniforms?

JOEL: Ab, league rules do not specifically prohibit the wearing of either greaves or targets of brass. As for the coats of mail and helmets of brass, that's left up to the judgment of the officials. The officials in this contest apparently feel that Goliath is merely protecting himself against the harassment we saw demonstrated by Harpo just a few moments ago.

ABNER: As you were speaking, Joel, the Godfearers chose to take another timeout.

JOEL: Coach Saul does not like what he is seeing. He's disturbed by the change of uniform.

ABNER: Now he's arguing with the referees. He's talking with Shadrach in a very animated fashion. Meshach is walking away.

JOEL: King Saul has to be careful, or he'll draw a technical.

ABNER: In the meantime, Abigail is down on the sidelines with Groucho. It's yours, Abigail.

ABIGAIL: Groucho, I talked earlier with God, and he mentioned the fact that the two of you were in the midst of some very difficult contract negotiations. I'm wondering if you have anything to say on this subject.

GROUCHO: Difficult, did he say?

ABIGAIL: I believe that was the word he used.

GROUCHO: God is a pussy cat.

ABIGAIL: So you would not characterize your contract negotiations with God as difficult?

GROUCHO: The only difficult part is when he tries to imitate the way I roll my eyes.

ABIGAIL: Thanks, Groucho.

GROUCHO: Thanks, sweetheart. Say, do you still run around with that churl Nabal the Calebite, evil in his doings?

ABNER: That was Abigail, discussing the matter of contract negotiations with Groucho, getting his take on things. Meanwhile, King Saul has just been hit with a couple of technicals and has been ejected from this game. As you can see, he's being escorted from the arena by an armed guard. Zeppo is turning cartwheels and leading the crowd in cheers. Joel, he does that so very very well.

JOEL: As well as anybody in the game.

ABNER: What's going to happen next, Joel? What's your expert commentary on this situation? Who will replace King Saul as coach of the Godfearers for the remainder of this, the seventh and deciding game of the AMEBA Championship Series?

JOEL: Under ordinary circumstances, Ab, it would be the captain, who in this case is Groucho. But Groucho, as we've been suggesting, has not been a factor in this game. Besides, he is in the midst of contract negotiations with God, which, despite his apparent disclaimer to the contrary, are in a very difficult stage, at least as reported in the press. Bear in mind that, number one, Zeppo knows this. He also knows, number two, that he is the alternate captain of the Godfearers and is thus third in command on this ballclub. And number three, he knows that he has recently become a factor in this game. Thus he fully expects to take over for the ejected Coach Saul. This in my opinion explains why he is turning cartwheels.

ABNER: Fine in-depth analysis, Joel. Now, could you further explain why God is now making his way down from his lofty perch, is proceeding toward the Godfearer bench, is being greeted by a standing ovation, and is smiling and waving his right hand in acknowledgment?

JOEL: There's a perfectly logical explanation for this. God is taking this opportunity to replace King Saul as coach of his own team, the Godfearers. Something he's always wanted to do.

ABNER: So what you're saying is, Zeppo was premature in his cartwheel exhibition?

JOEL: Exactly my point.

ABNER: There's a timeout on the floor as God gathers his players around him for a strategy session.

§

ABNER: WE'RE BACK, and here's Goliath at the line to shoot the two technicals. The crowd at that end of the court is waving tiny plastic surgical knives at the big man. All in good fun, of course.

JOEL: A way of reminding him of his hygienic disadvantage.

ABNER: Shoots the first. Ball bounces around, rolls off the rim. If he makes the second, the Philistines go up by one.

JOEL: The first critical point in this ball game.

ABNER: Goliath shoots the second. Misses the backboard completely, and the ball sails into the crowd.

JOEL: A souvenir for some lucky fan.

ABNER: Officials call a timeout. Why would they do that, Joel? Why would the officials call time when we had a timeout only seconds ago?

JOEL: Ab, basketball is a very difficult game to officiate even under the best of circumstances. And without a ball for the players to handle, dribble, shoot, fumble, and so forth, the game becomes practically impossible to officiate. This is why the officials have just called another timeout. They're going into the stands to retrieve the ball.

ABNER: They seem to be having a difficult time locating it. Your analysis, Joel.

JOEL: It appears that the lucky fan who caught the ball has run off with it.

ABNER: While the referees, Shadrach and Meshach, pursue the fan who has disappeared with the basketball, let's take a timeout of our own.

§

ABNER: THE REFEREES in tonight's game, Shadrach and Meshach, together with the two opposing coaches, Junior Khan and God, are huddled around Abednego's scorer's table. They seem to be discussing something. What do you think they might be talking about, Joel?

JOEL: I can't read lips, but my guess would be that they're discussing the case of the missing basketball. They're probably trying to decide what to do in the event the lucky fan who caught the ball Goliath hurled into the stands does not return.

ABNER: This is highly unusual. Have you ever seen anything like it, Joel?

JOEL: In all my years of basketball, first as a mascot, then as a player, then as a coach, and now as an expert commentator, I can honestly say, Ab, that I have never seen anything even remotely resembling this set of circumstances.

ABNER: Speaking of this highly unusual set of circumstances, what are the options faced by the referees and the two opposing coaches? Could you go through them with us, Joel, one by one?

JOEL: This is the way I see it. Number one, they could recapture the basketball.

ABNER: Wouldn't they first have to catch the fan?

JOEL: That is the tricky point. Once a fan has disappeared through this tumultuous Garden throng with a stolen object, such as a basketball, it's practically impossible to locate him or her without calling out the National Guard.

ABNER: Which the government does not have.

JOEL: Correct. Number two, they could call it a 12-12 draw and send everyone home semi-happy.

ABNER: Which would be like kissing your grandmother.

JOEL: There's so much at stake in this contest. Bragging rights. The championship trophy. The opportunity to spend an entire year feeling good about yourself.

ABNER: Plus political control of the Holy Land. Let's not forget that.

JOEL: Exactly. Number three, they could elect to make another basketball.

ABNER: Which would take time.

JOEL: Time the officials do not feel they have.

ABNER: I see your point.

JOEL: Manufacturing a basketball is a complex process.

ABNER: Could you just describe that process for us, Joel?

JOEL: It's actually quite simple. First you have to sacrifice a goat.

ABNER: A he-goat?

JOEL: A she-goat, if I am not mistaken.

ABNER: Then what?

JOEL: Then they have to surgically remove the udder, excise the teats, sew the whole thing up—

ABNER: In other words, perform an operation that only a qualified veterinarian could fully appreciate.

JOEL: Actually, it's a fascinating procedure. I've seen it done and could describe it in detail.

ABNER: That won't be necessary, Joel. Briefly, then, what you're saying is that the third option consists of one, finding a licensed priest and qualified veterinarian who are acceptable to both parties, two, locating a she-goat, or, as many of us were taught to call them, a nanny goat, three, sacrificing that nanny goat, and four, performing a delicate operation.

JOEL: Right.

ABNER: Which would take time.

JOEL: Time the officials do not feel they have.

ABNER: It might also be taken as an affront to our sponsor.

JOEL: Arnold's Goat Milk, which donates one hundred shekels, in the name of any player who slam dunks, to the Pituitary Research Division of the Ancient Israelite Medical Society.

ABNER: Are those the only three options?

JOEL: In my judgment, yes.

ABNER: Hold it right there. Abednego is asking for crowd quiet. Why is he doing this, Joel?

JOEL: I believe he's getting ready to announce the decision.

ABNER: Don't go away. We'll be back right after this message.

§

ABNER: GOLIATH AT MIDCOURT, still dressed in his coat of mail, plus greaves and targets of brass, topped off with a large brass helmet. He's brandishing his spear. Your analysis, Joel.

JOEL: The officials, with the blessings of the opposing coaches, have opted to waive the rule on illegal defense and have decided to let the two protagonists go one on one, decide this thing once and for all.

ABNER: Little David, now dressed in a rustic shepherd's costume and with a small holstered switchblade in his pocket, approaches, swinging a sling, key-chain fashion. What do you suppose could be in that sling, Joel?

JOEL: I can't be sure, Ab. It looks like a smooth stone.

ABNER: They're speaking to each other. What are they saying, Joel?

JOEL: More trash talk, Ab.

ABNER: Meanwhile, Goliath continues to brandish his spear. David still approaching, still swinging his sling. Now he stops, lets the smooth stone fly. It hits Goliath on the forehead. The big man goes down like ten talents of brick.

JOEL: It could be serious.

ABNER: David continues to approach, this time with more confidence. Draws his switchblade.

JOEL: If you have children at home watching, this might be a good time to send them to their thoughts and prayers.

ABNER: This is not a pretty sight.

JOEL: Just listen to that crowd.

ABNER: Have you ever heard anything like it, Joel?

JOEL: Never, Ab. Pandemonium has broken loose.

ABNER: They've been waiting a long time for this occasion.

JOEL: They pinned their hopes on little David, who came through in a big way.

ABNER: Little, yes, but only in terms of stature. In terms of heart, he's the one who's the giant.

JOEL: This young man gives you so many things. Scoring. Quickness. Ball-handling ability.

ABNER: Accuracy with a sling.

JOEL: The cool workmanlike expertise of a butcher.

ABNER: His only negatives are size and inexperience.

JOEL: He's truly the spiritual leader of this club.

ABNER: Charismatic is the word that comes to mind.

JOEL: Jerusalem has become his town.

ABNER: God has to be extremely pleased with what he's seen so far.

JOEL: The remaining members of the Gath Philistines have fled into the night.

ABNER: And now, this.

§

ABNER: INSIDE the Godfearers' locker room. Everyone congratulating everyone else. That's Zeppo there, pouring champagne on Chico. Chico pouring champagne on Harpo. Harpo pouring the bubbly stuff on Groucho. Now Groucho pouring it on God. Ernestine sitting in the corner, engrossed in her novel. The Commissioner of the AMEBA calling David over for the trophy presentation. David has exchanged his shepherd's costume for a towel. Let's listen to their conversation.

COMMISSIONER: Congratulations, young man. You've just been voted MVP of this entire championship series.

ABNER: As you can see, the Commissioner has just presented David with the Most Valuable Predator award. You might also notice that the trophy this year consists of Goliath's head. In case the Godfearer fans at home are concerned, I understand it will eventually be bronzed, in accordance with the local health code. There's David raising it aloft, triumphantly.

DAVID: Thank you, Commissioner. I couldn't have done it without my supporting cast. I'd like to thank. . . .

ABNER: Young David is now thanking his teammates, including Zeppo, Chico, Harpo, Groucho, Gummo—we can't forget Gummo, can we, without whose spear wound this come-from-behind finish would not have been possible.

DAVID: I'd also like to thank my father, Jesse.

ABNER: That's David's father Jesse, standing there with an expensive panatela between his teeth, holding an index finger aloft, indicating that the Godfearers are now Number One.

DAVID: Last but not least, I'd like to thank God, who had enough faith in me and my talents to bring me up from the farm system for the last four games of this crucial championship series. Besides being a generous owner and an astute coach, he's been like a second father to me.

ABNER: There's our very own Abigail, wife of Nabal the Calebite, trying to get close to David, have a few words with him. Abigail, could you just ask our young hero how he's feeling at this particular moment in time?

ABIGAIL: David. David.

DAVID: Yes, Abigail, wife of Nabal the Calebite?

ABIGAIL: And how is our young hero feeling at this particular moment in time?

DAVID: Just great. Great, great, great.

ABNER: Abigail, ask him about Goliath's body. What does he plan to do with Goliath's body, after the incident of the severed head?

ABIGAIL: David, what do you plan to do with Goliath's body?

DAVID: I thought I'd feed his carcass unto the fowls of the air, and unto the wild beasts of the earth.[72]

ABNER: The young man is so well-spoken. One of his many many talents, including of course kindness to birds and animals. All in all, a real credit to the game of basketball, as well as to the entire Godfearers organization. Abigail, ask him about his plans for the future.

ABIGAIL: David, what are your plans for the future?

DAVID: Right now I plan to take a shower. Wash the blood off.

ABNER: There's David, heading toward the shower, rolling his eyeballs, now being followed by Abigail, wife of the churlish Nabal. Joel should have made his way down there by now. Ah. There he is. Joel, can you hear me through the pandemonium?

JOEL: I hear you, Abner.

ABNER: Could you get hold of God for a moment, ask him a few questions?

JOEL: God? Sir?

GOD: Yes Joel, son of Samuel?

JOEL: A few words, please.

GOD: Yes.

JOEL: Earlier you ventured the opinion that Godfearer fans would be pleased by the ultimate outcome.

GOD: Yes.

JOEL: Is this what you had in mind?

GOD: Exactly.

JOEL: You mean you fully expected that King Saul would draw two technicals, be thrown out of the game, that you would replace him, that Goliath would hurl the basketball into the crowd, that a lucky fan would run off with it, that you would all gather around the scorer's table and finally decide to settle the matter once and for all by sending little David out to do battle with Goliath, *mano a mano*, that he would best the giant, that the rest of the Philistines would flee, that we would be standing here now, celebrating the occasion, and that the crowd would be pleased by all this?

GOD: Yes.

---

[72]See I Samuel 17:46.

JOEL: Sir, to change the subject, what about next year's crop of incoming rookies? Who do the Godfearers have their eyes on in the upcoming draft?

GOD: I wouldn't want to comment.

JOEL: What about Solomon, the young phenom from the Sheba School of Architecture, Poetry, and Philosophy?

GOD: I understand that he's a very intelligent young man, wise beyond his years.

JOEL: How do you think he'd fit in with your present rising superstar?

GOD: I wouldn't want to speculate.

JOEL: It's been suggested in the press that with those two, David and Solomon, you might have a dynasty on your hands.

GOD: It would be inappropriate for me to comment on that possibility.

JOEL: What about that pair of up-and-coming young men from Babylon State? Ezra and Nehemiah, the bookend forwards?[73] Down the line, wouldn't you love to see them in Godfearer stripes?

GOD: I understand that they are both fine team players. Very coachable.

JOEL: One more question, if I may. Clearly Groucho would not have been able to do what David has done tonight. Given that fact, how do you expect the negotiations with Groucho to go?

GOD: I'll say this. It's a whole new ball game.

JOEL: Thank you, Sir.

ABNER: Joel, could you try to get hold of Groucho and get his reaction to God's remark?

JOEL: Groucho. Where's Groucho?

GROUCHO: I'm here. Where else would I be?

JOEL: Groucho, you earlier characterized God as a pussy cat.

GROUCHO: Did I say pussy cat? I could have sworn I called him a lion.

ABNER: Joel, the fans might want to hear his reaction to the

---

[73]In the orthodox version of the history of Israel, Ezra and Nehemiah were instrumental in building the Second Temple and reestablishing the Jewish nation after the fall of Jerusalem (586 B.C.).

events of this evening.

JOEL: Groucho, your reaction to the events of this evening.

GROUCHO: I thought the best team won. Which is as it should be.

JOEL: Your reaction to two of the greatest players in the entire history of the AMEBA going head to head.

GROUCHO: Well, you have to like the kid, all right, his spunk and everything. But I've always been a big fan of Goliath. I really admired the way he turned down that lucrative job offer from the Lakers because of his principles, and I'm referring to his insistence that on certain occasions he be allowed to wear a brass uniform to protect himself from the roughness under the boards. Another thing I've always appreciated about Goliath was that he was a winner. At least, up until tonight.

JOEL: So what you're saying is, you have mixed feelings about the outcome.

GROUCHO: I do. As I may have mentioned, I was simpatico with Goliath because he stood up straight and tall for his principles, to say nothing of the fact that I like a winner. I know a lot of people enjoy cheering for the underdog, and I can see their point, but there's something about a winner that attracts my admiration. On the other hand, I've begun to appreciate the personal qualities of little David. I started out thinking he was just a smart-assed brat, but the more I saw of him the more I liked what I saw. The quality of confidence, I guess you could call it. But you could interpret this confidence in two ways, as poise and grit, on the one hand, or as cockiness, on the other.

JOEL: But the main thing is, isn't it, that he won.

GROUCHO: You noticed that too?

ABNER: Joel, ask him about his plans for the future, now that David has become for all intents and purposes the spiritual leader of this championship team.

JOEL: Groucho, one more question, if I may. What are your plans for the future, now that David has become for all intents and purposes the spiritual leader of the club?

GROUCHO: I'm currently negotiating with the producers of a TV quiz show. What's the capital of Arizona?

JOEL: Flagstaff?

GROUCHO: Arizona hasn't been discovered, so there *is* no correct answer. Sorry. And when they finally get around to finding it, Flagstaff will not be made the capital.[74] Sorry again.

JOEL: Thank you, Groucho. And now, back to Ab.

ABNER: There's Groucho, wrapped in his towel, heading off to the shower to congratulate the new spiritual leader of the God-fearers. Joel, your analysis.

JOEL: Ab, I'm not sure he went in there to congratulate David. Remember, Abigail's in there too.

ABNER: Excellent point, Joel. So there you have it, ladies and gentlemen. The seventh and deciding game of this, the AMEBA Championship Series, with its surprise ending. And outside, the celebration begins. Just listen to that crowd. Pandemonium has broken loose. They've been waiting a long time for this occasion. They pinned their hopes on little David, little of course only in terms of stature, in terms of heart he's a giant, a truly multi-dimensional young man who this evening has shown he can do it all—score, handle the ball, show charisma, decapitate a gigantic foe, feed the fowls of the air and the beasts of the earth, roll his eyeballs and attract beautiful women. . . .[75]

---

[74] According to Cardinal Micromentis, the later course of history proves that Groucho was at least a minor prophet.

[75] According to Ms. LaFemme, the rolling of a man's eyeballs is not what attracts beautiful women.

10 | Playing God

*T*HE SECOND MOST UNUSUAL SCROLL *in the Scriptures is Scroll #10,* "Playing God." *It consists of two parts, which appear to be composed in genres we have come to think of as uniquely contemporary. The first appears to be a soap opera synopsis, the second, an interview with a soap opera star.*

This scroll is the original version of the orthodox story of David and Bathsheba (2 Samuel 11:1–12:25). In that story, David, now the king and married to Abigail, happens to spy a sunbathing Bathsheba, who is wed to Uriah the Hittite, a soldier in Joab's army. King David wastes little time; only four verses later, Bathsheba informs him that she is pregnant. Shortly afterwards, David instructs Joab to "set ye Uriah in the forefront of the hottest battle." Joab obeys and Uriah is slain, leaving David free to marry Bathsheba. At this point God enters the picture, sending the prophet Nathan to rebuke the king for his vile behavior. David repents, Bathsheba has his baby, and God kills it. The royal couple, having been properly punished, proceed to have a re-placement, whom David names Solomon.

The superiority of this original version lies in (1) its tracing of the plot complications (including Queen Abigail's defensive tactics, which were later and unaccountably omitted), and (2) its inclusion of an interview with the fortunate actor who was given the chance of a lifetime, the opportunity to play God.

§

From Soap Monthly
Tammuz Schedule

THE BOLD & THE VENGEFUL

WEEK ONE

AN ALTERCATION WITH ABIGAIL sends David running to the Desert Lounge, where he comes to blows with the Canaanite mob boss Jerubbaal over Bathsheba. Abigail seeks spiritual guidance. General Joab declares war on the Ammonites. David puts out a hit on Jerubbaal. Rabbi Levi counsels Abigail to hire a PI. The police raid the Lounge. David escapes, surprises Bathsheba in her dressing room, and reads her the Twenty-Third Psalm; she feigns morning sickness but is persuaded by the lust-stricken king to take a rain check. General Joab ravages the Ammonites. Abigail hires Eglon [Adimelech, who played Adam on *The Young and the Beautiful*], a newcomer to the Jerusalem scene, to track the king's movements. David orders a background check on Bathsheba, only to discover that she is secretly married to a handsome brooding second lieutenant currently stationed at the Ammonite front. Abigail takes a moonlight walk and witnesses the murder of Jerubbaal by seven unknown assailants.

WEEK TWO

DAVID, DISGUISED in his old shepherd costume but trailed by Eglon, meets Bathsheba in a green pasture on the outskirts of town. Abigail reports Jerubbaal's murder to the police, but when she leads them to the scene of the crime she is astonished to learn that the body has mysteriously vanished. David astounds Bathsheba by reciting Psalm 119 from memory;[76] Eglon secretly

---

[76]Whether or not Psalm 119 was written by David himself, this was an extraordinary feat: that 176-verse chapter is the longest in the entire

tapes the performance. The police drag the River Jordan for Jerubbaal's body and come up with a pair of mismatched sandals. David and Bathsheba make love under a waterfall; after a night of passion he reveals his true feelings for her. The police begin to suspect Abigail of Jerubbaal's murder and put a tail on her. General Joab takes steps to besiege Rabbah. David confides his war strategy to a stunned Bathsheba, who reveals her love for him just after Eglon's hidden recorder runs out of tape. Abigail, feeling threatened, moves out of the palace and rents an abandoned fortress. David and Bathsheba wonder whether they have a future.

WEEK THREE

BATHSHEBA UNDERGOES A ROUTINE MEDICAL EXAM and learns that she is pregnant. The police discover that Abigail is married to David and is therefore the queen. Eglon shares the secrets of his investigation with Abigail, who fires him for letting his hidden recorder run out of tape. Bathsheba leaves an anxious message on David's machine, which he hears but forgets to erase. The police inform David of their suspicions about Abigail. David puts out a hit on Abigail and then goes over to Bathsheba's apartment for an unexpected visit, only to find Uriah the Hittite [Nehemiah, who played Uriah the Heep on Coveting], her second lieutenant husband on temporary medical furlough with spear shock, sleeping outside her bedroom door. A distraught Abigail discovers Bathsheba's phone message and plots her revenge. Eglon accosts Abigail with a bill for his services. General Joab besieges Rabbah. Abigail reconsiders her earlier decision concerning Eglon and gives him an I.O.U. and money for a long-play tape. David invites

---

orthodox Bible. Ms. LaFemme raised the possibility that a missing scroll recorded an earlier and perhaps shorter version of this psalm—which of course would detract from David's accomplishment (which, incidentally, she referred to as "pure corn"). But as Father Lecher rightly insisted, the briefcase containing the scrolls showed no evidence of tampering, a fact that guarantees that the Bear Lake Scrolls were delivered into his capable hands complete and entire.

Uriah the Hittite to a frank but friendly walk along the waterfront, where he is shocked to discover that Uriah is the son of Uriah the Hittite, Sr., a long-lost fraternity brother; they argue over whether "Hittite" is an ethnic slur. General Joab continues to besiege Rabbah. David schemes to get Uriah, Jr. in bed with Bathsheba so that it will appear that Bathsheba's impending child is legitimate, thus preventing a potentially-embarrassing paternity suit. The police, mistaking Eglon for the prophet Elijah, inform David of Abigail's puzzling behavior. Overcome by remorse, David removes the hit he had earlier put out on his wife the queen. Uriah refuses to sleep with Bathsheba, explaining that it is against his religious convictions to mix love and war; beginning to suspect David's intentions, he gets drunk while David and the police plot his death, a plot that Eglon secretly tapes.

WEEK FOUR

DAVID WRITES A LETTER to General Joab and asks Uriah to deliver it. Eglon attempts to blackmail Abigail. Uriah breaks the seal of the letter and tries to discern its contents, only to discover that he is unable to read Ur-Hebrew. Abigail reaches out to Eglon. David visits Bathsheba and pleads with her to buy an insurance policy on her husband; she promises to consider his request; once alone, however, she instead considers an abortion. Eglon seduces Abigail. Bathsheba is raped by a mystery intruder, who begs her to bring the child to full term. Uriah delivers David's letter to General Joab, who reads it and then, praising Uriah for his valor, puts him in the forefront of the hottest battle. Unbeknownst to Bathsheba, David takes out a large policy on Uriah's life. Eglon secretly records this purchase and sells the tape to the *Jerusalem Enquirer*. Bathsheba takes a sunbath and dreams of simpler times. Eglon records this dream and sells it to Abigail. The police discover the body of Jerubbaal in the city well. Uriah is killed by a stray spear. Bathsheba mourns his death. David collects on the insurance. The *Enquirer* publishes an exposé of the whole sordid mess. Bathsheba goes into seclusion to sort out her feelings.

David's approval rating plummets to four percent, necessitating a huddle with his advisors. Bathsheba gives birth to David's child.

WEEK FIVE

THE PROPHET NATHAN visits David and warns of divine retribution. Abigail files for divorce. A reporter from the *Star* overhears Eglon boast of his relationship with Abigail. Bathsheba's child is mysteriously murdered. All Jerusalem is grief-stricken, and the police draw up a list of suspects. The *Enquirer* runs a piece on Abigail's indiscretions and calls for her impeachment. Her approval rating plummets. Bathsheba goes on "Othniel Live" to give her side of the story. The police narrow the list of murder suspects to God. David fasts. Abigail attempts suicide but is discovered at the last minute by Eglon, who rushes her to the emergency room, where her life is miraculously saved by Abel, a handsome teen-aged brain surgeon [Sanballat, who played Nahum on *All the Young Doctors*], with whom she develops a close but Platonic relationship. God plays his trump card, conspiring with a fugitive Ammonite to frame David for the child's murder. David gets wind of the plot and takes steps to foil it. General Joab attempts a coup but is inadvertently thwarted by the police. Eglon mysteriously disappears, only to surface as a simple village rabbi. David and Abigail temporarily patch their differences and appear together on "Seven Days" to discuss the difficulties of modern marriage. Rabbi Levi appears on "The Gideon Show" as an expert on troubled relationships and vouches for his client. In exchange for clemency, General Joab appears on "Caleb!" and vouches for his commander-in-chief. Abigail's approval rating soars to ninety-eight percent while David's reaches an all-time high of ninety-nine percent.[77] Jerubbaal proves himself by rising from the dead; he then proclaims his devotion to Abigail, who, faced with an agonizing choice, declares her love for Abel. God

---

[77]See Professor Allbright's 684-page monograph, "Toward a Hypothesis on the Theory and Praxis of Ur-Hebrew Political Theory," (Reno [Unpublished], n.d.).

appears on "Othniel Live" and confesses to his part in the death of Bathsheba's baby, explaining that his vengefulness can be traced to a traumatic childhood experience and pointing out that because of his deeply felt pro-life convictions he had waited until the baby was actually born to kill it; his approval rating soars to 100 percent. Abel mysteriously disappears while hunting lions in the Negev. Abigail, heart-broken, seduces Jerubbaal, only to discover his mob connection. Rabbi Hillel writes a commentary downplaying God's confession; Rabbi Shammai writes a commentary congratulating God on his honesty; the Pope issues an encyclical condemning the destruction of the Ammonites. Abigail spurns Jerubbaal and joins a convent at the foot of Mount Sinai. Jerubbaal goes back to being dead. God, now at the height of his popularity, mysteriously disappears, prompting Abigail to reconsider her new lifestyle. David and Bathsheba come to an understanding; they cap off a busy week by making love under her dressing table and vowing that the fruit of their illicit passion will be a male child who will learn from their mistakes.

NEXT MONTH

SOLOMON IS BORN; God surfaces in a Buddhist monastery.[78]

---

[78]This first section of the Scroll gave rise to a vigorous but friendly debate on the question, Who is the hero, or heroine, in this story? Professor Allbright nominated Solomon; Ms. LaFemme nominated Abigail; Father Lecher, David; Cardinal Micromentis, both the Pope and God.

What is the significance of the story? Cardinal Micromentis concluded that this part of the scroll stands as evidence that the Ur-Hebrews possessed a highly-advanced culture. Professor Allbright maintained that it proved that *plus ça change, plus c'est la même chose* ("the more things change, the more they remain the same"), a sentiment to which Ms. LaFemme gave hearty approval. (The two construed this maxim in different ways, however. Professor Allbright was referring to human nature in general; Ms. LaFemme, to the injustice continually perpetrated on one gender by the other.) Father Lecher ventured the opinion that this synopsis could only have been composed by a creative genius, an insight from which this editor does not wish to dissent.

A Star is Born
By Deborah

MALACHI, WHO PLAYS GOD (*the awesome, enigmatic, and moralistic creator of the universe*) on The Bold and the Vengeful, *is an engaging, totally candid actor who enjoys nothing better than to sit down with a reporter around one of his three Olympic size swimming pools alongside his lavishly-furnished replica of the Temple on the shores of the Sea of Galilee to discuss his craft. The classically trained thespian, who served his apprenticeship as Moses's servant Jeeves on* Guiding Cloud *and then graduated to Goliath on* The Tall and the Lonely *before getting his big break as God on* B&V, *has been around long enough to have opinions on any number of subjects.*

DEBORAH: FIRST OFF, CONGRATS on your Esther nomination.
Malachi: Thanks.
D: Now that that's taken care of, let's get on with the obvious question. How would you describe yourself? I mean, in terms of your real life?
M: Well, I'm not at all like my character, if that's what you're getting at. Ironically, I'm a lot less like God than I am like David, who he's always crossing spears with. It's not that I don't enjoy a good round of revenge every once in a while, it's more that I'm . . . well, more of a romantic, I guess you could say, which is also one of David's main features. I enjoy composing psalms for my female acquaintances and swimming in waterfall-fed pools. Also, I'm somewhat younger than God's supposed to be.
D: If I may ask, how old is that?
M: Twenty-five.
D: It would seem that this thing of being not like God, personally, would create a problem—I mean, in terms of knowing how to approach the role.
M: Oh it does, yes, to some extent. But what I do is, first of all, I look inward. I try to put myself in his—God's—situation as a sort of general CEO of the universe. Then I read the script, trying to

figure out what the writers had in mind in terms of the emotional turmoil my character's been going through at the time—for example, how he feels when he finds out about Bathsheba getting pregnant and about David's brilliant scheme to get rid of Uriah because he wouldn't cooperate by shacking up with his own wife—and of course I try to figure out why he—God—decides to kill off the kid instead of just going the natural route and doing the abortion thing. In other words, I tap into the anger of a guy who's pretty upset by a whole lot of what he interprets as moral turpitude. Then, step number three, I try to apply my own experience, background and belief-system to the character. Anyway, that's sort of what I was taught in acting class at UJ. One, two, three.

D: You make it sound so easy.

M: I really don't mean to. My point is, it's actually quite difficult, playing God, especially for somebody who's basically a live-and-let-live kind of a person with maybe a little more interest than the average guy in the opposite sex.

D: So what's the hardest thing about playing God?

M: Hmmm. That's a tough one. I mean, there are so many hard things.

D: Just name one.

M: Well . . . there's of course the fact that he seems to have a difficult time adjusting to certain events, situations, etcetera, maybe because of his super-strict religious upbringing, or whatever. . . . But if I could name only one thing that's tough about the job, it'd probably be all the personality changes he goes through. For example, one day he'll be this really vengeful guy, then the next day he'll turn right around and repent of all the evil he's done, and of course in the upcoming month he's scheduled to put in a stint as a Buddhist monk, and after that, who knows? I don't think even Becky [head writer Rebecca] has decided yet where the storyline's headed.

D: In other words, your character lacks what you people in the industry call *definition*.

M: Exactly. Which makes it difficult for him to interact with the other characters on an everyday one-to-one basis.

D: Are you saying the show is maybe too plot-driven, with not enough attention being paid to character development?

M: Oh, no, I'm not trashing Becky or the writers, they're a really talented bunch of people, in terms of having degrees in creative writing, doing all the background research, plotting out a really fantastic storyline, etcetera.

D: Next question. Which of the other actors do *you* interact with?

M: Actually, I hang around a lot with Ruth [Abigail] and Sarah [Bathsheba]. We play a lot of ball together.

D: Say, speaking of playing ball, we get huge stacks of mail wanting to know what really happened between you and Eve [executive producer of *The Tall and the Lonely*]. The sharp pencils in the industry had you figured as pretty much set there on *T&L*, as the male lead [Goliath].

M: We had a discussion, Eve and I, and she killed off my part.

D: You mind telling our readers what the discussion was about?

M: She wanted me to put on a couple of inches. At the time, I didn't feel I was up to it.

D: Then it had nothing to do with the fact that storylines about giants aren't exactly big these days?

M: Absolutely not.

D: Or with the fact that you were jealous because the fans tended to identify with the little guy, David?

M: Rumors can be wrong.

D: For the record, do you have anything to say about the time you put in as Goliath?

M: Only that it was awesome.

D: Really. And what else?

M: Also, it prepared me for my present role.

D: In terms of. . . ?

M: I'm thinking of the size angle, mostly. Also, several personality traits.

D: Like, for instance?

M: Like being something of a bully.

D: Are we to take it, then, that you're not pleased with your present role, playing God?

M: Oh no, don't get me wrong. Fact is, I couldn't be happier. I tend to think of it as the perfect part.

D: In spite of the lack of character definition?

M: Actually, I'm learning to regard that lack, so-called, as part of the mystery of his personality.

D: One more question. I think I already know the answer, but here goes: has any other line of work ever tempted you?

M: Than playing God? Are you kidding? What other line of work provides as much job security? I mean, who in their right mind would want to kill off God?

D: Maybe Nietzsche?[79]

M: Who?

D: Never mind. Well, thanks much, I enjoyed picking your brain, and good luck on the Esther nomination for, what was it? Best Supporting Actor? If there's any justice in the world, you're a shoo-in.

M: Thanks, but that's a big if.[80]

---

[79]Professor Allbright pointed out that there are medical grounds for questioning whether Nietzsche was in his right mind when he spoke of the death of God.

[80]Three members of the committee were treated to a spirited debate over whether Malachi's final remark ("that's a big if," in reference to Deborah's apparently casual remark concerning the presence or absence of justice in the world) should be construed as coming from Malachi as Malachi (Father Lecher's position) or from Malachi in his role as God (Ms. LaFemme's theory).

11 | Solmark Cards, Inc.

"SOLMARK CARDS, Inc." became the basis for the Biblical book of Ecclesiastes. It was written by King David's successor, Solomon.

This short piece[81] proves that King Solomon was not a pompous, pedantic, morose, self-important, long-winded preacher, that he was in fact a man with a dry wit and waggish, sometimes black, humor. It also suggests that he might have made his fortune in the greeting card industry. If so, he was probably the first Ur-Hebrew to master the art of the punch line.

§

VANITY OF VANITIES, saith the Preacher, vanity of vanities;
all is vanity. . . .

> After that, I must have dozed off.

WHAT PROFIT HATH A MAN of all his labour which he taketh
under the sun?

> Probably the minimum wage.

ONE GENERATION PASSETH AWAY, and another generation cometh;
but the earth abideth forever . . .

---

[81]Father Lecher reported that this scroll was made from what he judged to be the hide of a newborn lamb.

      . . . or until the next really big meteor.

THE SUN ALSO ARISETH, and the sun goeth down . . .
     . . . or maybe it's the other way around?

THE WIND GOETH toward the south,
and turneth about unto the north.
    Looks like we're in for a few thunderstorms.[82]

ALL THE RIVERS run into the sea, yet the sea is not full.
      I wonder who pulled the plug?

THE THING THAT HATH BEEN, it is that which shall be;
and that which is done is that which shall be done . . .
      . . . are you following?

IS THERE ANYTHING whereof it may be said, "See, this is new?"
    sighs the Queen as she checks her closet.[83]

THERE IS NO REMEMBRANCE of former things,
       Your Honor.

---

[82]See Professor Allbright's extensive monograph, "Weather Patterns in the Ancient Near East: A Reconsideration, Based upon a Passage in Scroll #11," (Reno [unpublished], n.d.).

[83]This line caused an altercation between Ms. LaFemme and Father Lecher, an altercation that took on something of a personal tone. It is enough to report that Ms. LaFemme's position was that Father Lecher had tampered with the text; Father Lecher's position was that he had not.

I HAVE SEEN ALL THE WORKS that are done under the sun.
And they're *nothing* compared to what goes on
under the moon.

THAT WHICH IS CROOKED cannot be made straight . . .
. . . unless you can afford a good orthodontist.

AND I GAVE MY HEART to know wisdom,
and to know madness and folly.
Then I went for madness and folly.

I SAID IN MINE HEART, Go to now, I will prove thee with mirth,
therefore enjoy pleasure.
And that was the best decision I ever made.

I SAID OF LAUGHTER, It is mad: and of mirth, What doeth it?
Whom did I think I was kidding?

I MADE ME GREAT WORKS; I builded me houses;
I planted me vineyards . . .
. . . not necessarily in that order.

I GOT ME SERVANTS and maidens,
and had servants born in my house.
Think about it. There's a logical connection here.

I SOUGHT IN MINE HEART to give myself unto wine . . .
. . . and I'm now a card-carrying member of AA.

THE WISE MAN'S EYES are in his head.

That also goes for the fool.[84]

AND WHO KNOWETH whether he shall be
a wise man or a fool?

You can't really tell until
you've tried it out before a live audience.

FOR THERE IS A MAN whose labour is in wisdom,
and in knowledge, and in equity.

At least that's the rumor.

THERE IS NOTHING BETTER for a man,
than that he should eat and drink,
and that he should make his soul enjoy good in his labour . . .

. . . well, *practically* nothing.

THERE IS A TIME TO BE BORN, and a time to die.

The first is called a birth day. Ever wonder why
there's no word for the second?

THERE IS A TIME TO WEEP, and a time to laugh . . .

. . . and confusing these two can be
extremely embarrassing.

---

[84]Cardinal Micromentis cited this line as absolute proof that Ur-Hebrew civilization was the first to recognize the fundamental American principle of human equality.

I SAID IN MINE HEART, God shall judge
the righteous and the wicked . . .

> . . . but probably not in my lifetime.

THE FOOL FOLDETH his hands together,
and eateth his own flesh.

> There's probably a Latin word for this disorder.[85]

WHEN THOU OWEST A DEBT unto God,
defer not to pay it . . .

> . . . just try to get it restructured.

HE THAT LOVETH SILVER
shall not be satisfied with silver.

> And why should he,
> considering the price of gold?

NAKED CAME YE FORTH from thy mother's womb,
naked shall ye return, taking nothing with you . . .

> . . . and don't think your children don't know it.

A MAN TO WHOM GOD HATH GIVEN RICHES, wealth, and honour,
so that he lacketh nothing of all that he desireth . . .

> . . . if this description fits, why are you bothering to read *this*?

SORROW IS BETTER than laughter.

> Keep this in mind next time you're at a funeral.

---

[85]Professor Allbright was involved in extensive research on this matter
at the time of his untimely death.

WHOSO REMOVETH STONES shall be hurt therewith,
and he that cleaveth wood shall be endangered thereby.
                    So always wear your hard hat and a pair of goggles.

CAST THY BREAD upon the waters.
                    And if the fish don't bite, try salmon eggs.

WISDOM IS THE PRINCIPAL THING; therefore get wisdom.
                    Then use it to make a few shrewd investments.

A MAN'S WISDOM maketh his face to shine.
                    Strong drink also does a pretty respectable job.

12 | What Goes Around, Comes Around

THE DISCIPLES found this twelfth and final Scroll to be the most per-plexing of them all. There is nothing even remotely resembling it in the entire Bible. The puzzle was solved when Father Lecher mentioned its uncanny similarity to the story of the life of Gautama, the Buddha.[86] As we then discovered, that ancient story reports many of the events recounted in "What Goes Around, Comes Around": the gods in the Tusita heaven prevailing upon Gautama to descend to earth and become the Buddha; King Suddhodana, the Buddha's father, erecting a barrier of pleasure around the young prince in order to keep him innocent of life's sufferings; Buddha leaving his wife and young son in order to retire from the world; his achievement of enlightenment; his life as an itinerant preacher and founder of monasteries; his death, with his many disciples gathered around him.

Obviously, Scroll #12 is the original story, of which the Buddha story is a later and, one must say (throwing sensitivity to the winds), an inferior, though lengthier, version.

§

THE THING I REMEMBER MOST about him was maybe his drive, his push, his ambition. Achievement oriented, is how I'd describe him. Always wanted to better himself. And that's what eventually put him in a caste by himself. Most if not all of the other T's—

---

[86]The reader who has not mastered Pali (a dialect of Sanskrit) might wish to consult Henry Clarke Warren, *Buddhism in Translations* (Harvard, 1896), Chapter I, "The Buddha," pp. 1–110.

that's what we used to call the transfers, T's[87]—most T's were happy to take it one life at a time, just relax and smell the lotus blossoms. Not Buddha. Maybe I should say not the bundle of desire who ended up being this big success story who got written up in all the rags and mags as Buddha. Even way back then you figured he was gonna make something of himself. You could tell right off the top he was programmed to end up as maybe a king for some top-ten empire, and if that didn't pan out he'd make a big splash amongst the other fish in the religion pond.

I worked for Tusita, which was a five-star heaven specializing in employment opportunities for T's, people looking for a change of their lives, something a little more upscale. You don't hear about it much these days, Tusita, but it was the Big Blue of that particular time frame. I operated out of the Placement Office, which is why I happened to be in a position to keep an eye on the guy—I'll call him G for short. Started out as a lowly file clerk, I did, where I first perused this young phenom turning heads in the very low minors, the insect and lower vertebrate leagues. Worked my way up to Chief Personnel Officer, which is why I identified with the guy's positive attitude, myself being a go-getter, if I say so myself, moving up the ladder to the top. What this last job amounted to, I was in charge of interviewing the T's with worlds of potential and making recommendations to the upstairs brass as to what type of opening this or that T might be suited for—butterfly, toad, dog, rabbit, cow, horse, tiger, elephant, human being, whatsoever, and if human being, which one specifically, in terms of having a personal label.

Anyways, I took a personal interest in G's career, even before I met him in my official capacity as CPO. I used to do that in speci-fied cases, that is, take an interest. If a guy, or a lady—I did not discriminate, being way ahead of my time—if a guy or a broad showed unusual promise I'd take a personal interest. That'll give you some idea what type of a higher being I was back in my heyday, kind and caring, a real class act if I do say so. And as I mentioned, G showed worlds of potential, because of the drive factor.

---

[87]Buddhists came to refer to the transfer process as transmigration.

I remember the day I interviewed him for the Buddha job. We were looking for somebody—preferably a guy, though I personally, being several light years ahead of my time in the sensitivity department, would of recommended a lady, if she'd of had the right qualifications plus a few extra details going for her—we were supposed to be on the lookout for somebody with an unusually broad background and an outstanding track record in his or her previous lives, somebody who could do Buddha, *do* in the sense of not just going through the motions but playing the part like it was choreoformed.

"Let's see," says I to this G guy sitting across the desk from me, "it says here in the record you just got back from being a . . . Brahmin."

"That was in my *next*-to-last existence," says G, and he starts shifting his bulk around in the chair. Either nerves or boils on the sitting mechanism, I'm thinking. Probably nerves, because of the job-related stress, but on the other hand I always take pains to put my T's at ease, so it could of been boils, which would square with his having recently been employed as a Brahmin. Due to the fact that they sit around a lot, Brahmins do, reading books and meditating and chewing the metaphysical fat amongst themselves.

"Oh?" says I, looking in his file, which seems to lack a page with the details of his last existence. "Are we missing something here?"

"I don't know," he says, kind of smiling. "Are we?"

I smile right back at him, because my personal policy is not letting on to the fact of a missing page, which is a sure way to get you a fast demotion. "How'd it go?" says I calmly, showing a personal interest plus getting the conversation back on a safe track.

"It?" he says, shifting the bulk again. "Go?"

"The Brahmin stint," says I. "How'd it go?"

"Oh," he answers, and he seems to relax up a bit. "It's all there in the report."

"Hmmm, Hmmm, Hmmm. So I see. Says you did a damn fine job."

"Thank you."

"Don't thank me, I'm just reading what it says here in the report. Could be in arrears, as far as that goes."

"No, they monitor us pretty closely down there," he says, which I'm thinking wouldn't be hard to do in his case, because of the extra poundage the guy is lugging around, making him easy to pick out in a crowd. "What you have in front of you," he says, referring to the report, "is accurate to two-tenths of a decimal point."

This remark I coulda done without. I mean, the guy *was* a go-getter, you gotta hand it to him, but he was also a smart-ass intellectual, which goes with the territory, I'm referring to his formerly being a Brahmin, and I am not prejudiced against Brahmins, in fact some of my best friends have gone the Brahmin route, though I am partial to the Kshatriyas, having been one myself and proud of it.[88]

"Let's see," I says, "there don't seem to be any demerits, mostly just merits, is that right?"

"Well, there's a *minor* demerit," he says, fidgeting around in the hot seat. I'm thinking, it's got to be more than just boils, the wiggling does, he's dealing with a lot of stress, due to that ambition factor.

"Ah yes," I says, reading further on, "spilled a little soma[89] at a wedding, on the bride's dress, is that what we're referring to?"

---

[88]The reference is to the ancient Indian caste system, which places Brahmins (priests and scholars), over Kshatriyas (rulers and warriors), Vaisyas (merchants and farmers), and Sudras (peasants and laborers) in a rigid hierarchy. For an exhaustive list of the ways in which the Brahmin caste is inherently superior to the Kshatriya, see Professor Allbright's 589-page monograph, "I.Q. Determinants in Cross-Cultural Perspective: A Prolegomenon," (Reno [Unpublished], n.d.), which was found in his computer files after his massive and fatal brain hemorrhage on May 14, 1999.

Professor Mortimer Z. Z. Allbright was an exemplary disciple in almost every way, and enjoyed the admiration and respect of his colleagues. His wealth of learning will be sorely missed.

[89]A liquid intoxicant used for ritual purposes in ancient India. According to Father Lecher, it is similar to Mogen David, though of a somewhat higher quality.

"Right. I paid the cleaning bill, however, so it cancels out."

"*You* paid?" says I, looking for another demerit, which we were trained to do.

"Well, it came out of the slush fund."

"That's better," says I. "But on the plus side, you raised a couple million rupees for a new temple. That's got to have made you pretty pleased with yourself. Pret-ty pleased in-deed."

"Thank you," he says proudly. "I like to think of it as the most outstanding accomplishment of my last half a dozen existences."

"Compared to what, for instance?" I asks. If they'd of left it up to me, I wouldn't of bothered to ask compared to what, because I was already on the guy's side, and besides, I'd seen his papers for the last 500 and some existences except for the missing page, and what's the percentage in asking compared to what when you already have a pretty fair idea? But we were under strict orders from the mucks to ask those kinds of questions, we had standards to maintain, a fact which often got pointed out at staff meetings.

"Oh," says he, "compared for example to being a gentle elephant and giving kids rides on my back."

"That was certainly an impressive performance," I says, and in the meanwhile I'm writing it all down in triplicate.

"Thank you."

"So, what's next in terms of your career move?" I ask the guy. "Maybe another crack at being a Brahmin? One more spin at the fund-raising table?" I'm just testing him, of course, seeing if he's still got fire in the gut. I mean, I'm not really thinking of sending him down as another Brahmin, which nobody should have to go through twice, because of all the sitting involved plus the intellectual bullshit that's expected of you. I'm thinking of something of a higher scale.

"Don't you have something a little higher profile?" he wants to know, exactly according to plan.

"Well," I says like it just now occurred to me, "there's always Buddha."

"Buddha?" he says, perking up the ears.

"Correct," I says. "Right now we happen to be looking for somebody with a fair mount of *joy de vive,* which is Latin for being fun loving, somebody who can set a good example, stand up and give an upbeat twenty-minute sermon, maybe save the world if it comes to that. And of course be a team player all the way, that goes without saying. Would that be of interest?"

"How much meditation is required?" says he, like he's smelling a rat.

"Oh, just a coupla hours before breakfast every a.m. But other than that it's largely fun and games, a little entertainment by the scantily-clad ladies."

"What's the pay?" he wants to know, which is another sample of the ambition at work.

"I don't have the specifics right here, but it's somewhere in the, oh, nine figure range," says I, and I'm in the meanwhile thinking to myself, "Two figures, after the retirement."

"What about working conditions?" he asks, missing my thought.

"Stress-free environment," says I, on the chance it ain't boils that's making him twitch, hoping it's nerves, so he'll see the advantage of this perk. Hoping also to close the deal real quick, seeing as how it's almost time for lunch.

"How many dancing girls does that include?"

"Oh, about forty," says I, doing some fancy on-the-spot calculations.

"Make that forty thousand and I start to get interested," says he, twitching himself around in the chair again, "and make it payable on my sixteenth birthday."

"I'll have to see somebody about that," says I with a big frown, writing it down on my yellow pad and thinking to myself, It's got to be boils on that tender backside, not much evidence of nervousness at this point of time.

"What about palaces?" is his next request.

"Palaces?" I wants to know, followed by the question, "Did I hear you right, Mr. G, palaces? In the plurality?"

"Yeah, how many?" Said in a very cool way, looking at me peeper to peeper and all the time dragging on a Benson & Hedges while I'm thinking, It's boils, all right, it's definitely boils.

"Two?" This is my offer.

"Four." This is his counter.

"How about three?" I says, hoping the brass mucks upstairs'll cover me for a coupla extra palaces.

"Okay, three, but they gotta come equipped with wet bars, hot tubs, and brass bands."

To tell the truth, this was kinda getting to me. I really had to wonder if it was the greatest idea in the world to build a sixteen-year-old kid three palaces and give him forty thousand dancing girls and three brass bands for his birthday. Keep in mind I was from the old school. Make them *earn* it, was my philosophy, that's what *we* had to do. But it wasn't my decision to make, I was just a middle-level higher being in that point of time, the decision was in the hands of the brass upstairs.

Well, the short of it is, I made the recommendation to the top management, they accepted it except for moving the big birthday from age sixteen to age twenty-one, and next thing you know they had lanced his boil and given him a prescription for stress pills and sent him down to do the job. Which was easy, all he had to do was follow the instructions on the box.

§

THEN THERE'S DIMELDA. If you're gonna tell the Buddha story you gotta mention Dimelda, the two going together like fine wine and cheap beer.

The thing you remember most about Dimelda is definitely her gorgeous looks. She was always one of them kinds of female T's who pick up lots of positive comments, for instance about the unusually blonde hair and the cute little dairy air, which is Latin for the sitting mechanism. Even the mucks had their heads on a swivel when they passed her on the streets of Tusita, it being the kind of a heaven where stunners in the process of transferring tend to get accidentally detained because their paperwork always seems to be in the habit of misplacement.

A thing I recall is that Dimelda dropped by the office one a.m. about 10 o'clock, this was eleven years after the Buddha place-ment, looking for a change of situation. She was another one of them bundles of desire that I, being kind and caring, took a per-sonal interest in, due to her drive to succeed, which was pretty much along the same lines as G's, which is what gave me the idea of putting the two and two together.

"Let's see," says I, "you must be . . . Helen from Troy." I was lying between my teeth, of course, I knew damn well she was Dimelda from her file.

"Dimelda," says Dimelda accurately, and she's got her little mirror out to check for possible damage to the Maybelline.

"Dimelda," says I. "I stand collected. Hmmm. . . . Ah yes, you're fairly new at the game, aren't you. Working on just your twentieth existence, am I right?" All this time I'm moving papers back and forth on the desk, which creates the delusion of a heavy case load, as well as giving me something constructive to do with my itchy hands.

"Right," says she. "Twentieth time around."

"And last time you were a—"

"I've done all the major animals plus taken a shot as a human being," she says, chewing her gum rapidly. "But that was extremely early in the game, the human being stint, which explains the demerits. Check it out," she says, "it's in there somewheres. Under E."

Ordinarily I do not like being interpreted. I also do not allow my clients to chew gum rapidly in the office, it's like swearing and bad grammar, by the fact it creates a bad impression. But I let it pass that time, thinking alone to myself, This is Dimelda you're speaking with, old boy, God what a doll!

"A-*ha*," says I in answering her check-it-out-it's-in-there-some-wheres-under-E. "So it is, so it is. And what exactly did you have in mind this time around, in terms of a career move?" I fold my hands over my gut and smile when these words are being said, which is a way I have of showing personal interest.

"I figure I'm ready to give it another shot as a human being."

"Let's see," says I, dragging it out to keep the lady in my office for the maximum. "Let's . . . see . . . what we might have . . . for somebody . . . like . . . Dimelda. Hmmm."

I am not saying I was faking it, I was just slowing it down to keep from making arrears, also to give me time to think of a suitable situation that would take advantage of the lady's special talents. It's allowed, slowing it down is, *it* being the conversation, union rules don't specifically prohibit it, here *it* refers to the slowdown.

"Hows about a hooker?" is her next thought. "You got anything along those lines?" All this is being said between massages of the gum, which is moving from one extreme in her mouth to the other. You could say gum and mascara was what gave Dimelda defamation. Bubble gum, mascara, and romance novels, and you might also add chocolate-covered cherries to the list.

"Hoo . . . ker," I says, thinking, now *there's* a natural for the little lady, thinking also, why didn't *I* suggest it? And also some other thoughts.

"What's the matter," she wants to know, flapping several eyelashes in the breeze, "are the requirements too rigid, is that what you're thinking?"

No, I was not really thinking in terms of rigid requirements. I was thinking more the kind of thoughts that would make it hard for me to stand up real tall and straight when the interview is through with. Also thinking maybe I should have her over to the house, which would be in line with taking a personal interest. Then I followed this thought with another one that said, Well, maybe not, on account of the little lady not being necessarily that kind and caring due to the fact that she wasn't really in Dimelda's league in the knockout department.

"Here's something *close* to hooker," I says, probably under divine perspiration. "Hows about a go as a *hoofer*? Lots of jobs open for a lovely dancing girl these days. Fact is, several years down the line a young man by the name of Buddha is scheduled be in the market for them."

"Hoofer?" she says, and she stops to pop her gum. "I'm not a big dancer, and to tell the truth I'm nervous about getting in over my head."

"Over your head?" This is my curiosity at work.

"Well you see, I wanna do a good job, don't wanna blow it and have to come back as a cow, on account of once I had a bad experience in a previous life as a Black Angus."

"Bad experience as a *cow?* In this part of the world, where a cow is considered sacred?"

"This was in Omaha."

I mediately see her point. "Really don't think it's anything to worry about," says I. "Excellent risk/reward ratio, this being a hoofer gig has. You'd be one of forty thousand, which would cut down on the risk of having your mistakes noticed, with the potential reward being Buddha, who's heading up the ladder of success, if I am any judge, and I've had ten thousand years of experience in these things. Mark my words, lady, he's got major monarch written all over him."

"Are you sure?" she wants to know, and I can tell she's referring to the monarch part.

"Sure I'm sure," I says, which is close to the truth. "The guy's my client, I've been managing his career since Day One, when I got him placed as a worm."

"What's required, in terms of qualifications?" she asks next.

"Just a little *joy de vive*," I tell her, "plus the ability to spread it around."

She thinks about this dancing proposition for about five seconds and then agrees to give it a whirl. After which I get approval from upstairs to ship her down the chutes to her next destination.

§

ABOUT TWENTY YEARS LATER I ran across this scrap from the *Benares Times:*

BUDDHA-DIMELDA

Buddha and Dimelda, both of Benares, were wed Friday, June 3rd, at the Holy Names Stupa. Rev. Kondanna officiated.

The bridegroom is the son of King Suddhodana and Queen Mahamaya; the bride is the daughter of Trixi and an unidentified male.

The groom wore a saffron robe and carried a bright red lotus blossom, which was a gift from the bride. Matching accessories included a silver sewing needle and a porcelain begging bowl, which were gifts from the king.

The bride wore a white tent.

The newlyweds plan to spend their honeymoon in the maternity ward of St. Ananda's Hospital. Afterwards they will reside in Benares, where Buddha is king-designate and Dimelda works in the entertainment division of Palace Number Three.

Well well well, says I to myself while observing the honeymoon locale and the king's gifts. I wonder if there's a story here, and whether this notice gets filed or whether it gets itself misplaced. Keep in mind that the rules and regs state that all notices concerning the major events in the lives of a T are supposed to get filed. My own personal policy, however, was to protect the innocent, due to my class-act kindness. Because if the mucks got wind of something which wasn't meant for their specific noses, somebody might get a demotion, which would not look good on his record.

I decided to investigate. I waited for the right opening and then took advantage of a temporary layoff and went down the tubes myself, slipping into the skin of an experienced harem guard, who had the best perspective available for checking things out and getting the real scoop, in the interests of truth and accuracy.

It took me only one lifetime, but I got the full story piece by piece, on account of my cooperative sources, plus the fact that I wasn't born yesterday, coupled with a vivacious imagination.

It seems what happened was, Dimelda developed a plan early on. When she got to be fifteen, she figured she'd get Prince Buddha alone, discuss the news of the day in the area of politics, move on to the subject of religion, ask him about his life stories, tell him about hers, sob into a Kleenex for a little sympathy, offer to perform an exotic dance, press her naked young body against his twenty-four-year-old physique, get pregnant, and then refuse to have an abortion on moral grounds. It was only her second go-round as a human being but she was already street-wise, due to a previous existence as an alley cat. She saw the perfect chance to move directly from hoofer to princess without having to go through twenty-five extra lives. What should be kept in mind here is that people in my part of the world don't like to go through too many unnecessary existences—they consider life as basically painful, which means they try to cut down on the number of transfers. It reduces the misery, also saves wear and tear on the engine.

The plan worked to perfection. Dimelda got pregnant in the ordinary way, had her lawyer explain her pro-life convictions to the young prince's lawyer, and sent out the invitations.

She coulda saved the legal fees. The dance was so exotic that Buddha fell in love with her anyways, against his better judgment, and right away became pro-monogamy. This left the other hoofers with lots of spare time on their hands, which did nothing for their morals but helped me get the story.

The story is not headed for a happy ending. It turns out Dimelda did not like her job. She found being a princess was not what it was jacked up to be. Too many ribbons to cut, too many thank-you speeches to stumble through, too many flashing bulbs to get blindsided by, plus have you ever tried to find a decent daycare center for a kid? And worst of all, there was the age differentiation betwixt herself and Buddha, who was always being threatened with excommunication anyways, which explains the silver needle and begging bowl as wedding gifts, the king was trying to tell him it is not a good idea to get involved with somebody below yourself on the society scales.

So Dimelda decided it was a fine time to go with her first plan, which was to try her hand as a hooker. But this is not the kind of information you can keep secret for long, and Buddha was no fool, having been around the block well over 500 times, many of them as a human being, the majority as a guy. He found out about his wife's new hobby late one night when he was wandering around town looking for a poor miserable creature to preach a sermon to. He was just doing his job, the one he had contracted for back in the days when I and he went through the job description, which emphasized upbeat sermons to the down-and-out population. What happened was, he went into a high-class joint, where he ran across a guy who told him about this remarkable but unhappy blonde with a cute little bottom who worked out of

Maya Street. A blonde and a bottom which turns out to be familiar, because who should he find answering the bell at the Maya Street address but Dimelda herself, taking donations for a charitable cause.

"Buddha, darling," she says, suddenly giving the gum a rest while a junior customer is running around in the background looking for a pair of pants and the back door.

"Dimelda, you bitch," he says right back.

"You've come at last," she says nervously.

"Don't you have any shame?" is a question he suddenly wants an answer to.

But she tries to get the conversation moving in another channel. "I can explain," she says.

"What about the child?" he is curious to know. This is a reference to the kid, who is at home with the baby-sitter and may or may not be a factor in this situation, depending on which sources you happen to believe. Those that were sympathetic to the lady's cause tended to blame the kid and his colic for starting her on this adventuresome career, but the ones who suffered from her high-and-mighty attitude thought the kid was healthy, basically, and she was just using him as an excuse.

"I could not live on your take-home. I needed pin money," she says, avoiding the issue of the kid and getting on with the explanation.

"Is that the best excuse you can come up with?" is his answer to this question, according to one source.

"Pin money? What for?" according to another and more highly-placed source, who says her answer is: "Shoes."

"Shoes!" he says, and I'm going with the second source. "How many pairs have you already got in your closet?"

He is not playing games, he just does not know the count on the lady's shoes. This is because they have separate bedrooms, due to his having to get up early for the meditation requirement after a night on the town.

She thinks about this question for a minute. "Oh, about ten thousand," she estimates.

"*Ten thousand!?!?*" he says, and he is in the meanwhile multiplexing this number by the cost of shoes per pair and then

277

devising the result by the cost of services rendered, in terms of rupees, and he comes up with the number of johns—a number which pleases him not, averaging over a dozen per evening, assuming she is sometimes not laying it out on the cheap.

"Maybe it's closer to nine," she admits, and then she thinks to herself, What am I saying, he's always been good at figures, so she quickly adds, "Likely no more than eight thou, at the max."

Which would still come out to ten guys per night, well above the acceptable average.

And that's the factual scoop behind why Buddha decided to retire from the world at the tender age of thirty.

§

MY MAN did not really have a choice. Divorce was frowned at in that day and age, particularly if there was a kid involved, and of course divorce in the royal family was out of the question, they being expected to set a positive example for the down-and-outers, which was everybody else. This left only one option, retirement from the world—unless of course Buddha wanted to put out a hit on the lady. Which he had ethical scruples about, despite being a big admirer of Henry the Ape, because he'd be in danger of picking up a hundred demerits and in his next life would have to go back to being an insect.

So Buddha retired from the world.

Retirement from the world was not at that time considered religious per se, it was thought of more as a recreational activity. In fact, I believe it is now called a hunting trip. The plan was, he was gonna take five trusted employee buddies and spend two weeks in the woods, shoot a few tigers, then captivate a coupla elephants and bring them back for work in the transportation system. Then he was gonna go back to civilization and see if Dimelda had thought things over and realized the arrear of her ways. If so, it was on to the marriage enrichment weekend. If not—well, he didn't really have a contingent plan, being at that time a natural optimist due to his track record as a go-getter.

When they got out to the campground, however, they found

Buddha had forgot some supplies. He had packaged the pajamas and teethbrush and the sleeping bags and the ice chest and the Bug Off, but he had overlooked the food and shelter items of the budget. So Buddha had to send Channa the Chauffeur back to the palace with instructions to pick up several tents plus a two week supply of caviar.

There was nothing wrong with the instructions, they were spoken in plain Sanskrit. But Channa turned out to have lust in his heart for Babar. You can't really blame him, he'd been brought up deprived as a boy, with no elephants to drag Main Street with. If I or you ever got a chance like that we'd do exactly the same thing as Channa probably did, which was to light up a White Owl, bust out singing a few stanzas from the Drinking Song in *La Traviata,* and point Babar in the general direction of the Swiss border.[90]

Another thing Buddha had forgot to pack was the bow and arrows. Which explains why instead of spending two weeks in the hunting of tigers, he and his five buddies spent it in sitting around the campfire and empathizing amongst themselves, exchanging stories about their worst existences. One buddy, who had lost a substantive fortune in a market crash, consoled himself with cheap whiskey. One with crossed eyes had spent ten years in a graduate school getting the Ph.D. in Classics and ended up at the unemployment lines. One who had married a physical therapist noticed a peculiarity in their children, that the color of eyes and the pigment were in each case different. One veteran, who had lost two each of arms and legs in an unpopular war, took to memorizing transportation schedules. One guy who had

---

[90]According to Cardinal Micromentis, this sentence, together with the theory of continental drift, verifies the fact that India and Switzerland once shared a border, which explains why both nations now maintain a stance of strict political neutrality. The Cardinal made this astute observation just before his sudden and unexpected disappearance.

Cardinal August Micromentis was an exemplary disciple in almost every way, and enjoyed the admiration and respect of his colleagues. His astute comments are sorely missed, as are the cash reserves that disappeared at approximately the same time as he did.

misplaced important files in the Tusita placement office had been demoted to the statute of a human being. But when it came Buddha's turn to tell about his previous misfortunes, he was not anywheres to be found. He was off in the woods by himself, sitting under a Bay tree.

What Buddha was doing under a Bay tree is not known for sure. All that is known is what he later claimed, which is that he was meditating with himself. What he was meditating *about* is also not known, private thoughts being very difficult to monitor without state-of-the-art electronics, which had not yet been invented. But two weeks later he comes back to his five hunting buddies and treats them to a sermon on the subject of pain and suffering.[91]

There are four major points, if I remember—and keep in mind that the sermon was not his best effort, so the minds of his listeners would tend to wander. The first point being that life is *pain*. There is general agreement amongst the five friends on this thought, everybody nodding yes yes yes and murmuring how true how true.

The second point has something to do with the *cause* of pain, with the finger being pointed specifically at sexual desire, and he gives examples from his personal life, very melancholic. We all agree that the culprit is desire, but both the veteran and the former moneybags as well as the Ph.D. in Classics take issue with the sexual part. So to get the votes necessary for passage of Point Two, Buddha has to cut out the part about sex and just go with plain old desire, which makes everybody happy.

The third point is about the *end* of pain. His argument is that (a) if the cause of the pain is desire, then (b) the way to end the pain is to (c) quit desiring. "It's all very logical," agrees the Ph.D.

---

[91]The Buddhists later come to refer to this as "The Sermon at Benares," the centerpiece of which is the Four Noble Truths: (1) the truth of pain, (2) the truth of the cause of pain, (3) the truth of the cessation of pain, and (4) the truth of the way that leads to the cessation of pain. Readers not already well-versed in Buddhist teaching might consult E. A. Burtt (ed.), *The Teachings of the Compassionate Buddha* (New York: 1955), pp. 29-32.

in the crowd.

"Easier said than done," says the guy who has been married to a physical therapist.

"Hear hear," says the wise former placement officer.

But it passes anyways.

Then Buddha brings up point four, the *ways* to quit desiring, and afterwards he opens up the floor for suggestions as to the best eight ways to get the job done. It can't be seven and it can't be nine, he says, it has to be eight, no more no less.

"Vasectomy," is the first suggestion.

"That only increases the desire," says somebody who speaks from experience but shall remain nameless.

"Speak for yourself," pipes up the guy with a dozen kids of various hues.

"Hows about castration?" is the next suggestion.

"Get serious," says the guy with experience as a harem guard.

"It only works in the cases of *sexual* desire," points out the Ph.D. "We need something broader-based."

The bantering goes on and on like this, and in the meanwhile everybody is looking around for Channa to return with the basic necessities. But nobody knows yet that Buddha's chauffeur has probably taken off for Switzerland with the only elephant, so it is a long wait, with the time of day being taken up by contests for the most humorous suggestions about getting rid of the pain of life. It finally dawns on everybody, however, that Channa is gone for good and that we are stuck in the woods for a long period of time. This means if we don't want to spend the rest of our years wandering around scratching for roots and berries, drinking rainwater, and sleeping on pads of moss, we have got to come up with another living arrangement.

Which turns out to be a monastery. Maybe you've heard about monasteries—in fact, maybe you've even lived in one due to a demotion for past demerits. The thing about monasteries is . . . well, in the interest of briefness, let's just say don't believe everything you read in the scripture. If somebody should ever happen to hand you a brochure enumerating the oohs and aahs of monastic living, take it. Smile politely, take it, and cast it into the fire. My own experience has been that the only way you can get out of the monastic life is by transfer, becoming a T. Which usually involves a funeral.

Take Buddha, for example. He escaped his monastery and its rules and regs by being fed the wrong mushrooms. This was by an irate disciple, who shall remain nameless to protect the innocent.

I remember the deathbed scene like it was day before yesterday. All us monks bring lotus flowers up to Buddha's room and crowd around him. He is saying things like "This is my last existence" and "Now there is no rebirth"—pessimistic things in the extremis. Finally he looks up from his bed, this skinny, pale, shriveled-up eighty-year old man does, and asks us what we have on our minds. Everybody just looks around at each other and stifles a s.o.b. He probably thinks we're there for last-minute instructions or to show a special interest, maybe wish him well in his next life, but what most of the guys are there for was to meditate, the subject being Buddha's will and the possibility of having to go through probate.

He asks us again, "What's on your minds?" But everybody just keeps quiet. In those days it was considered rude to bring up the subject of the will in a hospital room. They recommended that you talk about pleasant things, like how nice-looking the nurses are and how great the food must be. In this particular case, however, the nurses are all men, it being a monastic hospital, and we all figure it would be in bad taste to bring up the subject of food with a guy who has just been poisoned.

So Buddha asks us again, "What's on your minds?"

Everybody just looks at the top of his toenails. He was getting irated, probably thinking, What's the matter, don't they know the answer or something? Why is it so hard to get good help? While he is probably having these thoughts, we original disciples are playing cat and mice. We notice he is getting whiter and whiter around the gills, so we put out the word that everybody is supposed to keep silent. "Look mournful if you can," we whisper amongst ourselfs, "but make sure to *shut up*. Don't mention the flowers. And don't even *think* of bringing up the subject of probate. Just play it cool, keep a closed upper lip, and let nature take his course."

Nature did, of course, don't he always. Which ended that episode in the career of the guy I'm calling G, for guy, go-getter, what have you.

§

AS IT TURNED OUT, Buddha's will was not quite what we'd hoped for. No mention whatsoever of the palaces, the wet bars, the brass bands, the dancers, the hot tubs. The theme was, keep the faith, don't slack off on the rules and regs, abstain from this that and the other, everything which causes pain.

It was about this time that I decided to give up on the monastic life. I figured I didn't want to be part of an organization which discriminates against the ladies. So I helped myself to a big bowl of mushrooms and pretty soon I was back at my old Tusita stamping grounds. I got my preceding job back by doing some fancy talking, misplacing a page or two to cover my tracks, pulling strings, getting my temporary replacement placed in a harem guard who later becomes a monk, etcet etcet. This was in plenty of time to help G with his transfer to the next career opportunity.

The day he comes in for the interview—this is after a well-deserved sabbatical from earthly cares—we happen to be looking for somebody to do Christ. The word from upstairs was, we needed somebody who had experience in the religion field, preferably international. Plus somebody with unweavering convictions about the difference between right from wrong. Which fit my G to a T. True, he had not done Buddha exactly according to specifications, having given up on the *joy de vive* message in favor of the gospel of suffering; but this could be traced back to a slight mix-up, over the difference between hooker and hoofer. True also, he lacked international experience. But that was as a human being. He'd put in an earlier stint in Europe, as a Saint Bernard, carrying brandy to unfortunate skiers. The point was, though, he was well qualified for the position, especially considering how rare it is to run across somebody which even *knows* the difference between right from wrong.

"Let's see," I says to G when he sits down, "it says here in the record you just got back from an Indian gig. Doing Buddha. Am I

283

right?"

"Right," he says, and this time around he does not wiggle around in the chair. More relaxed. Or maybe just tired.

"Looks like somebody has lost some weight," I says, which is meant for a compliment.

"Special diet," he says. "A meal a day. Fifty years."

"How'd it go, otherwise?"

I already know how it went, from the report on my desk. I'm making conversation, also checking for memory accuracy, which the brass mucks expect of us.

"*Déjà vu*," he says, showing off his Latin.

"Oh?" says I. "Am I missing something here?"

"A page," he says, with maybe a twenty percent smile.

I come right back with a ten percenter and then go right to the point. "Here's something that just came in," I says, shifting the papers back and forth on my desk to pick his curiosity. "Something a person with your qualifications . . . might . . . possibly . . . be interested . . . in."

"To tell the truth," he says, "I'm in no big hurry to go down again."

"What about . . . a go as . . . Christ?" I says, upping the smile to the high nineties and putting twinkles in my eyes.

"Christ!" he says, and in such a way as I don't know if he's swearing or showing an interest.

"Right," I says, voiding the issue, and I go on to sketch the circumstances: job description, perks, sermons on such basic themes as love one another and be ye perfect.

"How much suffering is involved?" he wants to know.

"Suffering?" I says. "In terms of what, for example?"

"In terms of pain. Agony. Mental anguish. The absence of pleasure."

It strikes me he is referring to any possible Dimelda types being sent his way, so I apologize for the last mix-up and go on to assure him that all the ladies Christ is due to run across will be high-minded types.

"For example?" he wants to know.

"For example, Mary, Mary Magdalene, Mary the mother—"

"And how's a guy supposed to tell all these Marys apart?"

This is a good question. It points to poor planning by the upstairs mucks. But I don't admit it, you never know who might be listening through the bugs. I just go on to tell him about the number of disciples budgeted (twelve, as opposed to only five for Buddha) and the lack of monasteries, which seems to spark an interest.

"Sounds too good to be true," he says when I am finished.

"Oh it is," I says, referring to the fact of it being true, up to a point.

"So tell me," says he, "how long's the gig?"

"The low thirties, in terms of years."

"Low thirties!" he says. "Why so short?"

"Light sermon schedule."

He thinks about this temporarily. Then he says, "And how's it set up to end?"

It's my turn to think about this for a while. "The good news," I finally remark, "is that the bottom line is, you get your body back in one piece."

"Hmmm," he says, and he scratches a little bald spot on his beard. "I think I'll pass on this one."

"May I ask why?" I says, out of courtesy.

"Frankly," he says, "I'd consider it a demotion."

"*De*motion?" I says. "Did I hear you right, Mr. G? You consider being Christ a demotion from being Buddha?"

"Him too," he says, and again he's putting on that damned low-percentage mystery smile which tells you to stay away from the subject.

"And what would you consider a *promotion*?"

"I was thinking in terms of maybe a job upstairs," says G, looking at me in the eyes. "I think I earned it."

I am left speakless by these remarks. Why would anybody in his right minds not want to play Christ and have a crack at saving the world, I'm wondering, and why especially would anybody want to retire upstairs and sit in on committee meetings and vote on merits and demerits and career paths?

"May I ask why?" says I.

"It's a matter," he says with that damned smile, "of retaining limited control over the running of the known world."

Another curious remark, I thinks, this G guy is full of them. But as they say, Ours not to wonder why, ours but to do and die.

"I'll see what I can do," I finally says, and I add, "but I promise you nothing."

So I write down this request in triplicate, staple it to the outside of the file which lacks the missing sheet, stand up and shake hands with the customer, send him out of the office and into the waiting room, give the file to my secretary with instructions to send it upstairs, and then forget about it.

§

A COUPLA MONTHS LATER I find something revealing behind the file cabinet. It's the missing page with the report on G's previous life, the one between being a Brahmin and doing Buddha. It says:

JOB DESCRIPTION: all-wise, all-powerful, all-good, willing to grow with the job; architectural consultant, real estate covenants in Israel, a.k.a. Holy Land.
TIME SERVED: 2,000+ yrs.
MERITS: Winning personality; kept in touch with clients.
DEMERITS: Broke vow to remain single by creating a wife (Eve), who turned around and cheated on him. Unpredictable; sometimes slew clients in fit of rage; currently wanted for murder of king's young son.

That explains everything, thinks I. The remark on wanting to retain limited control. The comment on playing Christ being a demotion. The *déjà vu* mention—being cheated on by Dimelda must of reminded him of how he was treated by Eve. But I don't do anything with this peace of information, I just crumble it up and throw it in the waist basket, because what if G happens to turn up at the upstairs job? Then he'll be my boss, and if I know him, he won't want the whole world knowing the true story.[92]

---

[92]This scroll became the subject of an unfortunate controversy between Father Lecher and Ms. LaFemme. It is enough to say that angry words

were spoken and recriminations exchanged, especially over the passage beginning, "If a guy, or a lady—I did not discriminate, I was way ahead of my time—if a guy or a broad showed unusual promise, I'd take a personal interest...," which Ms. LaFemme appeared to take personally.

While Ms. Emma LaFemme was with us, she was an exemplary disciple in almost every way, and enjoyed the admiration and respect of her colleagues. Her sardonic humor will be sorely missed. I am sure that, if Father Lecher could have rescinded one unkind word that he uttered in his entire life, it would be the characterization of his former disciple and close personal friend as a "[. . .] of a Judas."

CHURCH DOCTRINE

INTRODUCTION

WHEN, ON APRIL 1 ONE DECADE AGO, the angel Gabriella delivered the divine communiqué directing Father Lecher to found a new religion and build a theme park, she neglected to give him specific instructions. Thus he found himself faced with the responsibility of devising a strategy for completing these tasks.

The "game plan," as the good Father was fond of calling this strategy, required a division of labor among his four disciples. Cardinal Micromentis was assigned to assist him in promoting and advertising The Church of the Comic Spirit. Ms. LaFemme was to help him design and build Bear Lake World. My task, of course, was to edit the Scrolls and prepare them for publication. Professor Allbright was to compose a catechism detailing the doctrines of the church.

Unfortunately, Professor Allbright's untimely death prevented him from finishing the catechism. Thus it devolved upon me to complete the task for which he was eminently qualified.

As the author of this catechism, I have naturally relied on the insights of my former fellow disciples. I am indebted to Cardinal August Micromentis for his suggestion, made to me just before his retirement, that the catechism be kept short and to the point. As he persuasively argued, a long catechism would be an unnecessary waste of trees. For sacred doctrine requires words, and words require to be written down in order that scholars will have texts to interpret, and texts require paper, and paper requires wood pulp, and wood pulp requires wood, which is derived from trees. Moreover, no one reads sacred doctrine anymore, unless it is written by the Pope, and in that case they do not actually read it, they only buy it and put it on their coffee tables, which are made of wood, which is derived from trees. Therefore, sacred doctrine is a waste of trees: first, in point of the paper, second, in point of the coffee tables.

If I have not been as brief and concise as the wise cardinal would have wished, it is because of my belief that, were I to carry his insight to its logical conclusion, the Church of the Comic Spirit would be left without any written teachings—or, for that matter, without an easily-available translation of the Scrolls themselves.

I am also indebted to the late Professor Mortimer Z. Z. Allbright for his lengthy and perceptive monographs on each of the Scrolls. If I have not relied on those monographs to the extent he would have wished, it is because I have not given them the painstaking care they call for. I trace my negligence in this matter to my adherence to two superb maxims:

(1) "It is hard to say anything as good as simply nothing."[93]

(2) "Life is short."[94]

Furthermore, I wish to express my profound gratitude to Ms. Emma LaFemme, wherever she may currently be. I would be the first to admit that on the subjects that counted most, she was, as the saying goes, "right on the mark." If I have not followed her intuitions at every point, it is because I am, unfortunately, a man.

Last but far from least, I am grateful to Father Lecher himself, from whom I gleaned most of my ideas. Immediately before he departed this pain-wracked earth, he met with 500 members of his new booster club, who asked him many questions. "A Short Catechism" is an accurate paraphrase of the most frequently asked questions and his most coherent answers.

—B. S. Buller

---

[93] Attributed to the composer John Cage.

[94] Attributed to Methuselah.

A Short Catechism: Answers to FAQs

CONCERNING GOD

Is there a God?
Of course.

How can you be so sure?
I've had personal experiences with a number of angels. Angels are God's messengers. So there you have it: There's gotta be a God.

Maybe somebody's just been posing as God?
If he has, he's been doing a pretty good impersonation. And only God, or somebody like God, could pull it off. If it was God, it was God. If it was somebody *like* God, what would be the difference? So whether or not God exists, he exists.

Did God create the world?
The evidence is inconclusive.

What do you mean, inconclusive?
On the one hand, it's written, "You need lots of room outdoors to let them roam free." That's God speaking. He's referring to the pets. "Well," he goes on, "I took account of that need and created plenty of woods and pastures and gardens."[95] Also, you've got to

---

[95]"First Person Omniscient."

remember that he made Eve and Adam. So there had to be *some* creating going on back then.

But God also says that in the beginning, there wasn't much of anything. Just the basics: heaven, sun, moon, stars, wild birds, fish, animals, etcetera etcetera.[96] So it sounds to me like he didn't necessarily create *every*thing. And even if he did, he didn't take credit for it.

Then God isn't the all-powerful creator we've been hearing about all these years?

He was probably just being modest. Setting an example for the rest of us. There's nothing wrong with a little modesty. The world would be in a lot better shape if each and every day people would take a few moments of their time to be modest. Of course it's like everything else. It can be overdone.

And if he actually created everything, he was savvy enough not to take the blame.

So whichever way you cut it, God is everything he's cracked up to be, creation-wise. And more.

What is God like?

Male, for one thing. Transcendent, dignified, interesting, for another. Also, clever. And you can't forget funny.

Let's start with male.

You got a problem with that?

Many people do.

It's a free country.

Do you welcome women into the Church?

With open arms.

What about children?

Only adults. We've had to be pretty strict about that. There are laws.

---

[96]*Ibid.*

You also mentioned that God is transcendent as well as dignified and interesting.

It is written, "sitting there in his box high above the court, the owner and general manager of the Jerusalem Godfearers, God himself, very knowledgeable about this game of basketball, never missing a chance to see his team when they are in town."[97] That's about as transcendent as you can get. It's also written, "On August 13 past I requested of Mr. Jonah that he journey to Ninevah, Assyria, for the purpose of crying against her."[98] Isn't that a dignified way to put it? Sounds just like a lawyer. Then Moses writes, "Met God. Interesting experience."[99]

Case closed.

What about clever?

For example, "Hi. God here. I can't come to the phone right now, but at the tone please leave your message and I'll try to get back to you in the morning."[100] It's really him, you see, he's just screening his calls. And that's before the answering machine was even invented! Then there's the story about God working a sting on Satan.[101] Now is that clever, or what?

It doesn't bother you, God being clever?

Not a bit. I sleep better nights knowing he's clever.

But clever isn't necessarily wise.

You know what? Wise is way overrated. You can do a lot more things with clever, in terms of computer programs, portfolio management, winning hotly-contested games with time running out in the fourth quarter. With wisdom, you just *have* it. It's icing on the cake, a nice conversation piece, but that's about as far as it goes.

---

[97] "The Big Man in the Middle."
[98] "Love Boat."
[99] "Moshe's Diary."
[100] "The Secret of Long Life."
[101] "The Wager."

Bottom line. Clever has a huge advantage over its nearest competitor.

How about funny?

I'd go so far as to say that God is a comic hero.

What's a comic hero?

It is written, (1) "The comic hero imagines himself to be invulnerable and omnipotent."[102] He can't see the end result of creating a young knockout, not having any experience along those lines.[103] (2) The comic hero "indulges in wish fulfillment and fantasy gratification." Why do you think he bothered to make Eve?[104] (3) The comic hero "engages in play without any ulterior motive." That explains why he gives Abram the Holy Land and sets him up for a circumcision.[105] Which, as operations go, is pretty useless.[106] (4) The comic hero is "a realist who celebrates the body and affirms the life force." Flashes his backside to Moses, you may recall.[107] (5) The comic hero "cultivates comic paranoia, as if laughter were an essential defense against a hostile reality." That's how he gets through the divorce;[108] there's a lesson here for everybody. (6) The comic hero "may serve as the ritual clown of his society, acting as a scapegoat for its taboos." This explains the part about Abraham using God as a scapegoat for child abuse,[109] which was just then coming into its own as a

---

[102]Always the scholar, Father Lecher is quoting, throughout this paragraph, from Maurice Charney, *Comedy High and Low*, Chapter V, "Comedy in Theory and Practice: Seven Aspects of the Comic Hero" (New York, 1987), pp. 143-78.

[103]Father Lecher is thinking of "First Person Omniscient."

[104]*Ibid.*

[105]"Miss Holy Land."

[106]Father Lecher is of course speaking from the medical point of view, not the religious. Even so, Professor Allbright, himself a certified surgeon, would certainly have disagreed.

[107]"Moshe's Diary."

[108]"First Person Omniscient."

[109]"Miss Holy Land."

big taboo. The comic hero "doesn't eventually merge into the tragic hero, but represents an entirely different range of experience." Some major philosopher, I believe it was Aristotle, painted the tragic hero as being above average and the comic hero as being below average. Once again Father Lecher is absolutely correct.[110]

Isn't God supposed to be perfect?
Nobody's perfect.

Not even God?
He has faults, don't we all. For instance, it's written, "Broke vow to remain single by creating a wife (Eve), who then turned around and cheated on him. Unpredictable; sometimes slew clients in a fit of rage; currently wanted for murder of king's young son."[111]

But on the plus side, he confesses to the murder of Bathsheba's baby—and not just secretly, before a single priest, but before a live television audience![112] The point is, he's willing to learn from his mistakes. You also have to keep in mind that God had been around the block a few times, transmigrating from one available fetus to another.[113] And if you know anything about that kind of world tour, you know that the whole point is to better yourself.

So God's not perfect. But you have to hand it to him, he's always going for the big brass ring.

---

[110]Once again Father Lecher is absolutely correct. See Aristotle's *Poetics*, 2 and 5.
[111]"What Goes Around, Comes Around."
[112]"Playing God."
[113]"What Goes Around, Comes Around."

DOES THE CHURCH TEACH ORIGINAL SIN?
Yes. We strongly recommend that when you sin, you do it in an original way. Think of sin as an art form.

I mean, do you teach the doctrine *of original sin? The idea that sin entered the world at the very beginning, through Adam and Eve and their carnal lust?*

Absolutely not. The Church of the Comic Spirit teaches the doctrine of original innocence.

You put the blame on God?!
I mean we put the blame on nobody—not God, not Eve, not Adam.[114]

I don't get it.
Look at it this way. It's pretty clear that God was innocent. When he created Eve, he wanted a chess partner. He couldn't see what was coming down the pike. He just did what seemed the right thing to do at the time.

Eve? Also innocent. Sure, she wanted a masseur. But keep in mind that God left her home alone all day, reading French novels and eating chocolates. So she ended up having an affair. Wasn't that in the cards, given the combination of opportunity and God's age? Who can blame her? She hadn't *asked* to be created. She had no interest in chess.

And Adam? Look at it from his point of view. He was created, without being consulted, by an innocent, well-meaning God, and he ended up having an understandable affair. He had the perfect alibi.

Show me a jury in its right mind that would convict any of the first three persons.

---

[114]"First Person Omniscient."

Where does the Church stand on the gender issue?

Women are smarter than men.

What about woman's lack of self-esteem? Isn't it rooted in a male imposed awareness of intellectual inferiority?

No.

Where's the scriptural evidence?

In "First Person Omniscient," God says, "I created Adam. Perfect, except for one thing: not as smart as Eve. That's the way she wanted it." And in four of the other six Scrolls dealing with the issue, women are clearly the brains of the family. Elsie the Entrepreneur is smarter than Noah the Negev Nebbish ("The First Entrpreneur"), Sara the Siren is smarter than Abram the Schlemiel ("Miss Holy Land"), Jane the Satirist is smarter than Lot the Satyr ("The Tragedy at Sodom/Gomorrah"), Dorothy the Inquisitor is smarter than Job the Justifier ("The Wager"), Dimelda the Hooker is smarter than Buddha the Hunter ("What Goes Around, Comes Around"). But in the other two Scrolls, involving Zipporah vs. Moshe ("Moshe's Diary") and Abigail and Bathsheba vs. David ("Playing God"), the issue isn't clear. Therefore, in at least 71.4 percent of all Scriptural cases, women are smarter than men.

So why do men run the world?

Not true. Women run the world.

But beginning with William the Conqueror, England has had only 5.5 ruling queens, compared with 34.5 ruling kings, one of whom killed half of his wives.

Notice that, of the three most famous rulers, two have been women. And one of them had the bad habit of decapitating her generals. Besides, it is written, "the hand that rocks the cradle is the hand that rules the world."[115]

---

[115]William Ross Wallace, "What Rules the World."

Why don't men get smart and start rocking the cradle?
Beats me. My guess would be that it lacks a Scriptural basis.

CONCERNING THE CHURCH

WHAT IS THE PRIMARY PURPOSE OF THE CHURCH?
Running Bear Lake World, Inc.

What about preaching? Isn't it written, "Go ye into all the world, and preach the gospel to every creature"?[116]
It is also written, "people cannot stand much church—an hour and a quarter at the limit, and they draw the line at once a week."[117]

What about praying? Isn't it written, "Pray without ceasing"?[118]
If everybody followed that advice, nobody would have time for anything else.

What else does the Church do?
We have our hands full running the theme park.

Is the Church planning to expand?
Definitely. Number one, we now have new management in place. Number two, Bear Lake World, Inc., is the hottest growth company in America. People are busting the gates down to get in. Number three, our current thinking is, we should expand our enterprise into the most promising emerging markets—Tehran, Moscow, Beijing, Katmandu, the Ross Ice Shelf, you name it.

Should the profits generated by Bear Lake World, Inc., be tax free?
It is written, "Government has two basic secular purposes for granting . . . tax exemptions to religious organizations. First,

---

[116]Mark 16:15.

[117]Mark Twain, *Letters from the Earth* (New York, 1974), p. 18.

[118]I Thessalonians 5:17.

these organizations are exempted because they . . . contribute to the well-being of the community in a variety of nonreligious ways, and therefore bear burdens that would otherwise either have to be met by general taxation, or be left undone, to the detriment of the community. . . . Second, government grants exemptions to religious organizations because they uniquely contribute to the pluralism of American society by their religious activities."[119]

Our lawyers advise us that Bear Lake World, Inc., contributes to the well-being of the community in a variety of nonreligious ways, including but not limited to providing day care for the small children of the many tourists who derive benefit from its various activities. The same lawyers also point out that Bear Lake World, Inc., uniquely contributes to the pluralism of American society by its religious activities, including but not limited to the visiting of the sacred shrines by the devout flock in their semi-annual pilgrimages.

Add to that the fact that Bear Lake World, Inc., already contributes to the government indirectly, by providing jobs for tax-paying employees. Also, overhead costs are going through the roof. For example, in just the last month, management has built the House of Martyrdom and greatly expanded The Motel Whose Name Father Lecher Forgot. Moreover, the rise in the wholesale price of synthetic bear fur has exceeded the Producer Price Index numbers by 20.4 percent. And the price of plastic, from which we make the replicas of the Remington Model 700, has also exploded. Further, management has recently negotiated new multi-year, multi-million-dollar contracts with the angels Michelle, Cheri, and Gabriella.

That should do it. Next subject?

---

[119]Mr. Justice Brennan, concurring opinion in *Walz* v. *Tax Commission* (1970).

CONCERNING MORALS

WHAT IS THE HIGHEST VIRTUE?
Irreverence.

Where in the Scrolls do you find irreverence?
In "The Wager." After God had done his number on Satan, he laughed. It's generally considered irreverent to laugh in God's presence. When God laughed, it's a good bet that he was in his own presence. This means God showed irreverence. We should try to be like God, at least in some respects. That's common sense. So there you have it: Irreverence is okay.

But is it the highest virtue?
Can you think of anything higher than God?

No, but it's practically midnight. What are the other virtues?
I really can't think of any. But it's practically midnight.

Maybe we should all take a break.
Good idea. I know an all-night lounge down the street. Caters to insomniacs. Should hold most of us.

CONCERNING SALVATION

WHAT MUST ONE DO TO BE SAVED?
Laugh without ceasing.

What's the Scriptural basis?
It's written, "Laughter is the Best Medicine."[120]

I'll drink to that.
Cheers.

---

[120]The reference is to a popular feature in *Reader's Digest*, of which Father Lecher was an avid reader.

Does it have any negative side effects?

Does what have any negative side effects?

Laughter.

People have been known to split their sides laughing. I have time for two more questions.

CONCERNING LAST THINGS

WHAT WILL HEAVEN BE LIKE?

I don't know about you, but I like to think of myself as sitting in a hot tub, sipping aging grape fluid and exchanging playful banter with my angels.

How many angels can dance on the edge of a hot tub?

I've seen as many as half a dozen.

That's all, folks. Farewell. *Au revoir. Auf Wiedersehen. Adiós, Zayt gezunt.*

www.ingramcontent.com/pod-product-compliance
Lightning Source LLC
Chambersburg PA
CBHW071253170626
46809CB00001B/204